In The
Barrister's Chambers

Books by Tina Gabrielle

IN THE BARRISTER'S CHAMBERS

A PERFECT SCANDAL

LADY OF SCANDAL

Published by Kensington Publishing Corporation

In The
Barrister's
Chambers

Tina Gabrielle

ZEBRA BOOKS
KENSINGTON PUBLISHING CORP.

http://www.kensingtonbooks.com

ZEBRA BOOKS are published by

Kensington Publishing Corp.
119 West 40th Street
New York, NY 10018

All Kensington titles, imprints and distributed lines are available at special quantity discounts for bulk purchases for sales promotion, premiums, fund-raising, educational or institutional use.

Special book excerpts or customized printings can also be created to fit specific needs. For details, write or phone the office of the Kensington Special Sales Manager: Attn. Special Sales Department. Kensington Publishing Corp., 119 West 40th Street, New York, NY 10018. Phone: 1-800-221-2647.

Zebra and the Z logo Reg. U.S. Pat. & TM Off.

ISBN-13: 978-1-4201-2274-9
ISBN-10: 1-4201-2274-6

First Printing: September 2011
10 9 8 7 6 5 4 3 2 1

Printed in the United States of America

For my darling Laura.
May you always follow your dreams,
have the courage to believe in them, and
may your star always shine bright.
I love you.

Chapter 1

"They ain't whores!"

"What would you call seven women who live under your roof then, if not a brothel?" Prosecutor Abrams asked, stalking forward.

"Me lady friends, they are," Slip Dawson explained.

"All seven of them?"

"Me mum always said I 'ad a way with the ladies," Slip whined.

"Did your mother tell you to freely share your women with all the men of the City of London?" Abrams asked sharply, giving the accused a stony glare.

An imposing barrister at the defense table jumped up. "I object, my lord. The prosecution has not brought forth *one* man 'from the City of London' to testify as to bedding any of Mr. Dawson's lady friends."

The judge sighed and rested his chin in hand, a look of complete boredom on his face. Four of the twelve-member jury rolled their eyes; others snickered.

Evelyn Darlington sat perched on the edge of a wooden bench in the center of the spectators' gallery. Her eyes never wavered from the defense barrister—the only man in the room she knew—Jack Harding. He was the reason she was here, witnessing this spectacle, along with all the other observers in the packed courtroom.

The late-afternoon sun streamed in through the windows, raising the temperature in the crowded room by twenty degrees. Too many unwashed bodies in too small a space should have repulsed her.

Instead, she sat in her seat completely enthralled.

Jack Harding was precisely as she remembered him, as only a few lines near his eyes gave away the years that had passed since she had last seen him. He was tall—over six feet three inches—with chiseled features that gave him a sharp and confident profile. His eyes were a deep green that reminded her of the ferns that thrived during the summer months. His lips were curved in a smile, but she knew they could be either cunning or charming, or both.

Beneath his barrister's wig, she knew his thick brown hair had an unruly wave that he had often impatiently brushed aside when he was concentrating on a legal treatise. He was dressed in a black barrister's gown that would make the complexions of most men appear sallow, but the dark color only served to enhance his bronzed skin.

But perhaps his most fascinating appeal was his attitude of complete relaxation as if he were unperturbed by the judge, jury, prosecutor, and even the audience sitting in the courtroom staring at him. He was infused with a confidence that made one hang on every word that fell from his lips. Without a doubt, Jack Harding probably had women, from all stations in society, swarming around him.

A snort beside her drew her attention. "'E's got 'em by the throat, 'e does."

Evelyn turned to look at the man seated to her left, a squat fellow with beady eyes and fleshy jowls. The overpowering stench of onions wafted from his skin. He smiled, revealing no teeth and swollen gums.

She shifted inches to the right only to brush up against a heavyset woman with a bloodstained apron, sleeves rolled up to her elbows, and work-roughened hands. A butcher's wife, no doubt.

"'Tis a matter of time till old Abrams gives up." The woman laughed and rubbed the calluses on her hands. "Ain't nobody can git past that Jack Harding."

Just like old times, Evelyn thought. *Jack Harding could charm the habit off a nun and cunningly argue the most complicated legal points while doing so.*

But that's why she was here, watching him . . . waiting for him. For the years, it seemed, had only polished his raw talent.

The rest of the trial went as expected. Prosecutor Abrams argued about Slip Dawson's entourage of female inhabitants. Jack countered each argument by pointing out the prosecution's distinct lack of evidence followed by a number of witnesses who testified as to Slip's "stellar" character and good standing in the community.

Exactly eleven and a half minutes after the start of the trial, the judge cleared his throat, cutting off Prosecutor Abrams in midsentence.

"As all of the relevant evidence has been presented," Judge Tobias said, "I ask for the jury to deliberate on the charges and come to a verdict."

The jury, not bothering to leave the courtroom, huddled in the corner.

In what must have been record speed, the foreman stood—his barrel-shaped chest puffed up with self-importance. "We the jury find Slip Dawson not guilty of keepin' a brothel."

The spectators burst into cheers, turning the courtroom into a scene of chaos. Hands reached out to give Slip Dawson a hearty slap on the back as he proceeded out of the room—a free man.

The pounding of Judge Tobias's gavel was a distant thumping, completely ignored by the people.

Evelyn stared as Slip passed, a cockeyed smile on his face, and she wondered how many of today's observers were patrons of his "lady friends."

Her gaze returned to Jack Harding.

Jack extended his hand to Abrams. The prosecutor looked like he had sucked on a lemon, sulking in defeat, but he shook hands with Jack nonetheless. Jack then bent to gather his papers and litigation bag from the desk.

She waited until he turned to make his way out of the courtroom, then stepped into the aisle.

"Mr. Harding," she called out.

He stopped abruptly, his gaze traveling over her face, then roaming over her figure before returning to her eyes. His lips curled into a smile.

"I believe you have the advantage of knowing my name. How can I be of assistance, Miss . . ."

"Lady Evelyn Darlington."

His brow furrowed in confusion before his eyes widened in surprise.

"Why, Lady Evelyn! I don't believe it. You were a girl the last time I saw you. It's been a long, long time."

"Ten years since you were a student studying under my father to become a barrister at the Inns of Court."

"Ah, yes, my pupilage. From what I remember, you always had a voracious appetite for the law. You often visited your father's chambers, listening to his lectures. I have vivid memories of you following me around, taunting me with your extensive legal knowledge."

Heat stole into her cheeks at his words. "From what *I* recall, you needed the additional tutelage."

He laughed, a rich, pleasant sound. "Touché, Lady Evelyn. I probably did. Now please tell me, have you come today to watch the proceedings? Many do."

She shook her head, then looked up at him. "I've come to seek your services."

"My services? No one seeks out my 'services' unless they are in trouble. I cannot imagine you in trouble." A sudden frown knit his brow. "Last I heard, your father, Emmanuel Darlington, inherited his brother's title and is now the Earl of Lyndale. I understand he is currently lecturing at Oxford. Is he well?"

"It's not about my father, but a close acquaintance."

"Ah, I see. What crime has your friend committed?"

"None! He's been wrongfully accused."

"Pardon, Lady Evelyn," he said. "I meant no offense. What crime has he been accused of?"

She looked to both sides, her eyes darting nervously back and forth, then whispered, "Murder."

He cocked an eyebrow. "A serious offense, to be sure. Who is he?"

She took a deep breath and gathered her courage. "My soon-to-be betrothed."

He stiffened visibly, and a shadow crossed his features. "I'm very sorry, Lady Evelyn, but my docket is completely full. Murder trials take a significant amount of time to properly investigate and prepare, and I would be remiss to even consider representing your acquaintance."

A thread of panic ribboned through her. "But you must. If not as a service to an innocent man wrongfully accused, then as a favor to a girl you once knew."

"I can refer you to a number of proficient criminal barristers. I am not the only—"

"Then as a favor to my father, your former pupilmaster."

He hesitated, and she knew she had struck upon a nerve. Her father was a revered Master of the Bench—otherwise known as a Bencher—by many students, and she knew Jack was no exception. From what she recalled, Jack Harding owed Lord Lyndale even more than most.

He shifted the papers in his hands, then nodded. "I cannot promise anything, understand, but perhaps this conversation would be better suited elsewhere."

Relief coursed through her that he was even willing to further discuss the matter. "Yes. Certainly."

His hand cupped her elbow, and he led her out of the courtroom. As they weaved their way through the halls of the Old Bailey, she was conscious of his tall frame beside her, his firm fingers on her sleeve. She glanced up at the clear-cut lines of his profile and was once again struck by his air of authority. In this legal arena, he radiated a strength that drew her eye, impossible to look away.

He slowed his pace so that she could keep up, and a group of barristers waved as they passed. A voluptuous woman with a scandalously low bodice, a bright yellow flower tucked between her breasts, gave Jack a jaunty wave.

Evelyn couldn't help but ponder whether she was one of Slip Dawson's "lady friends."

"You are quite popular, Mr. Harding," Evelyn said.

"I am known as the people's lawyer."

"At the expense of the Crown's prosecution?"

His humor apparently returned, his eyes lit with laughter as he looked down at her. "You must not judge me too harshly, Lady Evelyn. From what I gather, my reputation is the very reason you sought me out today."

He was correct, of course. She had done her research. No other barrister, within the two jurisdictions covered by the Old Bailey—the City of London or the County of Middlesex—was a more successful criminal barrister than Jack Harding.

"You're right," she said. "I would be nothing short of lying if I said I hadn't followed your accomplishments over the years. I just never anticipated that I would so urgently require your services."

And she did *desperately* need his aid—a life depended upon it. For that reason alone, she refused to take no for an answer. She must convince Jack Harding to take the case, no matter the cost.

Chapter 2

Jack proceeded down a long hall, passing several more courtrooms, until he came to a stop before a door with a brass nameplate labeled CLIENT CONSULTATION. He reached for the handle, opened the door, and motioned for Evelyn to enter.

His gaze roamed once again over her form as she swept by. He had been stunned to learn that the beautiful woman standing in the middle of the spectators' gallery, waiting for him, was Lady Evelyn Darlington—the daughter of his pupilmaster when Jack was a mere student, striving to become a barrister. She had changed much in the ten years since he had last seen her poring over her father's papers. She had been a child then—close to twelve—now she was a woman full grown.

Her golden hair was piled in an elegant style atop her head. A few loose tendrils had escaped the pins and brushed the slender column of her throat. Her facial bones were delicately carved, and her lips temptingly plump. But it was the turquoise eyes, the shade of a tropical ocean—exotically slanted and tipped with thick lashes—that made his breath hitch.

She wasn't as tall as he preferred his women, but even

in the demure blue gown she wore, any man could see she was generously curved.

She made a circuit of the room, taking in her surroundings—a small desk in the corner, wooden chairs lining the perimeter of the room, and a bookshelf containing several well-used law books—with wide-eyed interest, and he was struck with a thought: Evelyn Darlington may have grown into a beautiful woman, but her scholarly aura seemed quite the same. She appeared quite serious, unaware of her beauty and how it affected men.

He closed the door, strode forward, and placed his bag and the papers he had been holding atop the desk.

Her eyes widened at the thick stack of litigation documents. "It's a wonder you can sort through such a voluminous amount of paper. Are they all pertaining to Mr. Dawson's case?"

He chuckled at the unmasked fascination in her voice. "Hardly. I was not lying when I said my docket was full. Truth be told, your friend will be better off with another barrister. There are several highly competent barristers we passed on the way here. I can escort you to any you choose today and request that they take the utmost care with the case."

"No," she rushed. "None other will do. You have not lost of late."

His gaze sharpened at her admission. "I'm flattered that you think so highly of me and that you have followed my career, but at the same time, I never anticipated that you would seek to hire me. Does Lord Lyndale know that you're here?"

Thick lashes lowered. "No. I haven't told my father of my intentions to retain you."

"He doesn't approve of your choice of betrothed, does he?"

She hesitated for a heartbeat before answering. "It isn't relevant."

"Ah, he doesn't." Her hesitation spoke volumes, just as when a witness paused those few critical seconds before formulating an answer on the witness stand. It usually meant a lie was forthcoming, or in Evelyn's case, an omission of importance.

He motioned for her to sit in one of the chairs in front of the desk. He ignored the chair behind the desk and occupied the one across from her.

Leaning forward, he said, "Tell me everything."

She took a deep breath, her breasts straining against the fabric of her bodice. "Mr. Randolph Sheldon, my soon-to-be betrothed, is under suspicion of murdering an actress in the Drury Lane Theatre."

"An actress? Was she his lover?"

Her cheeks flamed red. "No! She was a distant cousin."

"Why is he suspected?"

"He was seen fleeing from her bedroom window."

"Let me guess. Her body was found in her bedchamber?"

She shifted in her chair and twisted her hands on her lap. "Yes. She was to give him something."

He ignored her obvious discomfort and continued his questioning. "How was she killed?"

"She was . . . stabbed, wearing only her night rail."

"Who discovered her?"

"The neighbor heard screams, and she called the constable. Witnesses claim they saw Randolph jump from the window."

"That is enough evidence to cause concern," Jack said. "The prosecution will surely seek to indict him."

Evelyn's chin rose a notch. "But he's innocent! I've known Randolph for years. Our families were neighbors at our country estates in Hertfordshire. We took many summer strolls together."

"I still think it best that Mr. Sheldon be represented by another lawyer. I don't see how my representation would aid your father."

"Don't you see? If we are to be officially engaged and the reading of the banns begun, it would affect Father's career at Oxford, for his daughter to be engaged to an accused murderer!"

Jack leaned back in his chair. All his gut instincts warned him not to get involved with Lady Evelyn Darlington, but she was right. The resulting scandal *would* adversely affect her father's career.

And he did owe Lord Lyndale. If it was not for the eccentric Master of the Bench, Jack would not be practicing law, would not be enjoying his success, wouldn't have more money than he knew how to spend, and certainly wouldn't be basking in the fickle affections of the *ton*. In fact, it would be safe to say, Jack would be nothing at all; he would most assuredly be wenching, gambling, and drinking to excess.

But what disturbed Jack more than Evelyn Darlington's being besotted by a man who most likely killed another woman in cold blood was the fact that Lord Lyndale clearly was unaware of his daughter's intentions to seek out his legal services.

That and the undeniable truth that he was drawn to Evelyn himself.

Looking into Evelyn's mesmerizing blue eyes, Jack struggled to hold on to his firm resolve.

The lady is nothing but trouble, he mused. She had been a minx as a girl—an I-know-it-all-better-than-you-ever-will tormenter—and as a grown woman she was wildly beautiful. His attraction was its own warning. He never mixed business with pleasure. It always led to disastrous results in the courtroom.

His mind whirled with excuses. He would speak with her father, explain the circumstances to him, and he had no doubt in his mind that Lord Lyndale would understand that he did not have the time to take on a murder client. He would be doing his former pupilmaster a service by informing him of his daughter's clandestine activities.

Reaching out, she grasped his hand, her eyes imploring. "If it is a matter of money," she said, "please be assured that you will be paid."

Jack froze, every muscle in his body tensing. His blood always ran hot after a trial, and her touch—however innocent—tempted him to reach out and take the victor's spoils. A kiss, at the least. He wondered what her reaction would be if she knew the effect she had on him.

"It has nothing to do with money," he said tersely. "If I'm to consider taking on your friend's—Mr. Randolph Sheldon's—case, then I insist on speaking with your father first."

"My father? Why?"

"I owe him a great deal. I won't go behind his back and take on a case involving his own daughter, even if you are not the accused."

She sat upright as if her laces suddenly had been pulled tight. "Fine. If you insist."

"I insist."

She stood and turned to leave. "As I'm sure you're aware, my father is a busy man—"

He reached for his pocket watch with a flourish, then looked at her. "I'm available now. I had expected

Slip Dawson's trial to take longer and had cleared the remainder of my day. From what I recall, your father never liked to work through the evening meal and should be returning home soon."

Jack stood and opened the door for her. He gave her his most charming smile as they returned to the main hall of the Old Bailey. He would meet with Lord Lyndale, enlighten him as to his daughter's intentions, explain why he could not take on the case, help his daughter find a suitable lawyer to defend her anticipated betrothed, thus fulfilling any ethical obligations. He expected to be in his chambers at Lincoln's Inn of Court within two hours' time.

It was dark outside by the time they arrived at Lord Lyndale's town house in Piccadilly. They had traveled by separate conveyances, Evelyn choosing to take a hackney cab while Jack traveled in his phaeton. As soon as Jack was alone, he removed his barrister's wig and gown, laid them beside him on the padded bench, and ran his fingers through his hair. She had been worried about her reputation, traveling unchaperoned with a bachelor, and Jack was more than happy to accommodate her concerns. He didn't want to learn more than was necessary about her troubles.

Why bother? He didn't plan on taking them on.

They now stood on the front steps while Evelyn rapped on the door.

"Shouldn't your father's butler have opened the door by now?" he asked after a full minute had passed.

"Hodges is well into his eighties. His hearing isn't what it used to be," she explained.

Just like Lord Lyndale, he thought. *He would take troubled students under his wing and keep on an elderly butler when most other members of society would have let the old servant out to pasture years ago.*

Evelyn fished into her reticule, searching for her key. The task was made harder by the dusk, with only the dim glow of the street lamp to aid her. Finally she withdrew the key and was inserting it into the lock, when the door pushed easily open.

"That's odd," she said. "Hodges must have forgotten to lock the door."

They stepped inside the vestibule. It was dim here as well, and the lingering scent of a pipe filled the space. The distinctive smell of the tobacco triggered a memory of Emmanuel Darlington at the podium in the classroom, pipe in hand.

"Father?" Evelyn called out.

Jack took a step forward and bumped into a long-case clock in the corner. He heard Evelyn shuffle forward, then the sound of flint strike iron as she sought to light a lamp.

Hands outstretched so as to avoid walking into anything more, he made to reach her side, then tripped over something on the floor. He barely registered what sounded like a low moan, when Evelyn screamed and something shattered across the floor.

Jack twisted around, just in time to see a figure dart forward. Jack launched himself at the shape, grasping a fistful of coat, when a heavy object came crashing down upon his temple.

Chapter 3

Jack fell to his knees, his head pounding in pain. He could hear footsteps racing out the door and down the porch steps.

"Evelyn!" he shouted.

"Over here." Her voice was faint.

Jack crawled over to her side. "Are you hurt?"

"I'm all right . . . but my arm . . . I think I cut it on something when he pushed me down."

"Where is the lamp?"

"I dropped it."

He felt his way across the floor until he found the lamp and the tinderbox. As soon as he lit the lamp, Evelyn cried out, "Hodges!"

She flew to the side of the fallen butler. A crimson trail of blood oozed down his forehead and stained his white shirtfront. "Is he dead?"

Jack knelt down and checked the elderly man's pulse. "No, but he needs a doctor." Raising the lamp, he studied the door lock. "The door is not damaged. The intruder must have knocked, then forced his way inside when Hodges opened the door."

Evelyn's eyes widened like saucers, and she raised a

hand to cover her heart. "Good Lord! What about Father?"

She scrambled to her feet and started forward when Jack grasped her arm. She cried out in pain, and he realized she was bleeding. Looking around, he spotted a shattered vase on the floor. A jagged shard was embedded in her forearm.

"We need to get this out and stanch the bleeding."

"No . . . my father . . ."

His gut clenched. "Stay with Hodges. I'll be right back."

"No!"

Her glazed eyes revealed her panic. He understood her need to find her father. "I'll be a minute only to summon the constable and a doctor. Then we will go together and search for your father."

"Do you think there are more intruders?"

"No. They would have made their exit in the dark while we were down."

She nodded at his explanation.

He wasted no time taking to the street. It was late, but Piccadilly was a busy, upscale neighborhood. He spotted a hackney cab within seconds and flagged down the driver. "An intruder was just in Lord Lyndale's house. Summon the constable and the closest doctor," Jack directed, tossing a coin up to the driver who caught it in midair.

Jack ran back inside the house.

"We should check the library first," Evelyn rushed. "Father always goes to his office after arriving home."

Taking her hand, Jack made his way past the drawing room toward the library. He had been here years before, and he remembered that the library was located in the back of the house. It was a good bet that Lord Lyndale would be there.

It appeared that every candle in the house had been doused, and Jack held the lamp up high. When they came to the library, Evelyn sucked in a breath.

The room had been ransacked. Books had been ripped off the shelves and papers were scattered across the floor. Armchairs had been turned over and the leather upholstery slashed. Horsehair filling littered the carpet.

At first glance, Jack thought the room was vacant, but then a movement of the curtains caught his eye. He rushed forward and pulled the drapes aside. Emmanuel Darlington, the current Earl of Lyndale, was bound and gagged and thrust in the corner.

"Father!" Evelyn cried out and dashed to his side.

Jack immediately set to work untying the older man. "Lord Lyndale, are you hurt?" he asked, looking for signs of obvious injury.

Emmanuel Darlington's eyes widened as he looked up at Jack. "Jack Harding? What are you doing here?"

"It's a long story, my lord. I shall endeavor to explain everything once a doctor sees to you and Hodges."

"Hodges? Was he harmed?"

"Knocked unconscious in the foyer by the intruder who forced his way inside. Where is your manservant, your housekeeper, the rest of your staff?"

"They have one night off a week, save Hodges," Evelyn answered. "Father insists that we are quite self-sufficient and the staff deserves a respite."

Jack bit his lip at Lyndale's generosity.

Lord Lyndale stood with Jack's assistance and sat in a chair behind the desk. A solid wood chair, it had been spared having its cushions slashed open like the other chairs before the fireplace.

Evelyn set to lighting the candles in the sconces on the walls. A warm glow illuminated the library, and Jack was shocked to see how much his former teacher and mentor had aged.

Gone was the full head of dark hair and robust stature. This Lord Lyndale before him was balding with sparse tufts of gray hair, deep frown lines between his eyes. Whereas he used to enjoy a hearty meal and had a sizable paunch, he was now thin and had an unhealthy pallor. Jack mentally calculated Emmanuel Darlington's age as sixty-five, but he appeared in his midseventies.

An angry welt marred the back of his scalp, and Jack knew he had been struck from behind.

"Did you recognize the intruder?" Jack asked him.

"No. I was searching for a book, my back to the door, when I was attacked. When I stirred, he was still in the library, but I was bound, gagged, and stuck behind the curtains. I could hear him rummaging about, but I could see nothing."

Jack motioned to the ransacked room. "Has anything been taken?"

Evelyn spoke up. "It doesn't appear so, but it will take me time to sort through this mess and take inventory."

They were interrupted by a loud pounding on the front door.

"It must be the constable," Jack said. "I'll see to him; you look about for any missing items. They may give clues to the intruder's identity."

Jack left and opened the front door to find two men standing on the porch.

"I'm Constable Bridges and this is Lord Lyndale's personal physician, Dr. Mason. We were told there was a burglary."

"Who are you and where's Hodges?" the doctor asked.

Jack opened the door wide. "I'm Jack Harding, a fellow barrister and close friend of the family. There was indeed an intruder, and Hodges, Lady Evelyn, and Lord Lyndale all need your medical services."

The men stepped inside and soon every candle in the house was alight. Dr. Mason immediately tended to Hodges who had begun to come around. The elderly butler was not critically injured, but had been knocked unconscious when he had been thrown to the floor. Jack and the constable carried him up to his room to rest.

The doctor next examined Lord Lyndale to check for signs of concussion. Dr. Mason asked the elder man several questions and when he proficiently answered each one, the doctor nodded in satisfaction.

The doctor then turned his attention to Evelyn. When he rolled back her sleeve to reveal the embedded porcelain shard, she winced and paled.

Jack sat beside her and held the hand of her uninjured arm. "It must come out, Evie. You can squeeze my hand if you need to."

Wide turquoise eyes turned to him. "You used to call me Evie when I exasperated you with my knowledge of criminal procedure. No one's called me Evie since."

Jack grinned. "Good. I wouldn't want anyone to spoil your memories of me."

"Oh, I wouldn't worry about that. My memories of you are quite vivid."

He wanted to ask her to elaborate further, but just then, Dr. Mason pulled out the shard with a pair of tweezers, causing Evelyn to jerk.

"Ouch!"

"Hold still, Lady Evelyn." With the shard removed, the wound started bleeding anew. She squeezed Jack's hand as the doctor cleansed and bandaged her arm.

"It hurts more," she complained.

Dr. Mason handed her father a small vial. "If the pain persists, give her a little laudanum. If she becomes fevered overnight, send for me immediately." The doctor then snapped shut his black bag. "I'll return tomorrow afternoon to check on everyone."

Evelyn raised her hand. "Wait! Mr. Harding was injured as well."

The doctor's eyes narrowed at Jack. "Mr. Harding?"

"It's nothing," Jack said. "A slight bump on the temple is all."

The doctor set down his bag, his bushy brows furrowed. "Nonetheless, Mr. Harding, I should take a look."

Jack was forced to sit still as he was poked and prodded until the doctor was satisfied there was no serious injury. "Perhaps a dram of whiskey will do you good for any pain tonight. I'll leave now as I'm sure Constable Bridges has questions."

Young Bridges, who had been waiting for the doctor to depart, now stood and cleared his throat. In his early twenties, with the air of self-importance that typically surrounded new recruits, Bridges's spectacles had the thickest lenses Jack had ever seen.

"I inspected the first floor and no windows were broken. Mr. Harding's assumption that the burglar forced his way inside past Hodges appears to be correct." Bridges pushed his spectacles farther up his nose. "I have also conducted a walk-through of the house, Lord Lyndale, and only the library has been disturbed. It appears the burglar was interrupted by Mr. Harding and Lady Evelyn's arrival."

"You think it a common burglary then?" Lord Lyndale asked.

"I do. There have been two other burglaries in the

neighborhood over the past several months. But rest assured, Lord Lyndale, I shall recommend to my superiors that the foot patrols be doubled in Piccadilly."

Constable Bridges put his hat on. "I will keep you informed of anything we learn."

Lyndale nodded and Bridges made his way out, leaving Jack alone with Evelyn and her father.

"I don't agree with the constable that the intruder was a common thief," Jack said.

"Why not?" Evelyn asked.

"Bridges is a new recruit. I've seen it time and again in my criminal cases; freshly minted constables are quick to draw conclusions. They lack the sharp instincts that older officials have honed in the field."

"But Bridges said there have been burglaries in the neighborhood," Evelyn pointed out.

"There very well may have been. But not here. I've spent my entire career in criminal court, remember? I've picked up a few tips from my hired investigators over the years."

Jack strode to Lord Lyndale's desk and picked up a solid gold letter opener. "A common burglar would not pass this up." He pointed to an intricately carved silver snuff box in the corner of the desk, and said, "Or this either." He walked the perimeter of the room, noting other valuables in the library. A small mantel clock of exquisite workmanship, priceless rare books, a walking stick with a gold-tipped crown . . . all would bring a good price on the streets for a common criminal.

"It's possible our arrival interrupted the intruder and he fled before he could pilfer such items," Evelyn said.

Jack shook his head. "He had ample time to scour the room. The room was ransacked and the upholstery slashed while valuables left out in the open were untouched.

He was searching for something, and I don't think he was successful."

"Oh, my," Evelyn said, visibly shuddering. "What can this mean?"

Jack looked to his former teacher who had remained silent since the constable had departed. "Do you have any idea, Lord Lyndale?"

A still-dazed expression clouded Lyndale's face. "I cannot imagine. As a professor at Oxford, my life is quite public. I hardly have secrets."

Lyndale blinked, focusing his gaze on Jack. "You said you would explain why you had arrived here with Evelyn at this hour, Mr. Harding."

Jack ran his fingers through his hair in agitation. "I'm not sure now is the time, Lord Lyndale."

Lyndale cocked his head to the side. "I'd be lying if I said I'm not grateful for your presence here tonight, but I'm confused as well."

Evelyn came forward and rested a hand on her father's shoulder. "Perhaps another time—"

"It has to do with Lady Evelyn's betrothed, Mr. Randolph Sheldon," Jack said.

"Her betrothed!" Lyndale straightened as if a bucket of ice water had been dumped on his head. "Is that what Evelyn told you?"

"Father, I—"

"My apologies, Lord Lyndale," Jack interrupted smoothly. "She said her 'soon-to-be betrothed,' Mr. Sheldon. She sought me out specifically to represent him."

"Randolph Sheldon is one of my Fellows at the university," Lyndale explained. "We have also been friendly with his family over the years, and that is how Evelyn knows the man."

University Fellows, Jack knew, were scholarly students who achieved high marks and were recruited by professors to aid with their research. No wonder Evelyn was fond of the man.

And yet, by Lyndale's tone, Jack knew he did not condone the match.

Lord Lyndale turned to his daughter, his expression tight with strain. "Evelyn, I told you I would see to Randolph's defense if needed. I know all the criminal masters at the Inns."

"But none have Mr. Harding's trial record!" Evelyn protested.

At once, Jack saw his way out. He never wanted to get involved, and it appeared now, even more than before, that Emmanuel Darlington did not approve of his daughter's choice of a marriage partner or of her involvement in Mr. Sheldon's criminal defense. It would be easy for Jack to take his leave, perhaps send a polite note tomorrow morning inquiring into the Darlingtons' well-being, and then disappear entirely from their lives and return to immersing himself in his already-full docket.

But an unfamiliar guilt pierced his thick barrister's armor. Looking at his former mentor and pupilmaster, Jack couldn't help but notice his frailty, the lines of exhaustion around his eyes or worse yet . . . the subtle vulnerability beneath his façade of respectable Oxford professor.

And then there was Evie, the precocious chit from his past with the shrewd intelligence and sharp tongue who had inadvertently pushed him to study harder. The girl who had grown into a woman with the face and figure of a temptress. The contrast of brains and beauty was fascinating . . . compelling.

All that and the nagging suspicion that things were

not right here tonight. That somewhere lurked a real danger for both father and daughter.

Jack took a deep breath before asking the question that could very well bar his quick escape. "Is there a possibility that there is a connection between Mr. Sheldon's accused crime and the intruder tonight?"

Evelyn looked aghast.

Lord Lyndale's eyes clouded in confusion.

"A connection?" Evelyn asked incredulously. "No! It's nothing but a horrible coincidence."

"I don't believe in coincidences," Jack said dryly. "Years in the courtroom dealing with the underbelly of London have taught me such a thing rarely exists."

Chapter 4

After Jack left, Evelyn and her father finally retired. She had lain awake in her bed for over an hour, and more than once had tiptoed to her father's bedroom, pressed her ear to the door, and waited until she heard his muffled snores. He had sustained a nasty hit on the head, and despite Dr. Mason's examination, Evelyn knew at her father's age there were risks.

But it was Jack Harding's observations that had her tossing and turning the remainder of the night. He had rejected the constable's conclusion that the break-in was connected to a string of burglaries in Piccadilly. Jack had been correct in pointing out that valuables had been left behind. But even more disturbing, he had been suspicious of a connection between the intruder and Randolph's alleged crime.

Could it be true?

But what on earth would the murderer of the infamous Drury Lane Theatre actress, Bess Whitfield, want in her father's library office? It made no sense.

And then there was Jack himself. Handsome, devilishly charming Jack, who had turned out to be a safe harbor in which to anchor when deadly circumstances made her feel like grasping at driftwood like a drowning sailor.

After their run-in with the intruder, Jack had instantly taken charge, summoning the doctor and constable. He had not succumbed to the panic that had nearly overwhelmed her. He had been a source of strength and command when they had most needed it. Neither had he departed as soon as Dr. Mason or Constable Bridges had arrived, but had chosen to stay until Hodges and her father, as well as herself, had been examined, even holding her hand as the porcelain shard was painfully pulled out of her flesh.

The warmth of his palm as he held hers had sent a tremor of awareness down her spine. The faint scent of his shaving soap had filled her senses, and the heat emanating from the nearness of his body had offered a comfort that no amount of laudanum could provide. A delicate thread had formed between them. And when he had called her Evie, her mind whirled with unbidden memories . . .

Jack bent over a thick treatise, a lock of brown hair falling over his forehead. Jack standing outside the Inns, roughhousing with the other students. Jack flirting with the female clerks at the Inn, all of them responding to his smile.

She frowned at the last memory and shook her head at her foolishness. She was no longer a schoolgirl, but a grown woman who was more than able to resist the virile charms of Jack Harding. She must be more practical than to think of the past; too much was riding on the present.

There had been one good thing that had come of the evening: Jack's slight capitulation to take on the case. She had sensed it more than anything else. He was torn. If he truly believed in his suspicions, then he may feel obliged to take the case. For in representing Randolph Sheldon, Jack would be helping both her and her father.

She waited until the first streaks of sunlight filtered through her curtains before dressing and knocking on her father's door. She was surprised to find his room vacant, and when she rushed downstairs, she saw him dressed and sitting in the dining room. The servants had returned as expected, and the housekeeper, Mrs. Smith, entered carrying a steaming plate of eggs and biscuits.

At the sight of Evelyn, Mrs. Smith's eyes widened. "Lady Evelyn! I heard of last night's occurrences. You should not be up, my lady. Your maid, Janet, has just returned with the rest of the staff. Perhaps you should spend the day in bed. I'll send her to you right away."

"I'm well, Mrs. Smith. Thank you for your concern." Evelyn smiled, glancing at the plate of food in her hand. "That smells delicious."

"Right away, my lady." Mrs. Smith said, setting the plate on the table and rushing back in the direction of the kitchen.

Evelyn took a seat beside her father, aware of his steady scrutiny.

"I don't suppose I can talk you out of your plans? You know I do not believe Randolph would make a good husband for you," he said.

Evelyn knew how her father felt. Although he liked Randolph and kept him as his University Fellow, he believed Randolph was not a good spiritual or emotional match for his headstrong daughter. Despite her father's beliefs, Evelyn was convinced that she could change his mind regarding Randolph. If only the three of them could spend more time together, Lord Lyndale would see how truly intellectually compatible they were.

At her silence, his brows drew downward in a frown. "I take it your mind is set on your other plans as well?"

"If you mean my soliciting Mr. Harding, then yes, my mind is set," Evelyn said.

Mrs. Smith returned with a full plate and placed it before Evelyn. As soon as the housekeeper departed, her father spoke up.

"You have acted hastily. Randolph may never be arrested. Furthermore, you should not have approached Mr. Harding directly, but should have gone through a solicitor," he admonished.

Evelyn shook her head. She knew the formalities, of course. If a person had a legal dilemma, they were to approach a solicitor, who dealt directly with the public. The solicitor, in turn, contacted the barrister, who alone was permitted to appear in court.

"But I wanted to ensure Jack Harding's representation, not another barrister's chosen at will by a solicitor," she said.

"There are other barristers that owe me favors"— he raised a hand when she would interrupt—"but after last night, I do believe Jack Harding would be a good choice."

She took a quick sharp breath. "You do?"

"He is already acquainted with our family, and he was gracious enough to stay by our side last night. In addition, I too have been following his trial record. You are not the only one interested in such things, Evelyn."

Evelyn stiffened, momentarily abashed. "Of course not, Father. I never thought I was."

"Has Mr. Harding agreed to aid Randolph then?"

"Not exactly . . ."

"But he was here last night?"

"Only to speak with you."

"Ah, I see. He refused any subterfuge on your part."

"I believe that was his intent," she said dryly.

Lord Lyndale nodded. "Good. I'm even more comfortable with him then."

Evelyn watched him beneath lowered lashes as he finished his breakfast. Placing her fork down, she asked, "Father, do you believe what Mr. Harding said? That there is a connection between last night's burglar and Bess Whitfield's murder?"

Lyndale looked up, his eyes narrowed. "I do not, but I'm not surprised he did. Highly successful criminal barristers like Jack Harding do not achieve their results by leaving any stone unturned." Pushing his empty plate aside, he put down his napkin. "What I believe matters naught. Do you think you can persuade Mr. Harding to take Randolph on as a client?"

"If he believes you want him involved, then yes."

Her father stood and made to leave. "Good. I have a lecture at the university this morning that I cannot miss."

Evelyn rose. "I shall pay Mr. Harding a visit then."

Her father stopped and turned. "Alone?"

"I shall take Janet as a chaperone." She dare not tell him that she had already been alone with Jack Harding in the client consultation room of the Old Bailey Courthouse. Knowing her father, he would protest if he learned she had observed Jack's trial in the spectators' gallery with the general masses without a proper chaperone.

"Please extend my gratitude for his aid last night," her father said. "And invite him to dine with us one evening when we entertain the judges. I'm sure Mr. Harding would enjoy a meal with both Lordships Bathwell and Barnes."

"Of course," she said.

Evelyn waited precisely five minutes after her father's

departure before summoning a carriage. She had no intention of taking her maid.

Evelyn stepped out of the carriage and looked up in awe at the magnificent structure before her. She had visited Lincoln's Inn of Court many times in the past as it was her father's Inn, and he had maintained his chambers here before leaving to teach at Oxford. But it had been years since she had explored its hallowed halls as an excited and eager girl, lingering in her father's chambers and listening to him advise his clients and lecture his pupils.

Yes, she had been here dozens of times in her past, and yet Lincoln's Inn still enthralled her.

It was a compound more than a single building. She started down Chancery Lane and the Tudor Gatehouse came into view. Built in the sixteenth century, the brick gatehouse had massive oak doors with three coats of arms above its entrance.

The first coat of arms showed a lion rampant, which Evelyn knew was the symbol of Lincoln's Inn. But it was the memory of her father, sitting her high upon his shoulders as a little girl, pointing at the lion that made her smile. He had danced around and roared and she had giggled upon his shoulders as a giddy, carefree five-year-old. Years later she had learned that the lion was not only the symbol of the Inn, but the arms of Henry de Lacy, Earl of Lincoln. The other two arms above the oak doors belonged to Henry VIII, one of England's most controversial kings who ruled at the time the Gatehouse was built, and Sir Thomas Lovell, who was not only a member of Lincoln's Inn and the House of Commons, but the Chancellor of the Exchequer who funded the Gatehouse.

Stepping through the oak doors, she stood in Gatehouse Court, an appealing Tudor-style, half-timbered courtyard with turrets and flowering pots overflowing with fragrant blooms. Before her lay the Old Hall, the impressive library with its collection of rare and current law books, the dining hall, and the seventeenth-century chapel with its stunning stained glass, but she suppressed the urge to take a leisurely tour.

She turned to the left instead and headed for the Old Buildings, which housed the professional accommodations of the barristers.

If she had been born a man, she would have gladly entered the pupilage to become a barrister herself. The truth was, she had studied her father's books with a voracious hunger for knowledge and had been envious of the pupils that had come and gone, seemingly oblivious to their fortunes that only because they had been born male they could attain what she wanted most, but would never be able to have.

And then Jack Harding had come along.

He was the first student who made her not yearn to be born a male, but quite happily a female. He had been charming and carefree and quite horribly the worst pupil to enter Emmanuel Darlington's chambers. His Latin and Greek were sorely lacking, and he had never bothered to learn the basics of torts, contracts, or criminal procedure. But he had the gift of speech and a glib tongue like that of an experienced politician, and her father had instantly recognized his talent and taken Jack under his wing.

She herself had tried every trick she knew to gain Jack's attention. Unfortunately, without female guidance, no one ever told her the way to a man's heart was not through fluent Latin or a complete knowledge of William Blackstone's legal works.

Turning a corner, the heels of her kidskin shoes echoed

down a long hallway of doors bearing brass nameplates engraved with the names of barristers. She finally came to a stop at the nameplate announcing the Chambers of Mr. Jack Harding, Mr. Brent Stone, Mr. Anthony Stevens, and Mr. James Devlin. The first name was the only one of interest to her, and she knew the other three belonged to barristers who shared chambers with Jack.

Taking a deep breath, she reached for the handle and swept inside. She entered a common room, with rows of file cabinets lining the walls. A middle-aged clerk, seated behind a desk writing furiously on a legal-looking document, looked up and froze.

"May I help you, miss?"

"Lady Evelyn Darlington looking for Mr. Harding."

"Is he expecting you, Lady Evelyn?"

"Of course," she lied.

Adjusting his spectacles, he looked down at an appointment book, his ink-stained fingers traveling down the page.

Evelyn held her breath as her mind spun with excuses.

The clerk shook his head once and looked up. "I'm sorry, my lady, but I do not see your name in his appointment register."

"Then there must be a mistake," she said in a haughty tone she had heard her father use when addressing an unethical adversary. "Please advise Mr. Harding of my presence."

The clerk stood and strode down the hall, past several closed doors until he stopped before one. He knocked once, then cracked open the door. "A Lady Evelyn Darlington is here to see you, Mr. Harding. She claims she has an appointment, but I—"

Evelyn heard a murmur from behind the door, and

the squeaking springs of a chair, and then the door opened wide.

Jack stood in the entrance. He wore an impeccably tailored suit, the navy jacket of which emphasized the outline of his broad shoulders, and she wondered if he had another trial at the Old Bailey this morning. The familiar lock of wavy brown hair fell casually on his forehead as if he had styled it in such a roguish manner to enhance his appeal. But it was his unfathomable, emerald eyes that seemed to glow in his bronzed face that held her attention.

His gaze swept her figure, then returned to her face, and he grinned.

The pit of her stomach churned in response.

"It's quite all right, McHugh," Jack said. "Lady Evelyn is always welcome in my chambers."

The clerk nodded, and she handed him her cloak. He shut the door behind him on his way out.

She stood awkwardly in Jack's chambers, her eyes roaming the space. It was more impressive even than her father's chambers had been. With keen interest she took in the massive bookshelves lined with law books and the stacks of litigation pleadings and briefs piled on his mahogany desk. A luxurious Wilton carpet with a cut-velvet appearance and Turkish pattern covered the floor. Behind his desk was a stone fireplace, ready to be lit, and resting on the mantel was a bust of Sir Thomas More—one of the most prominent members of Lincoln's Inn—who had been tragically beheaded by Henry VIII for refusing to acknowledge the king as the Supreme Head of the Church of England.

"I was going to pay a visit today," Jack said, "to make certain you were all right after last night. How is your father faring?"

"He's quite well. He rose before me this morning and is delivering a lecture at the university as we speak."

Jack stepped close and reached for the hand of her bandaged arm. Looking down at her injury, he rubbed her fingers. "How about you? Does it hurt?"

Her pulse quickened at his touch, the stroke of his fingers against hers. "Less than last evening."

"Did you take a dose of laudanum like Dr. Mason advised?" he asked.

Evelyn wrinkled her nose. "No. I dislike the stuff. It clouds my thinking."

His lips twitched. "Many consider that a desirable side effect of the drug, although I'm not surprised by your aversion. You never could stop thinking."

She straightened. "Are you going to constantly remind me of the past?"

An easy smile played at the corners of his mouth. "Why not? You said yourself that your memories of me are quite vivid."

Heat flooded her cheeks. "Mr. Harding, I—"

"It's Jack. You always used to call me Jack."

"Yes, but that was years ago when—"

He raised her hand to kiss her fingers, and her heart slammed against her chest. His lips, firm, yet soft, brushed against her skin. He lifted his head, and his green eyes glittered intensely. Sunlight streamed in through the parted curtains, illuminating his face, and she was struck by a sudden serious set to his handsome features.

"I was furious that you were injured," he said, his tone hardening. "If I had been lucky enough to catch the intruder, I would have pummeled him senseless."

She swallowed hard. Uncomfortable with his keen probing eyes and the uncharacteristic harshness behind his words, she turned away, walking toward one of the large windows.

"I wanted to thank you for your assistance last evening," she said. "You went above and beyond any duty toward us when—"

She felt a big hand on her shoulder. "You're welcome, Evie. But tell me why you're really here."

She turned, and he was so close she had to tilt her head up to look into his eyes. There was no doubt in her mind that he knew the truth, and there was no sense trying to placate him with gratitude—even if it was heartfelt.

"Father changed his mind and agrees you would be the best barrister to take on Mr. Randolph Sheldon's case," she blurted out.

"He did?"

"Yes," she breathed, her voice sounding husky to her own ears.

Jack stepped closer. With her back to the window, she felt like a skittish doe being cornered by a large, dangerous predator.

"And what will be the terms of my retainer?" he asked.

She was finding it difficult to keep her wits about her with him standing so near. "The terms?"

"Payment, Evie. What are you willing to pay if I take on Mr. Sheldon's case?"

She blinked, hoping that her senses would reappear. "As I mentioned before, you will be adequately compensated."

He trailed his finger down her cheek, stopping beside her lower lip, and she froze, every nerve ending tingling at his touch.

"I'm not speaking of money."

"Whatever do you mean?"

"A kiss, Evie. I want a kiss as a retainer."

Chapter 5

"A kiss?" Evelyn asked, dumbfounded.

"Just between us. No one need know. Certainly not your Mr. Sheldon," Jack said.

She inhaled sharply, the fog that had previously shrouded her senses dissipating beneath his green gaze.

"I'm not certain what type of woman you believe me to be, Mr. Harding," she said sternly. "But rest assured I am certainly not like any of Slip Dawson's strumpets."

"It's Jack, remember?"

Straightening her spine, she raised her chin a notch and gave him her best glare. "I remember, *Mr. Harding.*"

He hadn't moved, and her back was still to the window with him mere inches away. He was challenging her, she realized, waiting to see if she would step aside, but she refused to show any cowardice.

"You're so urgent for me to take the case. Why?" he asked.

"I told you. Randolph and I are to be engaged. He's innocent."

"I don't think that's the entire reason, Evie," he said in a lower, huskier tone.

"I don't know what you are suggesting."

"That you were quite enamored of me once. You used to follow me around your father's chambers and wait for me outside the Inn."

"That was years ago," she blurted out. "I was little more than a girl." As soon as the words were out of her mouth, she realized the thought to deny his accusations had never occurred to her.

He grinned devilishly.

Evelyn felt her skin grow hot. How could she forget that Jack Harding was a skilled cross-examiner? And yet despite his ability to evoke an admission, his smile had a devastating effect on her.

It had always been hard to stay angry at Jack.

A sudden thought occurred to her. "You're jesting with me, aren't you? You weren't serious about a kiss in lieu of a retainer."

A predatory gleam flashed in his sharp eyes. "I wasn't joking."

"You honestly mean to take on the case if I kiss you?" she asked incredulously.

"Yes."

"Are you mad?"

"I'm perfectly sane, thank you."

"But I'm to marry another man," she insisted.

"So you keep saying. But where is he now? More importantly, where was he last night?"

He stepped forward, closing what little distance there had been between them. She swallowed at his nearness, the scent of his cologne. His body so close . . .

"That's not fair," she whispered. "You know quite well that Randolph could not come last night. He is in hiding. The Bow Street Runners would have arrested—"

"If you were my intended, I would have been there."

His words touched upon a primitive need long-buried

within her. When it came to Randolph, she had always had the more dominant personality. They had an intellectual connection that she treasured, but when important decisions needed to be made, she was inclined to take the lead and Randolph to follow. She had liked it that way, until Jack had pointed out the downside to such a relationship. She had needed someone to lean on last night, to take charge and make critical decisions, and Randolph had most definitely not been available.

But neither could she abandon Randolph Sheldon. She had searched for years for a man she could have a deep intellectual conversation with, and Randolph was never intimidated by her intellectual ideas or pursuits.

No matter how radical and unladylike such pursuits were viewed by the *beau monde*.

Evelyn's mind raced, and she came to a quick conclusion. What harm could one kiss do?

She and Randolph had kissed, of course, and the brief encounters had not been entirely unpleasant. But neither had she been swept away by passion or had lost her head as many of the lovesick debutantes of the *ton* had frequently gushed about in the ladies' retiring room at Almack's.

Looking up at Jack, she said, "Fine, Mr. Harding. A kiss. One kiss and you agree to represent Mr. Sheldon?"

He nodded.

Taking a deep breath, she tipped her head up and shut her eyes. "I'm ready."

Seconds passed and instead of the wet, smothering kiss she expected, she heard him chuckle.

She cracked open her eyes.

Jack stood still, his head tilted to the side. Slowly, ever so slowly, he reached out to touch her lips with a finger.

"Just as I thought. Have you been kissed by your Mr. Sheldon?"

"Of course."

"Hmmm." The pad of his thumb ran leisurely across her full bottom lip—back and forth—and her breath caught.

The urge to pull away was there, but not because his touch was unpleasant, but rather because it evoked a shivering along her spine.

"We had occasion to be alone," she breathed.

"I see. Then you know what to expect."

"Yes." *No.* Randolph had never looked at her the way Jack was gazing at her now, as if her mouth was a ripe strawberry waiting to be savored.

She watched in fascinated thrall as Jack's head lowered. She felt his lips touch hers like a whisper, and she marveled how his mouth—which had appeared chiseled out of fine Italian marble—could be so soft and gentle.

His tongue traced the fullness of her lower lip, and when she gasped he slid past her teeth and swept inside. Gathering her into his arms, he held her against him. And then his kiss changed. His mouth covered hers more firmly, and his hands explored the hollows of her back.

It was her undoing. Nothing had prepared her for the reality of the flesh-and-blood man. The feel of his chest—all hard muscle and sinew, so different from Randolph's slim build—felt sinful and intoxicating. Her body tingled from the contact; her heart raced.

Randolph's kisses had been overeager and sloppy, and in her mind she had likened him to an overzealous and panting puppy. The heavy breathing and awkward gasping had never raised this kind of physical response in her, and she had always believed a man's passions must vary wildly in degrees from a woman's.

Until now . . .

She felt her knees weaken at Jack's slow, seductive kisses. The tantalizing persuasion of his expert touch was as intoxicating as fine wine. He covered her lips with demanding mastery, and she was stunned by her response. In the deep recesses of her mind, she knew the kiss was wrong—the sensations coursing through her body were traitorous—and that she should end the embrace.

But it was Jack who pulled back first, a frown marring his brow as he gazed upon her upturned face. "So the legal scholar does have hot blood in her veins. Who would have thought?"

It was the last thing she had expected him to say, and the most damaging. Humiliation turned sharply into annoyance.

Pushing away from the window, she walked into the center of the room. "You misunderstand. I felt nothing. I was merely upholding my end of the bargain. Now will you uphold yours?"

Jack turned to face her. "Nothing, madame? I hardly call that kiss nothing," he drawled. "Do you feel the same when Mr. Sheldon embraces you?"

"You're wrong," she snapped. "And what I feel with Randolph is irrelevant." A sudden fear ran through her that Jack may still walk away. "You will take the case?" she asked, hating the way her voice took on a desperate tone.

His lips quivered. "Don't worry, Evie. I shall represent him. Despite my full docket, my instincts are telling me there is something amiss here."

Relief coursed through her. "On behalf of Mr. Sheldon, I want to thank you."

Jack's expression hardened. "Make no mistake, Evie, I'm agreeing not because of your Mr. Sheldon, but because I owe your father my career, and I always pay my debts."

A coldness centered around her chest at his words. She was confused by her reaction. She should be happy, thrilled really, that Jack Harding had agreed to represent Randolph. Instead, she felt a loss at his words.

Or more disturbingly, a loss at his touch.

It must be the stress, she thought. Her life had been turned upside down since Randolph had stumbled into her home mere days ago, incoherently babbling of Bess Whitfield's murder.

"About the kiss . . . I don't think it would be wise to do that again," she said.

Jack's head snapped up. "Don't worry. I wholeheartedly agree. I never mix business with pleasure. It always results in disastrous outcomes in the courtroom, and I take my trial record very seriously."

She met his stare with an effort, her voice wavering. "I understand."

"One last thing. Tell me when you have contact with Mr. Sheldon."

"But I told you, I don't know where he is."

"No matter. He has no choice but to reach out to you. Inform me immediately."

It was a command, not a request. Evelyn nodded numbly. "I shall see my way out."

As she left his chambers, she had the odd sense that even though she had successfully achieved what she had come for, she had lost something as well.

Chapter 6

"What are you hiding from us, Harding?"

Jack looked up from the stack of papers on his desk as the door to his office flew open. James Devlin and Brent Stone, two of the barristers that shared his chambers, strode inside.

Jack turned to Devlin, the more outspoken of the two men. "I don't know what you are talking about. It's impossible to hide anything from either of you; I wouldn't think even to try," Jack said dryly.

"Then what do you call the lovely lady that swept past us in the hallway on her way out of your office?" Devlin drawled. "The lovely *unchaperoned* lady, I might add."

Jack threw down his pen and leaned back in his chair. "She was here on legal business, nothing more."

Devlin and Brent exchanged a doubtful look.

"Legal business?" Brent asked. "Since when do you take on female clients that look like her? That's more in Devlin's line."

Devlin punched Brent in the arm. "Are you insinuating I'm unethical when it comes to my female clients?"

"I'm not *insinuating* anything, Devlin, merely stating fact," Brent said.

Devlin's eyes narrowed at Brent. "Perhaps it's been so long since you have entertained the thought of female companionship, your opinion has become skewed."

Jack suppressed the urge to laugh out loud as his two longtime friends and legal colleagues harassed each other. He also wanted them gone. He didn't want to talk about Evelyn or what had just passed between them.

"Enough, you two," Jack snapped. "I have work to do. Taking on a new murder client is time-consuming."

That got their attention. Devlin and Brent turned to look at Jack. In unison, they asked, "She's a murderer?"

"Not her. The man she intends to marry," Jack said.

Their gazes remained riveted.

"She's marrying a murderer?" Brent spoke up first.

"She believes he's innocent. Thus, my representation," Jack said.

Brent stepped forward. "Which brings me back to my original point. You never work for beautiful women. They are a distraction in the courtroom, remember? Why now?"

Jack sighed, his mind twisting with how much he should reveal. "She's Emmanuel Darlington's daughter."

Devlin's jaw dropped. "You're jesting?"

"That's the second time today someone has asked me that question."

"So you're making an exception to your rule because you feel indebted to your former pupilmaster and mentor?" Brent asked.

"I believe so, yes," Jack said.

"Have you bedded her yet?" Devlin asked.

For some reason, Devlin's remark grated on Jack, and he wanted to hit his friend square in the mouth. "Not all of us are like you, Devlin."

Devlin grinned. "I'll take that as a no. But I believe she will try your self-discipline."

"Don't listen to him, Jack," Brent said. "If you focus on the case, you'll have no time to think of her in a carnal manner."

Devlin's eyes flashed in a familiar display of impatience. "Not all of us are self-imposed celibates like you, Brent."

Jack studied the pair. He didn't have to be a woman to acknowledge that Brent Stone was a handsome man. With his tawny hair and blue eyes, Brent had always drawn the female eye. But for all his attractiveness, he hid a dark past behind his formal demeanor as a respectable barrister. As the Crown's leading patent expert, he spent long hours at Lincoln's Inn obtaining letters patent for wealthy, and oftentimes eccentric inventors. For reasons unknown, Brent Stone avoided the fair sex. Only once had Jack caught Brent with a woman. Jack had sensed Brent had wanted the liaison kept a secret from the rest of chambers, and so Jack had never mentioned the encounter to Devlin or Anthony Stevens, their other legal colleague and friend.

James Devlin, on the other hand, had quite the opposite personality. He was the illegitimate son of a duke, and even though he had been well provided for, he had been socially shunned by his father's family. He'd developed a thick skin and had been driven to succeed. Now that he was a successful barrister in his own right, Devlin enjoyed his wealth and freedom to act out his every whim—especially when it came to London's courtesans—while avoiding the marriage-minded ladies of the *ton*. Devlin's free-loving mind-set had gotten him into trouble in the past, but he had successfully fought more than one duel with a disgruntled husband. Dark, daring, and dangerous, women loved Devlin, and he adored them in return.

Yes, James Devlin and Brent Stone were opposite sides of a coin, but they were good friends nonetheless.

Devlin scratched his chin. "Wait till I tell Anthony. He's not going to believe it."

"Actually, I've been meaning to talk to Anthony about the case," Jack said.

Devlin frowned. "Anthony handles matrimonial matters. What does that have to do with your murder case?"

"He works with some of the best investigators in London. If a man's hiding a secret, Anthony's investigators can ferret it out."

"Even if that secret is a woman?" Devlin asked.

"Especially if it's a woman."

Devlin shrugged and turned to leave. "Perhaps Anthony can talk you out of this nonsense."

"I owe her father my career, Devlin," Jack's voice grated harshly.

"Then do yourself a favor and get yourself a mistress. And the sooner the better, from the looks of Lady Evelyn Darlington," Devlin shot over his shoulder on his way out.

Brent waved his hand, dismissing Devlin's speech. "No need for such measures, Jack. Working long hours will keep your mind off her. Just stay focused on the case."

Jack wanted to reassure his friend, but he held his tongue as Brent departed. As soon as the door closed, Jack let out a long held-in breath. Pushing his papers to the side, he stared at the surface of his desk as Evelyn's image arose in his mind.

He had initially wanted to kiss her out of need and simple curiosity. He had foolishly thought that if he kissed Evelyn, she would be stone cold—like a dried-out old book that had lingered too long untouched on the library shelf—and he would be able to get her off his mind and move on to focus on Randolph Sheldon's case. But to his astonishment, she had been anything but frigid. She had been as passionate and hot as an inferno; the kiss had been as smoldering as the heat that joins two metals.

It had also been just as jarring. His plan to satisfy his curiosity and quench his desire had failed. He had ended the kiss, knowing that if he had allowed it to continue, his resistance would have been lost along with his logic and legal ability. For a brief instant, panic had pierced him, and he had fought to suppress the urge to usher her through his door and out of his life.

But then cold reason returned, and he recalled his debt to her father.

Jack had been undisciplined until he had entered his pupilage under Emmanuel Darlington at Lincoln's Inn. Emmanuel had inspired Jack to learn and had taken him to task, but it was the taste of his first trial that had fully fired Jack's ambition. A trial victory was like an addictive drug, luring him to continuously crave the next one. To be able to persuade twelve jurors with only his words and a few props that his side was the righteous one—no matter how damning the facts—gave Jack a feeling of invincibility.

But it was not without cost. Jack worked long, unconventional hours, often leaving chambers with a heavy litigation bag and working well past midnight at home. He had longed for the next trial far more than he had longed for a wife.

He had known of barristers that had tried for both—a heavy trial practice and a family. Many failed to deal with the stress and too often indulged in alcohol as a way to cope. Their wives were bitter, their children neglected.

No, Jack Harding had sworn never to fall into the marriage trap.

His work was the most important aspect of his life. He had always enjoyed women, just not the tangle of relationships or the typical hysterics that accompanied them when he sought to walk away from a woman—all of which could weaken his focus.

He could work with Evelyn Darlington, he reminded himself. It would require that he keep a physical distance from her, but the fact that Evelyn was just as determined to maintain a professional relationship henceforth should aid his cause.

Devlin's and Brent's advice rushed back to him. Jack would take both. It shouldn't be hard to immerse himself in his work like Brent had suggested. His docket had already been full without the addition of Randolph Sheldon as a client.

As for Devlin's advice to take a mistress, the thought had a certain appeal.

Jack's prior mistress, Molly Adler, would welcome him back if he chose to pay her a visit. He had never officially ended relations with her; he had simply stopped calling. She had sent love notes, of course, but his interest had waned, and as an experienced London courtesan, she must have known to take another lover. But he had no doubt she would invite him into her bed if he chose to knock on her door.

It was a good idea, he knew. There was no easier way to get a woman off his mind than to bed another. They were all the same; Evelyn Darlington was just a woman, no different from any other. And when it came to the importance of his career, Jack refused to allow Evelyn to be the exception to his steadfast rule.

Chapter 7

A week after Evelyn had met with Jack in his chambers, she still had not heard from Randolph. Needing to distract herself, she decided to go on a long-delayed shopping excursion. Her maid, Janet, walked beside her as they passed Bond Street's well-known establishments—Hookham's Circulating Library, Ackermann's print shop, and Sir Thomas Lawrence's portrait studio.

They came up to Gentleman Jackson's boxing salon, and Janet craned her neck to get a glimpse inside.

Evelyn couldn't blame her maid. The pugilistic arts were presently in fashion, and she couldn't help but wonder if Jack Harding practiced boxing. At once her mind pictured him bare-chested and bare-knuckled, sweating in a ring. Her temperature rose of its own accord.

Biting her lip, she turned to her maid. "Janet, while I'm in the milliner's shop, I want you to go to the tea shop next door and pick up Lord Lyndale's medicinal tea."

Janet dragged her gaze away from the pugilists visible through the window to look at her employer. "'Ow will I know which one, m' lady?"

"The proprietor knows what I require for Lord Lyndale."

Evelyn's father had been looking tired of late, and

Evelyn was concerned that his hectic schedule was taking a toll on his health. Even though as an earl he need not work as a barrister or a lecturing professor, Emmanuel Darlington refused to act the titled lord and give up his love of teaching.

"Aye, m' lady." Janet bobbed her white-capped head, and left for the tea shop.

Bells on the milliner's door chimed as Evelyn stepped inside. From the outside, the shop appeared small, and indeed it was narrow, but it had considerable depth.

Evelyn wound her way through rows of display stands, holding everything from bonnets with dyed ostrich plumes to straw hats trimmed with ribbon streamers and artificial flowers, to gaudy jewel-studded turbans. Throughout the shop, expensively dressed ladies tried on hats and peered at their reflections in cheval glass mirrors.

Never one to be obsessed with fashion like many of her acquaintances of the *ton,* Evelyn's awareness of her attire had been heightened after her father inherited his title. Now the daughter of an earl, she was well aware of the importance of dressing the part.

A particular bonnet caught her eye. Periwinkle blue, with a ruched silk lining, it had a wide brim and ribbon edge. Beside it was a silk parasol with matching periwinkle fringe and a cane handle. The bonnet and parasol were exquisite and would be just the thing for walking in Hyde Park to shield her fair skin from the summer sun.

Evelyn reached for the hat, and her fingers caressed the fine material. Again an unbidden image of Jack Harding returned, and she pondered how he would react to seeing her in such finery. With the memory of his kiss, heat flooded her face. She remembered his lips, firm yet soft, and the tantalizing taste of his mouth. He was everything she had ever fantasized as an awkward girl and more . . . so much more.

She had desperately wanted to stand on tiptoe and press her body close to his, wanted to sink her fingers into his hair and then run her hands over his broad shoulders. It was as if he had drugged her, taken her will and turned it against her. Instead of being outraged at his demand for a kiss, as a true lady should have been, she had wildly wondered how she had compared to his other conquests, for surely there had been many.

Evelyn sighed, touching her lips with her finger, reliving the kiss in her mind.

An elderly matron with iron gray curls walked past, and the overpowering smell of her perfume wafted to Evelyn. When Evelyn looked up, the woman frowned as if she could read the inappropriate thoughts that passed through Evelyn's mind. Evelyn's finger dropped from her mouth, her gaze returning to the bonnet in her hands.

What was she doing?

It was one kiss. It was a mistake. And it would never happen again. Lust was meaningless and hardly the basis for a good future. The intellectual and respectful bond that she shared with Randolph Sheldon was irreplaceable and priceless. She refused to allow one kiss and a foolish childhood infatuation to distract her from her plans.

She made to return the blue silk bonnet to its stand, when a masculine voice came from behind.

"Evelyn."

She started and whirled around. "Simon! What are you doing here?"

He smiled and reached out to clasp her hand. "I've been searching for you, Evelyn."

Evelyn's eyes widened as she stared at Simon Guthrie in astonishment. Simon was Randolph Sheldon's closest friend, and Evelyn had immediately taken a liking to him. Simon was also a University Fellow at Oxford, but whereas Randolph was her father's Fellow, Simon labored under another professor. Of medium height and dark-haired, his narrow face looked older than his years. His brown eyes were sincere under drawn brows and he smiled reassuringly, showing straight teeth.

Simon pulled her behind a tall stack of mahogany drawers. Leaning close, he lowered his voice. "Randolph sent me."

Evelyn found her voice. "Where is he? Is he well?"

"He's fine. But he needs your help."

"I need to know where Randolph is."

"He's in a small house in Shoreditch."

"Shoreditch!" Evelyn's thoughts whirled like leaves in a strong wind. On the outskirts of London, in the County of Middlesex, Shoreditch was known for its many theaters and bawdy music halls. It was attractive to artists and theatergoers alike because it was out of the dominion of the more conservative London moralists. "Why is he there?"

"Bess Whitfield had a house there for when she wasn't performing in London. As Randolph's cousin, she gave him the key years ago."

At the mention of the murdered actress, shock flew through Evelyn. "Bess Whitfield! Is Randolph insane?"

"He had no other place to hide."

"He shouldn't have run in the first place." Her voice sounded brusque to her own ears.

Damnation. She hadn't intended to criticize Randolph's actions, but the words were out before she could stop them.

"Word is the Bow Street Runners are searching for him for Bess's murder."

"Perhaps if Randolph had stayed behind and answered the constable's questions, none of this would have occurred."

Simon's kind eyes studied her. "Do you really believe that, Evelyn?"

Evelyn exhaled. She didn't know what to believe. Truth be told, there was a good chance Randolph would have been arrested had he not fled from the constable. Randolph had been the one to find Bess Whitfield's body in her home. His presence there alone would have been suspicious.

"I need to speak with him," she said. "I have hired a barrister to represent him."

"A barrister? Who?"

"Jack Harding." She wondered if Simon had heard of Jack, being a university student.

"The jury master?"

She looked at Simon in surprise. "You know of him then?"

"Some of his cases and verdicts have been mentioned in the newspapers."

"Mr. Harding suspected that Randolph would reach out to me, but I thought Randolph would come to me himself."

"You must know that he could not. It is too risky."

"Mr. Harding needs to speak with him."

"I can arrange a meeting, but then Randolph will have to go back into hiding. Can we trust this Mr. Harding?"

"We have no choice."

Simon's face was grim. "I'll speak with Randolph and send you a note where to meet."

Simon nodded at the bonnet she held in her limp hands. Reaching out, he squeezed her shoulder. "Buy that one, Evelyn. It brings out the blue of your eyes."

Chapter 8

"Randolph wants to meet *where*?" Jack scanned the note in his hand and then glared at Evelyn.

"It makes perfect sense, really," Evelyn said.

"The hell it does." He was so irritated that he did not care if his choice of words was inappropriate before a lady.

Evelyn crossed Jack's chambers, sat in the chair across from his desk, and made a show of arranging her skirts before speaking.

"Surely you must understand that Randolph must be cautious," she said.

"I understand that he is evading the Bow Street Runners to avoid questioning regarding Bess Whitfield's murder. But I do not understand why he wants to meet at the infamous Cock and Bull Tavern in the frenzied fish market of Billingsgate on a busy Friday afternoon."

"It is a safe choice for him. Randolph will not be recognized there."

Jack felt his temper rise. "And he has no concern for your safety, your reputation?"

"I will dress appropriately."

Pressing both palms flat on the desk, Jack leaned into

them and glowered at her. "You think a quick change of your gown and all will be well? Have you not looked at your reflection of late?"

She swallowed. "We will travel together. It will be dark by the time we leave."

"No, Evie. *We* will not travel anywhere together. *I* will meet Mr. Sheldon alone."

Evelyn's eyes widened in alarm. "I must go. I have to see Randolph. And Simon said Randolph will not meet with you unless I am present."

"And just who is this Simon?"

"Simon Guthrie is Randoph's close friend and another Oxford Fellow. Simon is the one who delivered the note requesting us to meet at the Cock and Bull."

Jack glanced down at the now-crumpled note on the desk. Throughout his career he had met with clients in all types of establishments throughout the underbelly of London, but never had he been responsible for the welfare of a lady accompanying him.

And the Cock and Bull was a rowdy, bawdy tavern, in the center of the Billingsgate fish market. Part of the London docks, the place swelled with sailors, dockworkers, fishwives, buyers, prostitutes, thieves, and smugglers on a daily basis.

It certainly was no place for a lady.

Jack could blend in at the Cock and Bull if need be, and if by chance he was recognized, many of the tavern's patrons would look upon him as a hero from the Crown's overly aggressive prosecutors.

But to take Evelyn to such an establishment?

Unthinkable.

His eyes raked her face. Her golden hair was pulled back into a bun, but the severe style only served to emphasize her exotic cat-shaped eyes, which now flashed a glorious shade of blue.

Anger toward Randolph Sheldon—the man she intended to marry—escalated to a heightened pitch.

"I insist on traveling alone," Jack said. "I will tell you everything upon my return."

Evelyn sat forward in her chair, her spine visibly stiffening. "No. I will go with or without you."

"I am not offering a choice, Evie."

She met his hard eyes without flinching. "You must know that I do not take well to unreasonable orders, Jack. I intend to see Randolph no matter the risk."

No doubt, he thought. Evelyn would put herself in danger to aid her man. A foreign ache sprang up in the center of Jack's chest. No woman of his past acquaintance would ever jeopardize her safety on his behalf.

Could he be jealous?

Nonsense. In the cold, selfish world in which he practiced criminal law, he was merely unnerved by her loyalty.

She must have sensed he was debating whether to capitulate to her demands because she leaned across the desk and touched his sleeve.

"Please understand, Jack. I don't believe it to be a great risk. Not with you, Simon, and Randolph present."

Jack looked down to where her slender fingers rested on his arm. She would do it, he knew. She would go alone and the chances of her escaping unscathed without his protection were slim.

"I'll agree," he said, "but only because I don't want your father to become ill should anything untoward happen to you should you venture there on your own."

She removed her hand, and a secretive smile softened her lips. "Everything will be fine, Jack. You'll see."

His gaze dropped from her blue eyes to her full, bottom lip, curved now in a sensual smile, and his heartbeat hammered in his ears. Not for the first time, he wondered what he was getting himself into.

The most difficult part was slipping out of the house undetected. Evelyn had announced she wasn't feeling well and sought to retire for the evening after an early supper. Having long ago sent away her maid, Evelyn now restlessly paced her bedchamber.

The closed curtains shut out the late-afternoon sun, and a solitary candle stood lit on a nightstand. As she moved about, shadows loomed over the cream-colored walls like eerie ghosts.

The household routine was like clockwork as her father ordered his life with military precision. A familiar creaking of the wooden floorboards drew her to a halt, and she listened to her father's heavy footsteps first on the landing, then moving down the grand staircase. Lord Lyndale was headed for his library office where he would immerse himself in scholarly volumes, have his evening meal delivered on a tray, and remain until midnight. The servants, including Mrs. Smith, Janet, and Hodges, would perform their household duties, then linger in the kitchen until they retired. Only her father's valet would remain near to assist Lord Lyndale into bed.

She continued pacing for five minutes more, her eyes drawn to the mantel clock in thirty-second intervals.

Four o'clock.

Finally certain she could sneak out of the town house undetected, she rushed to her wardrobe. But instead of opening the wooden doors, she reached behind and pulled out a dress that had been carefully hidden.

Evelyn shook out the serviceable black fabric and eyed the garment. For a heart-squeezing instant, she felt a stab of guilt. But then she thought of Randolph and pushed the emotion aside.

The dress belonged to Janet, and Evelyn had taken it from the laundry when no one was about. She was thankful she had purchased Janet new dresses last month to supplement her wardrobe before Evelyn had ever dreamed of needing to borrow her maid's clothes. Nothing in Evelyn's own wardrobe was suitable for the Cock and Bull Tavern, and she had told Jack she would dress "appropriately."

The truth was she had no idea what would be appropriate attire for such an establishment. As a child, she had spent most of her time at her father's chambers at Lincoln's Inn or with her private tutor. And then later— after her father had inherited the earldom—she had begun to socialize with the *beau monde*.

Never had she strayed into the unfashionable areas of London, let alone the boisterous Billingsgate fish market.

"It is of no consequence," she spoke out loud to herself. "Randolph is depending on you."

Tossing the dress on the bed, her fingers reached for the buttons of her own gown. She stripped off the fine muslin, and the chilly evening air made her shiver. She pulled on black stockings and then struggled to don the maid's dress. She was glad it had buttons down the front instead of down the back—one of the reasons she had chosen it from the laundry.

A cheval glass mirror stood in the corner of the room, and she frowned at her reflection. The dress was a good two inches short and overly snug in the bosom. Evelyn knew Janet was shorter, but she hadn't considered the distinct difference in their chest sizes.

She looked again at the clock. The dress would have to do; Jack was waiting. She would wear a coarse wool cloak to cover the bodice, and the short hem would serve to showcase her economic straits. And along with the serviceable black shoes Janet wore, no one would mistake her for a lady of wealth.

Grabbing a black hat, she reached for the door handle and crept down the stairs.

Chapter 9

Jack was standing outside a hackney cab parked around the corner when Evelyn approached. His eyes raked her from head to toe, taking in her unusual attire with a wry smirk.

"What took you so long?" he asked.

"I had to wait until Father went to work in his library for the evening."

"Were you seen?"

"No."

He opened the door to the hackney and held out his hand. "I took the liberty of obtaining a cab. In the area of London where we are headed, my phaeton or carriage would draw a significant amount of unwanted attention."

She climbed in and sat on the bench across from him. In the small confines of the cab, her skirts brushed his knees. Jack watched as she fidgeted in her seat and retied the ribbons of her hat tightly beneath her chin, all sure signs that she was anxious and tense.

Some devilish part of Jack was glad she was nervous, but the rest of him wanted to reach out and touch her, reassure her that he would remain by her side tonight. He mentally shook himself. His warring emotions were becoming all too familiar when it came to Evelyn.

"I don't like this," he said. "Your father would not approve of where we are going. Is he aware that the Bow Street Runners are searching for Mr. Sheldon?"

She lowered her eyes and smoothed imaginary wrinkles from her dark cloak.

"I'll take your silence as a no."

She looked up. "Father isn't aware of the extent of the evidence against Randolph and that witnesses saw him fleeing from Bess Whitfield's bedroom window. He believes Bow Street wants Randolph for questioning. But Father fully understands Bow Street's aggressive nature, and he *wants* you to represent Randolph in case he is arrested."

"Then let me, Evie. I can go to Billingsgate alone. My representation as Mr. Sheldon's barrister will not be compromised by your absence tonight."

"We had an agreement, Jack. I go with you."

He threw up his hands and sighed. "Fine. Shall we then?" Leaning out the window, he gave the driver directions.

The leather harness creaked and the cab jerked forward, then settled into a sway as the wheels crunched over the cobblestone streets.

Jack returned his attention to her. The window shade was rolled up and the late-afternoon sun illuminated Evelyn's form. She was garbed entirely in a dark cloak. Her shoes were obviously a servant's, and the slight brim of her hat served to shield her eyes. It was not a bad choice of attire, and he wondered what she wore underneath. If he had any say, she would keep the cloak on the entire evening.

He noticed she was studying him as well. "Do you approve of my clothing?" he asked.

She grimaced. "I was wondering where your valet obtained such a horrid jacket."

Jack grinned. He was wearing a corduroy jacket, torn and badly stitched at one wrist, and a grubby shirt with enough grease stains to appear as if he had repeatedly wiped his plate with the dingy fabric. Coarse wool black trousers with frayed hems and scuffed boots completed his look. He hadn't bothered to shave that morning and had a shadow of a dark beard.

"My valet, Martin, is familiar with several second-hand clothing dealers. He adds his own personal flair, of course." Jack motioned to the awful stitching and grease stains. "But Martin's talent is remarkably helpful when I am investigating some of my clients' alleged griev-ances, and I need to travel to the scene of the crime."

A corner of her mouth curled upward. "I can only imagine."

"Don't be fooled, Evie. Our attire will aid us, but you must be aware that nothing will draw the eye like a beau-tiful woman."

She blinked, and the thought occurred to him that she had little idea just how stunning she was. Had no man ever called her beautiful before?

What a blasted waste, he mused. Her father had done her a grave disservice by permitting her to sequester her-self in his chambers.

The swaying of the hackney changed to a stop-and-go motion. The pungent odor of fish wafted through the window of the cab, and Jack knew they were close to their destination.

On impulse, he reached out and tucked a loose strand of blond hair behind Evelyn's ear. But as soon as he touched her, he felt an immediate and total attraction. His fingers lingered near her lobe, and he was mesmerized by the silky texture of her hair. He wanted to touch more of her, to take off the hat and explore the fine mass. . . .

He glanced at her face. She sat rigid, clearly surprised at his touch.

Feeling a sudden rush of frustrated annoyance at his lack of control, he jerked his hand back. "Stay close to me, Evie," he bit out. "Keep your hat on at all times. The last thing we need is your hair drawing unwanted attention. If any man approaches us, then you are to claim to be my woman. Understand?" His tone sounded unduly harsh to his own ears, but he didn't care, wanting only for her to heed his warning.

"But surely that won't be necessary?"

He leaned forward, his eyes piercing her with a hard stare. "Until we find Randolph Sheldon, then it is necessary for your own safety."

When she opened her mouth to protest further, Jack said, "Do you trust me?"

She looked taken aback and bit her bottom lip before looking him in the eye. "Yes. I trust you, Jack."

"Good, because we've arrived."

He opened the door, jumped down, and held out a hand to Evelyn.

She took it and alighted, her blue eyes wide as disks as she spotted the throng of people down the street.

"We can still turn back, Evie," he said.

She shook her head.

Jack tossed a coin to the cabdriver. "Stay in the area tonight and there will be double in it for you."

"Aye, gov'ner," the driver said, tipping his hat.

Then Jack took her hand in a firm grip and headed for the thickest part of the mob.

* * *

Evelyn couldn't believe her eyes. The fish market enveloped them in a malodorous crowd of activity. The overpowering stench of fish lay as heavy as the humid air on her skin. Fishmongers with gut-stained aprons waved fish above their heads and cupped hands around their mouths as they shouted their prices. Screeching seagulls hovered above and occasionally swooped down to pick at fish guts or slop thrown between the stalls.

"How will we ever find the tavern?" she shouted above the cacophony of voices to be heard.

"I know where it is," Jack said.

A burly sailor bumped into her and she stumbled. Jack steadied her with a hand at her elbow.

"We could lose each other in this crowd."

His grip tightened. "No, we won't. The tavern is just down the street."

"I didn't think it would be this busy. It's almost five o'clock in the evening."

"It's worse at five o'clock in the morning," he said dryly.

They passed a stall where a buyer haggled with a fishwife who had a dozen turbots strung around her apron. The brownish tails and white bellies of the fish swung around as the woman gestured wildly with her hands and yelled in the buyer's face. In the next stall a charlatan stood on a table, shouting out the benefits of a salve that could heal hemorrhoids as well as accidental cuts from fish knives in record speed. A milling crowd gathered around the charismatic man and the noise level increased.

Evelyn looked about flabbergasted, grateful for Jack's presence by her side. The market was like a living beast with a pulse of its own that could easily swallow an unsuspecting passerby.

"I can see why you did not wish me to come alone," she blurted out.

He stopped suddenly and looked down at her, his green eyes studying her with a curious intensity. "Is that an admission of weakness, Evie?"

"No, Jack. Merely a statement of gratitude for your escort."

A strange, faintly eager look flashed across his face, but as quickly as it had appeared, it vanished.

"I would have preferred to meet Mr. Sheldon elsewhere, but we're here now." He pointed past the table of the medicine man. "I can see the tavern up ahead. Let's be on our way."

They continued on through the market. As the end of the business day neared, fishmongers threw buckets of water in front of their stalls. Some mopped the fish guts and waste, others were content to let the gulls and stray dogs do the work. The cobbled street was slick and dirty, and Evelyn held up her already-short hem as they walked by.

Soon the murky, brown water of the Thames came into view, and the odor of fish and seaweed grew stronger. Shrimp and oyster boats were lined up at the wharf. Fishermen and porters scurried about at the direction of a burly wharfmaster, his weathered face as dark as tanned leather, whose shouts were mixed with ear-blistering profanity.

She first spotted the sign for the Cock and Bull Tavern before they rounded the corner and the building came into view.

"Stay by my side, Evie," Jack warned. "Every sailor in Billingsgate is going to be here on a Friday night."

They came up to the tavern door, and she could make

out the roar of voices within. Just as Jack reached for the handle, the door swung open and a sailor stumbled outside. Ruddy-cheeked and glassy-eyed, he barely glanced at them before making his way to the street and spewing up his latest meal.

Giving her no chance to stare, Jack dragged her inside the tavern.

A thick haze of smoke enveloped them. Her eyes stung, and she blinked several times until the scene before her cleared.

The tavern was crowded just as Jack had warned. It was a large room, with a long bar spanning the back wall and tables and chairs haphazardly scattered about. Groups of men were seated, their hands cradling tankards of ale or cups of gin while others held decks of cards. The crowd was coarse—made up of dockworkers, sailors, porters, and fishermen.

Candles sputtered from wall sconces and coals glowed in a corner brazier. A few women were present—barmaids scurrying about; other females with scandalously low bodices lingered at the tables, hanging over the shoulders of men who played cards.

The door closed behind Evelyn. The man behind the bar looked up and stopped pouring a bottle of gin. Other heads rose, and the occupants stared at the newest patrons with narrow-eyed interest.

Evelyn's heart pounded in her chest, and uncertainty flooded through her. She had tried to anticipate what she might encounter, yet no newspaper article she had read, nor even literature featuring the lower classes, had amply prepared her for this true life experience. Her senses were overwhelmed by the thick smoke wafting across her skin and the fetid air full of unwashed, perspiring bodies. The din of the crowd boiled down to a dull ringing in her ears, and her feet felt as heavy as if her borrowed shoes were filled with lead.

She was vaguely conscious of shuffling backward, making for the door, when Jack's hand tightened on her wrist. He pulled her firmly to his side, his breath hot in her ear.

"Don't, Evie. It's too late to run, and I'm with you."

The hard length of him pressed against her, reassuring her, and she nodded numbly.

Jack elbowed their way past the crush of bodies to an empty table in the rear of the room. Several broad-shouldered dockworkers eyed them, and Evelyn feared they were the type who enjoyed bar brawls. But Jack exuded a cocky confidence as if he belonged in such an environment, and the men remained in their seats. The man behind the bar went back to pouring cups of gin.

They were almost at the table, when a hand snaked out for Evelyn. Jack pulled her out of reach and glared at a young sailor with crooked, brown teeth who was far into his cups.

"Willin' to share?" the man asked, slurring his words.

Jack's face was fierce. "She's mine fer the night. Bought and paid fer. Find another."

The drunkard shrugged and turned his attention back to his gin.

Shock ran through Evelyn at Jack's comment, and she bit her lip. She recalled the promise Jack had her make, that if she were approached she would claim to be Jack's woman. She had assumed he meant his *wife,* but looking at her surroundings she realized that was never his intent—for no decent man would bring his spouse here.

They sat, and a buxom barmaid sidled over to Jack. The woman gave Jack a sly look, her greedy eyes raking his chiseled profile and broad shoulders. The shadow of his beard only added to his rugged, masculine appeal.

Jack did nothing to discourage the woman; rather he gave her a lazy wink and sent her off with a smile.

A streak of annoyance passed through Evelyn at how easily Jack could charm the female sex. Barmaids, librarians, courthouse clerks, and even high-born ladies—Jack seemed to know how to make them all respond with very little effort.

The barmaid returned with two tankards. Bending over more than necessary to place the ale before Jack, she displayed a huge amount of bosom for his view before walking away.

Just then, the door swung open and two men stepped inside, bringing with them a blast of wind.

Evelyn's tankard halted halfway to her mouth. "It's Randolph and Simon," she said to Jack.

Jack rested his hand on hers, staying her when she made to rise. "Do not draw attention to yourself. Let them come to us."

Chapter 10

Jack eyed the two men at the door. One was of medium height and dark-haired, the other was slightly taller with sandy-colored hair and round spectacles. Jack assumed the darker male was Simon Guthrie and the blonde was Randolph Sheldon as Evelyn had described them. Simon was the first to spot Evelyn in the corner. With a jerk of his head to his friend, the pair made their way to the back of the tavern and took seats at the table.

"Randolph!" Evelyn cried out. "I've been so worried."

Randolph Sheldon reached across the table and clasped her hand in both of his. "Evelyn, darling. Please forgive me." His blue eyes watered behind his spectacles, and his fair hair stood on end as if he had repeatedly run his fingers through it in angst. He wore a wrinkled coat with a limp shirt beneath, and his complexion resembled a dish of warm gruel.

Randolph raised her fingers to his lips and kissed them.

Jack grit his teeth, and a vicious thought popped into his head: *He does not deserve her.*

"Oh, Randolph," Evelyn sighed. "Are you well?"

"As well as can be expected. I never wanted this for you, Evelyn."

"Nonsense, Randolph," Evelyn admonished, her blue eyes gentle, understanding. "You did not bring this upon yourself. The murderer did."

At the mention of the crime, a painful expression crossed Randolph's countenance. He glanced nervously at Jack.

Evelyn looked at Jack, then at Randolph. "This is Mr. Harding. He has agreed to represent you."

"Simon told me about Mr. Harding," Randolph said. "But I don't know if it's necessary for—"

"Mr. Harding is extremely accomplished, Randolph," Evelyn said. "We are fortunate to have him."

Randolph still looked uncertain, and Jack spoke up before Evelyn had the chance. "Mr. Sheldon, if Bow Street is looking for you, then it's only a matter of time until they find you. Do not be fooled by their intentions. Bess Whitfield was a popular actress, and the head magistrate is under a considerable amount of pressure to make an arrest. The people *expect* a conviction. And from what I understand, the evidence against you is sufficient to give them what they want—whether you are innocent or not."

Randolph's eyes widened behind his spectacles. He looked young and scholarly, the type of man Jack expected Evelyn to be drawn to.

He is just a boy; what she needs is a man. Jack's gut twisted at his bitter thoughts. He knew Randolph Sheldon was not a boy, but was twenty-two, the same age as Evelyn.

"They have made up their minds then. They think I killed Bess," Randolph said in a choked voice.

At the common usage of the actress's first name,

Evelyn's hand fluttered to her chest. "You never explained the extent of your acquaintance with Bess Whitfield in the past."

"She was my uncle's daughter from his first wife. We were close as children, but then her mother died and my uncle remarried and they moved away. She wrote over the years, but it wasn't until she returned to London to take to the stage that we frequently saw each other again. My uncle died, you see, and I was her only living relative. She . . . she relied on me."

"Why did you not tell me?" Evelyn asked.

Randolph reached out to touch Evelyn's shoulder.

Jack wrestled with the urge to slap away Randolph's wayward hand.

"I wanted to, Evelyn," Randolph said. "But it was Bess who asked me not to. She was worried it would affect my chances at the university. She knew that I depended on my Fellowship with your father and that I had plans to one day become a professor myself. Bess was concerned her 'reputation' would hurt my advancement."

Evelyn frowned. "Her reputation?"

Randolph's face turned a mottled shade of red.

Simon came to his friend's aid. "Bess was known for her performances offstage just as much as those at the Drury Lane Theatre."

Bewilderment flashed across Evelyn's face. "Whatever do you mean?"

All three men looked at her.

Simon squirmed uncomfortably in his seat. Intelligent brown eyes glanced at her, then lowered, then looked at her again. "Bess Whitfield had many lovers. Some were men of influence and wealth while others were mere musicians and stagehands. Rampant rumors existed speculating that Bess's drove of lovers were the reason she had advanced in the theater so quickly. It's rare for a country girl to become a famous actress almost overnight at one of London's most popular theaters."

Evelyn cast her mind back and the image of Bess Whitfield focused in her memory. Evelyn had seen Bess on stage two years ago during the opening night of the newly rebuilt Drury Lane Theatre's production of William Shakespeare's tragedy *Hamlet.* Bess had played the role of Gertrude, King Hamlet's widow and the mother of Prince Hamlet, who marries Claudius, her husband's brother and murderer who succeeds to the throne. Bess had been a beautiful woman, but it was her charisma and provocative allure that had captured the audience. Evelyn would never forget the pivotal moment when Gertrude drank a cup of poison intended for Hamlet by Claudius. She had fallen to the floor, moaning in agony and reaching out for her son. The applause for Bess at the end of the performance had rivaled that of the lead actor, Robert Elliston.

Evelyn had heard competition for leading roles was fierce, but she had never suspected Bess Whitfield's performance *off*stage had aided her career.

Evelyn blinked, then focused her gaze on Randolph. "And you knew this about Miss Whitfield?"

"It's true, but that's not the side of Bess I knew. We were related, Evelyn, and we shared nothing but kinship."

Evelyn covered his hand resting on her shoulder. "I believe you, Randolph."

She coddles him like a helpless babe, Jack thought. Randolph could very well be guilty, an accomplished actor. Jack had seen it before; men so adept at lying, they could fool their own mothers while committing heinous crimes beneath the roofs they shared.

"Tell me what happened the night she was murdered," Jack said.

Randolph dropped his hand from Evelyn's shoulder, and his gaze snapped to Jack. "I was at the university library that night when a note was delivered. It was from Bess saying that she wanted to see me. She requested I come to her London lodgings. She said it was urgent, that there was something she had to give me. An item of great importance."

Randolph's hands twisted on the table. "I went right away. Bess rented the second floor of a four-story building. When I arrived on her doorstep, I knocked, but there was no answer. Then I noticed the door was ajar, and I let myself inside. I stood in the vestibule and called her name, but no one was about. The housekeeper was nowhere to be seen, and I later learned that she had left for the night. As I looked about, I heard a loud thump from upstairs. Concerned that Bess had fallen, I rushed upstairs. I found Bess in her bedchamber. She was . . . she was lying on the floor. She had been stabbed numerous times and there was blood . . . blood everywhere. On the rug, the walls, the furniture. I knelt down and held her in the crook of my arm, hoping to find her still breathing, but her life blood soaked through my shirt. She was already gone."

Randolph swallowed and ran his hand through his hair. "That was when I heard a man shout out. When I realized it was the constable, I . . . I panicked. The window was already open, and I jumped out and climbed down the trellis. The neighbor must have heard Bess's screams and summoned the constable. Looking back, the murderer must have still been in the house when I entered. He must have made the noise I had heard and escaped through the window moments before I had come upstairs."

"It's unusual for me to take on a client that is in hiding," Jack said. "If Bow Street comes to me, I have an ethical duty as a barrister not to present perjurous testimony. You should turn yourself in for questioning."

"No!" Simon and Randolph said in unison.

"You said yourself Bess Whitfield was popular with the people and Bow Street is under pressure to make an arrest," Randolph pointed out.

"Yes, but hiding is not aiding your cause. To the contrary, it makes you appear guilty. Eventually they will find you. If you return, I can be present when you are questioned and officially request to be kept informed of the outcome of any investigation."

"There is another option," Simon said as he withdrew a paper from his jacket pocket. Leaning forward across the table, he lowered his voice. "We have compiled a list of suspects. People that had both motive and opportunity to kill Bess Whitfield. We could investigate them ourselves while Randolph is in hiding."

"Yes," Evelyn said. "Mr. Harding and I can help look into them." Her face held an eager excitement like a puppy thrown its first meaty bone.

"Evelyn," Jack said, a silken thread of warning in his voice.

Evelyn spun toward Randolph. "You said Miss Whitfield wanted to give you 'an item of great importance.' What was it?"

Randolph shrugged. "I don't know, but I suspect the murderer was searching for the item when my arrival interrupted him."

"How do you know that?" Jack asked.

"Bess's bedroom was a mess. The bed had been torn asunder, the mattress sliced down the center. Furniture had been turned over, curtains had been pulled off their rods and vases had been shattered. The two cushioned chairs in the room had been slashed, and horsehair was scattered all over the carpet."

Jack's breath froze in his lungs. It was not every day that the description of a crime scene stunned him, but *this* crime scene, the way the room had been ransacked, was eerily similar to the way Emmanuel Darlington's library had been ripped apart days ago.

Jack had experienced a wary feeling in his gut then, had felt the crime had been somehow related to Randolph's problems. The inexperienced constable hadn't agreed and had called it a common burglary. But Jack had learned never to ignore his instincts—they had never failed him in the past. Now he had more than instinct to go on; he had coincidence. The two crimes were related; he felt it down to the marrow of his bones.

Whatever Bess Whitfield had planned on giving Randolph Sheldon was something that also involved the Darlingtons.

But what could it be?

Only one thing was certain: Evelyn and her father were in danger.

The constable would be of no assistance. Bow Street would turn a blind eye between the two crimes and would dismiss Jack's concerns. Rather, they would eagerly arrest Randolph and not look further for the true criminal. And once Randolph was arrested, Jack's time to search for the murderer was severely limited. Justice was swift. Within days after an arrest, a grand jury would find sufficient evidence to issue an indictment, and a trial at the Old Bailey would begin immediately thereafter. He had seen it time and again. The Crown's prosecution would be content with an easy conviction; it didn't necessarily have to be the right man.

Jack's gaze snapped to the list in Simon's hand. He had the resources to investigate the names. His fellow barristers and friends could aid him. They could find the killer, find whatever Bess had hid and had died for.

Only then would Evelyn and her father truly be safe.

Yes, she would be safe to live her life as planned with Randolph Sheldon at her side. . . .

Evelyn took the list from Simon and scanned its contents. "I know some of these people. I could look into them."

The corner of Jack's mouth twisted with exasperation. *She needs a firm hand. A man worthy of her mettle.* Jack scowled at his thoughts. *Don't be daft! Evelyn Darlington has made her choice.*

Jack turned his attention back to Randolph. "Do you still have the shirt?"

"The shirt?" Randolph asked.

"Yes. The shirt that was soaked in Bess's blood. Do you still have it?"

"I . . . I suppose so. I've been hiding at Bess's home in Shoreditch. I stowed it there. Why?"

"I'll need to examine it."

"All right."

"Does that mean you'll agree to help?" Evelyn's face lit with hope.

Jack plucked the list out of Evelyn's hand. "I'll agree to look into the names." He eyed Randolph. "I'll be in touch. Meanwhile, try to stay out of trouble and out of sight."

Chapter 11

Evelyn watched Randolph and Simon leave the tavern. She was disheartened to see Randolph depart and knew it would be a long time before she saw him again. But at the same time, she was eager to delve into the list of suspects that Simon had handed her and prove Randolph's innocence.

"Don't worry, Evie. You'll see him again."

Evelyn turned to find Jack watching her. She was struck by the firm set of his jaw, the intense green eyes.

She swallowed and nodded, unable to find her voice. How could she explain that she was more relieved that Jack had remained than she was upset that Randolph had returned to hiding? If Randolph stood any chance to return to his normal life, then Jack's services were essential.

Jack pushed his chair back. "We need to get you home."

She stood and cleared her throat. "Yes, of course. If I am fortunate, no one in the household will have noticed my departure."

She followed him to a rear door. He pushed the door open and they stepped into a narrow cobbled alley. Bypassing the main section of the fish market, Jack led her to where the same hackney driver that had brought them to Billingsgate waited.

Grasping her skirts, she climbed into the seat, and Jack sat across from her.

As the hackney started on their return journey, Jack lifted his sleeve to his nose and grimaced. "My valet is going to smell me coming."

She laughed. "The smell is quite horrid and clings to everything." Indeed, her "borrowed" clothing was destroyed by the slop and swill of the fish market, and she was thankful she had previously purchased her maid new clothing so those she was wearing might be disposed of without a pang of regret. Even her hat hung askew, damp from the humidity. She felt flushed and warm inside the coach, and she shrugged out of her wool cloak, which now lay wet and heavy against her skin.

Jack's gaze dropped to her chest, and Evelyn recalled the tight bodice. A sudden heat coursed through her, an awareness of his masculinity. The interior of the coach seemed to shrink as she focused on the attractive, virile man across from her.

Suddenly nervous, she pulled the coarse wool around her shoulders.

"I want to thank you for remaining as Randolph's barrister. I understand your predicament, your ethical duty not to lie to a Bow Street magistrate. But I am grateful that you did not insist Randolph return with us." The truth was she was so relieved Jack had agreed to stay that it felt like a lead weight was lifted off her chest, and she could freely breathe for the first time that evening. "I'm prepared to immediately look into the list of suspects that Simon provided."

"I don't think that's a good idea," Jack drawled. "It could be dangerous, Evie."

"But I could be of great assistance. As I said before, I recognized some of the names and—"

He held up a hand to interrupt. "I know better than to exclude you entirely. I suspect you would take matters into your own hands if I tried to stop you. I only ask that you do not look into any suspects by yourself and that you involve me in every step. We work together. Agreed?"

"Agreed," she said quickly, lest he change his mind.

"Even if you have the opportunity to see Mr. Sheldon, I want to accompany you."

Something in Jack's tone raised the hair on her nape. His eyes held a sheen of purpose and warning.

"You think Randolph is guilty, don't you?" she asked.

"It's possible."

She shook her head. "No. You asked me to trust you. Do you trust my judgment, Jack?"

"It's not the same thing. Mr. Sheldon could be a gifted liar. I've seen it before. Some people are so talented that they begin to believe their own version of the story."

"No, Jack. You have to believe me," she insisted. "I don't agree with what Randolph did after he found Bess Whitfield's body. I think he should have stayed and explained himself to the constable. But I would not remain by Randolph's side if I believed him capable of murder."

"I don't need to believe in my client's innocence to represent him," he pointed out.

"Yes, I know that too. But I trust Randolph's story that he went to Bess's home that night at her request. She planned to give him something. Perhaps if we learn what that item is, you will believe him."

Jack cocked his head to the side and gave her a grudging nod. The dying embers of the sun spilled through the open window of the cab, illuminating his extraordinary eyes, flecked and ringed with gold.

"My fellow barrister in chambers, Anthony Stevens, works with the best investigators in the business," he said. "If there was something in Bess Whitfield's past that she wanted to hide, they'll find it."

Jack strode into Gentleman Jackson's boxing salon at 13 Bond Street. Across the large salon, he spotted Anthony Stevens stripped to the waist in the center of a ring. Wearing padded gloves, he circled his opponent. The ring's heavy ropes were tied to four anchoring posts to form a square, and the boxers circled one another like scorpions with their tails raised, ready to strike.

The sparring pair rocked back and forth, their swift nimble footwork like rapid flashes across the hardwood floor. Both bent slightly at the waist, head and shoulders pressed forward, their gloves raised. They jabbed and punched as they moved, sweat running down their foreheads and onto their bare chests.

Anthony was tall, and his massive shoulder muscles bunched and flexed as he struck with each forceful punch. For such a large man, he moved with agility and grace in the ring. His opponent was as tall and powerfully built as Anthony, but one glance at the man's broken nose, missing front teeth, and purple bruising around one eye, pronounced him a seasoned boxer.

But Jack knew better than to underestimate Anthony's ruthlessly competitive nature.

To the side of the ring, resting his arm on the rope and shouting out instructions, stood John "Gentleman" Jackson himself. Before retiring, Jackson had defeated Daniel Mendoza to become the heavyweight champion in England. Since opening his own boxing salon, well-bred gentlemen flocked to Jackson for instruction in the pugilistic art.

Jack himself often sparred here, and he thrived on the physical exercise.

He watched the match from the far corner of the room. Near the end of the third round, Anthony surged forward and hit his opponent square in the gut, followed by a fierce uppercut to the jaw. Down and dazed, the other boxer lay flat on his back, and Anthony was declared the winner.

Jack waited to approach until Anthony stepped out of the ring, and an assistant untied his gloves.

"You fight like the devil, Anthony. By the experienced look of your opponent, I would have placed my bets against you," Jack said.

Anthony laughed as he wiped his forehead with a cotton towel. "You never were good with wagers, Jack."

Jack grinned. "I looked for you in chambers."

"Nothing like a good boxing session to ease the stress of the day."

"Ah, I see. An unpleasant encounter with a client?"

Anthony shrugged. "A particularly ornery fellow who is disgruntled with his spouse's spending habits." Anthony reached for his shirt and pulled it over his head. The fabric clung to his sweat-slicked skin. "I had planned to return to chambers after I bathed. But truth be told, I expected you to seek me out sooner. What took you so long, Jack?"

"Let me guess; Devlin and Brent gave you an earful."

"They told me about your latest female client. They warned me to expect you."

Jack cursed beneath his breath. "Bloody hell! Those two magpies gossip like old hags."

"I said the same thing, but there is truth to what they claim this time. Since when have you taken on beautiful women other than in your bed? I seem to recall you mentioning something about your trial concentration."

"I told them. Evelyn Darlington is my former pupilmaster's daughter. I owe Lord Lyndale." Indeed, Jack's youthful days at Lincoln's Inn touched upon a nerve. He had entered at his father's coaxing, and in little time he had found himself failing miserably and at risk of being thrown out of Lincoln's Inn. Without a willing pupilmaster to take him on, Jack would have had no choice but to leave and return to his father, head bent in shame. But Emmanuel Darlington, a revered Master of the Bench, had seen something in Jack and had quite simply been his savior. The man had been a phenomenal teacher, and he had ignited an appetite for learning in Jack—a near impossible feat at the time.

Anthony reached for a dented metal cup beside a water bucket, dipped it, and drank. Lowering the cup, he eyed Jack. "I assume both Devlin and Brent tried to talk some sense into you so I won't bother. What do you need from me?"

"The private investigator you work with. You once told me he was the best in the business."

Anthony was quick to supply the information. "He's a shrewd Armenian by the name of Armen Papazian, and he excels at his job. But I assume my needs for information are different from what you require. I use Mr. Papazian to delve into an adversary's bedroom antics and secrets."

Jack knew all about Anthony's unusual practices.

Anthony Stevens was an anomaly in their chambers. The truth was, Anthony was cut from a different cloth compared to every barrister Jack knew. Anthony had magically managed to obtain what so many of the married members of the *beau monde* fantasized about: the elusive divorce. Requiring an Act of Parliament, divorce was nearly impossible to obtain. Legal separation was more readily available, and even then the formal legal documents rarely were filed by the members of the *ton.* More commonplace and even expected was the fact that the husband and wife went on to live separate lives—some even on separate continents.

But Anthony had obtained divorces for three wealthy and respectable members of society, all titled men, all by proving the adultery of the wives. The fact that the men had kept mistresses throughout their marriages had been deemed irrelevant. The legal system, like society, favored men, and Anthony took complete advantage of that system.

Anthony's wealth and notoriety were well known, but he did pay a price for his chosen field. Seeing only the worst side of marriage, Anthony had become a jaded man who believed love an illusion pursued by weak fools.

Worse still, Anthony had developed a ruthless streak, a cutthroat manner that simmered beneath the surface of a respectable gentleman and barrister.

"Is it Evelyn Darlington's past you want searched?" Anthony asked.

"No. The victim's—the actress Bess Whitfield. She had numerous lovers and something to hide. Something worth killing for." Jack reached into his jacket pocket, pulled out a wrinkled paper, and handed it to Anthony. "This is a list of possible suspects and a place for Mr. Papazian to start investigating, although it is by no means complete."

"Who gave you this?" Anthony asked.

"Randolph Sheldon. The man suspected by Bow Street of the crime."

"Lady Evelyn's lover, I presume?"

Something about Anthony's statement irked Jack. "No. Mr. Sheldon is the man she is convinced she should marry, but he is not her lover," Jack said, unable to withhold the critical tone in his voice.

A bright mockery invaded Anthony's hawklike stare. "Come now, Jack. You do not believe they are lovers? What woman would zealously defend a man accused of murder if not her husband or lover? In my experience, there is no such thing as an altruistic and selfless female."

Except for Evie, Jack thought. She was unlike any woman he had ever known. Whether her behavior was irrational or completely altruistic as Anthony suggested, one thing was certain: She and Randolph had never been intimate.

Jack felt it in his bones—knew it just as he knew how to breathe. His instinct had homed in on the platonic relationship between Evelyn and Randolph. She had looked upon Randolph with concern and compassion, certainly not the heated look she had given Jack after he had kissed her . . . after she had experienced her first spark of passion.

Anthony eyed Jack narrowly. "Damn it, Jack. Don't tell me you're turning into one of those weak fools who allows a woman to get under your skin?"

Jack bit back harsh words. "Of course not," he snapped. "Just have your man look into Bess Whitfield's past."

"What about Randolph Sheldon's past?"

Evelyn wouldn't approve. But if Randolph was hiding

something, Jack wanted to know what it was. Jack nodded and said, "Yes, his too."

A satisfied light came into Anthony's eyes, and he slapped Jack on the back. "Consider it done, Jack. Finding out people's secrets is the best part of my job."

Chapter 12

After a night of fitful sleep, Evelyn woke late with the distinct odor of fish in her nostrils. Tossing back the covers, she immediately rang for Janet and ordered a bath.

Minutes later a brass tub and steaming buckets of water were delivered. As Evelyn lowered herself into the hot water, her thoughts drifted to last evening.

Thank goodness Jack had accompanied her to Billingsgate. She would have lost her nerve at the first glimpse of the crowded fish market, let alone the rough-and-tumble Cock and Bull Tavern.

Later, she had been fortunate to arrive home undetected. The first thing she had done was strip off her dress, tie it in a bundle, and toss it out the window. She planned on properly disposing of the ruined garment later today.

Resting her head against the rim of the tub, she let out a sigh. What was Randolph thinking to meet her at the Cock and Bull?

But the moment the thought crossed her mind, she felt a twist of guilt in her gut.

Randolph had been right. It was a safe choice for him.

No one had recognized him or had questioned his presence. He had blended in with the sailors, fishermen, and fishmongers in a sea of anonymous, faceless bodies whose only intent was to drown themselves in ale and gin after a long workweek.

Evelyn rose from the bath and dried herself off with a thick, cotton towel. Donning a morning dress of soft blue alpaca, she hurried down the staircase, intent on meeting her father in the dining room for nuncheon.

Her foot had just touched the vestibule when a knock on the front door sounded. Looking about, she didn't see Hodges and knew the chances of the elder butler hearing the door knocker were slim.

Striding to the door, she opened it, expecting to see an acquaintance of her father.

Jack Harding stood on the front steps instead.

"Good morning, Evie."

"Jack! What are you doing here?"

His chestnut hair was ruffled by a breeze in the doorway, and the shifting emerald lights of his eyes in the bright morning sunlight made her breath catch.

"I'm to meet your father for nuncheon. He sent a message to my home last evening inviting me."

"He did?" she asked incredulously. "He never mentioned it to me."

"Perhaps he truly believed you were ill and did not seek to disturb you. May I come inside?"

She started, realizing that she stood stock-still staring at him. "Yes, of course." Stepping back, she motioned for him to enter.

Jack strode inside and closed the door. "Will you be joining us?"

At the eagerness in his voice, she experienced a rush of pleasure. "I was on my way to meet Father."

She led the way to the dining room, all the while acutely conscious of his large, well-muscled body beside hers. She stole a sideways glance, noting how striking he looked in his finely tailored clothes and gleaming Hessians. She thought of the mended corduroy jacket and greasy shirt of last evening, and her lips curved in a smile.

Her amusement waned, turning to irritation, as she recalled how attractive he looked then too.

"Good morning, Mr. Harding," Lord Lyndale said, rising from his seat as they entered the room.

"Please call me Jack, my lord. There was never formality between us at Lincoln's Inn."

"That was before you became a barrister. But I am more comfortable calling you Jack. Please call me Emmanuel."

"Not Lyndale?" Jack asked, using the man's title.

"Not with you. I was Emmanuel Darlington for many years before my brother died, leaving me the title. I consider myself a teacher and barrister first, and I'm not much for the snobbish ways of the nobility."

Evelyn smiled, immensely proud of her father. He had refused to give up his position at Oxford, even after inheriting her uncle's earldom. He was a rare type of man, a true scholar at heart, dedicated to his pupils.

Jack and Evelyn sat, and Mrs. Smith entered and set plates of cold roast beef and rolls before them.

"Have you met with Randolph Sheldon yet?" Lyndale asked.

A shiver of apprehension ran down Evelyn's spine. Her father didn't know Randolph was in hiding at Bess Whitfield's home in Shoreditch, and he was completely ignorant of their escapade in Billingsgate. As far as Evelyn knew, her father believed Randolph was taking a brief sabbatical from the university until the business of

Bess Whitfield's murder was resolved, and Randolph had sufficient time to mourn the loss of his cousin.

Evelyn bit her lip and looked to Jack, fearful of what he would reveal. Her hands twisted the napkin in her lap, this way and that, in anticipation of his response.

"I have met with Mr. Sheldon," Jack said, "and I am looking into the best defense, as well as any alibis, should Bow Street decide to question Mr. Sheldon or seek his arrest."

Evelyn held her breath until her father nodded his head in approval. Exhaling in relief, she made a show of taking a bite of roast beef. Jack had managed to inform her father without telling him the most damning facts and had successfully hedged the truth without lying.

What an incredibly talented lawyer you are, Jack Harding, she mused.

"Truth be told," Lyndale said, "I am relieved you are on Randolph's side. Case law is full of tragedies in which men have been sentenced to death for lesser offenses, many of whom were probably innocent but without the means to pay for legal representation. I myself vividly recall a client who paid with his life. As a longtime criminal barrister yourself, I am sure you have experienced such injustices firsthand."

Jack's eyes darkened to a deep jade, and Evelyn knew he was recalling a memory. "I'm only too aware. Successful in the courtroom as I have been, I have lost trials and have been present at the execution of more than one client. Not all have been guilty of the alleged crime."

A tangible tremor passed across the table between Jack and Lyndale. Evelyn sensed their angst and shared bond of having witnessed the death of an innocent man, unable to prevent the deed.

A renewed urgency rushed through her veins, making

her light-headed. Randolph, too, could be an innocent man sent to prison—or worse—to the gallows.

Images flashed through her mind. Randolph with his fair hair and kind blue eyes as he listened to her theories on William Blackstone's works. All she ever wanted was a man who would look past her appearance and seriously consider her intelligence. And Randolph seemed to be perfect. He never minded her opinions, and he had even sought her help with research for his papers. That he never named her on his work or gave her credit for her research she knew was not his fault, but that of the male-dominated university.

And now, after years of searching for an intellectually suitable partner, there was a risk that Randolph could pay with his life for a crime he did not commit.

"Please keep me informed of your progress, Jack," Lyndale said.

"I have hired an investigator to assist with the investigation," Jack said.

Evelyn started, and her gaze snapped to Jack. He had wasted no time in seeking out professional assistance.

"Very well," Lyndale said, rising from his chair. "Before I forget, Evelyn and I host a monthly dinner with Lordships Bathwell and Barnes, and I will be extending an invitation for you to join us."

Jack stood and nodded. "I'd like that very much."

Lyndale glanced from Evelyn to Jack, and a keen look came into his eyes. "I'll leave you two to discuss the case." Then he turned and left the room, leaving them alone.

Jack sat and returned his napkin to his lap.

"You hired an investigator that swiftly?" she asked.

"My colleague, Anthony Stevens, works with a talented investigator with the instincts of a bloodhound; he arranged the matter. If Bess Whitfield was attempting to hide something, this fellow will learn the truth."

Jack rested his elbow on the table and leaned forward. "There's another reason I came here today, Evie. An opportunity has arisen."

"What opportunity?"

"It's Saturday."

"I don't follow, Jack."

"Tonight is Saturday evening, Evie. The busiest night of the week for the theaters."

"The theaters?"

"I thought we could start by questioning Bess Whitfield's personal dresser."

"Is the dresser on the list of suspects Simon gave us?"

"No. But I've learned that servants and the hired help should never be overlooked. Oftentimes they are the most knowledgeable."

"Are you suggesting I accompany you unchaperoned to the theater tonight?"

"Bring your maid if you must, but you may want to leave her in the carriage. We'll be going in the back door uninvited."

Chapter 13

On a busy Saturday evening, the Drury Lane Theatre could hold a little over three thousand people. Located in Covent Garden, the theater faced Catherine Street and backed onto Drury Lane. Built only two years earlier, it was the fourth Drury Lane Theatre on the site, the last having been destroyed by fire.

Jack's carriage pulled up, and Evelyn watched as a throng of theatergoers made their way inside. The newly installed gas street lamps illuminated the splendid clothing of the gentlemen and ladies dressed in high fashion. Some held opera glasses while others had playbills dangling from their gloved fingertips.

Rather than join the crowd, Jack directed the driver to turn onto Drury Lane in the rear of the building by the service entrance.

Evelyn turned to Janet who sat beside her. "Stay in the carriage. We'll be back shortly."

Janet's brown eyes grew wide, and she swallowed hard. Reaching up, she nervously smoothed wisps of frizzy, brown hair that had escaped her tightly braided coronet. "Is it safe, m' lady?"

Evelyn smiled and touched Janet's hand. "Please don't fret. I'll be back shortly."

Jack jumped down and assisted Evelyn. As they headed for the back door, he said, "Your maid doesn't approve of our clandestine activities."

"She'll do as she's told," Evelyn said.

"Ah, but where do her loyalties lie, Evie?"

Evelyn's stride slowed as she looked up at Jack. The lighting here was not as bright as at the front of the building since the expensive new gas lamps were not deemed necessary in the rear.

In the dimness, dressed entirely in black, Jack looked a dashing, but dangerous pirate.

"Don't worry, Jack," she said. "My maid's loyalties lie with me. She'll not whisper a word to my father."

He nodded, obviously satisfied with her answer. They came to the back door, and Jack reached for the handle.

At once the door swung open, and two men dressed in full costume as eighteenth-century noblemen stumbled out.

"'Ow the devil did I know they were plannin' to substitute Chester fer me? 'E don't know 'is arse from 'is head onstage!" the first actor said.

"Everything's been a bloody mess since Bess was murdered, what with the director changin' roles," the second man responded.

Evelyn held her breath, but neither actor paid them any heed. Jack took advantage and pulled Evelyn inside. The door closed behind them, leaving the two disgruntled actors to themselves.

They stepped into a dimly lit corridor. The strains from the orchestra warming up its instruments for the night's performance echoed off the walls. Actors and stagehands with single-minded purpose rushed to and fro, in and out of dressing rooms and gathering their props—before the curtain was raised.

To Evelyn's surprise, no one stopped them, everyone obviously too consumed with last-minute preparations. It was Jack who reached out and grasped the sleeve of a short man with a determined expression who attempted to scurry by.

"We're looking for Mary Morris," Jack said.

The man stopped short, his chest jerking with each in-drawn breath. He clutched a clipboard tightly to his chest and eyed Jack with annoyance. "Who are you?"

"I'm Mary's brother," Jack lied.

Jerking his head behind him, he said in a clipped voice, "Mary is in the second dressing room to the right. But I wouldn't bother with her tonight if I was you. She's been in a foul mood since the actress she worked for died. Mary's been lowered to dressing the seconds."

Jack grinned. "Thank you for the warning."

The man turned his back and scurried onward with a clipped stride.

Jack took Evelyn's hand and led her in the direction the man had indicated and stopped before a closed door. He rapped twice, then waited.

"What is it?" came a muffled voice.

Jack opened the door. A stout middle-aged woman, with steel gray hair and seamstress pins clenched between puckered lips, lifted her head and glared at them. She was hunched over, pulling the two ends of a gown together on the back of a skinny actress. With jerky movements, she removed the pins from her lips and proceeded to pin the actress's dress together. The bodice, clearly made for a more full-breasted woman, sagged drearily like two deflated balloons on the actress's chest.

"Bloody 'ell!" Mary swore. "Ain't nobody can fix this dress. You lack the titties to carry it off."

The actress's kohl-lined eyes narrowed, and with an indignant huff, she lifted her skirts and swept past Jack and Evelyn out the door.

Jack stepped forward, and Evelyn followed close on his heels.

The dressing room was small and crammed with a rack full of costumes, shelves of hats, and a counter crowded with facial makeup, wigs, and hairpieces. It smelled of sweat, smoke, and face powder.

"Who are ye?" Mary demanded.

"My name is Jack Harding. I'd like to talk with you about Bess Whitfield."

Two deep frown lines appeared between Mary's eyes. "Yer with the constable?"

"No. I'm a barrister, and this is a close friend of Bess's cousin." Jack motioned to Evelyn. "Has Bow Street spoken with you?"

"Not yet. I was wonderin' what was takin' 'em so long."

"They may not have thought to question you."

"Word on the street is they know who killed 'er. Some university boy seen jumpin' from 'er window."

"You don't sound convinced."

"Bess could 'andle a boy like that."

"You knew her well, then?" Evelyn asked.

"Bess was *my* actress. The day she walked in 'ere, I knew she 'ad what it took to make it big. Not like the dozens of girls that float through 'ere. Bess took a likin' to me. As she rose, my position in the theater rose with 'er. I owed 'er."

"They say she had many lovers. Do you think one became jealous and killed her?"

"I couldna say fer sure. All I knew is she liked 'er men. All sorts of 'em. Titled nobility, rich merchants, and even young, good-lookin' stagehands. Poor thing was neglected by her father as a child, and sought male attention like a moth seeks a flame. I knew all 'er men, all except 'er longtime benefactor."

"Her benefactor?"

"She kept 'im as a lover the entire time I knew 'er. 'E 'ad to be rich, probably nobility, fer 'e regularly sent 'er blunt and gifts, expensive ones too. But I never learned 'is real name."

"Do you know why someone would want to kill Bess?"

"No. There were rivals at the theater, but none that would advance straightway if she was dead. They knew the director would 'ire outside the theater, and 'e did just that after Bess was killed."

"Do you know if Bess had something to hide or something valuable? Something worth killing for?"

"None of 'er jewels were missin'."

"Anything other than jewels or money?"

"She kept a diary, but she was real careful never to use 'er benefactor's true name. As for 'er other lovers, they were all there."

"A diary? Do you know where it is?"

"It's missin'. I searched her dressin' room, but I knew it wouldn't be there. Bess always carried it with 'er."

"Do you recall any of her admirers she might have written about in her diary?" Evelyn asked.

Mary shrugged. "I knew 'em all as I seen 'em come to visit 'er backstage."

"Name them," Evelyn said. "Please."

"There was a fancy viscount with a curled mustache she called Maxwell, and the old, fat Earl of Newland.

Then there was a well-spoken commoner with dark hair named Sam. Never did learn 'is last name."

Evelyn took a quick breath of utter astonishment. "Maxwell Stanford, the Viscount of Hamilton, and Harold Kirk, the Earl of Newland!"

"There were others too. Some of the fools would pretend they were theatergoers who only wanted to meet Bess. Ha! As if old Mary can't tell when a man wants to bed a woman." Mary's wizened eyes studied Jack, noting Evelyn standing close by his side. "Just like ye two."

Evelyn took a step back. "We're not . . . lovers."

"Not yet?" She turned a hard eye on Jack. "Then it won't be long by the look of 'im."

Chapter 14

"Stop the carriage at the corner," Evelyn said.

Jack leaned out the window and spoke to the driver. Moments later, the conveyance stopped down the street from Evelyn's home.

Evelyn grasped her maid's sleeve, then reached for the door handle. "Kindly take a walk around the block, Janet. Knock on the carriage door when you get back."

Janet opened and closed her mouth like a fish, clearly surprised by the command. But at her mistress's stern stare, she scurried from the carriage.

Jack casually leaned back against the padded bench. He eyed Evelyn across from him, a knowing look in his eyes. "I take it you want a word with me alone?"

"I need to ask you something. When Mary Morris said she could surmise when 'a man wants to bed a woman,' and she referred to your inclinations toward me, you did not rebuke her or deny it. Why not?"

His stare was bold as he assessed her frankly. "Do you want to know the truth, Evie?"

"Yes, I do," she insisted. "For us to successfully work together there must always be the truth between us."

Ever since they had left the theater, Evelyn had pondered what Bess Whitfield's dresser had said—and very little of what was running through Evelyn's mind had to do with the murdered actress.

Mary Morris was old and shrewd, far more experienced than Evelyn when it came to men. Mary's comment that Jack wanted Evelyn in his bed had taken Evelyn by surprise.

But more shocking was that Jack had not denied the accusation, had merely shrugged in acceptance.

Did Jack truly desire her?

Instead of dissecting the valuable information they had learned about Bess's past interests since leaving the dresser's presence, Evelyn had been consumed with getting Jack alone and questioning him on *his* interests.

A mocking smile crossed Jack's lips. He sat forward, resting an elbow on his knee. "You truly are a fascinating contradiction, Evie. You ask me about my desires and in the next sentence you bring up our working relationship. Are you completely ignorant of a man's baser needs?"

"I . . . I don't know what you mean," she stammered, suddenly doubting her wisdom for bringing up the topic in such a forthright fashion.

The curtains were drawn, blocking out the street lamp, and in the dim light of the carriage, Jack suddenly seemed darkly illusive.

"I think you know exactly of what I speak." His voice, deep and sensual, sent a ripple of awareness through her.

He reached out to lightly finger a loose tendril of hair on her cheek. His fingers, tapered and strong, continued onward, trailing a leisurely path down her neck.

She gasped at his touch, her heart drumming in her ears.

He leaned closer until she could see the flecks of gold

in his jade eyes and feel his breath on her cheek. The scent of his cologne, sandalwood and cloves, filled her senses, and she sat perfectly still, entranced and weak-limbed. The idea to pull away did not enter her fog-enshrouded mind.

Kiss me.

The traitorous thought snaked through her head.

Slowly, ever so slowly, he lowered his lips to hers. Tender and seductively persuasive, his tongue slid lazily across her bottom lip, and he sucked on its plumpness, before delving between her parted lips. Overwhelmed by the taste of the man, she opened to him, reveling at the first tangling of their tongues.

Her hands rose of their own volition to his arms, the superfine texture of his jacket smooth beneath her hands. She leaned forward, into the kiss, and when she grazed his hard chest, a delightful shiver of desire ran through her. Her fingers inched higher, touched his neck, then speared through his thick hair.

He growled, low and deep in his throat, and captured her face in his hands, ravaging her mouth. Whatever logic or propriety remained flew from her mind.

His hands caressed her shoulders, then lowered to trace the sensitive skin above the bodice of her gown.

At the first brush of his palm against the side of her breast, she quivered and arched closer. Perched on the edge of the bench with her heart hammering madly, her mind told her to resist, but her body refused.

And then he cupped her breast.

The heat from his palm through the material of her gown nearly melted her bones. His touch was light, painfully teasing, and the shock of it ran through her body. Her breasts instantly swelled; her nipples hardened.

Ah. She wanted this . . . wanted more . . .

A loud rapping sounded on the carriage door.

Evelyn jerked backward like a stunned bird flown into a stone wall.

Jack cursed.

She reached for the door handle, then dropped her hand and touched her kiss-swollen lips. A horrid sense of shame and guilt flooded her veins.

She looked up at Jack. "We must never speak of this again."

"Don't try to deny what you felt, Evie," he said.

"It was a mistake, nothing more."

His eyes were like bits of stone. "Do you feel the same when Randolph kisses you?"

She lifted her head in horror. *Dear Lord, poor Randolph! How could I have behaved so wantonly?*

The rapping came again, more insistent this time.

Evelyn threw open the door, suddenly overcome with the need for fresh air and to escape the close confines of the carriage.

Janet stood outside, her pale face pinched. "M' lady?"

"Yes," Evelyn answered.

"Shouldn't we return?"

"Yes, of course. Father will be waiting." Evelyn made to step down with an urgency as if the carriage was on fire, when Jack grasped her arm.

"The step isn't lowered," he pointed out sharply.

He jumped out before her, lowered the step, then of-fered her his hand.

She alighted with his aid, but when she tried to pull away, he refused to release her hand.

"We need to discuss what occurred today," Jack said matter-of-factly.

For a heart-stopping moment, she believed he referred to their passionate embrace. But then she realized he meant what they had learned from Bess Whitfield's dresser.

By the smug grin on Jack's face, Evelyn suspected he knew of the true nature of her thoughts.

"I am available Monday," she offered.

"I'll be at the Old Bailey." Looking to Janet, he flashed a charming smile. "I'm certain Janet will enjoy viewing her first trial."

Jack's gaze hardened on Evelyn's stiff back as she hurried down the street with her maid rushing to keep pace by her side.

His body was tense, the blood pounding in his veins.

What the bloody hell had he been thinking?

Frustration roiled deep within his gut. It was simple lust. Evelyn was a beautiful woman. She had stared him in the eye and questioned him about his base desires.

What man wouldn't grow hot and heavy in similar circumstances?

And yet he had tasted her, tasted the rising passion within her. Beneath her no-nonsense and straitlaced façade simmered a passionate nature that was as challenging as a swift-footed deer darting past a starving hunter.

Ah, and there's the rub, Jack-boy.

She was untouchable. Not to be dallied with. And not just because she was a client that could possibly compromise his legal ability, but because she was Emmanuel Darlington's daughter.

His former pupilmaster deserved Jack's utmost respect. Seducing his daughter in a carriage parked on the man's street was not the way to show his gratitude or respect.

Not to mention the fact that Evelyn intended to marry another man.

Jack's mouth set in a grim line. The more he learned of Randolph Sheldon, the more he thought Evelyn's choice was a bad match. Intellectually compatible, perhaps, but Jack was certain they lacked even the merest spark of passion.

Then there was the messy business of the brutal stabbing of Bess Whitfield. The criminal still roamed free. And most disturbing of all, Jack was not yet entirely convinced of Randolph's innocence.

Chapter 15

He woke slumped over a rickety chair, his forehead resting on an old desk. A nearly empty bottle of whiskey rested in his hand.

The temperature in the room had dropped. The smell of smoldering ashes from the hearth comingled with rotting food roused him from his liquor-induced trance. He lifted his head and was seized by a shooting pain in his temples.

He pushed with his arms and tried to stand, but the pain slid to the base of his skull, demanding entrance to his brain, hovering like a demon.

Just like the curse that plagued him.

The chair creaked as he collapsed back down. He looked about the room. The floor was littered with crumpled paper, dirty clothes, and decaying food. Flies buzzed over an apple core.

His hand shook as he lifted the bottle to his lips and drank deeply. The cheap whiskey burned the back of his throat, every inch of his esophagus, and burst into a fireball in his belly.

The bitch was dead.

The fact should have given him joy, but the euphoria had waned.

He shut his swollen lids and pictured the killing. The initial fury on her face when she had walked in on him searching her bedroom had turned to bone-chilling fear at the first slice of the knife. He had been forced to act, to protect his future. And yet he had felt an excitement that had peaked at her horror when she realized she would die . . . her feeble struggles . . . the blood . . . the massive spray of blood.

Each time the well-honed blade had pierced her body, the crimson elixir of life had splattered across the walls, his clothing, his face, his lips.

She had betrayed him, and her death—although not planned—had left him unremorseful.

But now he had nothing.

Not entirely true.

There was another that could give him what he wanted. The beauty with the blond hair and blue eyes that he had been watching.

She was the one. She was pure. Innocent.

And unlike that tarnished actress, she would never betray him with another.

Chapter 16

There is no justice for the weak and poor.

At least, that's what Evelyn had always believed.

Two broad-shouldered guards brought the woman into the courtroom. Their viselike hold on her arms was entirely unnecessary, a pathetic show of barbarism.

Chained at the wrists and the ankles, the iron shackles dragged and clanked as she shuffled forward to stand before the judge. Her dress was torn and patched, her hem too short, her shoes pitiful pieces of leather that were held together with butcher's string. Whispers among the spectators placed her age around thirty, but the crow's-feet around her eyes, sagging skin of her neck, and gray in her hair, made her look twenty years older.

Six children and no husband, the whispers around Evelyn said.

Evelyn shifted on the wooden bench in the spectators' gallery.

The woman's crime: Guilty of theft of goods worth thirty-five shillings from a dwelling house.

Why ever else but to feed her six children? Evelyn thought. Life in the St. Giles rookeries was harsh on married women with a working husband, let alone a widow with half a dozen young children to feed.

Dear Lord, she could be sentenced to death for such a trivial crime. And what would become of her children then?

She'd heard enough from her father to know the answer: Pickpockets in training in order to survive.

"Hannah Ware," Judge Lessard began in a droll tone as he sat high up on his bench, "You have been found guilty of theft of goods from a dwelling house. Do you have anything to say for yourself before you are sentenced?"

The woman's mouth opened and closed. A raspy sound came forth, barely audible in the cavernous courtroom.

Evelyn decided right then and there to leave. She refused to watch such injustice. This was not the reason she was here today. She was here to meet . . .

Just then the doors in the rear of the courtroom opened and thumped against the wall. All heads turned to see Jack Harding striding forward, his black barrister's gown flowing behind him like a specter.

"If it may please the court, my lord," Jack said as he reached the woman's side, "I am the barrister for Miss Hannah Ware for her sentencing."

Judge Lessard straightened as if stuck with a pin between his shoulder blades. "You're late, Mr. Harding."

"Pardon my tardiness, my lord. I was in Lord Townsend's courtroom on a different matter."

"You're a busy barrister, Mr. Harding." The judge waved his meaty hand toward Hannah Ware. "I had asked the guilty party if she had anything to say before her sentencing. You may proceed on her behalf."

"Miss Ware is terribly sorry for her crime, my lord," Jack said. "She succumbed to a moment of weakness, stealing to feed her children when her eldest became ill. She agrees to pay full restitution for the amount taken. And she respectfully begs the court the benefit of clergy."

The spectators began rumbling. Evelyn clenched her fists in her lap. She knew enough of the law to understand that requesting the "benefit of clergy" meant sparing a guilty defendant the death penalty. Rather than the court issuing a punishment, it would send the defendant to the church for its own penalty.

"Benefit of clergy does not apply since the defendant committed theft from a dwelling house," Judge Lessard said.

"I beg to differ, my lord. Miss Ware was found guilty of theft of goods of thirty-five shillings. According to the new statutes, only those crimes of theft of *forty* shillings and more from a dwelling house are not eligible for benefit of clergy."

Evelyn held her breath.

The judge hesitated and made a show of sorting through papers on his immaculate desk before he finally raised his head. "In order to prove the defendant's affiliation with the church before benefit of clergy can be considered, the court requires she read the first and second verses from the 51st Psalm."

Judge Lessard turned to his court clerk who immediately brought forth a Bible and handed it to Hannah Ware.

Hannah's hands shook as she held the leather-bound book.

Jack took it from her, opened it to the correct page,

and returned it to her. "Go ahead, Hannah. Do the best you can."

Hannah's voice wavered as she stumbled over the verse familiarly known as "the neck verse" for sparing many the death penalty. "'Have mercy on me, O God, accordin' to yer unfailin' love; accordin' to yer great compassion blot out me transgressions. Wash away all me iniquity and cleanse me from me sin.'"

Judge Lessard nodded. "The court allows benefit of clergy in this case, Mr. Harding." The judge pointed to Hannah Ware and glowered at her above the rim of his thick spectacles. "You are fortunate indeed that branding was abolished."

Evelyn was aware that in the past guilty defendants who pled benefit of clergy were branded on the thumb so that they could not receive the benefit again should they commit more crimes in the future. Branding had been abolished thirty-five years ago—before Hannah Ware had even been born—but if it had still remained a regular practice, Hannah would have been branded immediately after her sentencing in front of the spectators.

"As promised by your barrister, I expect full restitution of the thirty-five shillings before you are released, Miss Ware," the judge said.

Hannah Ware paled and looked to Jack.

"The amount shall be paid immediately," Jack said.

"As the sentence is accepted, court is adjourned." Judge Lessard pounded his gavel.

Hannah Ware's shackles were removed and the judge rose. Spectators filed out of the courtroom.

Evelyn watched as Hannah Ware threw her arms around Jack and sobbed, repeatedly thanking him.

An elderly woman came forth with six children in tow. Their ages ranged from several months to eight years

old. They embraced their mother, joy and happiness—
and most of all, relief—written all over their tearstained
cheeks. The children must have been in the rear of the
room and Evelyn hadn't even noticed. What a travesty
that they could have been witness to their mother being
sentenced to death.

That is, if not for Jack.

She felt uncomfortable watching them, like an intruder
stealing glances into a private home.

She stood and quietly left the courtroom.

"Well, well, what have we here?"

Evelyn whirled around to see a tall, dark-haired man
standing behind her. His broad shoulders seemed a mile
wide. Unfathomable eyes, sinfully dark, looked down at
her. They held an ominous gleam that made her uneasy.

"Pardon?" she asked.

The stranger's mouth spread into a thin-lipped
smile. "I was told about you, but I really didn't believe it
until now."

Her discomfort increased. "Do I know you?"

Dressed in a telling black robe, he was clearly a barrister. He wasn't wearing a wig, and his dark hair was
cropped short and emphasized his square chin and bold
features.

He shrugged one big shoulder and again she was
struck by his massive size. Even through the robe, he had
the build of a boxer, all hard muscle and bulk.

"My name is Anthony Stevens," he said.

Realization dawned. "You're one of the barristers who
shares chambers with Mr. Harding."

"I assume you are Lady Evelyn Darlington, then? Jack
Harding's newest client?"

She nodded. "I'm here to meet Mr. Harding. I was told by a clerk he would be in Judge Lessard's courtroom today. Mr. Harding was late, and I had begun to believe I was in the wrong courtroom."

"Ah, you must have just seen Hannah Ware's sentencing."

She frowned. "Yes."

"Was Jack able to avoid the death penalty, then?"

"Yes, thank the good Lord. The judge allowed Miss Ware to plead benefit of clergy."

Anthony smirked. "Brilliant, really, that Jack was able to successfully obtain it. Judge Lessard is known for his harsh sentences."

"The judge did threaten Miss Ware with branding. I believe he would have carried it out, too, had branding not been abolished."

"Ah, yes. The delightful art of branding," Anthony drawled, his voice heavy with sarcasm. "Did you know it was not unheard of for some criminals to bribe the official to apply a cold iron? That way, they could effectively continue to steal repeatedly with no fear of a big fat letter "T" for theft so obviously imprinted on their thumbs. It was a big sham, really. Some officials were in on it too and received their cut from the stolen goods. Quite a lucrative business. Were I reborn a member of the lower classes, I would surely participate in such a cunning scheme."

"I hardly believe such was the case for Hannah Ware. She meant only to feed her offspring," Evelyn argued.

"The woman hasn't a shilling to her name. Did Jack promise restitution?"

The question struck her. Evelyn had heard Jack offer restitution for the thirty-five shillings. Hannah Ware had looked stricken when the judge insisted the amount be immediately paid in full.

So where would the money come from? And more to the point, how could such a client pay for Jack Harding's services?

"You look confused, Lady Evelyn. Let me guess. You are wondering why such a prestigious and expensive criminal barrister like Jack Harding would represent an impoverished thief such as Hannah Ware."

His careless words unleashed her fury. "I'd hardly call an unfortunate widow with six starving children a thief!"

"Sympathetic to the lower classes, are you, Lady Evelyn?"

"What would you know of a woman's plight?"

"Nothing. But from the looks of your expensive gown, neither would you."

For a heart-stopping moment, she wondered about Anthony Stevens's true intent, and then she realized he was baiting her, judging her reaction to his inflammatory speech. She had seen it before. Opposing solicitors and barristers who had strode into her father's chambers with belligerent attitudes, twisted facts, and misinterpreted statutes all in an attempt to throw their adversary off balance and tip the scales in their favor.

She lifted her chin, meeting those hard, dark eyes straight on. "Are you always this confrontational, Mr. Stevens?"

"If I'm having a good day."

She couldn't help herself. She burst out laughing.

A glimpse of astonishment touched Anthony's expression before it was replaced with its familiar mocking indifference. "I'm beginning to understand why Jack agreed to help you. A lady with a sense of humor is hard to find."

"I've seen your kind before, Mr. Stevens. You should know that I'm not easily intimidated."

"In that case, I'll satisfy your curiosity. Hannah Ware is one of Jack's *pro bono publico* cases."

"*Pro bono?* He represents her for free?"

"You sound very surprised."

"I just thought . . . I mean I believed . . . barristers of Jack's caliber could name their price."

He shot her a penetrating look. "He can. But unlike me, Jack Harding still has a soul and a conscience."

Evelyn didn't know how to respond, but she was saved from having to answer by the approach of another man.

"Anthony! Are you bothering the lady?"

Evelyn turned toward a masculine voice. Her breath caught as a gentleman strode forward.

She stared at his face, unable to tear her gaze away.

Sweet Lord, this was a handsome man.

Thick, light-colored hair and piercing blue eyes met her stare. Smooth bronzed skin stretched over high cheekbones. His chiseled features looked as if his creator had taken extra time to craft his visage. He wasn't garbed in a barrister's gown, but rather wore a tailored navy suit that revealed a sinewy frame.

The man stopped before her and eyed Anthony Stevens. "Leave her alone, Anthony."

Anthony faced his accuser with a mocking look. "What makes you think I was harassing the lady?"

"I know better." The handsome man turned his gaze upon her and smiled.

Her heart skipped a beat at the devastating effect.

"Please pardon my colleague, my lady. His manners can be abominable," the man said.

"No apologies are necessary. Mr. Stevens was quite enlightening," Evelyn said.

Again, surprise crossed Anthony's expression, and he swept into a mockingly low bow, as if Evelyn were the Queen of England herself. "A true lady." Anthony rose and turned to his accuser. "May I introduce Mr. Brent Stone. He is a fellow barrister in our chambers. Brent, this is Lady Evelyn Darlington."

Brent Stone's eyes twinkled. "Jack's latest case. You must be special indeed for Jack to agree to aid you. His docket is quite full. Are you here to see him then?"

"I was supposed to meet with Mr. Harding, but he appears quite busy this afternoon."

"He has his charitable cases today."

"Yes, Mr. Stevens told me, but I cannot help but find it surprising."

"Jack handles dozens of such cases throughout the year. Jack and I are board members of the London Legal Aid Society, an organization dedicated to providing necessary services for the destitute."

Evelyn looked to Anthony. "Are you a member as well, Mr. Stevens?"

"Alas, but no, Lady Evelyn. The impoverished have no need for my legal expertise," Anthony drawled.

"And what exactly is your expertise?" she asked.

"Exploiting the fairer sex for their partners' gain."

"Pardon?"

"Disposing of unwanted wives," Anthony said bluntly.

"I see," Evelyn said.

"Anthony's reputation precedes him," Brent Stone said.

"Are there any more barristers in your chambers I should be aware of?" she asked.

"Mr. James Devlin is the only other. He is not at the Old Bailey this afternoon. But you will have the privilege of meeting him soon, I'm sure," Anthony said.

"I'm looking forward to it." After meeting these two, Evelyn couldn't help but wonder what the remaining barrister was like.

The doors to Judge Lessard's courtroom opened and out came Hannah Ware and her six children followed by Jack.

Jack stopped in his tracks when he spotted Evelyn. He looked at Anthony Stevens and Brent Stone beside her, and then cursed beneath his breath.

Chapter 17

"What the devil are you two doing?" Jack glanced from Anthony Stevens to Brent Stone.

"Don't panic, Jack," Anthony said. "We were just introducing ourselves to Lady Evelyn."

"That's what I'm afraid of," Jack drawled.

Evelyn spoke up. "Your fellow barristers are quite charming, Mr. Harding."

Jack rolled his eyes. "Charming? I've never heard Anthony Stevens referred to as charming before."

"She must have been referring to me, then," Brent Stone said, a teasing note in his tone.

Evelyn smiled at the handsome barrister. "You have both been very informative." She turned to Jack. "They advised me of your charitable activities. I had no idea."

Something akin to admiration crossed her beautiful face. He felt a curious pull at his innards like a boy seeking the approval of an attractive governess.

Ridiculous.

"It's nothing," Jack said.

"I'd hardly call your activities nothing. Father is a firm believer that justice, in the form of legal representation, should be available to all. Not just those wealthy enough to afford it," she said.

Anthony whistled between his teeth. "Look out, Jack. She is beginning to believe you her champion."

Jack shot Anthony a dark stare. "Don't you two have somewhere else to be?"

"Truth be told, I was looking for you when I spotted Lady Evelyn," Anthony said. "I'm waiting for my Armenian investigator, Armen Papazian, to arrive. He's unearthed information that may be of interest to you."

Jack eyed Anthony. "Let's speak with him elsewhere. The client consultation room is best."

Anthony arched a brow. "Why? Don't you want the lady to be present?"

Jack itched to punch Anthony in the mouth. The bastard was baiting him and anticipated Evelyn's outraged response. The problem was Jack didn't know what information the investigator had discovered.

What if it concerned Randolph Sheldon's past secrets?

"I want to hear what Mr. Papazian has to say," Evelyn insisted.

"Of course you do, my lady," Anthony said.

"Let's get on with it then, shall we?" Jack said tersely. He'd take a piece out of Anthony's hide later. He couldn't do it in front of Evelyn.

Brent Stone bowed to Evelyn. "Unfortunately, I must miss this meeting as I have an appointment. It was a pleasure, Lady Evelyn." He turned and left, his lean frame gracefully turning a corner and disappearing from view.

Jack turned to Evelyn. "Where's your maid?"

"I left her in the carriage. Janet had no interest in viewing the Old Bailey."

"Will you never bring a chaperone?"

"I did. She's in the carriage."

Jack looked at Anthony Stevens, then back to her. "Forget the client consultation room. I'll not take you in there without your maid."

With two unmarried barristers remained unspoken.

They chose a vacant corner in the hallway instead.

"Where's your man?" Jack asked.

Anthony withdrew a pocket watch. "I expect him any minute now. He's always prompt. Ah, here he is now."

Jack glanced up at the sound of approaching footsteps. A short man with a furrowed brow and a head of jet, curly hair approached. Olive-black eyes, hooded like those of a hawk, regarded them keenly before he greeted them, and Jack suspected his watchful inquisitiveness made him excel in his profession.

Anthony made the introductions. "May I introduce Mr. Harding and Lady Evelyn Darlington. This is Mr. Papazian."

Jack shook the investigator's hand. "Please tell us what you have discovered."

"I'm still looking into the list of possible suspects for Bess Whitfield's murder that Mr. Sheldon and Mr. Guthrie provided. What I have discovered, however, is that there is a man who visits Bess Whitfield's grave each afternoon. I spoke with the cemetery gardener who said the man is obsessive in his behavior. He arrives exactly at one o'clock each afternoon and exhibits conduct unusual to that of the average mourner."

"What on earth does that mean?" Jack asked.

"I'm not certain. But upon further investigation, I learned the man's identity."

"Who?" Anthony asked.

"Harold Kirk. The Earl of Newland."

Evelyn gasped. "He's one of the lovers identified by

Mary Morris, Bess Whitfield's dresser at the Drury Lane Theatre!" Evelyn said.

"Mary knew her mistress's secrets, then," Papazian said.

Jack eyed Evelyn with a calculating expression. "It's time we paid Bess Whitfield our respects."

"The man is obsessed," Evelyn whispered.

"More like cracked," Jack responded.

Evelyn glanced sideways at Jack, then returned her attention to the man placing roses, one at a time, on Bess Whitfield's grave.

Jack and Evelyn were a good twenty feet away, crouching behind a towering gravestone of someone of importance, spying on Harold Kirk, the aging Earl of Newland. In the distance behind the earl, loomed the shape of a gray stone mausoleum.

The earl's behavior was strange indeed. He circled round and round the grave, placing one rose on the top of the gravestone with each circuit. He mumbled beneath his breath as he did so. Evelyn could see his lips moving in what appeared to be a sort of eerie chant, but from this distance she couldn't hear the words.

"I've been here watching him every afternoon this week," Jack said. "His routine hasn't varied. He's cracked, I tell you."

This was the first time Evelyn had come along with Jack. Newland's repetitive behavior was truly alarming. Despite it being a pleasant May afternoon, Harold Kirk wore a heavy wool coat. His pallid complexion resembled ash from a fireplace gone cold. Sparse, gray hair protruded from his scalp like unkempt weeds. He was of average height and appearance, save for a bulbous nose that resembled a ripe tomato.

Evelyn smoothed damp palms over her black mourning dress. The outfit was from her uncle's funeral, and she had chosen it not only because she was to visit a cemetery, but because of the black hat and net veil that concealed her face. Jack wore a dark jacket as well, and with the collar up and the curled brim of his hat down, he gave the appearance of a nameless mourner.

"What is the man saying?" she asked.

"I passed by him yesterday, pretending to pay my respects to another grave. He mumbles Bess Whitfield's name, date of birth, and death. Exactly as it's written on the stone."

Anxiety raced through her. "Could he be the killer?"

Jack shrugged. "If not the killer, then an obsessed lover. Either way, there are cases in which murderers feel compelled to visit the graves of their victims, much like infatuated lovers."

Newland suddenly stopped his circuit of the grave and began coughing. Pulling a handkerchief from his waistcoat, he hacked and gasped horribly for over a minute. One hand held the handkerchief over his mouth while with the other he grasped his side as the coughing fit reached a crescendo. His face turned an alarming shade of red, matching his nose. His struggle to breathe seemed endless, but finally the gasping subsided and he withdrew the handkerchief.

Even from this distance, Evelyn could see the blood on the cloth. "Sweet Lord," she whispered.

"They say he has advanced consumption," Jack said.

"Consumption!"

"He doesn't have long to live. That's why this troubles me. I don't think he's the murderer," Jack said.

"Why?"

"He has no motive. He's been a widower for over ten

years. He has no children. If he was having an affair with a notorious actress, and his sexual antics were detailed in her diary, who would care?"

"He's an earl. Society would still be harsh. Doesn't he have an heir?" she asked.

"A nephew that's currently in India. From what I understand, they were never close. Newland cares naught for the nephew save that the man is getting his title and fortune," Jack said.

"You said yourself he's cracked. If he's mentally unstable, he could be dangerous," Evelyn said.

"Yes. I've seen it before."

Just then, Newland stopped his circuit and turned to where Jack and Evelyn stood partially concealed behind the tall gravestone. His lips twisted into a thin-lipped smile, and he took a step toward them.

Chapter 18

Evelyn gasped.

"Let's go," Jack barked. "Now."

"But—"

Jack grasped her arm and pulled her around. "Don't look back. Don't acknowledge him."

With a firm hold on her elbow, Jack led her down the stone path between the graves. Evelyn rushed to keep up with his long strides.

"He saw us, Jack," she said.

"Keep your hat on and your veil over your eyes. He has no idea who we are."

"How can you be certain?"

"He thinks we are mourners come to grieve over another deceased."

"Then why are we rushing away?" She was panting now, and they were only halfway down the stone path.

Jack's steps never faltered or slowed. "I don't want you seen up close and recognized. Whether Newland is Bess Whitfield's murderer or not, he is still demented."

They reached the entrance of the cemetery and their hired hackney cab came into view. The driver spotted them, jumped down from his perch, and opened the door.

She had a mad urge to turn around to see if the earl had followed them this far.

"Don't, Evie," Jack warned. He ushered her inside the cab, then gave the command to depart. The driver hopped into his seat and the carriage jerked forward.

She glanced out the window.

There among the last row of graves before the road, stood the Earl of Newland. His burning eyes, like those of a feral animal, took her completely by surprise, and she froze in her seat. Then he raised his hand and waved his bloody handkerchief at them.

In the thick stack of social invitations and legal correspondence on Evelyn's desk, one envelope stood out— not because of its costly, cream vellum, fine calligraphy, and gold-embossed seal, but because it bore the crest of Viscount Hamilton.

Evelyn broke the gold seal and tore open the envelope. Inside was a formal invitation for one of the most anticipated costume balls of the Season given by Cecilia Stanford, the Viscountess Hamilton. This was not just an ordinary costume ball. Cecilia hosted a masquerade where all the guests' identities were guarded with vigilance appropriate to top military maneuvers.

Evelyn was a friend of the Hamiltons' daughter, Georgina. A fourth-year debutante, she was close to twenty years old, just two years younger than Evelyn.

Georgina was an intellectual who read voraciously on the controversial subject of women's rights. Georgina had been quite vocal about not wanting a Season, but because of her family's social status, her wishes were ignored. Georgina's mother, Cecilia, a renowned hostess, had been aghast at her daughter's beliefs. She was determined to parade her reluctant daughter through Season after Season and find her a suitable husband.

Evelyn, like Georgina, hadn't any desire for an official coming out either, and because her father had not inherited the earldom until after she had reached the ripe old age of twenty, Evelyn had been spared.

Evelyn's mother might have impressed the importance of a Season on her daughter had she been alive, but she had died when Evelyn was an infant. Evelyn's father had been far too busy at Lincoln's Inn to concern himself with such frivolities. Evelyn had been grateful for her father's legal distractions.

An endless Season of balls, soirées, garden parties, masques, and Wednesday evenings at Almack's marriage mart at the mercy of its frightening patronesses, all in the hopes of finding a fitting husband, was not a fate Evelyn would wish for any lady, let alone herself.

No, she had found her match in Randolph, a man with whom she could hold an intellectual conversation without his needing to reach for his snuff box.

A sudden image of Jack Harding flashed through her mind. Would he seek a rosy-cheeked debutante as a bride?

Although Jack wasn't titled, he was very wealthy and many aggressive mamas of the *ton* sought out rich men before titled ones for their daughters. Ideally, a husband with both wealth and title was preferred, but if given a choice between the two, many went after money like bloodhounds during hunting season.

Jack didn't seem the sort to seek out a young, virginal debutante with an overreaching, interfering mother. What would he have in common with such a girl?

But then again, men acted completely irrationally

when choosing a spouse. Perhaps Jack was after a wealthy wife from a respectable or titled family.

Evelyn frowned at her thoughts. Jack Harding's marital prospects were none of her concern.

She skimmed the rest of the invitation, noting that the masque would be held in a fortnight. The ball offered the perfect opportunity to learn more about the viscountess's husband.

Mary Morris, Bess Whitfield's dresser, had named Maxwell Stanford, Viscount Hamilton, as one of Bess's lovers. Unlike the mad Earl of Newland, Maxwell had a wife and daughter. Both would suffer from the humiliation if Bess's diary became public. The scandal sheets would relish printing any outrageous story about the viscount and the notorious actress. Gossip would be rampant.

In short, Maxwell had more than sufficient motive to kill Bess for her incriminating diary.

Evelyn wondered if either mother or daughter had any idea about the viscount's extracurricular activities with the actress. Perhaps they wouldn't be surprised. Many married men of the *beau monde* had mistresses.

Just as the wives had lovers.

Evelyn didn't want such a marriage for herself. She could not picture herself cuckolding her husband, and she knew she would be distraught if her spouse took a mistress.

She turned her attention back to the invitation. She had never wanted to be paraded about as a debutante, but she did enjoy an occasional masque or party, and Cecilia Stanford's yearly costume ball was one of Evelyn's favorites. Like all the guests, she could don a costume and shed a part of the rigid propriety that constrained members of polite society.

Evelyn contemplated what to wear. Cleopatra came to mind. She loved the Egyptian period.

She thought of Jack and wondered if he was on the guest list. What would he wear?

Instantly, Mark Antony sprang to mind.

Good Lord.

What was she thinking?

She didn't know if Jack was invited. She only knew that she wanted him there. The opportunity to observe Viscount Hamilton could be invaluable to their investigation. But if she were truthful to herself, that wasn't the only reason she wanted Jack Harding to attend.

She was becoming accustomed to having him around, and that was a bad, bad thing.

She shifted in her desk chair, reached for a piece of foolscap, and penned a note.

Mr. Harding,
   Received an invitation to Viscountess Hamilton's costume ball. Will you attend?

                                        Lady Evelyn

Evelyn needn't mention the viscount himself. Jack would make the connection to Maxwell Stanford, the viscount that Mary Morris had said was one of Bess Whitfield's lovers.

Hours later, Hodges entered the drawing room carrying a silver salver with an envelope addressed to Evelyn. She waited until the butler departed before opening the envelope. Bold, black script dominated the page.

No invite as of yet. What can you do?

Jack hadn't bothered to address the note or sign his name.

Shrewd barrister.

She tore his note into tiny pieces and threw it into the fireplace.

It had been weeks since Evelyn had last paid Lady Georgina Stanford a visit. Evelyn stood on the steps of a magnificent Berkeley Square mansion and raised the brass door knocker.

Within seconds, a dour-faced butler opened the door.

Evelyn looked up at the servant in surprise. *Hodges would have taken forever to reach the door, assuming he even heard the knock,* she mused.

"Good afternoon, Lady Evelyn. Lady Georgina is expecting you," the butler said.

Evelyn stepped inside a stunning marble vestibule with a vaulted ceiling. Sparkling chandeliers holding dozens of candles drew her eyes upward. Sunlight from the open door bounced off the chandeliers' crystal prisms, creating magnificent iridescent images on the marble floor.

She followed the butler down the hall, past two sitting rooms and a music conservatory. Peering momentarily into each room they passed, she hoped to catch a glimpse of the viscount, but all were empty. She doubted whether he was in. Whenever Evelyn had visited in the past, he had never been home, and only rarely had she seen him out.

The butler opened a door into a formal drawing room, and Evelyn entered. Royal blue silk settees matched the curtains, and the same shade was in the Aubusson carpet. Priceless artwork from Dutch and Flemish masters Rembrandt, Jan Steen, Sir Anthony Van Dyck, and Peter Paul Rubens lined the walls.

Georgina Stanford stood as soon as she spotted Evelyn.

"Evelyn!" Georgina's face lit with a smile. She rushed over to embrace Evelyn. "It was such a pleasant surprise to get your note asking to see me."

Evelyn hugged her friend. An attractive young woman with abundantly thick chestnut hair and hazel eyes, Georgina was tall, slender, and quick to smile. If she was a fourth-year debutante, it was not for lack of offers, but for lack of interest on her part.

The two women took seats side by side. A maid carried in a tea tray with scones and crumpets. Georgina poured two cups of steaming green tea and handed one to Evelyn.

Evelyn waited until the door closed behind the servant before speaking. "I received your mother's invitation to the masquerade ball."

"I take it you are attending?" Georgina asked.

"It's my favorite event of the Season. What will you be?"

"I was thinking of Diana, Goddess of the Hunt," Georgina said.

"Diana! Didn't Roman mythology depict her with one breast bared?"

"Exactly."

Evelyn shot her friend an incredulous look. "Georgina Stanford, you wouldn't dare."

"Why not? That would surely push Mother over the edge."

"Who has she been pressuring you to marry now?" Evelyn asked.

"Lucas Crawford, the son of the Earl of Haverston."

"Lucas Crawford is merely a boy."

"Ah, but he is heir to the earldom. And from the looks of Haverston, he hasn't long to wait."

"What will you do?"

"Thumb my nose at him. I've been meeting with a group of feminist women and we are currently reading Mary Wollstonecraft's book *A Vindication of the Rights of Woman,* in which she argues women are regarded inferior to men because of their lack of education. Even though Wollstonecraft has been dead now seventeen years, her ideas still provide endless fodder for discussion, and we currently are debating her beliefs on marriage."

"The conversation must be fascinating," Evelyn said.

Georgina's voice rose an octave. "It is! There are women in our group who believe the poets—including Byron—spout nonsense merely to trick young girls into believing in love. These girls then marry and sacrifice their identities, their very souls, to their husbands. Men are not taken over by such poetic fancy; rather, they use it in order to control women until they have legally relinquished all their rights in matrimony. They compare marriage to slavery."

Evelyn laughed. "It doesn't sound like a group that would interest your mother."

Georgina rolled her eyes and reached for one of the scones on the tray.

Evelyn felt an instant's guilt tighten her chest. What if Georgina's father *had* murdered Bess Whitfield?

Evelyn truly liked Georgina. They were friends, and friends didn't seek to harm each other. But then again, there was Randolph's very life to consider. He was an innocent man, and unlike the viscount, Randolph didn't have a title or wealth to favorably influence a Bow Street magistrate.

With renewed conviction, Evelyn tucked her guilt away and pressed on with her plans.

"Are your parents home today?" Evelyn inquired.

"No. Father is at one of his clubs as usual, and Mother is attending Lady Litmanson's garden party. I claimed a headache to escape Mother's constant nagging on the subject of Mr. Crawford."

"Do you ever want to marry?" Evelyn asked.

"Only if there is a meeting of the minds."

Evelyn thought of Randolph. "I understand."

"Tell me about your Mr. Sheldon."

Like the rest of society, Georgina had no idea Randolph Sheldon was in hiding. Or that he was a suspect in the Drury Lane Theatre's lead actress's murder. Evelyn wanted to keep it a secret for as long as possible.

That is, until Bow Street Runners found Randolph and gave her no choice.

"Randolph is away researching a subject for my father," Evelyn lied smoothly.

"You must miss him then?"

The innocent question stopped Evelyn for a moment. If she was truthful to herself, she didn't miss Randolph as much as she would have thought.

Before the murder, they had routinely conversed in the evenings when Randolph stopped by to speak with her father. Other days, she had visited her father's offices in Oxford when she knew Randolph was present. Oftentimes, Randolph was grading papers or researching a topic for her father. They had spent countless hours together talking, poring over volumes in the university library, working side by side.

Evelyn was concerned for Randolph, yes. His situation was constantly on her mind, yes.

But did she miss him? Truly miss him?

No.

Georgina was looking at her curiously. "Is something wrong, Evelyn?"

"I ah—"

"There is another man," Georgina said matter-of-factly.

"Not in the way that you mean," Evelyn said.

Georgina placed her teacup in her saucer and leaned forward. "Tell me."

"I came today to ask a favor. I want to ensure a certain man is on the guest list for your mother's costume ball."

"Name him and I will have an invitation immediately sent out if it hasn't been already."

"A Mr. Jack Harding—"

"The barrister and jury master?" Georgina asked.

"Yes, how did you know?"

Georgina waved a hand. "Rest assured he's on the guest list. If he has not already received it, his invitation should arrive any moment. He gets invited to all the *ton* functions, you see, but he rarely attends. Apparently he is extremely busy. But he is in favor with the *beau monde*—he has aided a few in legal matters. Any society matron would be thrilled to have him in attendance. It seems his chosen discipline has been quite lucrative."

Evelyn frowned. Jack was not the money-grasping barrister she had initially believed. An image of Hannah Ware and her clinging children came to mind—like six small starving street urchins desperate for their next meal. Their mother would have been executed, lost to them forever, if not for Jack's volunteered services.

Jack was proving to be a complex man.

"If Mr. Harding rarely attends that would explain why I haven't seen him at past functions," Evelyn said.

"Other barristers of his chambers are invited as well because they have curried favor with my father," Georgina added.

Interesting, Evelyn thought. What types of favors would a viscount require of three other barristers?

Had Maxwell Stanford been involved in troublesome behavior in the past? Evelyn wondered.

"Why are you interested in Mr. Harding?" Georgina asked. "Has he caught your eye?"

"No," Evelyn answered quickly. "Absolutely not."

Georgina eyed her curiously. "He is a handsome man. It wouldn't be unusual if you—"

"No, you are mistaken. It's not that at all. Father is interested in having Mr. Harding as a guest lecturer at Oxford. I thought to help him." The lie came too easily to Evelyn's lips.

"Then why doesn't your father speak with him?"

"He has. He will. I thought to as well," Evelyn rushed.

"I see," Georgina said in a tone that implied she didn't believe her one bit. "Do not be too hard on yourself, Evelyn. Mary Wollstonecraft says a woman needs to explore all aspects of her inner self—even the sensual side—in order to find the freedom to be truly happy."

Chapter 19

"Cleopatra was an excellent choice. I do believe your barrister will be struck dumb."

Evelyn whirled around to see Lady Georgina. Her friend smiled slyly, and her hazel eyes shone behind her half mask. She had indeed dressed as Diana, Goddess of the Hunt, but thankfully, her white tunic covered *both* breasts. Strapped to her back was a dainty bow and quiver of golden arrows.

Evelyn returned Georgina's smile. "He's not *my* barrister, Georgina, but an acquaintance. And it's not me that has to be on guard. With your bow and arrows, you look quite like Cupid. Lucas Crawford best be wary."

"Ha!" Georgina laughed. "Dressed as you are, every man in attendance will be looking at you and trying to discern your identity when the arrow hits them. You look stunning, Evelyn."

Evelyn felt a thrill of excitement at the compliment. She *had* dressed with care tonight. She wore a sheath dress of gold tissue with a low bodice. Without a restraining corset and the heavy, voluminous skirts of a traditional ball gown, the dress felt as light as air. Thong sandals laced up her daringly bare ankles. Gold serpent bands with emerald eyes wrapped around each of her upper arms. She had contemplated wearing a wig of straight black hair, but at the last minute had chose instead to style her own hair. A jeweled headband with emeralds that matched the eyes of the serpent bands held her hair while the rest cascaded down her back in a platinum waterfall. A sequined, gold half mask hid her identity, making her feel bold and brazen. Had Evelyn not told her friend she was to dress as Cleopatra, Georgina would scarcely have recognized her.

Evelyn knew she looked attractive, and she admitted to herself that she wanted Jack Harding to see her this way, wanted him to look upon her as a beautiful woman and not just as the scholarly child who had followed him around conjugating Latin and Greek verbs.

Don't be reckless, her inner voice warned. *Such an attraction is perilous.*

"Do you know what costume your barrister is wearing?" Georgina asked.

Evelyn scanned the crowded ballroom and the masked guests. "I have no idea. And he's not my barrister."

Two giggling women, one dressed as a shepherdess and the other as an angel, held the arms of a portly man dressed as Henry the Eighth. The trio stumbled, then pushed past Evelyn and Georgina.

"There is such a crush. It will be difficult to find anyone tonight," Georgina said.

Normal etiquette required the announcing of the guests by the Hamilton staff, but tonight was a masquerade ball, and that formality did not apply. A charge of mystery and excitement hummed through the ballroom. The guests' costumes were extravagant, and many had taken great pains to hide their identities. Every area of the globe seemed to be represented, from Arabian sheiks and harem girls, to Chinese monks, to medieval knights and their ladies.

Liveried servants wove through the crowd, passing out flutes of bubbling champagne as the guests mingled in an orgy of self-indulgence. Behind masks, eyes glittered with lustful intent—searching for partners with similar dissolute plans to indulge their own guilty pleasures while remaining blissfully anonymous.

The entire ballroom was a kaleidoscope of brilliant color and flickering lights. Combined with the laughter and music, it amplified Evelyn's senses.

Just then a pair of strong hands encircled Evelyn's waist from behind and boldly lifted her up to stand on a wooden chair beside her.

"A queen deserves to be up on a throne," a masculine voice said.

Evelyn gasped as she looked down on Jack. Dressed as a pirate, he wore black from his gleaming boots to his plumed hat. The top three buttons of his shirt were undone, revealing his bronzed throat and a sprinkling of dark hair. A sword and eye patch completed his look.

Evelyn recalled another time she had thought Jack the perfect pirate. In the dim back alley behind the Drury Lane Theatre, Jack had been dressed entirely in black. He had looked like a dashing, but dangerous pirate then as well.

"Dear Lord, Jack. You scared me half to death," Evelyn said.

She realized her slip with formality as soon as his Christian name left her lips. Evelyn looked to Georgina who no doubt would believe her prior assumptions that Jack was *her* barrister were true.

With as much dignity as she could muster, Evelyn stepped down from the chair.

"May I introduce Lady Georgina Stanford." Motioning to Jack, Evelyn said, "This is Mr. Harding."

Jack swept off his hat and bowed formally. "A pleasure, Lady Stanford."

Georgina smiled charmingly. "Formal introductions are not necessary tonight, Mr. Harding. Mother believes it will add to the fun if her guests pretend anonymity, but I am pleased to meet you."

"Your mother is wise. But pray tell me, rumors abound that she knows what costumes her guests selected before tonight and that she knows every guests' identity behind their masks. Is it true?"

"You can ask her for yourself, Mr. Harding. She approaches with my father as we speak. Pardon my early escape, however, before my mother can barrage me with questions about a particular guest." Georgina curtsied and hurried away.

Evelyn turned as a couple came forward.

Lady Cecilia, Viscountess Hamilton, was dressed as Queen Elizabeth, complete with neck ruff, voluminous skirts, white-powdered face, and towering red wig—a formidable presence, much like the queen she imitated. A renowned *ton* hostess, Cecilia took her annual masquerade quite seriously.

Maxwell Stanford, on the other hand, had not bothered with a costume. In his late fifties, he was still a handsome man with a full head of jet hair and trim build. His curled mustache reached far past his lip, from cheek to cheek.

The viscount's eyes traveled from Jack and came to rest upon Evelyn. Instantly his gaze sharpened. His mustache twitched as one corner of his mouth twisted upward.

"Mr. Harding," Lady Cecilia said. "I trust you are enjoying yourself."

"Your ball is quite spectacular as are you yourself, my lady," Jack said. "No other hostess can do it justice."

Lady Cecilia smiled, instantly charmed. Her cheeks flamed as red as her wig. "I'm flattered, Mr. Harding."

Evelyn wanted to roll her eyes. Only Jack could make the severe hostess blush.

The viscount spoke up, his rapier gaze boldly passing over Evelyn. "I know better than to ask the true identity of this lovely Cleopatra, but I hope you are enjoying the festivities as well."

"Your champagne is exceptional, my lord, and the guests' costumes are a feast for the eyes."

"As are you. I've always been fascinated with anything Egyptian," the viscount said.

Despite his attractive demeanor, Evelyn was unnerved by his intense stare. There was more than lust shining in his jet eyes, there was also a cold efficiency that made her heart thump against her rib cage.

Could he have brutally stabbed a woman to death in her own home?

Evelyn was keenly aware of the viscountess's stiffening spine at her husband's blatant interest.

Lady Cecilia reached out to take the viscount's arm, and Evelyn was certain she saw the woman pinch her flirtatious husband.

Their marriage is hardly amicable, Evelyn thought. If her husband openly pursues other women, no wonder the viscountess is bitter.

Jack spoke up, breaking the awkward silence. "I've heard that you know the secret identities of all your guests, my lady. Is it true?"

"What nonsense!" Lady Cecilia said. "Someone is pulling your leg. I recognized you, Mr. Harding, only because you chose to wear an eye patch and not a mask.

How in the world could I know what costumes my guests decided to wear beforehand?"

Jack grinned. "A theory is all, my lady."

Cecilia's cold eyes sniped at Evelyn. "I couldn't begin to guess the identity of our Lady Cleopatra."

A devilish look crossed Jack's face. "Ah. Neither can I."

Lady Cecilia relaxed and pulled her husband alongside her. "Come along, dear. We must greet our other guests. It's been a pleasure, Mr. Harding."

Jack nodded and their host and hostess disappeared in the throng of costumed revelers.

Evelyn turned to Jack. "What on earth was that about?"

"She has a fireplace poker up her arse, and he's a perverted whoremonger."

"Jack!"

"I didn't like the way he looked at you."

Evelyn felt her face grow hot. "Do you think him capable of killing someone?" she whispered.

"I think anyone is capable of killing. The question is: Is Hamilton capable of sadistically murdering a helpless woman?"

"That is the reason I wanted you to attend tonight. To observe him. Although I have seen the viscount at society functions in the past, I never had reason to study him as a suspect. I was hoping your knowledge of criminal behavior would help."

"My experience can shed light on a person's behavior. But even I will admit that the savviest criminals have a dark side that is inherent in their nature and can be difficult to detect. Just like a chameleon, they can camouflage their dark thoughts and blend with their environment."

"Still, you know more than most."

He cocked his head to the side and measured her with a cool appraising look. "Let us go our separate ways tonight. When Hamilton goes into the card room, I will engage him in conversation. It's the best way to study his mannerisms."

"But—"

Jack held up a hand to interrupt her in a fashion that was becoming irritatingly familiar. "We should not be seen together tonight. We will attract untoward attention."

Surprise siphoned through her. Jack Harding worried about society gossip? Surely he wasn't expressing concern for *her* reputation. She, more than he, knew about propriety. It would defy all the rules for her, the daughter of an earl, to fraternize with a bachelor.

Or was Jack worried that they would draw Viscount Hamilton's curiosity?

Either way, Evelyn felt as if Jack had put her in her place, had slapped her on the wrist like a wayward child.

"I didn't intend to be your shadow," she said, her voice sounding strained to her own ears.

"I didn't think you did. I'm merely suggesting you should consider wagging tongues. Even though your true identity is craftily disguised and you arrived with your father, I've learned never to underestimate vicious gossipmongers."

"Concerned for your reputation, are you, Jack?" she snapped.

He shot her a sly wink. "Always, Evie. I wouldn't want the *ton* to see me with one lady. They might erroneously conclude that I'm considering relinquishing my coveted bachelorhood."

With a click of his booted heels, he donned his plumed hat and disappeared into the crowd.

Chapter 20

The nerve of the man.

Evelyn sipped her champagne as the colorful swirl of dancers whirled past on the dance floor. After Jack had arrogantly strode off, she had been determined to ignore him. She had taken advantage of her full dance card—where she was anonymously listed as Lady Cleopatra—and had danced most of the evening until she was breathless and her feet ached. Her partners consisted of a diverse group, from an army captain on leave from Brighton wearing his own uniform, to the son of an earl dressed as Genghis Khan.

Only when the long-case clock in the corner of the ballroom struck one in the morning did she stop for another glass of champagne and to chat with Georgina and friends. She was most proud of her valiant efforts not to think of Jack or what, if anything, he had learned about the viscount. And yet, despite herself, she glanced at the entrance to the card room.

A flash of black at the corner of her eye was all it took.

She spotted Jack saunter to the back of the room, whiskey in hand, and join a group of gentlemen. Although all wore masks, she recognized Anthony Stevens from his height and the breadth of his shoulders, and Brent Stone from his chiseled chin and swath of golden hair. A third man with dark hair and an easy smile was among the group, the remaining barrister in Jack's chambers, she assumed.

After a full minute, she looked away, lest she be caught staring.

What did you discover about the viscount, Jack? And why the change in attitude?

They were supposed to be partners. Investigate the suspects together. But Evelyn knew a part of her was angry that he so easily dismissed her after she had taken great pains with her appearance. She wanted him to notice her, society be damned. Instead, *he* had reminded *her* about propriety, for goodness' sakes.

A sudden sense of insecurity seized her, and she was drawn back in time to the twelve-year-old girl again, desperately seeking to gain the attention of her father's newest pupil.

Lord, no.

She refused to think of herself in this manner. She was a woman full grown, a woman who had found her intellectual equal in Randolph Sheldon—a man who *sought* her attention. Taking a deep breath, she decided it was time to act like a mature adult, confront Jack in a businesslike manner, and find out what he had discovered.

But when she spun around, he was gone.

"If you're seeking your pirate, he went toward the terrace. Perhaps you can both take advantage of some fresh air," Georgina drawled.

Evelyn didn't bother to argue with Georgina. She excused herself and headed for the open French doors leading onto the terrace.

As she wove through the crowd, it was impossible not to notice that many of the guests were intoxicated, deep into their cups, at the late hour. Eyes glittered through masks and women trilled with high laughter. A portly man dressed as a medieval jester reached out for her. Deftly, she evaded his grasp, her gaze never wavering from the French doors.

She didn't dare look away for fear of Jack walking out and disappearing in the crowd.

Stepping onto the terrace, she stood a moment to allow her eyes to adjust to the change in lighting. Lit torches lined the terrace; a full moon hung low in the sky like a giant pearl. She moved to the balustrade and glanced at the meticulously kept gardens below. The scent of roses and other flowering shrubs wafted to her. A cool breeze blew loose tendrils of hair at her nape. Coming from the hot, brightly lit and noisy ballroom, the terrace was a refreshing respite.

"Mr. Harding," she called out.

No answer.

The terrace was empty save for two gentlemen in the far corner smoking. The red glow of their cheroots winked at her, like twinkling lights.

She looked for others, but saw no one. Could Georgina have been mistaken? Perhaps she saw another darkly clad man of Jack's height venture outside.

Leaning over the balustrade, she studied the gardens below. Had she not been eyeing the view so carefully, she would have missed the shadow.

There. Just behind the rosebushes, skirting the maze. A black-dressed figure moved stealthily, not at all like that of a guest taking a garden stroll.

She leaned forward as far as she could without falling over the balustrade, until the shadow passed by.

It was Jack. She was certain.

So what was he up to?

Deciding to follow, she rushed down the stone steps leading to the gardens. She knew her costume offered little concealment, like a white flag waving in a breeze, but thankfully, the soft soles of her sandals were silent on the path. She fell as far back as she dared without losing complete sight of him. She prayed he wouldn't look back.

She trailed him to the back of the mansion. The gardens sloped upward here, and stone a shade lighter than the rest of the home's façade revealed a newer addition. The architect had cleverly included French doors leading from several of the rear rooms that opened to the gardens.

But the farther Jack moved away from the terrace, the less illumination the torches provided, and at one point she was afraid she had lost him. Then, hearing a door handle rattle, she darted behind a statue, and from there watched Jack open a set of glass doors and slip inside. Seconds later, a match flared and a lamp glowed dimly.

What on earth was he doing?

Suddenly Jack's face appeared behind the glass and heavy drapes were pulled over the doors, obstructing any view of the interior.

She crept up on the doors and tried to peek through a crack in the drapes, but the dark interior revealed nothing.

Frustration roiled inside her. Frustration and annoyance at his secretive activities.

She turned the door handle and pushed it open soundlessly.

The moment she stepped inside, a strong hand clamped over her mouth and gripped her from behind. He kicked the door shut with a boot.

The lighting was dim, but she didn't panic or struggle. His scent, his touch, his strength were by now imprinted in her mind.

"Don't make a sound," he whispered in her ear.

His warm breath sent a shiver down her spine. She nodded to let him know she understood. He released her and took a step back.

"What are you doing here?" he demanded, his tone harsh.

"What are *you* doing here?" she countered.

"I plan on searching Hamilton's private library."

Evelyn looked around and noticed that they were indeed in a library. Rows of leather-bound books lined the walls. A desk and a leather chair sat in front of a bay window, and combined with the glass doors, she could picture Hamilton conducting business here with plenty of natural light.

"You were going to search without me?" she asked.

Jack's eyes narrowed. "Quite frankly, yes. I was fortunate enough to find this garden entrance without having to wander through the main part of the house. So if you will just step outside and return to the festivities, I will continue with my endeavors."

"No."

He cocked a dark eyebrow. "Pardon?"

"Why didn't you tell me of your plans? I can assist. Two people can search twice as fast as one."

"That's precisely why I failed to mention it. It's risky, Evie." His eyes darted to the glass doors through which she had just entered, and then to a solid door that led to the main part of the house. "There're two entrances to the library; a servant or Hamilton could walk through either one at any moment."

"I'm willing to assume the risk."

"Don't be daft. Be gone, woman."

Her chin jutted forward. "Is this why you insisted we go our separate ways tonight? You hadn't the slightest concern for your reputation or mine for that matter?"

"I knew that you would be just as stubborn about this as everything else."

"We are supposed to be partners."

"Has your safety ever entered your brain?"

"We're wasting time. I assume you plan on starting with Hamilton's desk."

He hesitated, and she felt a twinge of fear that he would physically oust her from the room. But then, carting her over his shoulder like a sack of potatoes would draw significant attention.

"You search his desk," Jack said tersely. "I'll start with the bookshelves. Keep an eye out for small secret compartments—anywhere a diary may be hidden."

Evelyn quickly stepped to the desk. She didn't say a word, lest Jack change his mind and demand she leave. She searched quickly, her heart hammering, as she checked every drawer and glanced at every paper. Discovering a stack of bills, she skimmed each one. Her brow furrowed as she reached the middle of the stack, and she hesitated.

She looked to Jack who was balanced on a footstool, reaching up high, his fingers tracing the edge of the top bookshelf, no doubt searching for a hidden latch. From this angle, the muscles of his broad shoulders strained against his black shirt. She swallowed, her mouth gone dry. What would it feel like to touch his shoulders without the barrier of clothing?

He stepped down and turned around. Too late, she realized she stood still behind the desk, bills in hand, staring at him like an awestruck girl.

"What is it?" His gaze lowered to her hand. "What did you find?"

She blinked, clearing the enticing picture of him shirtless from her mind.

She raised the handful of bills. "There are invoices for jewelers, flower shops, and dressmakers. All are for delivery to Bess Whitfield's London address."

"Let me have a look." Stepping close, his fingers brushed hers as he took the stack from her.

He studied each bill carefully. "The last delivery from the dressmaker's was for the day before Bess was murdered."

"Why would he have a gown made if he planned on killing her?"

"I don't think he planned it," Jack said. "I think it was a crime of passion, carried out in the heat of the moment. The killer repeatedly and viciously stabbed the victim. There was no forced entry into her home. She let him inside. She knew him. The murder was personal."

"Oh, my," Evelyn whispered.

"I've found something as well." Jack went back to the bookshelf and reached for a packet of papers he had left on a lower shelf. Turning around, he opened the packet to reveal a group of letters. He spread them across the desk, a dozen in all. "Love letters from Bess Whitfield to Maxwell Stanford, Viscount Hamilton."

Evelyn's mind whirled as she skimmed the letters. All were written in a flowing script and scented with a cloying floral fragrance. It was clear that the couple had a love-hate relationship, for the contents of the letters varied from scalding anger to vivid descriptions of promised erotic acts. Evelyn's eyes widened at the scorching words.

Could a woman truly do such things to a man?

Would Jack like them? her inner voice asked.

She inwardly cringed. It should be Randolph in her thoughts, not Jack.

"Here." Jack pointed to the date in the right-hand corner of the last letter. "Bess saw Hamilton with another woman, other than his wife. She was furious. The letter coincides with the dressmaker's invoice. Hamilton had arranged to have a dress delivered as an apology gift."

"Maybe she rejected his gift and refused to accept his apology," Evelyn suggested.

"And he retaliated by stabbing her to death. It's a likely scenario. Strong attraction between the sexes is animalistic in nature and can stir up dangerous, sometimes deadly actions."

Yes, my attraction to you is animalistic, without logic and entirely dangerous, she thought.

"Either way," Jack said, pointing to the letters spread out on the desk, "they are not Bess's missing diary."

"Perhaps he never found it, or he was unaware of its existence," she said.

"It's possible, but we don't have time to discuss that theory now. Put everything back exactly as you found it." Jack gathered up the letters and moved to the bookshelves.

She sensed an urgency in him, and she made quick work of putting the bills back in the order she had found them and returning them to the drawer.

As she closed the drawer, a nagging thought pierced her brain. Her earlier confidence regarding their surreptitious search was suddenly shattered like broken glass.

"What about Georgina?" she whispered.

Jack stepped down from the stool and faced her. "What about her?"

A sudden knot rose in her throat. "I consider her my friend. What if we prove her father guilty of murdering Bess Whitfield? It would destroy not only Viscount Hamilton, but Georgina and her mother as well. The scandal would be horrendous, the gossips ruthless."

In three strides, Jack stood before her. Reaching out, he gripped her shoulders and forced her to face him. His eyes blazed and glowed in the lantern light.

"Don't you dare for one minute believe this is your fault or that you did any wrong. You did not ruin anything. If Hamilton is guilty of murder, then he is solely responsible for the ruin of himself and his family. Besides, we did not prove anything tonight other than that Hamilton and Bess Whitfield were lovers with a tumultuous relationship. He is no different from half the married men of the aristocracy. The letters and the invoices do not place the knife in his hand. Any defense barrister worth his salt would successfully argue such."

"But—"

His large hand took her face and held it gently. The touch of his palm was almost unbearable in its tenderness.

"*Shh,* Evie. If by chance Hamilton is guilty, then as a titled lord and powerful member of the nobility, there is a very real possibility that he would not be indicted and never see a jury trial. It's extremely difficult to convict a viscount. He'd have to be tried in the House of Lords, and those stuffed shirts take care of their own. Charges may never even be pressed and a scandal avoided. Could you say the same if Randolph Sheldon was charged with the crime? He lacks both a title and influence."

He was right. But still, Georgina had been nothing but kind to her.

"Do not forget, the crazy Earl of Newland is just as likely a suspect." Jack's soft breath fanned her face as she stood close.

She nodded. His logic, his very presence was reassuring, and she had a maddening urge to lean close, to have his arms embrace her, to rest her aching head against his firm shoulder. For someone who was always the strong one, her feelings were disconcerting.

"Come," he said, stepping back. "We've been in here too long. We need to leave before we are discovered."

He must have sensed her vulnerability, the myriad jumble of emotions whirling in her and the comfort she gained from his nearness for he extended his hand.

Without hesitation, she slid her palm into his.

Jack doused the lantern and cracked open the French doors. Glancing in all directions to ensure no one was lurking about, he pulled her into the gardens and closed the doors behind them.

They walked side by side in silence, down the sloping lawn until the blazing torches of the terrace came into view.

Jack's steps faltered. He dropped her hand and patted his shirt pockets.

She stopped and looked up at him. "What is it, Jack?"

"I forgot my bloody eye patch. I have to go back."

"To the library?"

"It was there the last time I saw it."

"It's risky to return twice in one night. Can you not leave it? No one will know."

"Both Viscount and Viscountess Hamilton saw me in

costume wearing that eye patch. How many pirates can there be tonight?"

None that look as memorable as you, she thought.

He turned to leave. "Get back to the ball before you are missed, Evie. I shall be in touch regarding the case."

"When?" she called out as loud as she dare.

But he was gone, melting into the night.

Chapter 21

Jack sped through the gardens, retracing their steps until he stood outside the entrance to Hamilton's library once again. He slipped inside.

The eye patch was where he had left it resting on a bookshelf. He slipped it into his pocket.

He cursed himself for his stupidity, his carelessness. He never should have allowed Evelyn to stay and search the place.

But once again, when she stood up to him with fiery challenge, she was a magnificent sight to behold, and he was helpless to refuse her.

When he had first spotted her in the ballroom tonight dressed as the Egyptian seductress, Cleopatra, she had stolen his breath. His fingers itched to stroke her bare shoulders, the curve of her hip through the white satin, the curtain of golden hair.

He was getting sloppy. Tonight wasn't the first time he had illicitly searched a residence. Sometimes Jack would "follow" his investigators inside a dwelling and take a look around the crime scene before the constable could arrive and "alter" the evidence in their favor.

But never had Jack left behind so obvious a clue as to

his identity. Knowing Hamilton had seen him in costume not more than two hours ago, Jack might as well have left his calling card.

It was Evie. All Evie. Her catlike blue eyes, her sharp intelligence, and fearless courage. And when she had become all teary-eyed at the thought her actions could harm her friend, Jack had instinctively responded.

But the truth was Evie's distress *had* disturbed him. He found himself genuinely wanting to comfort her. He had consoled clients or their spouses in the past, but his efforts had been superficial and selfish. He needed solid witnesses in the courtroom, not broken ones riddled with the guilt of their crimes. Other than as a barrister determined to influence a jury, he hadn't truly cared about their sorrow.

But Evie was different.

Not entirely true.

His selfish streak had remained. Yes, he had been moved by her torment as he never had been before, but his desire for her simmered in his blood. He wanted her now more than when he had kissed her in the carriage. Each time he touched her, the attraction grew stronger. Yet, her innocent lack of awareness of her effect on him tantalized him.

If by brushing her lips with his roused his lust, what would it be like to feel her naked flesh against his, to have her in his bed?

Footsteps sounded outside the door of the main part of the house.

Jack jerked to attention.

Damn.

His mistake, his distraction, could cost him dearly. No time to flee through the French doors into the gardens. He would be spotted. A guard summoned.

Grasping a heavy, brass candlestick from the desk, he hid in the corner, concealed by the end of a bookshelf.

The door opened. A servant entered and emptied the wastepaper basket beside the desk. But instead of leaving, the servant stopped to stare at the bookshelves.

Jack ceased to breathe, his fist clenching the candlestick until the decorative brass bit into his palm. His heart pounded in his chest, and he held his breath. Two steps closer and Jack would have to attack, strike the man unconscious.

The servant moved to the center bookshelf, straightened a book, then turned and left, closing the door behind him.

Jack exhaled, returned the candlestick to the desk, and wiped a bead of sweat from his brow. He slipped out the French doors and blended into the shadows.

"Have the invitations been sent yet, my dear?"

Evelyn's head rose at her father's voice in the doorway. She was sitting in the dining room, pushing eggs around her plate in an unsuccessful attempt to eat.

"Pardon?" she asked.

"The invitations to Lordships Bathwell and Barnes. Have you sent them?" Emmanuel Darlington asked.

Comprehension dawned. Her father's monthly dinner with the judges. It was part of his routine to stay in close touch with the judges even though he no longer had chambers at Lincoln's Inn or appeared in court. His time was consumed with lecturing students at Oxford.

With Randolph's troubles, however, she had forgotten the invitations entirely.

She had always enjoyed the dinners and the discussions ranging from the most current judicial opinions to courtroom blunders and antics committed by new barristers. But today she felt nothing but a stab of annoyance—not at her forgetfulness—but at her father's reminder of her duty to make all the arrangements.

The idea of spending an evening in the judges' company seemed, well, quite boring.

At her father's solemn expression, she sat straight and pushed her wayward thoughts aside. She had always been a dutiful daughter, one considerate of her father's needs and career.

"It must have slipped my mind, Father. I'll send them out at once," she said.

"Do not forget to extend an invitation to Mr. Harding."

Despite herself, excitement hummed in her veins at the notion of Jack attending. With him at the table, the scene would be much more stimulating and, for once, the thought of intellectual conversation did not play a role.

Stop this nonsense! she thought.

She had to stay focused. It had been four days since the Hamiltons' costume ball, and she had not heard from Jack. She assumed he was busy with his other cases. After all, Randolph Sheldon was not his only client. But she wanted to know what Jack intended as his next course of action. She refused to admit she missed him.

"Send them today, my dear. They are all busy men," her father said on his way out of the room.

Evelyn remained to finish her tea before heading for her desk to see to the invitations. Hodges stopped her at the foot of the stairs.

"You have a gentleman caller, Lady Evelyn," Hodges announced.

For a split second, her heart jolted. Was Jack here?

"A Mr. Simon Guthrie," Hodges continued. "I put him in the sitting room. Shall I arrange for refreshments?"

Bewilderment replaced her earlier thoughts. Why on earth was Simon here? Was Randolph in more trouble? Had the Runners finally found him?

She became aware of Hodges staring at her; the elderly butler's brow furrowed. "No, thank you, Hodges. I'm certain Mr. Guthrie's visit will be brief."

The last thing we want is an interruption by the servants, she thought.

Hodges nodded and shuffled past, his gait slow and uneven.

Evelyn rushed to the sitting room and threw open the door.

Simon jumped to his feet as she entered. He looked the same as the last time she had seen him in the Billingsgate tavern. His dark hair was neatly parted to one side and his brown eyes were gentle and contemplative. Of medium height and average features, he had the common appearance of a man who could blend in anywhere. But the first time Evelyn had met Simon at Oxford, she knew he possessed a sharp intelligence. He was a University Fellow like Randolph, only Simon worked for a different professor. She had always liked Simon, and the fact that he was standing by Randolph's side, despite mounting adversity and criminal consequences, told her that Simon was loyal to his friends.

Evelyn motioned for Simon to sit and she took the chair across from him. "Is something amiss, Simon?"

Simon twisted his hands in his lap. "Randolph wishes to see you."

"But the danger—"

Simon looked up, his expression sincere. "He's desperate, Evelyn. His days in Bess Whitfield's Shoreditch home are spent in solitude. I brought him his books, and he has been able to continue some of his work. But he's suffering from melancholy and stress. He says he misses your time spent together."

Evelyn's heart sank as memories assailed her. "What did Randolph have in mind?"

"There's a small bookstore on Bond Street, Smithy's Books. It's not busy most afternoons and there is seating in the rear of the store where customers can peruse their selections in comfort."

"I'm familiar with the place."

"Tomorrow at four o'clock?"

"Tell Randolph I will meet him then."

"Oh, and Evelyn—"

"Yes."

"Randolph wants to see you alone. Without Mr. Harding present."

She hesitated, her thoughts swirling wildly. What an unusual request for Randolph to make.

She recalled her promise to Jack that she would not investigate matters on her own or meet with Randolph without him present. But how would either Randolph or Simon know about that?

"Is that a problem?" Simon asked.

She thought of Randolph, poor Randolph, isolated and worried in Shoreditch. She did miss him, she realized. Perhaps they could discuss his last project before this mishap had sent him scurrying into hiding. Their meeting would have to be brief. And why on earth would Jack want to waste his time? By his own admission, Jack was an extremely busy barrister, and the thought of him acting as a chaperone was quite ludicrous.

She raised her eyes to find Simon watching her. "It will not be a problem. Please tell Randolph tomorrow afternoon cannot arrive quickly enough."

Chapter 22

Bond Street offered a tempting array of establishments where a lady could shop. Evelyn walked past the newest attractions: a goldsmith's who specialized in broaches of rare jewels, and the shop of Madame Fleur, the current French couturiere who was all the rage. But for the first time, it wasn't the shops that had her pulse quickening in anticipation.

She had sent Janet on a venture to procure her father's weekly supply of medicinal tea, only this time, Evelyn had written down the name of an extremely rare blend, one that would occupy the maid for over an hour.

Evelyn stopped before a small shop. The wooden sign above read SMITHY'S BOOKS. She opened the door, and a tinkling bell chimed as she entered. The smell of books was immediately comforting and reminded her of the university's impressive library.

She spotted the shopkeeper, an elderly man with a white walrus mustache and thick spectacles, mending a book's binding on the front desk. He glanced up as she passed by, nodded distractedly, and went back to his work. As she wove her way among tall shelves crammed with volumes to the back of the shop, she acknowledged that Simon had been correct. The rest of the bookstore was vacant in the late afternoon.

Her hand flew involuntarily to her heart when she saw Randolph. He sat on an old settee of faded green velvet reading a book held up to his face. But there was no mistaking the shock of fair hair.

"Randolph," Evelyn whispered excitedly.

He lowered the book and smiled. Pale blue eyes twinkled behind gold-rimmed spectacles.

"Evelyn," he said, and it was as if no time had passed between them. She felt as she used to when she had walked into her father's Oxford chambers and found Randolph laboring over his latest paper.

He stood. She rushed forward, and they embraced.

He was small-boned and slightly above average height. As he held her, she became aware of his slender frame, as if he had lost weight since the last time they had embraced.

"I've missed you dearly, Evelyn," he breathed.

"Me too," she said, and she acknowledged that she did miss him. He was her closest friend, her confidant.

He took her hands in his and they sat side by side on the worn settee.

She touched his face, noting the gauntness that had not been visible a month before. His fair skin magnified the dark circles under his eyes. Renewed concern for his well-being surfaced.

"How have you been faring?" she asked.

"It's been difficult, Evelyn. Quite horrid, actually." His eyes welled up, and she feared he would cry.

She squeezed his fingers. "Oh, Randolph. Tell me everything."

"I rarely leave Bess's Shoreditch home for fear of being recognized or grabbed by a Bow Street Runner.

I'm grateful that the residence has not yet been sold, mind you, but Bess's things are still there and I cannot get the sickening thought out of my head that she is dead . . . murdered."

"Rest assured that we are doing everything we can, Randolph."

He looked up. "We?"

"Mr. Harding and I. You do recall we retained his services?"

"Yes, yes. I just don't like that you are spending time with another man. It makes me uncomfortable." Across his pale skin a dim flush raced like a fever.

"Don't be foolish," she chided. "I'm doing it solely for you."

Randolph's face crumpled; he appeared more bereft and desolate than before. She was assailed by a piercing guilt.

"Do you see Simon Guthrie often?" she asked, hoping to change the topic.

"He is my only visitor, my best friend." Randolph's voice was hushed and full of despair, like an echo from an empty tomb.

Her heart sank at his words. Wasn't she his best friend? Or was she being selfish? Simon was free to visit Randolph, whereas she, an unmarried daughter of an earl, could never be allowed to travel to and from a murdered actress's home in Shoreditch to see a man.

"Do you remember the time we spent together in the university library?" he asked.

How could she forget? Her thoughts filtered back. She recalled when they had worked on one of Randolph's projects that required esoteric research on the Roman aqueducts. Heads bent and shoulders touching, they had whispered for hours, until the head librarian had threatened to throw them out at fifteen minutes past the closing hour.

Her father had been busy with a faculty meeting that had taken longer than anticipated, and Randolph had taken advantage, urging her to accompany him to a Grecian coffeehouse in the Strand. They drank coffee late into the night in a dim corner of an establishment where no proper ladies were present and no one had a care as to her identity. Emboldened by the atmosphere, she had leaned across the table and initiated a kiss. It had been horridly improper, daring, and quite exciting.

Bells chimed from the front door, startling Evelyn out of her thoughts and alerting her to the presence of another shopper in the store.

"Come with me." Randolph rose and pulled her to her feet.

"Where—"

"Shh," he said, placing his finger over his lips and leading her to a back exit.

He pushed the rear door open, and she found herself in a back alley behind the shop. The faint odor of rotting garbage reached her nostrils. A scrawny calico cat drank rainwater that dripped from the roof shingles of an adjacent building. The feline dashed down the alley as the back door closed. All was quiet save for the sound of a shutter slamming shut in the distance.

"Randolph, is it safe—"

He pulled her roughly into his arms. "I must have a moment alone with you without the threat of prying eyes or I'll go mad." Lowering his head, he kissed her.

Momentarily stunned by his uncharacteristic aggressiveness, Evelyn's first instinct was to push him away, but she stopped herself. Randolph needed her in his despair. He had never been physically assertive in the past, and she recognized that his behavior was fueled by fear and insecurity.

But truth be told, she needed this too—but for entirely different reasons. An insistent—albeit shameful—curiosity welled in her breast.

Could Randolph's kisses be like Jack's?

Closing her eyes, she raised her mouth to his.

The pressure of his lips was pleasant. She leaned into him and placed her hand above his pounding heart. At her touch, Randolph moaned, his actions became more urgent, and the kiss changed. Sloppy, wet kisses slanted over her mouth and down the column of her throat, leaving a slick path on her skin. His breath tasted like coffee and she wasn't surprised knowing his fondness for the beverage. But a nagging voice pointed out it wasn't like Jack's hot taste. And Randolph's slender build felt nothing like Jack's solid, muscular chest.

The dreadful truth was, Randolph's kisses were inexperienced, lacking the seductiveness of Jack's lips that had skillfully aroused her passion.

She stepped back, holding him at bay with a raised hand when he tried to close the distance.

"I need this, Evelyn," he begged. "I need to feel some part of my life is the same."

"It's the same, Randolph. I stand by your side now as always." But her voice was shaky, lacking conviction even to her own ears.

"Am I the only one not to have been formally introduced to your lady client?"

Jack eyed James Devlin across the table. He had joined his friends and fellow barristers for drinks at a tavern near their shared chambers at Lincoln's Inn. Their weekly gathering was a routine, and they often discussed their most complex and troublesome cases and legal strategies. But from the smirks and grins on both Anthony Stevens's and Brent Stone's faces, the last client Jack wanted to discuss was Evelyn Darlington. He could do without further male teasing and ribaldry.

A tavern maid set four tankards of ale on the table, and Jack took a swallow before answering. With his dark looks and carefree attitude, James Devlin had always been the most outspoken of the group. Jack was well aware that Devlin fully enjoyed his freedom and bachelorhood and took advantage of London's many amorous courtesans. He was especially skilled at avoiding the marriage trap and the overeager mamas of the *ton*. The idea that Devlin wanted to meet Evie raised Jack's hackles.

"Why would you care to meet Evelyn Darlington, Devlin?"

"Quite simply because I feel left out. Brent said she was as striking up close as from a distance. Even Anthony was smitten."

Anthony choked on his ale and slammed down his tankard. "Smitten? Where the bloody hell did you hear that?"

Devlin turned his smile up a notch. "Brent told me. Said she wasn't intimidated by your bullying and had you grinning like a simpleton after a few choice compliments."

Anthony's hard eyes narrowed, and he turned to Brent. "You told him that?"

Brent shrugged, not in the least disturbed by Anthony's size or menacing expression. "I told Devlin what I had witnessed."

Jack spoke up before the conversation progressed to fisticuffs. "Aren't there other cases we can talk about?"

"Yes, but we all want to know how Lady Evelyn is faring," Brent said.

As Jack eyed Brent over the rim of his tankard, he felt a suffocating sensation tighten his throat. Brent Stone was a handsome man. Did Evelyn find him attractive when she met him at the Old Bailey? Despite Brent's proclaimed celibacy, the memory of Jack accidently walking into Brent's chambers and finding him with a woman in a compromising position was not easily forgotten.

Jack mentally shook himself. He was thinking like a fool. His friends were trustworthy and they had been together for years. Jack had never exhibited a jealous bone in his body over a female in the past, and Evie wasn't even his woman.

She was Randolph Sheldon's.

"The investigation is progressing, but far from over," Jack muttered.

"What about the Earl of Newland? Did you follow up on the lead from Investigator Papazian?" Anthony asked.

"Newland's a crackpot and obsessively visits Bess Whitfield's grave," Jack said.

"He's obsessive, you say?" Devlin asked. "I've known of murderers who feel compelled to attend their victims' funerals, even repeatedly visit their graves. He may be your man, Jack."

"I'm not convinced," Jack said. "He lacks motive. What would a dying old man with no close relatives care about a notorious actress's diary, no matter how sexually explicit?"

Curiosity got the better of Jack. He had previously told his fellow barristers of the search for Bess Whitfield's missing diary. If Jack was unable to prevent talk of

Evelyn or the case, then he may as well pick his friends' brains for information.

Jack turned to Anthony. "What about the supposed list of suspects that I gave you from Randolph and his friend Simon Guthrie? Has Investigator Papazian unearthed anything suspicious?"

Anthony shook his head. "One is deceased of natural causes, two were out of the country at the time of the murder, and the last has an alibi for the entire day. The list was full of dead ends, a waste of time."

"I'm not surprised," Jack said. "Randolph is desperate, and he must have been grasping at straws when the list was put together."

"Do you believe they fabricated the names?" Devlin asked.

"No, but my gut has told me all along that Randolph knows more than he has let on." Jack looked to his friends. "What do any of you know of Viscount Hamilton?"

"Maxwell Stanford?" Brent asked. "I've prepared several letters patent for him."

"And I drafted the contract to purchase a hunting lodge on his behalf," Devlin said.

"He was one of Bess's lovers," Jack said. "I found letters in Hamilton's library that revealed that a tumultuous relationship had existed between them. Viscount Hamilton is middle-aged, in good health, and has a family who would suffer if a scandal arose. He has more to lose if the diary was revealed."

"You searched his library?" Brent asked incredulously. "Did Lady Evelyn learn of your underground activities?"

"She accompanied me."

Devlin let out a hoot of laugher. "I said from the beginning that a tempting woman like her would give you a run for your money, Jack."

Brent leaned across the table. "Did you find the diary, Jack?"

"No. Bess Whitfield's dresser said there was a commoner who went by the name of 'Sam' who was also one of the actress's last lovers. If I can find the diary, I can question him to see if he had motive."

"It seems to me you're overlooking the obvious," Anthony drawled.

Jack sat back in his chair. "And that is?"

"Randolph Sheldon interrupted the murderer, causing him to flee out of the window. Based on how you described the murder scene—the bedroom ransacked and violently torn apart—the diary may still be in Bess Whitfield's London home."

Realization dawned. "You're right. I need to search it."

"Will Lady Evelyn go with you?" Devlin asked, a cynical twist to his lips.

"Knowing her stubborn nature, I would guess yes," Jack said.

"Have you bedded her yet? It would be easier on you if you exorcised your lust," Devlin said.

"Ignore Devlin, Jack. He's an ass," Brent said. "Just continue to follow my earlier advice: Work hard and you won't have time to think of her in a lasvicious nature."

"You're both daft," Anthony muttered. "Since when does lust have to complicate anything? Jack can have a tumble without losing his legal head."

Brent scowled at Anthony. "Your matrimonial and divorce cases have skewed your beliefs. It's obvious you've never cared for or fallen in love with a woman."

"And you have? Your total lack of female companionship tells a different story," Anthony said.

Jack rolled his eyes. Despite their cutthroat words, they enjoyed taunting each other like close brothers.

But they did give him a new idea: To search Bess Whitfield's London lodgings. And Evelyn *would* insist she come along. He should be annoyed, troubled by her anticipated interference, but instead his pulse pounded in anticipation.

He couldn't wait to see her again.

Jack departed soon after finishing his ale. Devlin waved at the barmaid and ordered three more tankards and he, Anthony, and Brent discussed what Jack had told them.

"What's Lady Evelyn like?" James Devlin asked the two barristers that had already met her.

Brent shrugged. "I only spoke with her once at the Old Bailey. As the daughter of a barrister, she was familiar with her surroundings and understood the meaning of *pro bono,* but on the other hand she seemed surprised when I said Jack volunteered his services for the poor."

"You think she's after his money?" Devlin asked.

"Hardly," Brent said, shaking his head. "Emmanuel Darlington inherited an earldom and all the estates that came along with it. And he was a successful barrister before then. No, I believe she is completely genuine and naïve and believes a poor scholar accused of murder would make a good husband."

Devlin looked to Anthony. "What about you? What do you think about her?"

"She's more than just a beautiful woman. She has spark. I think Jack's taken by her already, the poor fool," Anthony said.

"Why do you say that?" Devlin asked.

Anthony leaned back in his chair. "She's more trouble than most. Not only is there this murder business to resolve, but she's smart, stubborn, and independent.

Combined with her looks, she's a force to be reckoned with. It will be interesting to see how Jack handles her."

"There's more than Jack's heart to worry about here. From what I understand, both Lady Evelyn and her father could be in danger," Brent said.

Anthony crossed his arms over his chest. "It's a possibility. But the further Jack digs into the murder, the chances are he could be in danger as well."

Chapter 23

Weeks passed and yet the glorious memory of the slaughter did not fade. Rather it was like costly whiskey strengthening over time.

The killer circled his desk in his private room when the pounding in his head began anew. Holding his temples, he dropped to his knees, taking in great gulps of air. It didn't help. The pain heightened, threatening to crack his skull in two, roaring like an infernal beast.

Time was running out.

He had to find that diary.

It was the key to the power that he craved and coveted.

But in his enemies' hands, it was the weapon that could cause him to lose all that he had attained.

At first, Bess had denied all existence of the diary. Once, when he had surprised her in her bedroom, he had caught her writing by candlelight at her escritoire. When she had noticed him, she had slammed the plain, nondescript cover shut and shoved it away. But it was too late; he had known of its existence.

Even with her death, the thought of the diary in its hiding place taunted him.

He needed to finish what he started. Get his hands on

that diary, and use it to blackmail his rivals. Then he needed to replace Bess Whitfield with another. The magnificent, blond female who wouldn't dare lie to him—whom he could easily control with pain and fear.

"You want to search where?"

"Bess Whitfield's home in Mayfair. It is a four-story building with tenants on the second, third, and fourth floors. My sources say the second floor Bess had been renting has not been inhabited since her murder."

Evelyn looked at Jack. Hodges had announced Jack's arrival a half hour earlier, and when she had entered the drawing room, she had found him gazing out the window overlooking the street. Her eyes had immediately been drawn to his broad shoulders straining against the meticulous cut of his moss-colored jacket. His trousers fit like a second skin over muscled thighs. And when he had turned and smiled, she felt a curious swooping pull at her innards.

Just like a breathless girl again, she had been excited at the prospect that Jack Harding had come to see her.

"Well? What do you think, Evie?" he asked.

She became aware of Jack's stare, waiting for her response. He sat in a winged-back chair, his long legs crossed before him, and she occupied the settee across from him. Gathering her wayward thoughts, she smoothed imaginary wrinkles from her skirt.

"I'm not surprised that the landlord is having difficulty finding a new tenant considering a woman was savagely stabbed to death in her bedroom," she said.

"It's to our advantage. There is a good possibility that the diary is still there."

"But Randolph said the place was torn asunder. Surely the murderer found what he was looking for," she argued.

"I had originally believed that as well, but after speaking with Anthony Stevens, I realize we may have prematurely jumped to the incorrect conclusion."

"What do you mean?"

"Randolph said that he had received an urgent note to go to Bess's home to receive 'an item of great importance.' When he arrived, the door was ajar and the housekeeper was absent. As he looked about the vestibule, a loud noise sounded from upstairs, and when he investigated, he found Bess's body. By then he heard the constable and panicked. The window was already open and he climbed down the trellis. The noise Randolph heard on the second floor must have been the murderer escaping through the window moments before Randolph had come upstairs. Randolph interrupted the murderer's search, and there is a good chance the diary was never found."

"I want to go with you."

"I had a feeling you would insist. But still—"

"Bess's lodgings are vacant. There is no threat to my safety. I told you from the beginning that I want to be actively involved in any investigation on behalf of Randolph's case. Short of tying me down, I insist on going with you."

His jade eyes darkened with an unreadable emotion. "Believe me, Evie, the image is quite tempting."

She felt her cheeks grow hot, but she refused to be waylaid. "Two people can search faster than one, remember?"

"Trust me when I say that I haven't forgotten Viscount Hamilton's library escapade. But this time, I don't want you sneaking up on me. Since the place is vacant, there will be no anticipated danger of discovery."

"How do you plan to get inside?" she asked.

"That will be the easy part, and I assure you I will not need the services of one of my lock pick clients."

"You have represented professional burglars, then?"

"Of course. I do not discriminate on the type of criminals I represent. I take pride in my work."

Her brow furrowed. "You must be jesting."

He shrugged. "Only partly." He held up a hand when she made to argue. "Don't fret, Evie. I spoke with Bess's landlord and made inquiries as to the availability of the home. He thinks I'm an interested renter and is more than happy to loan me the key to take a look around. The most challenging aspect will be for you to accompany me without Janet trailing as your chaperone."

Evelyn smiled a secret smile. "Don't worry about that, Jack. At my age, I know how to dodge an unwanted chaperone with no one the wiser."

Chapter 24

It was a simple matter. While Janet and Mrs. Smith were occupied cataloging the pantry, Evelyn slipped out the back door of the kitchen and cut through the garden to the main street. Walking swiftly, she flagged down a hackney and soon was in Mayfair. As Jack had instructed, she told the driver to stop across the street from Bess Whitfield's home.

Evelyn paid the driver, stepped from the cab, and studied the four-story brick building across the way. It looked like many others in Mayfair with its flower boxes and sturdy brick façade. The only difference was that a brutal murder had occurred inside its walls.

She shivered despite the warm May afternoon.

"Evie!"

She whirled around as Jack stepped from an alley behind her.

"I take it you had no difficulty on your journey here and that no one questioned your leaving?" he asked.

"They'll never notice me gone."

He smiled and offered her his arm. "Shall we, then?"

They crossed the street and stood on the porch, but instead of using a key as she had anticipated, Jack pulled out two thin rods from his sleeve—one straight and one with a slight hook—and inserted them into the lock.

"What on earth are you doing?" she asked.

"Lower your voice and act as if you own the place," he said in a low, composed voice.

It took every ounce of willpower not to turn around and see if they were being observed. "Are you picking the lock? What happened to the landlord happy to show you the place?" she whispered vehemently.

"I was told an urgent family matter arose, and he had to leave town. I saw no need to wait for his return."

A second later, the lock clicked, and the door swung open. With a firm hand low on her back, Jack ushered her inside and closed the door behind them.

Dimness surrounded her, and a musky scent permeated the space. Evelyn blinked, her eyes adjusting from the bright afternoon sunlight to the poor lighting inside the small vestibule. She looked about, noting the heavy velvet curtains drawn closed at every window.

"Where are the tenants on the third and fourth floors? This place appears uninhabited."

"They've all left since Bess's murder."

Jack cracked open the drapes, permitting just enough light to see, without alerting the neighbors of their presence. She could make out the flocked leaf pattern of the wallpaper. A staircase loomed ahead.

"You had said Bess rented the second floor. Where should we start there?" she asked.

"In Bess's bedroom. It's where the murderer had last searched before Randolph's arrival."

She nodded and followed Jack. The stairs creaked as they ascended to the second floor, and Evelyn made a conscious effort to stay an arm's length from Jack. Shadows flickered off the flocked walls—spooky images like dancing specters. Despite knowing that the building was vacant and that Jack was close by, the hair on the back of her neck stood on end.

They reached the second-floor landing and faced a closed door. A brass plate on the door labeled with a large *B* identified it as Bess Whitfield's lodgings. Before she could ask, Jack pulled out his lock picks and got to work.

He really was skilled at it, she thought, for within less than five seconds, they were inside.

Unlike the velvet curtains downstairs, Bess's quarters had been decorated with Venetian lace at the windows, and plenty of sunlight illuminated the interior. Most of the furniture had been removed. Only a few select pieces remained, and Evelyn suspected they were the better pieces that the landlord had retained when Bess's only living kin, Randolph Sheldon, had never showed up to claim them. They consisted of a settee of gold fabric beneath the window, a small dining table of solid workmanship with matching chairs, and small vases and collectibles artfully displayed on a bookshelf.

Noticeably absent were any books or reading material of any kind, and Evelyn assumed that Bess Whitfield hadn't a care or use for them.

How odd, Evelyn thought, *that Randolph, who was obsessed with books would have grown close to a woman who had no interest in them.*

The hardwood floors gleamed from a recent cleaning and the smell of lemon polish filled the air. A bucket and mop rested in the corner, and it was clear that the landlord had made efforts to clean and stage the place to attract a new tenant and compensate for the fact that a heinous crime had occurred here.

"The bedroom must be in here," Jack said as he opened the first door on the left.

She walked inside, and a canopy bed with a missing mattress met her eyes. Evelyn recalled Randolph's description of the crime scene, how the mattress had been sliced down the center in search of what they now suspected was the diary. Here the floors did not gleam, but a dark stain in the center of the room drew the eye. A large bottle of white vinegar and a scrub brush rested by the stain—additional proof that the landlord was trying to remove evidence of the murder.

Her hand fluttered to her chest. *This was where Bess Whitfield bled out.*

Evelyn could imagine the blood splatter on the white walls and curtains . . . the gruesome killing as Randolph had described it. *No wonder Randolph ran! If I walked in on a murder victim, would I have the fortitude to stay and explain myself?*

She had always believed Randolph was wrong in fleeing out the window and climbing down the trellis, but now she wasn't certain she would have done otherwise.

"Are you all right?" Jack asked.

She looked away, at the frame where a large mattress should be. "I . . . I was just thinking. Maybe Randolph's reaction in fleeing wasn't that . . . that cowardly."

Jack's hand cupped her elbow, and he turned her around. "People react differently under stressful conditions. But knowing you, I don't believe you would have run, Evie."

Her eyes snapped to his face, and her heart pounded an erratic rhythm. There was some tangible bond between them at the moment that was frightening.

"Perhaps you don't know me as well as you think," she whispered.

His lips twisted in a smile. "In this, I'm sure. You wouldn't run from a challenge, but would fight till the end. Randolph Sheldon has no idea how fortunate he is to have a woman like you stand by his side."

His nearness, his words, kindled strong feelings of warmth. Her heart fluttered wildly in her breast.

"Come, Evie. Let's search this place and be gone."

She blinked, coming to her senses. "What should we look for? It's obvious that the landlord cleaned the place. Do you think he found it?"

"I don't think it was kept out in the open. Bess Whitfield was not stupid. She was cunning and would have hidden her diary where it would be least suspected."

"I take it we're to look for hidden compartments again?"

He flashed a grin. "You catch on quickly, Evie. Perhaps you should consider a future as an investigator for hire."

At his humor, the tension in her shoulders eased a notch. "An unlikely occupation for a woman, Jack. I can only imagine my father's reaction."

She eyed a closet and a tall chest of drawers in the back of the room. She decided to search the chest first and walked over and opened the top drawer. Empty. Knowing the landlord had been through the place, she wasn't surprised, but she checked the others just to be sure. All were bare. Starting over with the top drawer, she ran her fingers along each edge, searching for a crevice or nook out of place, but found nothing.

The sound of a chair dragging across the wood floor drew her attention. She turned to see Jack stand on the chair and reach up to the corner of the ceiling.

"There's a patched seam," he said.

Slipping a hand into the inside pocket of his jacket, Jack pulled out a small pocket knife. She watched as he inserted the knife into the seam and began to chip away. Bits of plaster fell on his head, and soon a small crevice became visible. Evelyn was surprised at Bess Whitfield's ingenuity. A thick coat of plaster could easily conceal such a clever hiding place. An ordinary person would miss it, and only someone with a sharp eye like Jack's could catch it.

Jack reached inside the crevice. His brow furrowed in concentration as his fingers searched inside. "Damn. It's empty."

"Are you sure?" she asked.

"There's nothing here. She must have moved the diary and plastered over the crevice."

"Why would she do that?"

"She must have feared it would be discovered," Jack said as he stepped down from the chair.

"It all makes sense now. No wonder Bess wanted to give the diary to Randolph, her only living kin, for safekeeping. She was murdered before she could tell him where she hid it."

The distinct noise of a door closing downstairs and the sounds of the stairs creaking jerked their heads around.

"Someone's here. We have to leave," she whispered urgently.

Jack shook his head. "No time. In the closet. Now."

He took her by the arm, jerked open the closet door, and thrust her inside. He stepped in but left the door slightly ajar.

It was a small, cramped space with shelves on both sides. The cracked door allowed a thin shaft of illumination. Lily sachets could be dimly seen, hanging from overhead hooks and filled the space with a cloying, flowery scent. Evelyn was pressed close to Jack, aware of his strength and warmth.

Heavy footsteps echoed off the hardwood floors, coming closer. Her heart thundered in her chest and perspiration trickled between her breasts. She strained to see, all the while praying the intruder stayed out of the bedroom.

But the footsteps came closer, stopping on the threshold.

Jack pressed a finger to his lips, warning her to keep quiet, a moment before the intruder entered the bedroom. Jack shifted to the side, and she saw his pocket knife clenched in his fist.

Evelyn bit her lower lip to stay silent.

Through the small crack, she was able to make out a face.

Viscount Hamilton.

Dear Lord, what is he doing here?

The question barely registered in her mind before he spotted the chips of plaster on the floor beneath the chair Jack had used. Hamilton strode to the corner and looked up at the damaged ceiling. But instead of investigating the revealed hiding place, he whirled around to face the closet.

Icy fear twisted around her heart.

She was certain he would march over to the closet and tear the door open.

Hamilton strode forward with purpose, but stopped short in the center of the room. Standing in apparent contemplation, he rocked back and forth on his feet.

Her mind whirled, wondering what he was doing, and then she heard it: a creaky floorboard.

Hamilton dropped to his knees, withdrew a chisel from his coat pocket, and began to pry up the board.

He worked for a full minute, curses tumbling from his lips, until the board came loose, snapping in half, the sound reverberating like a gunshot off the bare walls.

Evelyn watched as he reached down below the floor. *He's looking for the diary!*

More curses, louder this time, and he withdrew his hand. Empty.

Hamilton's face turned a mottled shade of red, his nostrils flaring with fury. A vein in his forehead swelled like a thick snake. His mustache twitched, and he slammed the chisel on the floor. Muttering beneath his breath, he rose, picked up the chisel, and stomped out of the room.

Seconds later, they heard another door open down the hall.

Jack opened the closet door and took her hand. "Quick. Before he returns."

She followed Jack out of the bedroom and they crept past another room where Hamilton was on all fours, his back to them, as he pried another floorboard loose.

Together they fled Bess's second-floor lodgings, and Evelyn rushed down the stairs behind Jack. Holding her skirts high, her heart pounded so loudly she feared Hamilton would hear it.

The vestibule came into view. Almost there . . .

Halfway down the stairs, she tripped, a surprised screech escaping her. Jack's reflexes were lightning quick, and he whirled around to steady her.

For a heartbeat they stared at each other. Then the dreadful sound of pounding footsteps above.

Hamilton was in pursuit.

They flew down the remaining steps, and Jack opened the front door. But instead of hurrying outside, he turned around and dragged her into the far corner. Pulling her into his arms, he covered her with his body and kissed her firmly on the mouth.

Chapter 25

Jack's hand slid onto Evelyn's nape and held her close. Her bonnet, which had loosened during her mad flight down the stairs, fluttered to the floor. He entwined his fingers in the silken mass of hair, and his thumb found the rapid beat of her pulse.

Her body was soft and warm pressed against his. For a moment, he could easily forget the imminent danger—then the sound of Hamilton's heels thudding on the wooden steps pierced his consciousness.

Evelyn made a small incoherent sound.

Jack used his weight to pin her in the corner, and shielded her body with his. Increasing the pressure of his lips, he smothered her protests.

From the corner of his eye, Jack saw Hamilton step into the vestibule.

Hamilton glanced in their direction, then his attention snapped to the open front door. He bolted out the door, his footfalls echoing down the street.

Jack raised his head, but his body stayed pressed to Evelyn's.

"He's gone, Evie."

Evelyn's full lower lip trembled, her azure eyes wide with fright. "What happened?"

"We fooled him into thinking us lovers in the midst of a passionate embrace. Obviously, he has no idea the third and fourth floors are uninhabited. When he spotted the front door wide open, he must have assumed we fled, and he followed in pursuit."

"That was so close. If he is the murderer, we could have been his next victims," she said in a small frightened voice.

A wave of protectiveness hit Jack in his chest. The thought of Hamilton—or anyone—hurting Evelyn made his blood boil. There was no doubt in his mind that he would have killed to protect her.

"Don't even consider it, Evie. I wouldn't have let him touch you," he said in a harsh, raw voice.

He was aware now of her soft, full breasts pressed against his chest.

"Jack, I—"

His eyes lowered to her mouth. With Hamilton gone, he wanted to kiss her for real, to trace the soft fullness of her lips with his tongue. To unbutton the bodice of her gown and trace her breasts, to hear her moan for him . . .

She rested her hand against his chest where his heart pounded. He waited for her to push him away, but her resistance never followed.

"Jack," she breathed.

She tilted her head to the side, exposing the slender column of her throat. He couldn't help himself. He kissed her neck, the wildly beating pulse that matched his own.

She was pliant against him, pliant and receptive.

But he was aware of their surroundings. Aware that

they had illegally entered a private dwelling and were completely exposed with the front door wide open. His overheated and aroused body raged against logic and caution.

He took a step back, away from Evelyn and temptation.

"We should get you in the hackney."

Her eyes were glazed. She blinked, and he saw the moment her thoughts cleared. "Do you think Hamilton will return?"

"He wasn't carrying anything, and I don't think he found the diary. I want you safe and away from here."

She nodded woodenly, and followed behind him. Jack left the house first, looking about from left to right until he was certain Hamilton was gone for good. Only then did he motion for Evelyn to follow, guiding her across the street and into the waiting hackney.

Her skirts brushed his trousers as she settled on the bench across from his. Her blue eyes were wide, her disheveled hair loose around her shoulders. His fingers itched to touch the golden mass. She licked her lips, and despite the threat from Hamilton, and their near escape, his arousal throbbed in his trousers.

Jack gave the driver instructions to Evelyn's home, and then made to step out of the cab.

"You're not coming with me?"

"I have to go back."

"Back? Why on earth? You said Hamilton didn't find the diary."

"Yes, but we interrupted his search, remember? I want to take another look around. See if I can pick up where he left off."

She grasped his sleeve, her eyes imploring. "What if

he returns? There's a good chance he is Bess Whitfield's killer, Jack."

He touched her face, his fingers lingering on her cheek. "It's unlikely he'd risk returning here today. And if he does, I can take care of myself, Evie." He gave her a sly wink. "Don't worry. You can't get rid of me that easily."

As soon as the hackney drove out of sight with Evelyn safely ensconced within, Jack slipped back into Bess's home. He studied every creaky floorboard, every seam of plaster with a keen eye, but detected no other hidden compartments.

Dropping to his knees, Jack examined the board Hamilton had been in the process of prying up when he had stopped to pursue them. Hamilton hadn't finished with the board. Jack pried it off and reached within.

Nothing.

So Jack's assumption had been correct. Hamilton hadn't found the diary.

But the man clearly desired to find it, and badly.

Viscount Hamilton had been deeply involved with Bess Whitfield. The actress's dresser, Mary Morris, had told them as much. The letters Jack had found hidden in Hamilton's library attested to their tumultuous relationship, and Hamilton's presence here today confirmed he was desperate enough to burglarize a private residence to get his hands on that diary. Hamilton also had motive and opportunity for the murder.

He was, without a doubt, their most likely suspect.

It would be extremely convenient for Viscount Hamilton should Randolph Sheldon be tried and hanged for the crime. Hamilton could continue to search for the diary without the watchful investigative eyes of the Bow Street constables.

Jack frowned as an image of Earl Newland circling Bess Whitfield's grave, madly muttering, came to mind. Viscount Hamilton may be the most likely suspect, but Newland could not be entirely ruled out.

Jack recalled James Devlin's comment. Newland's motive in finding the diary wasn't as strong as Hamilton's, but insanity went a long way in justifying murder.

Jack finished his search of Bess's home and hailed a hackney cab. He gave the driver directions to his chambers at Lincoln's Inn and sat back in his seat. Thinking back, Jack recalled the number of times both aristocrats— Viscount Hamilton and Earl Newland—had come close to identifying Evelyn. Newland easily could have seen her face at the cemetery, and Hamilton had almost caught her here today. The threat of near discovery made Jack's temper flare.

Holding Evelyn in his arms, kissing her, had heightened his attraction for her. He wanted more, needed more. He wanted to watch her disrobe for him, to savor the feel of her naked flesh against his, wanted to be inside her so badly he could taste it.

He didn't know how much more he could stand. Working close by her side, yet refraining from touching her. Worse still, knowing she meant to give herself to Randolph Sheldon.

Again James Devlin's words came back to him. It *had* been too long since Jack had been with a woman. That was his problem, and it could easily be rectified. This fierce response for Evelyn must be due to a combination of the excitement of danger comingled with an overly long dry spell without a willing woman in his bed.

His last mistress, Molly Adler, was outrageously curved,

hedonistic, and beyond eager to do anything in bed to please. Focusing on Molly's image, lying in bed with her legs splayed wide open, he couldn't remember why he had ever grown bored. He shook his head at his foolishness.

Why was he torturing himself when sexual release could be easily bought?

It was time to pay Molly a visit.

Jack had sent a note in advance. After all, he wasn't a fool, and he had no desire to knock on his former mistress's door only to find her entertaining another man. It had been a little over four months since he had last seen Molly Adler, and he hadn't a doubt that she had found her next lover and benefactor.

Jack stood on a porch of an elegant town house— a residence he had helped purchase for her—and raised the brass knocker.

The door opened and Molly stood on the threshold, her servant nowhere to be seen.

"Jack," she sighed in a husky voice that oozed sensuality and promised all sorts of bedroom sport. Dressed in a sheer concoction of scarlet that outlined every womanly curve, she leaned to the side, and her rich curtain of mahogany hair draped over a bare shoulder. It was a well-practiced stance, calculated to enhance her physical assets and simultaneously tease and arouse.

"It's been a long time, Molly," Jack simply said.

She pouted, her painted, red lips portraying disappointment while her shrewd, black eyes raked over his body. "I was quite upset with how you ended things."

Despite her words, she stepped back and opened the door wide. "But I've decided to forgive you, darling."

She smiled slyly and raised her hand to show the emerald bracelet he had sent along with his note.

Ah, Jack thought, *predictable as always.*

Jack strode inside, and she closed the door behind him and leaned against it. "I've missed you, Jack," she drawled. "I haven't met a man that can compare to you."

His gaze lowered to her large breasts. She had rouged her nipples and they stood out like drops of dark chocolate through her sheer gown.

"I regret staying away," he said gruffly.

She sashayed forward and rested her arms on his shoulders. "We have much time to make up for, don't we, darling?"

He followed her up the stairs, discarding articles of clothing as he went. His cravat, his jacket, his waistcoat.

Her rounded hips swayed before him, and he could make out the full globes of her buttocks and the crevice between them.

They reached her bedchamber. Dozens of candles had been lit. It was clear she had been waiting for him, waiting and ready. She let the gown slip off her shoulders, and it swished down her abundant curves to fall to her feet. She had shaved herself, and the V between her legs was shockingly bare. She sat on the edge of the bed, and provocatively raised her legs to give him a full view of her glistening mons.

She was a skillful courtesan, a sexual creature. Everything a man could want to slake his lust.

But she wasn't Evie.

Could never be Evie.

The truth was Molly Adler was the antithesis of the blond innocence and intelligence that had tied his guts in knots.

He tried, damn it. But the mahogany hair was all wrong,

and the round dark eyes were far from the slanted Persian blue that were imprinted on his brain.

He closed his eyes and tried again, tried to focus on his body's needs, but instead a vivid picture of Evelyn grew ever clearer in his mind. Her flawless skin, her long golden hair like strands of lustrous glass, her eager response to his kiss. She was refreshingly honest and innocent, without contrivance, and the complete opposite of the woman before him.

He opened his eyes and looked at Molly, her legs splayed open on the edge of the bed. She licked a finger and rubbed the swollen flesh between her legs.

His lips twisted in distaste, and his arousal deflated like a punctured balloon.

Christ! What had he ever seen in her practiced sexuality?

His friends would never let him live this down. Devlin and Anthony would laugh. Brent would shake his head and tell him he told him so.

But the truth was far worse than his friends' anticipated ridicule.

If he couldn't exorcise his lust for Evie with another woman—an eager and experienced whore at that—then what was he to do?

Chapter 26

Two days after their encounter with Viscount Hamilton, Hodges delivered a letter to Evelyn. She reached eagerly for the envelope on the silver salver, thinking it was from Jack.

Letting the cream vellum stationery flutter to her desk, she read the letter, her distress mounting with each word.

Dearest Evelyn,
    It was wonderful seeing you again both at my home and at my mother's costume ball. I cherish our renewed friendship and do not want to wait as long as in the past to spend time together. I am having friends at my home Thursday afternoon for tea and some insightful feminine conversation. I would be thrilled if you would attend. My mother will be away attending Lady Borrington's soirée.

Your friend,
Georgina

Evelyn knew how she was going to respond, but she wasn't comfortable with her decision, having never acted the coward in the past.

Evelyn closed her eyes as a sickening sense of despair knotted in the center of her chest. She liked Georgina. She admired her kindness, her sense of humor, and most of all her insistence on being her own person and not succumbing to her mother's marriage demands. Georgina's invitation—although vaguely worded—was clear to Evelyn. While Viscountess Hamilton would be away Thursday afternoon, Georgina would have her feminist friends over for some rollicking conversation.

Under different circumstances, Evelyn would have loved to attend. She was sympathetic to their cause and agreed with many of Mary Wollstonecraft's opinions.

God only knew how many times she envied the male pupils that had passed through her father's Lincoln's Inn chambers. They had the opportunity to study and become barristers when she could do no more than sit by and voraciously read her father's books. They had thought her a funny little girl whose nose was always buried in a book. They were completely oblivious to the notion that a female should crave more education than how to play a few chosen tunes on the pianoforte, properly pour tea, and thread a needle.

Despite her fondness for Georgina and her desire to attend her Thursday gathering, Evelyn would be forced to decline. She felt like a traitor, for never could she forget the sight of a fervid Maxwell Stanford, Viscount Hamilton, on his hands and knees as he pried up a floorboard in Bess Whitfield's bedroom.

Georgina's father was most likely a killer.

How could she ever face her friend again?

She couldn't tell Georgina what she knew. It would devastate her friend to learn that not only had her father had an affair with an actress who went through lovers the way a dandy tossed aside used cravats, but that Hamilton may have murdered Bess Whitfield.

Evelyn knew enough of the law to understand that the evidence against Hamilton was circumstantial at best. Jack himself had said all they had discovered was that Hamilton and Bess were lovers. It seemed as if half of London had been in Hamilton's position.

But now, combined with Hamilton's presence in Bess's home, it was even more unnerving for Evelyn. They couldn't very well go to Bow Street with what they had witnessed since they had illegally broached Bess's home themselves. Even if a constable did believe their story, it still did not prove Hamilton was the killer, only that he wanted to unearth the diary before it was found by another and released to the newspapers.

Her thoughts, as always of late, turned to Jack. It had been two days since she had strained to watch him from the window of a hackney cab as he had returned to Bess's home to search for the blasted diary.

Had he found it? Or heaven forbid, had Hamilton returned when Jack was inside?

Her face burned as the memory of Jack's kiss came back to her, of his chest pressed so firmly against hers. Even though they both had been fully clothed, she had felt the heat of his body as though nothing had separated them. She had been acutely aware of more than the pleasure of his kiss, but of his familiar, alluring fragrance, his tall, muscular frame so different from Randolph's.

Despite the imminent danger—of both Viscount Hamilton and public discovery—she had been fascinated. It had been Jack who had withdrawn, reminding her of their surroundings. She dared not think of how far she would have allowed him to go if not for his restraint. It dawned on her that the more time she spent with Jack, the more perilous to her heart he was becoming.

Evelyn laid her head in her hands, feeling a wretchedness of mind she'd never known before. She bit her lip until it throbbed like her pulse. She needed to prove Randolph Sheldon's innocence, but at what cost?

Three days later, Evelyn refused to wait any longer for Jack to contact her. She had never been a patient person and the waiting had her stomach churning with anxiety and frustration. She had to know the outcome of Jack's search of Bess's home. Perhaps he had found the mysterious diary. Her mind whirled with images of Jack squirreled away in his chambers, avidly reading its illicit content at his leisure.

It was late afternoon by the time she arrived at Lincoln's Inn.

Stepping through the oak doors, she walked through the Tudor-style Gatehouse Court, only this time she did not spare a glance for the impressive architecture of the tall turrets or fragrant flowerpots. She headed for the Old Buildings, which housed the professional accommodations of the barristers. She strode down the halls, scanning the brass nameplates on the doors until she came to the one she sought.

Reaching for the handle, she swept inside and ran straight into a solid body.

"Oh!" she cried out.

A firm hand steadied her. "My apologies, miss. Are you all right?"

Evelyn looked up into the sinfully dark face of a tall man. Carrying a hat in one hand and a litigation bag in another, he was clearly on his way out when she had rushed inside.

She cleared her throat. "I'm fine. Just a little stunned."

He smiled, and she couldn't help but notice he was quite attractive with blue eyes, dark, curling hair and lean, strong features. "I apologize again. I was in a hurry and had no idea such a beautiful lady was on her way inside. May I help you?"

"I'm here to see a barrister."

"Then it is your lucky day since I am quite a competent barrister." He bowed low and said, "James Devlin at your service. Your wish is my command."

She smiled at his charming demeanor. "You misunderstand, Mr. Devlin. I'm here to see a certain barrister."

"Who is the lucky one, may I ask?"

"Mr. Harding."

Amusement flickered in his cobalt eyes. "You must be Lady Evelyn Darlington."

"Yes, how did you know?" Her voice rose in surprise.

His grin turned to a chuckle. "Jack and I share chambers."

"I've met your other two colleagues, Mr. Anthony Stevens and Mr. Brent Stone," Evelyn said.

James Devlin leaned close and whispered in her ear, "Let me tell you a secret, Lady Evelyn. I'm better than all of them."

She pulled back and met his sharp gaze. Despite his outrageously inappropriate and flirtatious behavior, she couldn't help but find him amusing. "No doubt the ladies find you hard to resist, Mr. Devlin, but I require Mr. Harding's services."

James shrugged matter-of-factly. "Should you tire of Jack, I'm always available. My docket's not as full as his, you see." He winked, put on his hat, and walked out the door.

Evelyn shook her head. Were all of Jack's fellow barristers such characters?

Putting James Devlin out of her mind, she turned the corner and came to the common room of the chambers. Just like her last visit, the clerk, McHugh, was bent over his desk, writing on a lengthy legal document. Stacks of paper were piled on all four corners of his desk, and Evelyn surmised one of his tasks was to file legal correspondence in the dozens of file cabinets that lined the walls.

McHugh glanced up as she came close. His bushy brows knit, and with ink-stained fingers he pushed his spectacles farther up the bridge of his pinched nose.

"Lady Evelyn," he said. "I assume you are here to see Mr. Harding?" He made to reach for the appointment register.

"I'm afraid I do not have an appointment." Evelyn held her breath, expecting him to protest, but unlike the last time she had shown up unexpectedly, McHugh rose and motioned for her to follow.

"Right this way, my lady."

They passed three closed doors, and Evelyn read the brass nameplates that identified Brent Stone's, Anthony Stevens's, and James Devlin's offices.

McHugh noticed her interest. "The other barristers are at the Old Bailey. You are fortunate that Mr. Harding did not have any courtroom appearances this afternoon and is in chambers," he said, a note of censure in his voice.

Evelyn bit her cheek to keep from smiling. Despite his seemingly polite behavior, the clerk made no effort to hide his disdain for unannounced client visits.

They reached Jack's door, and McHugh knocked.

"Enter."

The clerk cracked open the door. "Lady Evelyn is here, Mr. Harding. If you do not need anything else from me, sir, the chambers are empty, and I'd like to leave for the day."

"Of course, McHugh." She heard Jack's voice from behind the door.

Seconds later the door opened, and she stepped inside Jack's office.

Chapter 27

Jack tossed Evelyn's cloak on a chair and motioned for her to sit on the settee next to his desk. He casually leaned against his desk, one booted leg crossed over the other, and leveled his gaze upon her.

Without a jacket, waistcoat, or cravat he looked magnificent. His shirtsleeves were rolled up, the top two buttons of his shirt undone, revealing the corded muscles of his neck and a sprinkling of hair on his bronzed chest. It was clear he hadn't expected company and had discarded his formal business attire to work privately in his office for the remainder of the afternoon.

"I take it you couldn't wait until I contacted you?" he asked.

Despite his teasing tone, she lifted her chin. "You must know I'm anxious to find out what occurred after you returned to Bess's home."

"I can only imagine."

He grinned, and her heart gave a little jump. *Don't be a fool, Evelyn! You must keep your wits about you and not succumb to his easy charm.*

She was reminded again of all the female clerks and

wives of clients at Lincoln's Inn that had practically swooned when Jack Harding had entered the room. The years had only honed his rugged appeal. Hadn't the barmaid at the infamous Cock and Bull Tavern in Billingsgate eagerly displayed her enormous breasts for his viewing pleasure?

No, she must not let childhood fancy pervade her thoughts. She was a woman now, fully in control of her faculties. She had to focus on her goal of marrying a man who valued intelligence and independence in a woman. Such a male was an anomaly, and the arrogant Jack Harding did not fit this description.

She craned her neck and peered at his desk. "Did you find the diary or not?"

He arched a dark brow. "Do you expect I'd keep it out on my desk if I did?"

"Don't tease me, Jack. I have thought of little else since fleeing Bess Whitfield's home."

His face grew serious, and he pushed away from the desk and walked over. Sitting beside her on the settee, he cradled her gloved hands in his. "I'm sorry if my teasing distressed you, Evie. I never found the diary, and I'm convinced Bess moved it before she was murdered."

The heat of his hands seeped through her gloves. His thumb caressed her palm in a circular motion through the thin kidskin, and her pulse skittered alarmingly. Looking into his handsome face, she felt an unwelcome surge of excitement, and she knew without a doubt that her conflicting emotions were dangerously close to melting her firm resolve to keep Jack Harding at a safe distance.

Why did he have to be the most attractive and compelling male she knew?

Fighting an overwhelming need to be close to him, she stood and stepped to his desk, her back to him as she struggled to compose herself. She looked down and noticed the thick book of statutes open on his desk.

"What are you doing?" she asked.

"Research." He stood and followed her to his desk.

The book was open to the criminal code and a thought occurred to her. "You're doing legal research for Randolph's case?"

"I'm looking into defense theories should he be tried for the murder."

"Do you think it will come to that?"

"It's my job to be prepared, and truth be told, Randolph lacks the funds and savvy to hide from Bow Street forever."

She spun to face him. "I can assist you," she blurted out. "I'm highly proficient at legal research and have already come up with several theories of defense. And if Randolph is forced to go to trial, I can help you prepare for the courtroom as well."

He held up a hand. "Wait a minute, Evie. I work alone. I'm quite aware of how proficient you are at research. But book knowledge and practical lawyering in the courtroom are completely different."

"What on earth do you mean?"

"I mean you cannot learn in university how to handle a twelve-man jury."

"But the statutes and rules of evidence and hearsay, they all must apply."

"They are just the basics, Evie. But how you deal with people, how you present a case in a favorable light, it's all something you must learn by practical experience. It's just as important, if not more, in influencing the outcome," he said.

"You're an actor."

He shrugged, not in the least perturbed by her accusation. "Perhaps that is the best description."

She changed tactics. If a logical argument wouldn't move him, then revealing her true plight might. "Please let me do something, Jack. My mind is awhirl, and I haven't had a good night's sleep in weeks."

He sighed with exasperation and ran his fingers through his hair. "Very well." He turned the book around and pushed it across the desk. "You start by looking into the statutes. I'll check the case law to see if anything relevant appears."

"Thank you," she said.

"Would you like wine?" he asked. "It's the end of the day, and I had planned on having a drink before you arrived."

She nodded, and Jack went to a sideboard in the corner of the room.

Evelyn pretended to read, turning the pages in the book, as she stole glances at him as he poured two glasses. Without his jacket, his broad shoulders appeared a mile wide, his muscles rippling beneath his white shirt. The latest men's fashion allowed for padded jackets, but Jack would never need such artifice like most men of the *ton*.

He returned to the desk, handed her a glass and raised his. "A toast," he said. "To the most beautiful research assistant I've ever had."

"To finding what we need," she added as she raised her glass to his. "I'm quite proficient at this, you know."

His gaze caught and held hers. "You always were, Evie."

She sat on the settee with books spread around her. Jack sat behind his desk. They worked together for over an hour. They shared ideas and theories until Jack was comfortable that they had not overlooked anything relevant for Randolph's anticipated defense.

The wine heated her blood, and Jack's conversation eased the tightly coiled knot in her stomach that had been present since walking into his chambers. He discussed his prior murder cases, and how he had struggled with those clients whom he knew were innocent, but the evidence was stacked against them.

Then there were the other cases—the ones where the defendant was truly guilty of the crime—but Jack gave them the best representation he could. She sat enthralled as he spoke. Unlike the many male members of society that she had encountered, Jack did not talk entirely about himself. He was truly concerned with providing the best legal representation for the clients who so desperately depended on him, no matter how difficult the case.

He had an air of efficiency about him, and she was fascinated by his keen intelligence and strategic ingenuity in the courtroom. She made suggestions for Randolph's case, and took delight in Jack's positive response to several of them.

He refilled her wineglass, and they continued to work for another half hour. It was a cool May evening and a refreshing breeze blew in through the open window. At one point, she sneaked a peek and caught him brush a lock of brown hair from his eyes. She couldn't help herself, and her thoughts traveled back to his early days at Lincoln's Inn when he studied a treatise.

Old habits don't die, she thought, as she recalled his same mannerism.

He looked up and found her watching him. "What is it, Evie?"

"I was worried sick when I didn't hear from you," she confessed. "Images of Viscount Hamilton creeping up behind you in Bess's bedroom kept running through my mind."

His green eyes darkened. For a heart-stopping moment, she feared she had gone too far, blurting out her true feelings.

He slowly rose and pushed back his chair, and her fingers tensed on the book in her hands.

Closing the distance between them in three long strides, he knelt before her on the settee. He took her hands in his once again, but this time, her gloves lay discarded on the settee, and the touch of his fingers on hers made her skin tingle.

"You needn't have worried, Evie," he said. "I was serious when I told you that I can take care of myself."

Beneath his heated gaze, Evelyn couldn't help but compare Jack to Randolph. Jack was strong, shrewdly intelligent, and competent whereas Randolph's bookish smarts and youth had left him desperate and unprepared for the crisis that had fallen in his lap.

She knew with certainty that Jack could handle Viscount Hamilton just as he could master any complex legal dilemma.

He lowered his gaze to her mouth, and she recalled the pleasure of being held against his body, of his lips caressing hers. Something intense flared between them, and she recognized the spark of desire in his eyes. Her heart pounded, her breath quickened, and she feared that with one encouraging word from his lips, she would kneel down and join him on the velvet-soft Wilton carpet at her feet. Her lids lowered, and she waited for him to pull her closer, to hungrily cover her mouth with his.

Chapter 28

Raising his hands from hers, Jack trailed them up
Evelyn's arms to the edge of her puffed short sleeves. His
touch sent her senses spinning, and again she was helpless against her traitorous thoughts. Jack's palm was
much rougher than Randolph's. Rougher, larger, and oh,
so much more arousing.

"Careful, Evie," he said in a hoarse voice. "You
shouldn't have come to see me without your maid."

She understood exactly what he was insinuating. His
eyes gleamed like emeralds, and she acknowledged that
she'd never truly lusted after Randolph like she did Jack.
This longing for Jack was wicked, sinful. Her feelings
for him had nothing to do with logic, for to abandon all
propriety, all morals, to give herself to a man to whom
she was not wed, a man who knew she had plans to
marry another—was foolish and reckless.

Moving close, he cradled her face between his hands.
"Evie," he whispered gruffly. "I have tried to exorcise this
desire I feel for you—believe me I have—but I've failed.
Your beauty and intelligence—your very essence—have
bewitched me."

She gasped. How had he probed the deepest recesses of her mind to discover her most secret desires? Could he be that talented, that intuitive? She struggled to quench the joy she felt in her chest at his words, but his nearness was thrilling. She breathed in his familiar, alluring scent and clenched her skirts in her lap to prevent her fingers from reaching up to hold his hands against her flushed cheeks.

"When I kissed you in Bess Whitfield's vestibule, I was going mad inside and not because Hamilton was hot on our heels. All I could think about was kissing you more, kissing you *everywhere,*" he said huskily.

"Jack, I—"

"Let me kiss you, Evie."

She didn't protest, didn't make a sound. She watched entranced as his head lowered and his lips touched hers. Whisper soft and seductive, he kissed her. She opened to him, and his tongue swept inside. She came alive then and met his tongue with her own. Her fingers speared into his thick hair and urged him to deepen the kiss. With a low growl, he slid his hand around her neck, drawing her closer, and took her mouth with a savage intensity that left no doubt that he desired her.

Jack Harding desiring her? The irony was not lost on her. She would have given anything years ago to have him want her.

She tasted the rich wine on his tongue, and it was headier and more intoxicating to her than if she had consumed the entire bottle. He touched her only with one hand and his lips, yet it seemed as if his heat wrapped around her like a glove, caressing her body. If she felt this way from one kiss, what would the touch of his hands on her flesh feel like?

His head lowered to kiss a hot trail down her neck, and lower still, to the lacy bodice of her gown. When his lips hovered over the swell of a breast, she sucked in a breath. With lids half closed, she watched him kiss her breast over the fabric of her gown. The heat was scorching and arousing at once.

She'd always behaved like a lady in the past, had held to a strict code of propriety. But now with Jack Harding kneeling at her feet, propriety was the furthest thing from her mind. What did it matter when her body was burning from the inside out?

Touch me, she thought. *Touch me more.*

His nimble fingers reached behind her to unfasten the buttons on the back of her gown. Then her gown and shift slid down her arms, baring her breasts to his gaze.

He sucked in a breath. "You're so fair, Evie."

It was the reverence in his voice and the fierce desire in his heated gaze that was her undoing. And when his lips grazed the side of her breast, then her nipple, her senses reeled.

Sweet Lord, she'd never expected pleasure like this before.

She clenched his shoulders as his mouth took possession of her breasts. He was ruthlessly thorough in his seduction, first teasing, then laving each nipple, giving equal attention to each breast. Her head fell back, her back arched, and through lowered lashes the colorful bindings of the law books lining the shelves blurred like a fiery kaleidoscope.

She was perched on the edge of the settee, her fingers digging into Jack's back. Feeling the solid muscle beneath his shirt, she kneaded his skin and pulled him closer. She wanted more. She wanted to feel his naked flesh beneath her fingers, to explore him as he was her.

There was a rustle of skirts, and then his fingers glided up her silk stocking, past her thigh, to the top of her garters. She stiffened at the shock of his touch, but he gave her no time to think and pulled her closer still to suck a nipple full in his mouth. She whimpered as pleasure radiated straight from her breast to flood her loins with a liquid heat. Working through her clothing, he reached her woman's center and threaded through the curls to finger the sensitive flesh.

She cried out as shivers of delight spiraled from the soft core of her body. It was wicked, sinful, and oh, so miraculous. Her senses reeled. Her hips arched against his hand of their own accord, and she clawed his shoulders.

"Easy, Evie," he murmured against her breast.

Easy? She wanted anything but easy.

He stroked with his fingers and eased the tip of one inside her, wresting an outcry of delight from her lips. He found her sensitive nub and his thumb glided over it, once, twice. Passion rose in her like the hottest fire, clouding her mind. She squirmed on the settee, whether to pull him closer or push him away she didn't know.

He lifted his head, his intense green eyes meeting hers.

"Let me love you, Evie. It will be good between us. I promise you'll never once think of Randolph, and he never need know."

Yes, she thought. *Randolph would never know.*

Her mind whirled. She could be with Jack, know him intimately as a woman, and slake this maddening lust she had for him. The thought did not shock her as it once would have. At that moment, all she knew was her body's crying out for a release that she knew Jack had the skill to give her.

She slid to the carpet in a pool of skirts. Kneeling face-to-face, she pressed against his hard length. "Yes, Jack."

Surprise flickered in his eyes, but was quickly replaced with fierce satisfaction.

"Don't move, sweetheart." He rose and went to the door. For an instant she feared he would walk out on her, leave her kneeling, half-naked on the carpet. She clutched her gaping bodice to her breasts and watched him.

He turned the lock and the sound reverberated through the quiet room like a gunshot. The noise should have snapped her to her senses, but when Jack turned and stalked back to her with grace that reminded her of a large, predatory panther her misgivings vanished.

"The chambers are empty, but I want to be certain," he said.

He came to her, and she was rewarded when he swept her into his arms and took her mouth with a searing kiss. Her gown fell back to her waist, and her nipples instantly hardened against his cotton shirt. She moved restlessly against him, suddenly anxious to touch him. Her fingers rose to the buttons of his shirt, but he reached up to pull the fabric apart, sending buttons flying across the carpet. Pulling the shirt from his waistband, he shed it impatiently.

She greedily studied him. He was everything her childhood dreams were made of and much, much more. Even though she had never seen a naked man before, she innately knew no other could compare to Jack Harding. He was in his prime, and the most attractive male she knew. He was muscled and sinewy, a sprinkling of hair on his chest and down to the waistband of his trousers.

She swallowed at the bulge that appeared there, nervous, but curious.

He cradled her face in his hands, and forced her eyes to his. "Are you certain, Evie? I may not be able to stop if we go any further."

Oh, yes, she was certain. She thought she might die if he stopped. Here was her chance to be with Jack, the male she had pined after as a girl, the man she desired as a woman.

Still, a tiny voice had to ask, "You will tell no one?"

"I promise."

"You can prevent an unwanted child?"

He hesitated, then nodded. "There are ways."

"Then make love to me, Jack."

His face was fierce as he reached out to tug on the last button that held her clothing in place, and her gown and shift slid down her hips to the carpet. Her drawers followed and then she was naked beside him, clad only in black silk stockings and garters. His eyes widened in appreciation as they traveled down her body.

"Lord," he murmured. "You're perfect, Evie."

He went for the top button of his trousers, and quickly discarded them. It was her turn to stare. The trail of hair down his chest did indeed continue lower, and his manhood stood erect from a nest of black curls. A frisson of misgiving stabbed her brain at his size, but then he took her into his arms and laid her on the soft carpet.

Stretching his long length beside her, he kissed her thoroughly. He was tender, then savage, and he kissed her as if he was committing her to memory.

His hand slid down her taut stomach to the swell of her hip, and lower still to stroke the sensitive nub between her legs. This time she anticipated the pleasure, and her body sang beneath his skillful touch. He continued his seductive onslaught, kissing her everywhere until she was desperate for more. Only then did he move atop her, bracing his weight with his arms and inching her legs apart with his thigh. His manhood grazed her swollen mons, and she gasped and opened her eyes.

She might have been alarmed by the savage, hungry look in his eyes. But it was Jack—Jack whom she had known and adored since childhood. Without hesitation, she reached up to pull him close.

Skin to skin, they lay panting against each other. She heard his sharp hiss, then felt him pressing against her core, gliding inside her. The sensations were pure and explosive. Inch by inch, he pushed farther until he stopped. Digging her heels into the carpet, she arched upward, wanting more, needing something . . .

"Dear God, Evie. Don't move," he groaned. She frowned in confusion, her brain sluggish with the strength of her lust.

"Jack, I need . . ."

He groaned again, but then plunged all the way within her. She cried out from the sudden stab of pain.

"Stay with me, Evie," he said hoarsely.

He sounded in pain as well, but he pulled back and thrust forward. Her pain ebbed and warm honey flowed to where their bodies were joined. An urgency overtook her, and she raised her hips to meet his rhythm. The pleasure built in intensity. Passion pounded the blood through her heart, chest, and head, and she feared she'd shatter into a million pieces.

Then her body did explode. She arched her back, her nails raking his shoulders as she was hurtled into blissful oblivion. His answering groans echoed around her, he thrust twice more, then stiffened above her and abruptly pulled out of her body. She felt something hot and wet spurt across her belly and breasts.

Exhausted and drained, she lay heavily breathing in

the warmth of his arms. He brushed a kiss across her forehead.

Opening her eyes, she gazed at the chiseled planes of his face. Her mind was sluggish to return; her first coherent thought was that she had immensely underestimated how difficult it would be to get Jack Harding out of her system.

Chapter 29

After using his handkerchief to gently wipe away the evidence of their lovemaking from Evelyn's body, Jack lay on his side, his hand resting on the lush curve of her hip. She curled into him, and he inhaled the intoxicating scent of lavender on her heated skin. Her eyes were closed, and she breathed heavily through parted lips. Gazing down at her, he couldn't help but marvel at what had happened between them.

There had been women in his past, but never had he experienced such a combination of physical and emotional satisfaction. When she knelt before him in all her naked splendor, his mind had drained of reason and his masculine instinct to claim and possess had raged through him like a beast. Her uninhibited response, her fierce climax, had been the catalyst that had heightened his own arousal.

He had no delusions as to what existed between them. She had hired him to do a job, to defend the man she wanted for her husband. Nothing that had occurred on the floor of his office, no matter how earth-shattering, had changed that fact.

She would leave here and go to Randolph Sheldon with the knowledge that no one would be the wiser as to what had transpired here. His jaw clenched, and a foreign stab of jealousy pierced his chest where his heart now felt like a lump of granite.

He should be grateful for her loyalty to another man because it served his purpose. He didn't want to feel this possessiveness for a woman, even if she was the precocious, but oddly charming girl from his past. He had always strived to maintain an emotional distance, as his career was the most important aspect of his life. If he had any sense, he would rise, help her dress, and send her on her way. Instead, his fingers lightly traced her breasts, her nipples firming under his touch.

She opened her eyes, and he was drawn by their mesmerizing blue depths. She pushed herself up on her elbows, and her hair, which had tumbled free from the knot she usually wore at her nape, curled over her shoulders and around the fullness of her breasts in thick golden waves. Dusky pink nipples thrust through the strands.

His cock instantly stiffened to iron as rampant need seared through him. His hot gaze traveled the length of her body.

Evelyn's cheeks flamed red, and she nervously bit her full, bottom lip. Reaching for her dress, she made to rise.

"Wait." His hand snaked out to hold her arm.

She turned back. "I must leave."

"Don't do this, Evie."

"Do what?"

"Do not regret what happened between us."

She glanced away. "It was wrong."

"No, it was perfect."

"You won't tell Randolph or my father?" she whispered several heartbeats later.

"I'll never breathe a word of what happened between us to anyone."

She let out a long, audible breath. "Thank you."

"Tell me, how did you come to be here without your chaperone?" he asked.

"I told everyone I was attending Lady Eaton's tea party. I arrived at your chambers by hackney."

He grinned. "I trust this was much more enjoyable?"

Her lips trembled with a smile, and she laughed. "Jack Harding, how is it you can make light of anything?"

He shrugged. "It's part of my charm."

He was relieved at the sight of her smile. He didn't want her distraught or—heaven forbid—wallowing in self-regret.

She stood and looked about for her undergarments. He had never bothered to remove her black silk stockings or garters, and when she bent down to retrieve her shift and drawers, he nearly groaned out loud at the tempting sight of her lush buttocks. She was perfectly formed, with the face of an angel and the body of a temptress. He had bedded her, and yet the need to bury himself deep within her again remained stronger than before.

She donned her undergarments and gown and gathered her hair in one hand across her shoulder. Turning her back to him, she said, "Will you help me with my buttons?"

It was an innocent request, and he knew she had no choice but to ask his aid as the tiny row of buttons ran down the entire length of her back. He stood and slipped on his trousers. Stepping close, his mouth watered at the sight of her creamy skin, and his fingers itched to delve inside the gaping fabric. He finished with the last button—and unable to resist—he leaned down and brushed his lips over her neck.

She shuddered and turned in his arms. Thick lashes lowered and her attention riveted on his mouth. Her tongue licked her lower lip, wetting it. His already snug trousers grew painfully tight, and that was perilous. She needed to return home at once before he swept her off her feet, stripped her of her clothing, and made love to her again.

By sheer force of will, he stepped back and yanked her cloak off the chair and handed it to her.

"Go now, Evie," he said hoarsely.

A probing query came in her eyes. "Jack, will what happened between us change anything?"

Her question was clear, but it felt like a solid punch to his gut. "Nothing will change. I'll be in touch regarding the case."

She nodded, unlocked the door, and fled the chambers.

For long moments Jack stood still, staring at the door, as sweat beaded on his brow. He breathed in and out, willing his brain to resume control over his arousal. The seconds ticked by on the mantel clock.

Sheldon, she wants Randolph Sheldon, he repeated the mantra over and over in his mind.

It made things much simpler for Jack Harding, the jury master. But the problem was, now that he had tasted her, how was he going to walk away and watch her go to another man?

How could she have misjudged things so badly? Some deep part of her had truly believed that being with Jack intimately would have put an end to the maddening attraction she had for him.

But she had been terribly wrong.

"Are you well, m' lady?"

Evelyn's gaze snapped to Janet walking beside her. They were halfway down Bond Street, heading for the tea shop. Once again, Evelyn was on an errand for Lord Lyndale's newest medicinal tea. This time she sought a blend to assuage the painful varicose veins that plagued her father of late.

Her maid was looking at her curiously.

"I'm fine, Janet. Ah, here we are," Evelyn said as they came to the tea shop.

Snapping her parasol shut, Evelyn opened the shop's doors. The bells chimed, announcing their presence to the shopkeeper. The man waved from behind the counter, recognizing his frequent customers.

Evelyn strolled around tables, perusing random tins of tea. Her mind was elsewhere as thoughts of yesterday returned. She had made it home without any member of the household suspecting her true whereabouts. She had immediately requested a hot bath and a dinner tray, and then went straight to bed.

She had dreamed of Jack.

She relived their brief time together. The warmth of his arms around her had been so male, so bracing, and she had soared higher and higher until she had exploded in a firestorm of sensations. And when he had touched her after they had already made love, she had wanted to do it all over again.

As the erotic images flashed through her mind, her blood pounded and her cheeks burned. She looked up, acutely conscious of the people milling about the crowded shop.

I must be a deviant, she thought, *to have been so consumed by lust.*

How could she have allowed him to make love to her? Or more disturbingly: How could she have desperately wanted him to? Perhaps that's what happened to women who waited too long to marry or to bed a man. Once they finally succumbed to passion they thought of little else.

But she knew it had more to do with Jack Harding than her age and lack of experience. He was a rare type of male. Handsome, confident, intelligent, and slightly dangerous. The combination was irresistible. She was not the first woman to be drawn to him.

She could blame the wine, but she was old enough to know better and to be honest with herself. She had been crazed with need. His power of persuasion in the courtroom had carried over into the bedroom. His seduction had been as ruthless as any legal campaign. He had stoked a growing fire within her until it had burst into flame, and her whole being had been consumed with wanting him.

Then there was her subconscious. That nagging voice that had needled her into her final capitulation for she knew it was her only chance to be with him before the true murderer was found and Jack's services were no longer required.

And with that thought, an image of Randolph Sheldon crystallized in her mind.

Dear Lord, what about Randolph?

Crippling guilt squeezed her heart like a tight fist.

Dare she tell Randolph what had happened? Although they weren't yet officially betrothed, they had an understanding. Her father liked Randolph and had kept him as his University Fellow, but he didn't approve of her marrying him. Evelyn had been confident that she could change her father's opinion, but then Bess Whitfield had been murdered and all her well-laid plans had come to a halt—which had led her straight to Jack Harding.

Jack had promised that nothing would change, that he would continue to represent Randolph and keep her apprised of the case. And then he had thrust her cloak in her arms and told her to leave. Her throat seemed to close up, and a new anguish seared her heart.

What did she expect? That Jack profess his undying love for her?

Jack had made no promises of affection, and why should he? She had repeatedly proclaimed that she wanted Randolph's name cleared so that they could marry.

And Jack was *not* the marrying kind.

But the question was: Could she keep what had occurred on the floor of Jack's office a secret forever and go through with her plans to marry Randolph?

She knew she wouldn't be the first woman to do so. Many were forced to marry men they didn't like, men many years their senior, even men they feared. She had heard of women that had successfully faked their virginity on their wedding nights.

But she had never wanted that for herself. She had thought she had found her perfect intellectual mate in Randolph. Could she have been wrong?

Don't be a fool, Evelyn, her inner voice warned. Despite her guilt, she feared giving up Randolph because of one reckless experience. There was no future with Jack. He would move on to his next female conquest, and she would be left with nothing.

No Randolph.

No Jack.

Just spinster Evelyn.

A heaviness centered in her chest at the dreadful

thought. She didn't want to be a spinster. Although she loved her father dearly, she wanted her own home, her own family. She didn't want to spend the next decade organizing her father's mountain of legal books on his library shelves, arranging his monthly dinners with the judges, or buying his medicinal teas.

So what was she to do?

"I found it, m' lady!"

Evelyn's attention was snapped to the present as Janet approached clutching two tins of tea to her bosom.

"Lord Lyndale is going to be pleased. This blend assures relief from varicose veins, and the other," Janet said, thrusting forth a second tin in Evelyn's face, "promises comfort from constipation by loosening the bowels."

Evelyn forced a smile, feeling as if her face would crack from the effort. "Splendid, Janet. Let us pay and be on our way."

Evelyn made the purchases and they left the shop. No sooner had the door closed behind them than did another cry startle her.

Chapter 30

"Evelyn!"

Evelyn whirled around to spot Georgina Hamilton waving from three shops down. Wearing a vivacious orange walking dress and bonnet with matching ostrich feathers, Georgina rushed toward them, the plumes of her hat bouncing wildly.

"I thought that was you, Evelyn. I missed you at my tea. Please tell me you are feeling well?" Georgina asked.

Evelyn knew Georgina was referring to the illness she had faked in order to excuse herself from Georgina's feminist gathering.

"I'm feeling much better, Georgina. Thank you for inquiring. I hope you had an entertaining afternoon with the other ladies?"

"I was concerned by your letter. Your condition sounded alarmingly like my uncle who suffers from incurable consumption." Georgina turned a worried glance to Janet standing beside them. "Has a doctor seen Lady Evelyn?"

Janet looked to Evelyn, then back to Georgina. The maid's brown eyes were wide with uncertainty. Her mouth floundered open and closed.

Evelyn quickly entwined her arm with Georgina's and drew her aside. "Janet upsets easily. But I'm fine now, and I apologize for alarming you. Now tell me about yourself. Has your mother relinquished hopes of a match with Lucas Crawford?"

The diversion worked, and Georgina's face twisted with displeasure. "No, Mother has invited his family to visit our country residence in Somersetshire next week. It's not the thought of a full week of Lucas's courtship that distresses me, but rather the dreaded anticipated scrutiny of two overbearing mothers!"

"Oh, Georgina."

A glimmer of hope lit Georgina's eyes. "Will you come with me to Somersetshire, Evelyn? It would be delightful to have a friend. Father wouldn't mind."

Panic welled in her throat accompanied by an overwhelming urge to flee. A vivid image of Viscount Hamilton crouched on the floor of Bess Whitfield's bedroom, prying up floorboards, blasted through Evelyn's mind.

Dear Lord, to sleep under the same roof as Hamilton! The notion was unfathomable. But worse yet was the thought that her friend's father was their lead suspect in the murder of his own mistress.

How could she ever confess such information to her friend?

Evelyn held up her recent purchase from the tea shop. "I'm so sorry, Georgina, but I cannot leave Father and go to the country with you. He hasn't been feeling well of late, and I am not free to leave him alone. I must return home now as he is waiting for his medicinal tea."

"I understand. Please send Lord Lyndale my best." Georgina hugged her and waved as she stepped inside a carriage bearing the Hamilton crest.

Evelyn headed back to where Janet waited. Sourness

settled in the pit of her stomach, like an old wound that ached on a rainy day. There was no question, she was suffering from guilt.

Guilt over her actions with Jack. Guilt over keeping secrets from Randolph. Guilt over her treatment of Georgina.

The simple had become complex. She had started out seeking to protect Randolph from prosecution until the true murderer was arrested so that she could proceed with her marriage plans. Now, the lives of others she cared deeply for could be ruined and—solely because of her recklessness—her heart lay in perilous danger.

It was a Friday evening in early June when Lord Lyndale's monthly dinner party with the judges arrived. Evelyn's father and the Lordships Bathwell and Barnes were comfortably seated in the drawing room, brandies in hand, engaged in a heated debate over the controversial Corn Laws while Evelyn rushed about seeing to the final details of the evening meal. She was just leaving the kitchen with Mrs. Smith when a knock on the door drew their attention.

"Hodges is in the cellar fetching the wine," Mrs. Smith said as she started for the door.

Although Mrs. Smith's large girth blocked Evelyn's view of the doorway, the deep timbre of Jack Harding's unmistakable voice washed over her like warm spring rain.

It was the first she had seen him since they had made love in his chambers days ago. He stepped inside, and Mrs. Smith took his cloak. He thanked and smiled at the housekeeper, and the elder woman beamed at the attention and bobbed a curtsy. Then spotting Evelyn, his grin flashed briefly, dazzling against his bronze skin.

Striking in his impeccably cut black-and-white evening attire, his tall, well-muscled frame moved with an easy grace as he approached Evelyn.

"Lady Evelyn, my apologies. I had a court appearance that lasted longer than anticipated. I trust I am not too late."

Aware of Mrs. Smith's presence, Evelyn politely smiled. "Not at all, Mr. Harding. The others are in the drawing room engaged in a lively discussion over the repeal of one of Parliament's laws."

"Splendid."

She led the way to the drawing room, aware of the power that coiled within him as he walked beside her.

Lord Lyndale rose to greet Jack.

"Jack, you are just in time to set the record straight. Pray tell us your opinion of the Corn Laws."

Jack took an armchair between Lordships Bathwell and Barnes. Both judges eyed Jack with calculating expressions.

Evelyn held her breath as she sat beside her father and wondered how Jack would handle himself with the two opinionated lordships.

Bathwell, a squat fellow with beady eyes, had a ring of gray hair around a shiny scalp and small, yellow teeth that resembled a ferret's. Barnes, on the other hand, was a brawny man with a thick neck and a chest as broad as an armoire. Seated between the two judges, Jack's tall physique and commanding air of self-confidence distinguished him from a typical barrister.

"I must confess I am agreeable to the growing movement of repealing the Corn Laws. They may have been useful in the past, but the market is changing, and the country would benefit from increased imports of wheat from the Baltic region," Jack said.

Lord Lyndale and Barnes nodded in agreement, while a cold, congested expression settled on Bathwell's face.

"I'm not surprised by your opinion on the matter, Mr. Harding," Lord Bathwell said, his voice heavy with sarcasm. "As a seasoned criminal barrister who has ensured the freedom of countless criminals at the expense of the Crown's prosecution and the good citizens of London, I understand why you would favor the repeal of a vitally important law. Criminal barristers always do what's expedient and in their best monetary interests."

Evelyn stifled a gasp. She knew Bathwell was hard-hearted when it came to a defendant's pleas at sentencing. Hannah Ware came to mind. The indigent widow had admitted to stealing. Her reasons for committing the crime—to feed her six starving children—wouldn't have mattered if Bathwell had sat on the bench. The dogmatic judge would have denied Hannah benefit of clergy. But to accuse Jack of being a selfish criminal barrister, devoted to amassing his own wealth at the expense of the Crown and the citizens of London?

Ludicrous.

At one time, she had ignorantly thought the same. Now she knew better. Yes, Jack Harding did get paid to represent defendants accused of crimes, but he also selflessly volunteered his services for the destitute. His *pro bono* activities had spared Hannah Ware a harsh sentence, perhaps even the death penalty.

Quiet descended in the room. Barnes and Lord Lyndale looked at Bathwell, then at Jack. Evelyn thought Jack would take offense to Bathwell's inflammatory statement.

What barrister wouldn't?

But Jack sat back in his chair, his mouth twitching with amusement. "I appreciate your sentiments regarding my success in the courtroom, my lord, but I can assure you this: Criminal barristers such as myself do perform a most valuable service for the Crown's prosecution."

"What might that be?" Bathwell asked.

"Top prosecutors would find how easily they would be able to obtain convictions tedious. They would leave in droves out of sheer boredom. Imagine what would become of the Crown's prosecution then?" Jack said.

Barnes guffawed at Jack's outrageous statement. "A point well made, Mr. Harding."

Lord Lyndale chimed in. "There's no more effective method of losing talent than through boredom and tediousness."

Bathwell nodded grudgingly. "I should have known better than to debate you, Mr. Harding. Despite my comments, I'm glad you decided to join us this evening."

The tight knot within Evelyn eased. Whatever anxiety she had about Jack Harding fitting in with the imposing judges was clearly misplaced.

He's a smooth talker, no matter the situation thrust upon him, she thought.

Dinner was announced, and the men rose to follow Evelyn and her father to the dining room. Evelyn had carefully set out the seating arrangements, but at the last minute, Lord Lyndale altered her plans.

"Evelyn, as our new guest, I would like Mr. Harding to sit beside me tonight. I'm sure Lordships Barnes and Bathwell will be amenable."

The judges nodded, affirming the decision, and Evelyn had no choice but to sit beside Jack. If she didn't know any better, she would have thought her father planned it that way.

Nonsense. Father isn't coy or overly subtle. If he wanted Jack Harding to sit beside his daughter, he would come right out and say so.

Or would he?

She frowned at her thoughts. She knew her father didn't approve of Randolph as a future son-in-law, but that didn't mean he wanted Jack Harding to step in and assume the role. Father had never suggested such a thing in the past. It was her overactive imagination.

That and her mounting guilt over what she had done.

She sat still as the first course of turtle soup was served. The legal discussions that had interested her in the past barely registered. Instead, she was highly conscious of the man seated beside her.

The first course was taken away, and the second served. Droll conversation drifted around her, failing to penetrate her hazy senses. She stole sideways glimpses of Jack's strong hands holding his fork, reaching for his wine goblet. Images of those hands stroking her breasts, the curve of her hip, and lower still . . . pervaded her mind.

Jack turned to Evelyn. "Eat something, Evie," he whispered in her ear. "Are you well?"

Evelyn met his stare. His inquiring green eyes, serious face, and the clear-cut lines of his profile, were devastatingly handsome. His aquiline nose, square jaw, and firm sensual mouth would captivate the attention of any woman.

"I'm not hungry."

"You don't want your father to worry, do you?"

She dutifully raised her fork.

He placed his napkin on his lap, and his thigh brushed her skirts. The scent of his shaving soap—clean and masculine—reached her, and her reaction was maddeningly swift. A slow swirl grew in the pit of her stomach.

The meal was endless. A footman took her dinner plate, but she knew dessert was yet to arrive—strawberries and Devonshire cream. She tried not to glance at Jack as he consumed the fragrant berries.

At last her father set down his fork, and she sighed with relief as the dessert plates were cleared from the table. Coffee in the library, accompanied by cigars and port would follow.

She stood, and the guests followed Lord Lyndale to his prized library. The judges and Jack took seats by the fire-place, her father sat in an armchair before his desk.

Evelyn had always remained in the library in the past, serving coffee. Even though women never interrupted the men's after-dinner cigars and port, her father was not conventional when it came to his daughter and had allowed her to stay. Barnes and Bathwell had known her since she was a child and were both accustomed to her father's eccentricities. The fact that both judges were fond of their coffee—and she dutifully kept their cups full—no doubt aided her cause.

But tonight was different for Evelyn; she was restless and agitated. Jack's presence disturbed her senses and served to add to her mounting guilt. The significance was not lost on her that she would have previously found tonight's conversation intellectually stimulating. Rather than listen intently, however, she felt as if the library walls were closing in on her, and the high collar of her gown was slowly squeezing off her air supply.

Barnes asked for more coffee. Evelyn reached for the half-full coffeepot.

"I'm afraid it is empty, my lord." she lied. Rather than pull the servants' cord, she murmured an excuse, grasped the pot, and rushed from the room.

She hurried to the kitchen. Her chest was tight, her

lungs lacking adequate oxygen. Since the meal was over, the kitchen was empty save for a young scullery maid. The air was redolent with the aroma of roast lamb and potatoes from the evening meal. Evelyn handed the pot to the maid with instructions to send a full pot back to the library. The maid scurried to do her bidding. Rather than return to the library, Evelyn hastened past the ovens still radiating heat, long worktables laden with various kitchen utensils, and pots hanging from iron racks, to the back door leading out of the kitchen.

She needed fresh air and the garden would do nicely. She reached for the knob.

"Evelyn."

She recognized his voice instantly, and her hand froze on the knob. Slowly she turned.

Jack stood, leaning against one of the tables, his steady gaze riveted on her face. "Where are you going?"

"Why are you here?" She answered with a question of her own.

"You ate close to nothing in the dining room, and you were alarmingly pale in the library. I was concerned."

"I'm fine. Nothing a bit of fresh air won't cure. Go back to the library before you are missed, Jack."

"We need to talk."

"Talk? About what?"

"About what happened between us in my chambers."

Horrified, her face grew hot with humiliation. Try as she might, images of their bodies entwined on the Wilton carpet of his office rose within her like an ocean wave. She had acted no better than a common doxy.

Her embarrassment quickly turned to annoyance and she replied irritably, "There's nothing to talk about. We had agreed nothing would change between us."

He stalked forward and stopped in front of her. "I'm

afraid that's no longer possible, Evie. I haven't been able to stop thinking about it."

Dear Lord, neither have I, she thought.

Her heart pounded in her chest at his words. With sudden clarity she knew she had been fooling herself all along. After experiencing Jack Harding, how could she ever continue with her plans of marrying Randolph? Worse still, how would any man measure up to Jack?

I'm falling in love with him. Or have I always been in love with him?

In that instant Evelyn knew what she had to do: Confess all to Randolph and beg his forgiveness. She knew now that she could never marry Randolph. Her last hope was to hold on to her friendship with him. It was a friendship she treasured and held dear, and despite what had occurred between her and Jack, despite her growing feelings for the man who stood before her, she would not abandon Randolph without ensuring his innocence and freedom. Randolph may despise her after she confessed to an illicit affair, but she would not disclose with whom she had the affair and pray that Randolph retained Jack as his barrister.

She cleared her throat. "Jack, I've thought of it as well. But it was a mistake and must never happen again."

His expression darkened. "It didn't feel like a mistake to me."

"I'm sure it has happened to you before."

"No, it hasn't. I've never made love to a woman in my chambers."

"That's not what I meant." She was not ignorant of Jack's reputation of charming the ladies. "You said you would continue to represent Randolph."

"I meant it at the time."

"At the time?"

He shoved his fingers through his hair. "It will be difficult for me to represent him when I am distracted by you. Perhaps Mr. Sheldon would be best represented by another barrister. I know many competent—"

"No. You promised," she insisted.

"Why is it so important to you that I represent him?"

"Because of your trial record. Because Randolph is innocent." *Because my conscience will never be assuaged should Randolph be found guilty if you failed to defend him because of our affair.*

"All right, Evie. I'll do it. But it will not be easy." He laughed beneath his breath. "Anthony and Devlin were right."

She didn't know what he meant by his last comment, but then she lost her train of thought when he reached out and cupped her face with his hand.

"I need you to know something, Evie. What we shared was different for me. Special."

His gaze was soft as a caress, and he stepped closer, his palm sliding behind her neck. His eyes lowered to her lips, and she sensed he was about to kiss her.

She didn't protest. Didn't move.

"Evie," he whispered.

Yes, Jack. Kiss me one last time.

His mouth brushed hers, once, then twice. She parted her lips and closed her eyes.

A pounding on the kitchen door sounded.

She jerked back and opened her eyes. "Dear Lord, who could that be?"

"Step aside," Jack instructed as he reached for the knob and swung the door open.

A lone man stood in the doorway. Dressed in a black

coat with the collar turned up around his neck and the curled brim of his hat pulled low, it took Evelyn a moment to identify him.

"Simon! What are you doing here?" Evelyn asked.

Simon Guthrie glanced at Jack, then Evelyn. "I've come with bad news."

"Randolph?" Evelyn asked, afraid of the answer.

Simon nodded, his face grim. "There was a scuffle with the Bow Street Runners. Randolph escaped, but he was injured."

Evelyn's stomach clenched. "Has he seen a doctor?"

"He's refused. He's back at the Shoreditch town house, and he's asking for you."

Her voice frozen with fear, Evelyn could only stare.

"I'm going with you," Jack said.

Chapter 31

On a Friday night, Shoreditch's theaters and music halls were crowded with partygoers. Evelyn sat across from Jack and Simon in Jack's carriage, and she gazed out the window at the brightly lit music halls and streets teeming with revelers. Shoreditch was far from London's Drury Lane Theatre, and the quality of the productions lacked the city's polish, the patrons of the music halls a loud, rough lot.

"This is a bad idea, Evie. Your father wouldn't approve."

Evelyn glared at Jack seated across from her in the carriage. Simon sat still beside Jack.

She raised her chin a notch. "I have no choice."

Evelyn knew she was taking a great risk fleeing her home in the middle of the night to see Randolph. The waiting had seemed endless until the judges had departed for the evening, and she had been able to slip out of the house undetected. Simon had hid in the gardens and Jack in his carriage around the corner.

They left the theater district and soon alehouses, inns, and gambling houses appeared. The noise from the establishments spilled into the streets, and the scent of sewage wafted through the carriage window. A scantily clad woman waved a colorful scarf and called out a window of an inn. Even from across the street, Evelyn could see the woman's enormous breasts resting on the windowsill—her unnaturally red hair matching her painted lips.

A quick glance at a group of drunken sailors rollicking across the street sent Evelyn's pulse racing. She realized what she took to be an inn was indeed a brothel. Shocked, she stared at the scene with wide eyes.

The Cyprian's plying her trade quite successfully. They're like hounds drawn to the scent of bloody meat, she mused.

The cobbled street they were currently traveling was in horrid disrepair, and it was not long before the wheels of the carriage hit a rut.

Evelyn jerked forward, grasping Jack's thigh for support.

"Careful, Evie." Jack's hand steadied her.

Her cheeks burned, and she removed her hand as if she had clutched a hot poker. She was more conscious than ever before of Jack's presence mere inches away.

Simon coughed, and Evelyn turned to him.

"Randolph is staying here?" she asked in a choked voice.

"No, Bess Whitfield's town house is closer to the theater district, but this is the safest route at the moment. Constables rarely travel this road."

She didn't know how to respond to that comment so she remained silent. Soon rows of town houses came into view. The buildings were better maintained here, and Evelyn was relieved to know Randolph hadn't been staying with the riffraff they had passed. Yet the thought that he was living in the dead actress's home, the same woman he was suspected of murdering, struck Evelyn as past the bounds of good sense. It was clear that Simon and Randolph did not share her sentiments.

The carriage came to a stop. Evelyn and Jack followed Simon up the front steps and into a dimly lit vestibule. Simon lit a lamp, and a low glow illuminated the area. Flocked wallpaper with a floral design and dainty furnishings revealed a woman's touch. But the place was dirty with rubbish littering the floor and dead flowers in a porcelain vase on a corner end table. Cobwebs already clung to the rungs of the banister. Had they not bothered to clean the place since Bess Whitfield had last lived here?

"Where's Randolph?" she asked.

"Upstairs."

They reached the top of the stairs, walked down a narrow hall until Simon halted by a closed door and turned to Evelyn. "I must warn you that Randolph has taken a large dose of laudanum for the pain."

She nodded. She didn't care if he was coherent, she wanted to see him. She reached for the doorknob.

Jack touched her sleeve. "Do you want me to go with you?"

"No, I must speak with Randolph privately."

"I'll be outside the door."

Evelyn slowly opened the door. The interior of the room was dimly lit, and it took her a moment to make out a figure on the high four-poster. She tiptoed closer, seeing Randolph lying still, a rose-patterned sheet that matched the curtains pulled up to his chin.

"Randolph," she whispered.

He jerked at the sound of her voice and opened his eyes. "Evelyn? Is that you?"

She rushed to his side. "Yes, I'm here. I came as soon as I heard."

He lowered the sheet to reveal the bandage around his chest. "I cracked some ribs. It hurts like the devil."

His slurred words and glassy, bloodshot eyes alarmed her. He was obviously still under the effects of the laudanum. Her eyes traveled his face, noticing the bruises around his left eye and swollen bottom lip. But the purplish, egg-sized knot on his temple was what truly alarmed her.

She placed her reticule on an end table next to a pitcher of water, and sat on the edge of the bed. Pushing his fair hair from his forehead, she was relieved that he was not hot to the touch. His injuries were severe enough, but a fever could kill him. She caressed his head, careful not to touch his injured temple.

"Tell me what happened," she said, her voice compassionate.

"Simon and I went to an alehouse. We drank too much and decided to try our hands at a game of cards. I was up ten pounds. I knew I should have walked away, but we are in need of money so I stayed. When I won the next hand, I couldn't believe my luck, but the brute across from me accused me of cheating. Me, cheating! Imagine that!" Randolph cried out, his gaze intense. "That's when the brawl started. Someone called the constable, and the Bow Street Runners showed up. One of them recognized me and a simple bar fight turned into a fight for my life. The Runner struck me in the temple with his truncheon. That's when Simon came to my aid and hit the Runner with a chair and stunned the man. We ran from the alehouse. Simon saved my life."

"What were you thinking going to the alehouse, Randolph? You are supposed to be in hiding."

Randolph flushed miserably. "You don't know what it's

like staying here. I couldn't stand to be banished any longer. I used to have a life. I used to have *you*."

Pain squeezed her heart at the desperation in his voice. "Oh, Randolph. After Bess Whitfield's murder is resolved, you will be able to go back to your previous life. Your Fellowship at Oxford, your research, your friends, all will return."

"And you, Evelyn? When this is all over, as you are so certain it will be, will you stay with me? Will all return to normal between us?" There was a tremor in his voice.

She swallowed. The moment was here. The time to tell him of her indiscretion, her illicit affair, to confess she was not the perfect woman for him and would not make a perfect wife. She opened her mouth, then closed it as a terrible tenseness seized her.

I have no choice. I must tell him!

Taking a deep breath, she tried again. "Randolph, I've been thinking. I'm not certain we should marry."

His brow creased, his eyes unfocused. "What are you saying?"

"I no longer wish to marry you. Please understand. It is not because of your cousin's murder and the resulting circumstances, but because I—"

He grasped her arm and pulled her close, his blue eyes flashing. Despite his injuries and drugged state, he was surprisingly strong. "Please, Evelyn. Help me. You aren't going to leave me, are you?"

Any words she would have spoken died on her lips. How could she continue to argue when he was injured, drugged, and desperate?

She smoothed back the sandy blond hair from his forehead with a shaky hand.

"Please don't upset yourself, Randolph. I'll take care of everything as usual."

She did not answer his question, yet he failed to notice and somehow her words comforted him. His viselike grip on her arm eased.

"Try to rest now, Randolph." She rose, refilled his water glass from the pitcher on the end table, and left the room.

Jack and Simon were waiting outside.

"Are you all right?" Jack asked.

She nodded woodenly.

"I'd like to speak with him," Jack said. "A while back I had asked for the shirt he wore the night of the murder."

"The bloody shirt? Why do you need it?" Simon asked.

"It may prove critical to my investigation," Jack said.

Seconds passed, then Simon nodded. "Randolph has it. You can see him if he is awake."

"He's awake, but he's exhausted and needs to rest," Evelyn said.

"I won't be long." Jack opened the bedroom door and slipped inside, leaving Evelyn alone with Simon.

Evelyn turned to Simon. "What were you thinking, going to the alehouse?" she asked, unable to keep the censure from her voice.

"Randolph was restless and in need of fresh air. I thought it best if I accompanied him rather than allow him to venture into Shoreditch alone. I couldn't have stopped him."

Evelyn sighed, feeling selfish for venting on Simon. Her nerves were raw, her emotions tangled by guilt and fear. It wasn't his fault that Randolph had gone to the alehouse. "You're a good friend, Simon. How can I ever repay you for saving his life?"

"He needs you, Evelyn. You will not abandon him?"

She was taken aback, not so much by the question itself, but by the intense look in Simon's eyes. Her instincts flared, and she knew her answer was important to Simon, as important as if Randolph had asked her himself.

"No, I will see him through his troubles," she said.

That much was true. She would do everything in her power to aid Randolph until he was free to return to his prior life. As for the fact that she would never marry him, that was not something she was prepared to admit to Simon.

Jack approached the four-poster with reserve. "It's Jack Harding, Mr. Sheldon."

Randolph's eyes flew open; he struggled to raise himself on his elbows.

"Don't sit up," Jack said.

"It's my broken ribs. They hurt like hell."

"Pain is good. It lets you know you're still alive."

"What good is alive when I'm hunted?"

"You're right about that much. Eventually Bow Street will look here."

Randolph flinched at Jack's tone. "You're my barrister. Can't you do something?"

"The best thing we can do is find the killer. Tell me, do you know of a diary Bess Whitfield had kept?"

"A diary?"

"Yes, her dresser at the theater had said she diligently wrote in a diary, including the names of her lovers. Do you know where she kept it?"

"I don't know of any diary."

"Think back, Mr. Sheldon. If we can find the diary, the killer's name might be written on the pages. We know of two of her last lovers, both of whom we are investigating, but there were others—a commoner and a mysterious benefactor. I want to question them both."

Randolph shrugged. "I can't help you."

"How about the shirt you wore the evening you found Bess's body?"

Randolph let out a long, audible breath. "I was going to burn the shirt. I kept it only because you had asked for it. It holds horrible memories for me."

"Where is it?"

"I stuffed it behind the wardrobe."

Jack strode to the wardrobe in the corner. Crouching down, he reached behind it, his fingers brushing the back panel and wall until he felt a soft fabric. He pulled the shirt free and shook out the wrinkled, stained cotton.

"How can that help?" Randolph asked.

"Leave that to me," Jack said.

The bedroom door opened and Jack came out, a white cotton shirt in his hand. The fabric was saturated in areas with Bess Whitfield's dried blood. Inky black. The sight of the old blood made Evelyn's stomach roil.

"Is that it?" Evelyn asked.

"We're fortunate he kept it."

She wanted to ask why, but Jack spoke. "Randolph needs to see a doctor. I know of one who lives close by. I'll send a note for him to visit."

"Can he be trusted?" Simon asked.

"Yes, the man is a former client. He owes me a favor."

Relief coursed through Evelyn. "Thank you. His ribs will heal, but I am worried about the hit to his head."

"My man will see to him. We need to leave, Evie," Jack said.

"I'll stay the night with him," Simon said. "Just in case he needs someone."

Evelyn held her raw emotions in check. She should be the one to care for Randolph, to see him through his time of need, not Simon.

"I'll be in touch soon," Jack said.

Jack took Evelyn's arm and escorted her down the stairs. He reached to open the door when she realized she had forgotten her reticule.

"I left my reticule in Randolph's room. I'll be a moment." She grasped her skirts and turned toward the stairs.

"Wait. I'll go with you," Jack said.

They made their way back up the stairs and down the hall when raised voices drew them to a halt.

Simon and Randolph were arguing.

Evelyn looked at Jack in surprise, but he held his finger over his lips and silenced her.

"He asked about the diary," Randolph said.

"What did you tell him?" Simon asked.

"That I had no idea what he was talking about."

"Why did you do that?"

"Bess never wanted the existence of her diary known. I'm the only one she confided in, the only one she could trust. I never betrayed her in life, and I won't betray her in death."

"Where is the diary now?" Simon asked.

"I don't know."

Evelyn looked at Jack. A swift shadow of fury swept across his face. Lips thinned with anger, eyes narrowed, he opened the door with such force it slammed against the wall. Chips of plaster flew across the room.

"What the hell is going on here?"

Evelyn rushed after Jack, and grasped his sleeve. "Wait, Jack—"

He brushed her aside and glared at Randolph. "You denied knowledge of any diary. You lied. I want answers. Now."

Randolph's eyes widened. "I swore to Bess that I would never tell a soul."

"I'm not any soul. I'm your barrister. The only person between you and Bow Street at the moment."

"You must understand."

"Where is it now?"

"I don't know. I've never seen it."

"You're lying."

"I'm not. I swear it!"

"Your swears mean nothing to me. You lied to me once about the existence of the diary. Let me tell you this: I have one rule and that is my clients must be truthful to me, no matter how damning the truth. You broke that rule. I'll no longer represent you. You should find another barrister and soon." Jack's voice was quiet, yet held an undertone of cold contempt.

Randolph sat stunned. Simon didn't move from the corner.

Jack strode from the room. "Let's go, Evie."

She snatched up her reticule and rushed to follow. He was down the stairs and holding the door open by the time she caught up with him.

"You can't be serious." She was out of breath, trying to keep her fragile control.

"Get in the carriage."

"Please don't do this."

"*I* didn't do anything. Randolph did."

Jack turned his back, strode from the town house, and proceeded to his carriage. His driver straightened to attention as his master approached. Jack held the door open, and she had no choice but to follow and step inside the carriage.

She waited for the door to close behind him and the carriage to start forward before whirling on him.

"Randolph did not murder Bess Whitfield. He's innocent and not capable of taking a human life. Surely you must know this by now."

"I know no such thing. He's lied once, and quite convincingly. You must face the possibility that he's capable of lying about the actress's murder and that he is guilty."

"I'm not a fool, Jack. As the daughter of a former criminal barrister, I know there are those capable of intentionally taking human life and skilled at lying to cover their deeds. But Randolph is not one of those people. I can't explain it other than to say I feel it to be true in my gut. He's innocent, I tell you. He may have lied about the existence of the diary, but that is entirely different from lying about overpowering and butchering a helpless woman."

"Then why would he lie about the diary? If he's truly innocent, wouldn't he want the diary found? The name of the killer may be written on the pages."

"He explained that his cousin never wanted the diary known, and he swore to her that he wouldn't speak of it."

Jack gave her a look that suggested she was acting as naïvely as the twelve-year-old girl she had been when they first met.

"Evie, it's one thing for a man to swear to keep a secret to a living woman, and quite another for him to uphold the vow after the woman has died and all that may be keeping his neck out of the hangman's noose is the truth."

"It may not make sense to you, but Randolph is a man of honor, and that is exactly something he would do."

Again, that look of disbelief crossed his face.

"Nothing I say will convince you he's innocent?"

He sat forward, his eyes green chips of stone. "I don't care about his 'innocence.' I have represented guilty men in the past and have ensured that they get a fair trial. What I cannot tolerate is a client lying to me. If I'm to assist him, I insist on the truth."

"You are abandoning him. He'll be tried and executed without you by his side."

"That's no longer my concern."

The coldness of his words shocked her. A sudden fury enveloped every fiber of her body. "You want a reason to abandon him."

"What?"

"You want Randolph out of the way because of our illicit affair. You said it yourself when we were in my father's kitchen. You said it would be difficult for you to represent Randolph when you are distracted by me. You went so far as to strongly suggest Randolph be represented by another barrister. I'm a distraction because of our . . . our lovemaking, and you were looking for an excuse to be rid of Randolph!"

He stilled. "Do you truly believe that?"

Her thoughts were jagged and painful. "I don't know what to believe anymore, Jack. I tried to confess my indiscretion to Randolph tonight. I would not have mentioned your name, but I would have admitted to the affair and that I had breached his trust."

"Why would you do that?"

Her misery was like a steel weight. "Because I cannot live with myself anymore. Because my heart is heavy and my conscience is screaming out for redemption. But when I saw Randolph lying in bed, so desperate, so needful of me, I couldn't bring myself to wound him more." She held her tears in check, her eyes imploring. "Don't you see? If Randolph is convicted and punished because of my behavior, I could not survive such guilt."

He touched her hand. "You're right, Evie."

"I am?"

"I was harsh, too quick to react. I'll continue to aid him, but henceforth, he must be honest with me."

"Yes, yes! I'll speak with him. Thank you, Jack."

She threw herself in his arms and kissed him on the cheek. When she went to move back, his arms stiffened around her, and he held her against him.

"Perhaps your insight is correct, Evie. Subconsciously I may have been looking for a way to walk away from Randolph's case. I find myself more and more captivated, wanting to touch you, wanting to make love to you again."

She gasped and pulled back. Despite everything, her emotions were as volatile as a volcano, and her pulse throbbed at his evocative words.

"I'm not going to marry Randolph. I told him tonight, but he was drugged, and I fear he refused to hear. I must tell him again the next time I see him."

"I know."

And then he swept her from her seat, settled her on his lap, and kissed her.

Chapter 32

Jack couldn't have stopped himself from kissing her. Her simmering emotions, her crippling guilt, had pierced his defensive armor. At the sight of her tears, invisible bands had squeezed his chest.

Evie, *his* Evie, was suffering. He wanted nothing more than to ease her pain and for Randolph and his burdensome troubles never to bother her again.

Selfish bastard. You want to touch her too. To bury yourself so deeply within her that she will never think of another man.

His heart had hammered at her admission. Her plans had changed, and she no longer intended to marry Randolph. She had finally realized that Randolph Sheldon would not make her the perfect husband.

But what did that mean?

For years Jack had told himself he was not the marrying kind. Hadn't he always wanted to focus on his career? A wife and family would undoubtedly take precious time away from his legal practice. And Evelyn was an earl's daughter. She should marry a titled member of the nobility. She could marry a duke—be a duchess.

Good Lord, what could a barrister offer in comparison to a duke?

But then Evelyn squirmed in his lap and desire ran through him with the vigor of a shot. None of his misgivings mattered, only the overwhelming need to possess and claim the woman in his arms. He was helpless against her allure, and he had to have a taste of her.

Just a taste.

His mouth covered hers. Whisper soft, his lips brushed back and forth while he caressed her cheek. Their time was limited, and he feared she would push him away, but she did not. Her arms wound around him instead, and she leaned close, her full breasts pressed against his chest.

He groaned. Tearing his mouth from hers, he reached up and pulled the pins from her hair. The heavy mass fell down onto her shoulders. Such golden, shimmering hair. Silken strands slipped through his fingers. He looked into her eyes, their color changing from blue to deep azure with desire. The knowledge that she wanted him thrilled him to his core.

He kissed the corner of her mouth, then licked a path down the slender curve of her neck to her throat and felt the wildly beating pulse beneath his tongue.

She moaned, and grasped fistfuls of his hair and pulled his mouth to hers. She kissed him back as if all her fears and pent-up longings melted into the kiss. He sucked on her lower lip, and she rubbed her bum cheeks against his arousal.

His control snapped. He kissed her, hungrily, greedily. His hands went to the fastenings on the back of her gown, and he had her breasts free and in his hands. His lips brushed her nipples, the rosy peaks growing to pebble hardness. He was like a man starved. With each stroke of his tongue, her cries of pleasure drove him on, and he didn't think he had ever been as painfully aroused. The interior of the coach grew hot and steamy, and sweat beaded on his brow.

"Evie, love, I need you."

"I know, Jack. Yesss."

He delved beneath her skirts and ran his hand up her slender calves and found the V of her drawers. His fingers grazed her heat and her incredible wetness. She cried out and clutched his shoulders.

Madness overtook him.

"Sweet Jesus, Evie. I need you now."

Pushing her skirts to her waist, they both struggled to remove her drawers in the cramped space of the carriage. He bumped an elbow, she a knee, and finally she was free of her drawers. He threw them on the opposite bench. He made quick work of his jacket and cravat, but it was Evelyn who reached for his shirt buttons.

"Let me."

He hissed as her fingers touched his heated flesh and her hair teased his nipples. The shirt gaped open, but neither of them bothered to remove it in their haste. Instead, she reached for the button of his trousers and freed his arousal.

She touched him then. Tentatively at first, then more fully, encircling him from base to head. Her eyes were large pools of appeal.

"Evie, I don't know how much I can stand."

"We cannot fully disrobe."

"We don't need to, love."

He moved her hand, guiding her, showing her how to stroke him while his fingers stroked her and her pleasure spiraled. He slid a finger inside her, then two, his thumb gliding over her slick flesh. He watched her eyes close, her back arch, and her breasts sway before him.

As her moan of ecstasy slipped through her lips, he buried his face in her neck and sucked her skin into his mouth in a raw act of possession. Then his body went rigid, and his hot seed spurt into her hands. Breathing heavily, he collapsed against her.

Evelyn held Jack to her breast, his breath warm against her skin. The steamy air inside the carriage was thick with the scent of their lovemaking. Her breathing was ragged. Her legs were numb below the knee where they were crammed against the side of the carriage, but she couldn't summon the energy to move.

Jack stroked her hair and caressed the length of her back. "Evie, love. There is a handkerchief in my coat pocket."

He reached across her to pull the handkerchief from his coat and cleansed her hands. Raising her chin with a finger, he kissed her briefly and looked in her eyes.

"I'm sorry for what you had to go through tonight, but I'm glad you are not marrying Randolph. You do not belong with him."

Her heart raced. Still perched on his lap, with his handsome face inches from hers, her emotions whirled and skidded. She dropped her lashes quickly to hide her raw emotions. She knew Jack was not saying she belonged with him. Only that she had made the right decision concerning Randolph.

"It was the right thing to do," she whispered.

"But difficult nonetheless."

Speaking to Randolph had been trying and stressful, but it had freed her mind. She had told him that she did not wish to marry him. Randolph had refused to comprehend, and she knew the laudanum was not entirely to blame, but he had no choice but to acknowledge what she had said when she spoke to him again, for her mind would not change.

And then there was Jack. Even though he had never mentioned words of love, when Jack had swept her into his arms, she had responded with a startling fierceness.

She was a grown woman, she told herself. Life was brief, happiness fleeting. She could make the decision to be with Jack intimately. No one need know what had transpired on the floor of his chambers or inside his carriage.

Jack would undoubtedly go on with his life, with his successful legal career, and she with her own existence.

She was a realist, a pragmatist, and would survive to take care of herself and mend her broken heart. And even if Jack was the marrying kind, she wouldn't want to spend the rest of her life with a man who couldn't commit his entire heart, couldn't love her as much as she loved him.

Such a fate would be a prison of its own making.

Chapter 33

It was still dark outside when the carriage arrived at Evelyn's home.

"Where do you intend to enter?" Jack asked.

"The back door into the kitchen," Evelyn said.

"I'll see you there."

"No! There's no need. I don't want to wake anyone."

"Don't worry, Evie. I can be stealthy when the need arises. Besides, I want to ensure your safety."

"Don't be ridiculous. Piccadilly is a good neighborhood." But even as the words left her mouth, a vivid memory of Hodges bleeding and unconscious in the vestibule and her father bound and gagged in his library sprang to her mind. By the expression on Jack's face, she knew he recalled it as well.

"Very well," she sighed. "You can walk me to the back door."

They alighted, and Jack gave instructions to his driver to wait at the corner. As they made their way around the side of the house, the light from the street gas lamps faded and failed to illuminate the gardens. A sliver of moon provided little light.

Evelyn grew thankful for Jack's presence. Landscape

familiar in daylight was completely different at night. The shadows of the trees and shrubbery were distorted, exaggerating their size. She had never ventured out this late alone and certainly not in the back of the house in the gardens. Whenever she returned past midnight from a ball or party, she had always had a chaperone, and Mrs. Smith had kept a lamp lit on an end table by the stairs.

Evelyn felt in her reticule for the key. On her fourth try, she managed to unlock the kitchen door.

She stepped inside, and Jack followed. The kitchen was black as pitch.

"Where's the tinderbox?" he asked.

"I don't need one. I know the layout of my own home and can find my way to the main stairs. You should leave now," she whispered.

"Not yet. I'll see you further."

She whirled around, trying to make out his features in the darkness. "Now you are acting ridiculous. I'm safe here. I don't want to wake the household, especially my father."

"It's too late for that, Evelyn," a deep male voice said.

At the sound of the all-too-familiar voice emanating from the bowels of the kitchen, Evelyn froze. Panic welled in her throat.

"I presume that's you, Lord Lyndale," Jack said.

There was the sound and flash of a match lighting, and then a glow of a lamp revealed her father in the far corner. He held the lamp high as he approached, his stride stiff and indignant. He halted at a worktable, set the lamp down, and crossed his arms in front of his chest.

Lyndale's face was pale and his brow creased. His clothing was terribly wrinkled, and Evelyn noted it was the same suit he had worn to dinner with the judges.

Tufts of sparse, gray hair stood on end as if he had repeatedly ran his fingers through it in agitation.

"I expected better of you both," Lyndale said.

Evelyn spoke up. "Mr. Harding is not to blame."

Lyndale's glare turned on his daughter. "You're probably correct. I've indulged you, Evelyn. I admit I was negligent during your childhood. I was immersed in my work, first at Lincoln's Inn and then later at the university. I allowed you unusual freedoms for a female and encouraged your intellectual pursuits. Looking back, I should have remarried and given you a mother figure and a proper Season."

"That was never important to me, Father."

"You went to see Randolph Sheldon, didn't you?"

The abrupt change in topic startled her.

"Barnes and Bathwell informed me that a Bow Street magistrate issued a warrant for Randolph's arrest for the murder of Bess Whitfield after he failed to appear for questioning. Christ, witnesses heard the victim's screams and then saw Randolph jump from her window! When were you going to tell me? Here I was thinking Randolph took a sabbatical to mourn the loss of his cousin, when he is wanted for her murder instead. Thank goodness the judges have no idea of your marital notions toward the man. They informed me solely because Randolph is my Fellow."

"Father, I planned on informing you. I'm sorry—".

Lyndale cut her off with a curt wave of his hand. He looked to Jack. "I wanted you on Randolph's side, in case he was questioned, but it has gone too far. Are you aware he is in hiding?"

"Yes, my lord."

"What else?"

"There was a scuffle with a Bow Street Runner and Randolph was injured."

"Injured?"

"Some broken ribs and a good hit on the head."

"Does he need a doctor?"

"I'm arranging for one to see him."

Lyndale sighed wearily. "We must be prepared for the possibility that Randolph is guilty."

Evelyn was startled. Jack had said the same thing. Yet her instincts still balked against the notion that Randolph was a murderer.

"I asked Jack to take me to Randolph. I needed to see his injuries firsthand," Evelyn said.

"How did you learn of the confrontation with Bow Street and that Randolph was hurt?" Lyndale asked.

Evelyn's eyes darted nervously back and forth between her father and Jack. How much to confess? "Simon Guthrie delivered the news. He accompanied us tonight."

Lyndale blinked in surprise. "Guthrie is involved in this as well? He is not my Fellow, but I wonder what his professor would think of this mess."

Her mind fluttered away in anxiety. "I would hope you would not speak of it and jeopardize Simon's Fellowship."

Lyndale straightened; the line of his mouth tightened a fraction more. "After learning everything that I have tonight, combined with your unforgivable behavior, I insist this madness cease and Randolph surrender when he is well enough to do so. I never wanted him for you."

She looked away, unable to meet her father's eyes. "I understand. But I still believe Jack should represent Randolph."

"Nothing will change in that regard. Go upstairs now, Evelyn. I need to have a word alone with Mr. Harding."

Grateful and relieved that her father's lecture ceased and that he agreed Jack could continue to aid Randolph, she fled the kitchen.

Jack watched Evelyn depart before approaching Lord Lyndale.

"I apologize for taking your daughter to see Mr. Sheldon tonight, my lord," Jack said.

Lyndale turned with a start and strode to a corner cabinet. "Would you like some whiskey, Jack?" he asked over his shoulder.

Jack eyed his mentor warily. He had just been caught alone with his daughter well past midnight without a chaperone in sight and the man was asking him if he wanted a whiskey?

"Whiskey sounds fine," Jack said.

Lyndale opened the cabinet doors and withdrew a bottle. "Good old Hodges always keeps a bottle in the kitchen." Reaching farther inside the cabinet, Lyndale pulled out two mismatched glasses, poured a good amount of amber-colored liquor in each, and handed a glass to Jack.

Jack took the whiskey and swallowed a goodly amount. Both men placed their glasses down on the worktable and leaned against it.

"You have feelings for Evelyn," Lyndale said. It was a statement, not a question.

Jack hesitated, careful with his words. "I would never hurt her."

"I didn't believe you would. Otherwise, I would insist you leave my house at once and never contact her again. Randolph Sheldon's defense be damned," Lyndale said, his tone chilly.

Ah, this is the scalding lecture I expected from an outraged father, Jack thought. "I understand, my lord."

Lyndale sighed. "I never wanted Randolph Sheldon for Evelyn. Intellectual and bookish, he makes the perfect Fellow for a professor who is too busy with research to give the proper amount of attention to the tedious task of grading student papers. But Randolph is weak at his core. He needs a mother figure, someone to tell him what to do and make all his decisions for him. He is a follower, never a leader."

Lyndale withdrew his spectacles and rubbed his eyes before continuing. "Evelyn's mother died when she was just a babe, and she learned how to run the household at an early age. I realize I am to blame. She is an invaluable help to me and organizes my library and my life so that I do not have to think of such trifle matters. But I want more for her than to marry and become another man's 'mother figure.' Evelyn is strength and responsibility and beauty and brains. I will not live forever. I long to see her find her match and be truly happy, impulsive, and free."

Jack swallowed. Evelyn had been just that, impulsive and free with her passion moments ago in his carriage. His pulse throbbed just thinking about it.

But he could never tell her father.

"I do believe she is reconsidering her feelings for Randolph," Jack said.

"Good. Randolph won't make her happy. He will only burden her with more responsibility and trouble."

Jack nodded. He had felt the same when he had initially taken on Randolph's case.

Lyndale reached for his whiskey. "I may be an old man, but I remember when I first met Evelyn's mother. Logic and reason, be damned." He took a sip and set the glass down. "It reminds me of the way you look at Evelyn."

"Pardon?"

"Evelyn was besotted by you when she was a girl. Oh, I had many pupils pass through my chambers at Lincoln's Inn. But she never went out of her way to memorize all those Latin and Greek verbs until you became my pupil. What I'm trying to say is I would encourage a match between you and my daughter."

Jack was stunned. Did the man suspect what had occurred in the carriage? Or was he like any other father who would insist Jack act honorably? After all, Evelyn had been alone with Jack in the middle of the night and there was no doubt her reputation had been compromised—whether her father knew to what extent or not. It didn't matter that no one saw them. In the eyes of society, Lyndale could legitimately claim that his daughter's reputation was tarnished and insist Jack do the right thing. But Lyndale was unusual with the rearing of his daughter.

"I know not to force anything on Evelyn. She can be quite stubborn. She also cares naught for society, rank, or the incessant gossips of the *ton*. But *you* can convince her."

"I don't know what to say, my lord."

"I'm guessing marriage was not in your immediate plans. You're ambitious and believe your legal career is your calling card, your purpose in life."

"Is that wrong?"

"The law is important to a barrister, but it will not comfort you when you are ill, support you when you lose a trial, or celebrate with you when a jury returns a verdict in your favor, and most important of all, it will not love you until you grow old. And if you are to be truly blessed, the law will not give you children to carry on your legacy."

Jack had never wanted those things. He could handle bad verdicts and victories. He couldn't handle emotional entanglements or the demands of a wife if he needed to work a long day.

"Think about what I said. If she has decided on her own that Randolph Sheldon is not the man she wants to marry, then I am pleased. I see the way you look at each other. I have every right to insist you marry my daughter after tonight. But like any barrister worth his salt, why force the issue when it can be amicably resolved? Besides, could you bear the thought of her marrying another?"

The killer walked the streets, careful to avoid the light of the gas lamps. He needed to release his roiling emotions before the pain took over.

Too late, he felt the tension build in his skull, like a pair of hammers pounding against each of his temples. He needed privacy, before his body revolted and he spewed his guts on the closest street corner.

Sweat poured down his forehead; his breathing came in ragged gasps. Spotting the first empty alley, he stumbled inside.

Two brick tenements lined each side of the alley. Windows covered thick with grease concealed the view inside. He hated this neighborhood with its dark, dank underworld of crime, prostitution, and poverty. If he had a choice, he would never step foot here.

At a slight sound at the end of the alley, his head snapped around. A pair of brilliant green eyes shone in the dimness. He picked up a stone and threw it at a black, stray cat. The feline hissed, then darted behind a discarded barrel.

He picked up another stone, heavier this time, and repeatedly tossed it in the air and caught it in his fist as he stalked forward.

"Pssss. Little pussy."

He spotted the tail from behind the barrel, then kicked the barrel aside and hurled the stone at the cat's head. Not even a whimper, and the feline dropped to the ground.

Ah, death was medicinal, and for several quick heartbeats his headache subsided.

Then the pounding returned.

Hell. The killing of an animal no longer comforted him.

Blinded by the pain's return, he sat on the overturned barrel and rested his throbbing head in his hands.

For the hundredth time that day, he thought of the diary. He needed it now more than ever before as his debts were mounting. Within those handwritten pages was power he could use to blackmail and control Bess Whitfield's influential lovers like dangling puppets on a string. A different thought crossed his mind.

His prize. The beautiful blonde.

He had believed her pure, loyal, virginal. But she, like every other woman he had known, had disappointed him.

She was no better than the actress.

Coy, seductive, teasing, selfish . . .

Bess Whitfield's punishment had not been planned, but had served to temporarily ease his torment.

Perhaps another killing would ease that torment again.

Chapter 34

"Lord Lyndale wants me to marry his daughter."

Three pairs of eyes turned to Jack. Anthony Stevens, James Devlin, and Brent Stone had met Jack at the local tavern for a Saturday afternoon gathering. After his second tankard of ale, Jack had found the courage to broach the subject that had been on his mind since leaving Lord Lyndale's home last evening.

Anthony spoke first. "What the devil do you mean Lyndale 'wants' you to marry?"

"He caught us returning home together alone late last evening," Jack said.

James Devlin slammed down his tankard. "Ha! I told you that you wouldn't be able to resist temptation. You should have crawled back to your former mistress like I advised."

Christ, I tried! Jack thought. But the fact that he could not maintain an erection with Molly Adler was not something he would ever admit to any of his colleagues.

"It's not what you think," Jack said. "We learned that Randolph Sheldon was injured in a bar brawl by a Bow Street Runner. Evelyn insisted she see him. I didn't want her traveling to Shoreditch alone in the middle of the night so I took her in my carriage. It was still dark by the time we returned to her home, and Lyndale was waiting for her."

Anthony smirked. "How could you be so foolish as to get caught, Jack?"

"You've compromised her reputation for certain. My only question is: Why hasn't Lyndale demanded you marry?" Devlin asked.

"Two reasons. He's aware of his daughter's stubborn nature, and Lyndale is not conventional by any standard. That's what makes him an exceptional teacher and mentor."

Devlin loosened his cravat with a forefinger. "I'm glad it's not me. I've dodged the marriage trap one too many times."

"Tell Lyndale to sod off," Anthony said. "I'd never allow anyone to force me to do anything, let alone shackle myself to an unwanted wife."

"Do you love her, Jack?" Brent spoke for the first time.

The question and the serious tone of Brent's voice caught Jack off guard. Anthony and Devlin's skepticism and sarcasm on the topic of marriage had been expected. But Jack could never predict what Brent Stone would say regarding the fair sex.

It was a fair question. Did he love Evelyn? He knew he cared deeply for her. He was fascinated by her quick wit and keen intelligence. He desired her. But love?

Was there even such an emotion or was it all fancy, concocted by women and weak men?

He'd never known Anthony, Devlin, or even Brent to fall victim to love. Jack was not a young fool. He was a seasoned barrister who had witnessed firsthand every human emotion—whether in the courtroom or in his chambers.

No plaintiff or defendant he had ever encountered had acted out of pure, unselfish love.

No, he was too jaded, too pragmatic, to believe in such nonsense.

But Lyndale's words haunted him. *Could you bear the thought of her marrying another?*

No. He couldn't. But that was jealousy and possessiveness, not love. He wanted far more from Evelyn than a barrister-client relationship. But why couldn't he have what he desired—Evelyn in his bed—and still maintain an emotional distance?

"I care for her. I respect and owe her father a great debt," Jack answered Brent.

"What of the man she was to marry?" Brent asked.

"She's had a change of heart regarding Randolph Sheldon," Jack said.

Devlin slapped Jack on the shoulder. "I was right. You bedded her. Anthony owes me ten pounds."

Anthony shrugged a massive shoulder. "I guess I do."

Jack glared at Devlin and Anthony. "You made a wager whether I would bed Evelyn Darlington?"

"I won," Devlin said with a mocking grin.

Jack should have expected Devlin and Anthony's antics, but it was Brent Stone's close regard and knowing eyes that were most disturbing.

"Does her father know you've been intimate with her?" Brent asked.

Jack shook his head. "I don't suspect he does. He believes only that we are working together. Even Lyndale would demand we marry if he knew."

"Will you propose to Lady Evelyn, then?" Brent asked.

"That's just it. Evelyn is not a typical woman. Her

father knows she won't jump at any proposal. He asked me to *convince* her."

The corner of Brent's mouth lifted. "You'll have to woo her."

Jack sighed and rubbed the back of his neck. "I will do Lyndale's bidding, but the ultimate decision will be up to the lady to decide."

The troublesome truth was the thought of wooing Evelyn excited Jack. Thankfully, she had come to her own conclusion that Randolph Sheldon did not suit her, and now with her father's blessing, Jack was free to pursue her.

"What about your career? A demanding wife?" Brent asked.

"I've decided marriage need not interfere if I keep my head. As for matters of the heart, that's utter nonsense."

Brent laughed. "It may not be as easy as you think, Jack."

Evelyn had immersed herself in the mundane household task of cataloging and organizing the linen closets alongside Mrs. Smith in a vain attempt to keep her thoughts from the previous evening. It wasn't until the afternoon, when they opened the last closet, that Evelyn succumbed to a fierce sense of urgency. She had to tell Randolph the truth without delay. She had tried last night, but he lay injured, drugged, and when he had clutched her hand and pled, she had lost her nerve.

She could no longer afford such weakness.

She hurried to her room and changed from a plain, serviceable dress to a walking dress of white muslin with a pink pelisse and rushed down to the dining room. Her father was already seated with a plate of stew before him, reading *The Times*.

Her heart lurched at the sight of him, thankful that he didn't berate her last night when she and Jack were caught sneaking into the kitchen. Any other parent would have thrust a pistol into Jack Harding's back and escorted him to the altar.

But then he was ignorant of her relationship with Jack. No doubt her father would behave differently if he knew.

"I'm going to see Randolph this afternoon," she announced.

Lyndale lowered the paper. She was struck by the deep circles under his eyes and his sallow complexion. He appeared to have aged ten years overnight. Guilt seared her breast that his already-fragile health may have suffered due to her careless behavior.

"Why?" His steady gaze bore into her.

"I attempted to tell Randolph that I no longer wish to marry him, but he had been dosed with laudanum, and I fear he misunderstood."

"Does your change of heart regarding Randolph have anything to do with Mr. Harding?"

Evelyn worked hard to maintain a blank expression. Despite his health and busy schedule at the university, Lyndale still had moments of great perceptiveness. She reminded herself that years ago he had been a distinguished trial barrister who was skilled at obtaining confessions from adverse witnesses on cross-examination.

She dare not confess her illicit affair with Jack.

"I, ah. I'd rather not say, Father."

"Come close, Evelyn."

She obliged and took the seat next to his.

He reached out to clasp her hand. "Evelyn, I'm getting

old, and I want nothing more than to see you happy. I have regrets in my life, but marrying your mother was never one of them. You look so much like her. You have her golden beauty and rare intelligence. I'm thankful that you have come to your own conclusion regarding Randolph, but I also know you have been fond of Jack Harding since you were a child."

Sweet Lord, did he know she had been with Jack? She would die of humiliation. Schooling her expression was much more difficult now, and she stirred uneasily in her chair.

"Go see Randolph. Tell him it's over between you, but have Jack Harding take you *and* have Janet accompany you as a proper chaperone."

She leaned forward and kissed him on his cheek. "Thank you for understanding."

Lyndale squeezed her hand. "If Randolph's well enough to travel, Jack must convince him to turn himself in to Bow Street."

Evelyn opened the bedroom door with foreboding. Her eyes immediately went to the four-poster.

A portly middle-aged man was bent over the bed, stethoscope in hand, listening to Randolph's breathing.

The doctor straightened as she approached and pushed his spectacles farther up the bridge of his nose. "I'm Dr. Astor. Mr. Harding sent me."

"Yes, Doctor. Thank you for coming. How is Mr. Sheldon?"

"Three cracked ribs and a mild concussion. He should cease taking the laudanum. There can be dangerous side effects from the drug after trauma to the head."

She nodded, and couldn't help but wonder what favor the respectable-looking doctor owed Jack to convince him to attend a murder suspect.

"Mr. Harding is waiting for you downstairs," she said.

The doctor left and the door closed behind him.

Evelyn walked to the side of the bed. Randolph's pupils were back to normal size, his face a healthy color. She sighed, relieved he was no longer drugged.

Randolph's gaze roved and appraised her, and he reached for her hand. "Evelyn, what would I do without you?"

A cold knot formed inside her, and she paused to catch her breath. "I'm glad you are feeling better, but there is something I must tell you. I no longer wish to marry."

"So last night wasn't a nightmare! You meant what you said. Is it because I'm accused of Bess Whitfield's murder?"

"No. I've betrayed our trust. I've had an affair."

"An affair! With who?" He released her hand and struggled to sit.

"It doesn't matter now, Randolph. What matters is you deserve better. I'm certain you will meet another woman someday. Despite everything, I won't abandon you, and will do everything in my power to see you through your troubles. My dearest hope is that we can remain friends."

"Friends! After you behaved like a strumpet?"

He threw the words at her like stones, and she flinched as if he had struck her.

"I trust Mr. Harding will still act as my barrister," Randolph said.

"Yes, yes."

"Then tell him that I'm ready to surrender to the authorities. Leave now, Evelyn."

"Randolph." She reached out, tears in her eyes, but he pulled away.

"Leave, please!"

By the time Evelyn came down the stairs, the doctor had departed and Jack was pacing back and forth on the floral-patterned carpet. Simon was nowhere to be seen, and Janet was waiting in the carriage.

"I spoke with Dr. Astor. Randolph suffered a concussion," she told Jack.

"I know. I spoke to the doctor on his way out. He assured me Randolph will be fine and is able to travel," Jack said. "Tell me what else happened."

"I broke off our engagement."

"Evie, love, you were never officially engaged. There was no reading of the banns and you never had Lord Lyndale's consent."

"Don't mock me, Jack."

"I apologize. It was not my intention to do so. What did you tell Randolph?"

"That my feelings for him have changed. That I wish to maintain our friendship."

"And?"

"That I had an indiscretion. I never named you, of course. But he spurned my friendship nonetheless. I doubt he'll ever speak to me again."

"He may not have whether or not you confessed to an affair. I've never known of a man and woman to remain close friends after one has broken off a relationship and the other continues to have romantic feelings."

"Randolph agreed to surrender to the authorities, and he wants you by his side as his barrister."

Jack nodded. "I've contacted a Bow Street constable

who is a friend and owes me a favor. He will return with Randolph and hold him in custody for as long as he possibly can before escorting him to Newgate so that we can finish our investigation. He cannot hold him for too long as Randolph's trial will have to start. But he has connections and will ensure Randolph is treated well in prison."

"Does everyone owe you a favor?"

He grinned. "It comes with the profession."

"I doubt that, Jack. What will we do if we can't find the killer?"

"We're close, Evie. Even if we never find the blasted diary, I can argue that others, such as Newland and Hamilton, had more motive than Randolph. In any case, Randolph cannot stay in hiding forever. He has to surrender."

"But doesn't he appear guilty by running and hiding from the authorities?"

"Yes, but I will do everything in my power to explain his actions. Meanwhile we must look into all our leads." He took her arm and steered her toward the door. "Come, Evie. We need to leave. I don't want you present when the constable arrives."

They stepped outside, and sunlight momentarily blinded her. The street appeared completely different in the daylight hours. Jack's carriage and driver waited; the matching team of bays stood obediently, their sleek muscles gleaming beneath the late-afternoon sun.

Evelyn looked up at Jack. His dark, curling hair, the elegant ridge of his cheekbones and his green-flecked eyes, combined with his firm command and competence, made her instinctive response to him so powerful. She could no longer deny that the warm friendship she felt for Randolph had never compared to the sizzling passion that she experienced every time she set eyes on Jack.

I love him. And when this is all over, he will leave.

"Thank you," she murmured.

"For what?"

"For arranging for Dr. Astor to see Randolph, for the constable to bring him in, and most of all, for not abandoning Randolph despite our . . . our indiscretion."

The smile in his eyes contained a sensuous flame. "We need to speak of the future, but now is not the time and place."

Chapter 35

"Lady Georgina Stanford waits in the parlor," Mrs. Smith said.

Evelyn had just returned from Shoreditch when the housekeeper informed her of Georgina's surprise visit.

"Is anything amiss?" she asked Mrs. Smith.

"I don't believe so. Lady Georgina said you were expecting her."

Expecting her? Evelyn couldn't recall sending a note. The last time she had seen Georgina was outside a Bond Street tea shop. Georgina had invited Evelyn to her country home and Evelyn had declined, unable to stomach the thought of sleeping under the same roof as Georgina's father, Viscount Hamilton.

Evelyn handed her cloak to Hodges. "Please bring tea," she instructed Mrs. Smith, and then made her way to the parlor.

Georgina sat in a chair gazing out the window. She spun around when Evelyn entered.

"Thank goodness!" Georgina cried as she rushed to meet Evelyn and embraced her. Her thick chestnut hair was pulled back, revealing a pale face and hazel eyes. Evelyn always knew Georgina as quick to smile, but today her expression could only be described as one of anxiety and apprehension.

"Georgina, what has happened?" Evelyn asked.

"You will think me terribly weak after I tell you."

"Nonsense." Evelyn guided Georgina to a settee and she sat beside her. "Tell me everything."

"I fear I must marry Lucas Crawford and quickly."

"What are you talking about? I thought you decided against marrying Lucas?"

"There's been an unfortunate change of circumstances. I've discovered my family is in debt and sorely in need of money," Georgina said.

"Money? But your father is Maxwell Stanford, Viscount Hamilton. Surely your family must have resources."

"My father has been behaving strangely for quite some time. My mother and I have only recently discovered he has been zealously gambling. Our country estate in Somersetshire, the Berkeley Square mansion, and our other properties have all been encumbered. Mother didn't realize the full extent of the damage until her diamond necklace, an heirloom from her great-aunt, was missing. That's when my father confessed he sold it to pay off one of his debts. He even admitted to taking the jewels from her other pieces and having the stones replaced with paste."

"I'm so sorry, Georgina. But what does this have to do with you marrying Lucas?"

"Lucas Crawford is the son of the Earl of Haverston. His family has a fortune. Mama believes the way out of our predicament is for me to marry Lucas before he learns of our financial troubles."

"Oh, dear," Evelyn said.

Unspoken pain was alive and glowing in Georgina's eyes. "I apologize for burdening you and stopping by without notice, but I desperately need a friend to talk to, and my suffragist acquaintances would be horrified. The idea of marrying for money, of bartering my body, is not a novel notion among the *ton,* but they would judge me for my weakness nonetheless."

There was a soft knock on the door, and Mrs. Smith entered with a tea tray. Evelyn waited until the maid departed before embracing Georgina.

"Oh, darling. There is nothing wrong with saving your family. What your father has done is wrong, not the sacrifice you are prepared to make to save your family. Do you know what started Hamilton's bout of gambling?"

"He's had mistresses for years. I've known this since I was a child. My mother knew as well, although she has never mentioned it to me or led Father to believe that she has been aware of his lovers. I have since come to the conclusion that his unfaithfulness was acceptable to her so long as he kept it private. But his last lover had irked her like none of the others."

Evelyn held her breath. "Who was she?"

Georgina looked down at her hands. "Her name was Bess Whitfield."

Evelyn kept her features deceptively composed. "Bess Whitfield? The famous, murdered actress?"

"Yes. It was no secret that his mistress had numerous lovers. I think my father grew jealous and there was an incident when gossip came back to my mother. Mother's status in the *ton* means everything to her, and she refused to tolerate the slightest humiliation. My parents had a terrible row over Bess Whitfield one night. I couldn't help but overhear."

"What did your father do?"

"After she was murdered, Father started acting strangely. He always enjoyed gambling and his clubs, but never before had he been reckless with his spending habits. After her death, he changed. His moods have been unpredictable, dark. He's been drinking too much. Some nights I was afraid to approach him."

"Do you believe he would harm you or your mother?"

Evelyn knew she was asking an inappropriate question, but if there existed any chance Georgina or Viscountess Hamilton were in danger, she would reveal the truth to her friend. Any man desperate enough to pry up floorboards and search for Bess Whitfield's diary after her death could be capable of violence.

Evelyn often wondered what Viscount Hamilton would have done had he caught them fleeing Bess's home that fateful day.

Had he been armed? Would he have shot them?

Georgina shook her head. "No, I don't fear physical harm from my father, only his temper. When he is roused, he rants and yells at any unfortunate soul that crosses his path."

"What will you do about Lucas Crawford?"

"I've resigned myself to marriage. At least he's young and not unattractive. I've never found him repulsive or distasteful, but I thought to choose my own spouse."

"How does he feel?"

"I do believe he's infatuated with me. He sends flowers daily and notes requesting strolls in Hyde Park."

Georgina was beautiful and poised, and Evelyn could understand why Lucas was drawn to her. "Perhaps you should accept his invitation and get to know each other. Hyde Park is stunning this time of year."

"I shall take your advice," Georgina said.

Evelyn leaned close, her eyes piercing the distance between them. "But should you find you still do not wish to marry Lucas after a time, then please return to me. My mother left me a small inheritance and I will give you every last shilling. It will not be enough to cover all the debts, but I'm certain my father would offer his assistance. You could travel to France with your mother."

A tear rolled down Georgina's cheek. "I could never take your money, but you are a true friend for offering."

A note arrived the following morning.

Evie,
  Please come to my home around one o'clock. I have made a vital discovery. And do bring your maid as chaperone.

Just like Jack, he hadn't bothered to sign the note. Evelyn and Janet took a carriage to Jack's home on St. James Street—a prestigious address for a wealthy bachelor's home. They passed the popular male establishments, Brooks's, Boodle's, and White's. Despite the early-afternoon hour, two well-dressed men stumbled out of Boodle's. One slapped the other heartily on the back, and they both rocked with the laughter of drunken revelers.

The driver lowered the step and they alighted. She had never seen Jack's home before, and she was full of curiosity about his living arrangements. Lifting her skirts, she made her way to his town house, her inquisitiveness growing with each step.

They reached the porch and Evelyn lifted the heavy brass knocker.

The door swung open, and a butler with a solemn expression looked down at them.

"Lady Evelyn Darlington to see Mr. Harding."

The butler's expression changed, and he nodded in welcome. "He's been expecting you, my lady." He opened the door wide and stepped aside. "I will inform Mr. Harding at once."

Evelyn and Janet stepped inside and handed their cloaks to the butler. Evelyn's eyes were drawn to the beautiful Italian marble in the vestibule. They followed the butler to the formal drawing room where he asked them to wait, and Evelyn noted the fine rosewood furniture and Brussels carpet. Several paintings from sporting artists George Stubbs and John Wootton hung on the walls and displayed the majestic lines of thoroughbred horses. It was clear that Jack Harding was quite successful in his chosen profession, and he lived in elegant luxury.

Moments later the door opened and Jack strode into the room. He looked strikingly handsome with an exquisitely tailored dark blue jacket and trousers. His eyes, normally brilliantly intelligent, held a gleam of eagerness that she found compelling and exciting.

"Good afternoon, ladies," Jack said.

Evelyn stood. "Your note mentioned a discovery. What is it, Jack?"

"If you would but follow me, I will explain." Jack looked at Janet. "Perhaps your maid would prefer some refreshment here while we speak?"

It was a statement more than a question. Janet blinked nervously and looked to Evelyn.

"Yes, Janet, do stay here. Legal nuances would bore you, and we will be back shortly."

Evelyn followed Jack from the room. She assumed he would take her to his library, but they passed room after room—a conservatory, the library, a billiard room—until they stood in the doorway of the kitchen. It was after nuncheon, and no servants were present.

"Where are we going?"

He grinned. "Trust me. This is something you want to see."

She followed him into the kitchen, and he stopped before a long worktable and a water pump.

He studied her thoughtfully for a moment. "Before I begin, I want to apologize for not believing you and not trusting your instinct."

"Whatever are you talking about?"

"Randolph's innocence."

Her head swirled with doubts. What was he up to?

Jack reached for a large sponge, roughly a foot square, and a butcher's knife and placed them on the table. Opening a cupboard, he retrieved a jar containing a thick, crimson liquid.

"What on earth is that?"

"Pig's blood from the butcher. I experimented early this morning and sent you the note afterward."

"What experiment?"

"Watch and see."

Jack removed his jacket, and his white cotton shirt molded to his broad shoulders. She had no idea what he was about to do, but her pulse quickened.

He opened the jar and poured the pig's blood over the sponge. She wrinkled her nose at the metallic scent as it was quickly absorbed by the once-dry sponge.

"Step back, Evie. I don't want to ruin your gown."

Curious and bewildered, she obliged.

Jack picked up the long blade and repeatedly and viciously stabbed the sponge. Blood splattered everywhere— over the worktable, the water pump, the walls, his face and hands, and most of all, his shirt, turning the white fabric into a gory display.

She stood there, blank and amazed.

Jack threw down the knife and turned to her, eagerness flashing in his eyes. "What did I just prove?"

At once she knew what he was after. "The bloody shirt!" she cried out.

He jerked his head to the corner of the kitchen. "Randolph's shirt is lying on the second table. Would you be kind enough to retrieve it?"

She rushed to the corner, retrieved the shirt, and held it up for their view. Bess Whitfield's blood stained the white cotton of the entire right sleeve and underarm a deep maroon. There was no blood splatter. The opposite sleeve and most of the shirtfront remained white.

"Randolph claimed he arrived after Bess already lay dead. He held her in his arms. If he was the true killer, this shirt would be covered with blood splatter," she said.

Jack pulled a handkerchief from his pocket and wiped the blood from his face and hands. "Yes, Evie. This shirt is a pivotal piece of evidence that can exonerate Randolph. Juries love courtroom dramatics."

"Will it help the damning fact that Randolph fled the murder scene and later went into hiding?"

"I don't have to prove *who* killed Bess Whitfield; I only have to show that Randolph did *not*. This," he said, pointing to Randolph's shirt, "will help."

She wanted to throw herself into his arms, to thank him for his craftiness and brilliance. He must have sensed her intention for he held out a hand. "As much as I'd love to hold you, my dear, I don't advise it right now."

She laughed. "I'm so relieved and excited I don't care!"

"I need to wash and change. Will you wait for me?"

"Yes."

She would follow him to the ends of the earth. He had singlehandedly provided the greatest defense for Randolph, and most importantly, Jack believed her. Her instincts regarding Randolph's guilt had been correct.

"Please wait in the library. There's more we need to discuss and I prefer privacy without your maid's presence."

Chapter 36

Jack escorted her to the library before leaving to change. Evelyn strolled the perimeter of the well-appointed room, noting its rich mahogany bookshelves lined with legal volumes, statutes, and priceless rare books. A massive desk with stacks of papers beneath polished stone paperweights was situated before a large bay window. She breathed in the familiar scents of leather-bound volumes and old books.

It was a masculine room, clearly designed as his working office away from chambers, and she pictured Jack bent over the desk in deep concentration.

She sighed and sat in one of the two hammerhead leather chairs arranged before a stone fireplace.

Less than fifteen minutes later, there was a knock on the door and Jack entered. He had washed and changed to another white shirt with lace cuffs. He wore black Hessians and buckskin trousers that hugged his muscular legs. He hadn't bothered with a cravat or jacket, and the top button of his shirt was undone, revealing the corded muscles of his bronzed throat.

He sat in the chair beside her and crossed his long legs

before him. He appeared quite serious and she wondered what other legal conclusions he had in mind.

"Your father wants us to marry," he said.

"What?" Her mind skidded to a halt. Whatever she had expected him to say, it was not *that*.

"After much consideration, I do believe it is the proper course of action."

"You do?"

"Yes, although Lord Lyndale is unaware of the extent of our relations, my behavior warrants honorable intentions."

"Your behavior?"

"Yes, that and the fact that we were caught alone by your father sneaking into his home well past midnight."

She straightened in her seat. "I had hoped to marry for love, not because my father made a decision."

"We're too old to subscribe to such nonsense," he said, his tone arrogantly dismissive.

Her mood veered sharply from disbelief to anger. "Too old? You may be past thirty, sir, but I am not."

"I apologize. It is the expedient thing to do."

"Expedient?" Her temper rose hotter and hotter.

"Are you going to keep repeating everything I say?"

"Since it is completely ludicrous, then yes."

"Evie, I don't understand. You said yourself that you no longer wish to marry Randolph. I know you admired me as a girl, and you are now free to marry with your father's blessing."

She stood. "You are a jackanapes, Jack Harding."

He rose, his brow furrowed. "What is wrong with you? Do you require me to go down on one knee?"

"I told you what I require. I expect any future husband to love me," she said, bristling with indignation.

Please tell me you love me like I have loved you forever. The bitter thought crossed her mind that as a young girl, she would have jumped up and down with joy at the thought of Jack Harding proposing marriage.

But this was different. Jack was proposing out of obligation because his mentor had advised him to do so. Because he believed it honorable to do so.

He stepped close and trailed his finger down her cheek to her lower lip. Despite her anger, she shivered at his touch.

His eyes smoldered. "We desire each other. That's much more than most couples ever hope to achieve."

Pain squeezed her heart, and she stepped away. "Lust and obligation are not enough for me. The answer is no, Jack."

Early Monday morning, Jack drove his curricle to the Bow Street magistrate's office. He was in a foul mood and not fit company to meet with other clients at chambers.

Evelyn's refusal of his marriage proposal had infuriated and aroused him.

She had stood before him, her blue eyes flashing, her magnificent breasts heaving in indignation, her voice firm and final. He had to hold himself back from jerking her into his arms and kissing her senseless. He had fantasized of throwing her on his desk, spreading her golden hair across the surface, lifting her skirts, and mounting her right then and there. He may have done just that if her uptight chaperone hadn't been sipping tea two doors down.

He had been certain that she would have preferred a logical proposal. After all, she prized reason above all else.

But she had surprised him.

She wanted love. What had possessed her?

As if intellectual compatibility and hot lust weren't more than sufficient grounds for a healthy marriage. Many couples lacked the slightest spark, not to mention mental communion.

He clenched his jaw. He should have told her he loved her. He was an accomplished actor in the courtroom. He had only to step before a jury and the persuasive words flowed freely from his lips. But the truth was he had no intention of permitting himself to fall further under Evelyn's spell. It was disturbing enough that she was never far from his thoughts.

He needed to maintain his wits, to keep a safe emotional distance and retain the sharp focus he'd always had in the courtroom. He refused to beg or compose sonnets or write lovesick poetry. She'd have to accept what he offered.

Jack stopped the curricle at the corner and jumped down.

A strong gust of wind blew between the buildings and Jack tightened his grip on the papers in his hand. Distracted by the task, he collided into a tall man leaving the magistrate's office.

"Jack!"

Jack looked up into Brent Stone's cobalt eyes.

Damn. Brent was the last person he wanted to run into.

"Jack, what are you doing here?" Brent asked.

"I'm here to see a client. Why are you here? You handle letters patent, a far cry from criminal matters."

"I'm handling a *pro se* case. Petty thief."

Ah, yes. Brent's volunteer matters for the London Legal Aid Society. Brent should be canonized, yet there was something sinister about Brent Stone that Jack never could put his finger on.

There was more to the man than the handsome, upstanding, and respectable barrister. No one in chambers knew his past and whenever the subject arose, Brent clammed up. But his inquisitiveness, his shrewdness, told more of a story than that of a barrister ensconced in chambers drafting patent applications all day long.

Jack's voice was heavy with sarcasm. "Don't waste too much time on the fellow. Petty theft makes for a hard defense before a jury."

He attempted to pass by, but Brent clasped a heavy hand on his shoulder. Piercing blue eyes probed his soul.

"Why are you in such a foul mood? Pray tell me, does it have anything to do with Lady Evelyn?"

"Sod off, Brent."

Brent's lips twisted wryly. "So the smooth-talking Jack Harding failed to charm a woman?"

"She'll only marry for love."

"Don't be a fool, Jack. A woman like Evelyn Darlington only comes once in a man's life. She's the perfect match for you."

Jack shoved off Brent's hand. "What would you know of women or love? You're celibate, for Christ's sake."

Brent stilled. "I was married once."

Jack was momentarily speechless in surprise. "No one knew."

"It was years ago. She died. It was my fault."

Brent delivered the words matter-of-factly, but Jack was not fooled. There was anguish there, just beneath the surface, and for the first time Jack understood why Brent Stone preferred to bury himself in his boring patents day after day.

"I'm sorry," Jack said, at a loss for further words.

"I'd appreciate if you kept this in confidence. There's no sense Stevens or Devlin should learn of my past."

Jack nodded. "Why tell me, man?"

Brent's earnest eyes sought his. "Because life is too short. Tell her you love her, Jack."

After Brent departed the magistrate's office, Jack went in search of the constable who had returned Randolph to London.

Floyd Birmingham was an ordinary-looking man of medium height and build with brown eyes and dishwater brown hair. His unmemorable appearance aided him as a constable who walked the streets at night.

Jack found Floyd in the first office down the hall.

"How's Randolph Sheldon faring?" Jack asked him.

"His health has improved even though he's in Newgate awaiting trial. I'm glad you're here, Mr. Harding. If there are any witnesses who can testify as to his whereabouts the day of Bess Whitfield's death, then find them quickly. The magistrate is under public pressure for a conviction and he is pushing for a speedy trial."

Jack understood. After the grand jury indictment, a trial could begin immediately thereafter. Bess Whitfield had been a highly popular actress and the public would demand quick justice. It was one of the reasons Jack had not protested when Randolph had gone into hiding. Jack knew it would take time to investigate Bess's murder and build Randolph a successful defense.

"Do what you can to look after him. He's a university student and unaccustomed to harsh living," Jack said.

"He's lucky he has you on his side, Mr. Harding," Floyd said. "You know I owe you, and I'll do what I can for the man."

Jack had represented Floyd's brother, Brian Birmingham, also known as Burn Birmingham on the streets for his fascination with starting fires. Burn had set fire to a brothel two years ago, which had resulted in the destruction of the building. All six prostitutes had escaped with their lives, but a patron that had died in the fire was one of the six Commissioners of the Treasury.

The magistrate had only been slightly concerned by the survival of the women or the property loss, but the death of the public official had been a different issue. It did not matter that the commissioner had been a regular abuser of the women. Swift justice had been demanded by the Crown's prosecution, and Jack had managed to obtain a prison sentence for Burn rather than the death sentence.

In short, Jack had saved the man's life, and Floyd Birmingham was eternally grateful.

Jack shook Floyd's hand. "I appreciate your assistance."

Just then, the front doors of the entrance slammed against the wall and fierce shouting followed. Jack and Floyd rushed toward the clamor.

Two constables dragged a man between them. The prisoner violently struggled, thrashing his limbs from side to side. The sounds of his shoes scraping on the hardwood floor reverberated through the sparsely furnished entry. Strands of dirty hair hung limply over his face, and he cursed incoherently.

"Who is he?" Jack asked.

At the sound of Jack's voice, the man's head whipped upward; his hair parted to reveal his face.

Shock flew through Jack at the sight of the Earl of Newland.

Newland smelled of earth and perspiration. He was covered in dirt, with smudges on his face, hands, clothing and even his hair. His spectacles were twisted and askew on his face. His clothing was disheveled, his dark eyes fevered and wild.

"What's going on here?" Floyd asked the two constables restraining the earl.

The men came to a stop, yanking Newland upright between them.

"We caught this bugger digging up a grave in broad daylight. If he's a grave digger, then he's crazed if you ask me," said the constable on Newland's right.

"That's no grave digger. He's Earl Newland," Jack said.

The constables exchanged looks of disbelief.

"An earl? Are you certain?" Floyd asked.

Jack stepped close and looked Newland in the eye. "Tell them, my lord. Tell them who you are."

"Aye, I'm a bloody earl," Newland hissed.

"Whose grave was he digging?" Jack asked.

"Bess Whitfield, the murdered actress. Dead for a while now. The stench would have been terrible," the short constable said.

Jack grasped Newland's shoulder. "Why? What was Bess Whitfield to you?"

Newland's eyes narrowed to slits. "She was to be my wife. I sought to move her to my family plot so that after I die we can be buried together."

Jack recalled the old man had advanced consumption. And Bess Whitfield had told this rich, old earl she would marry him?

It made sense. She knew he was dying. Why not marry, produce an heir, and take his fortune? The likelihood was that Newland was Bess Whitfield's longtime lover and benefactor.

Jack grasped Newland's shirtfront. "Did you kill her?"

Newland's eyes flashed hatred. "I recognize you. You were at the cemetery. You and your woman. Pretty little blond thing. What would you do if she was murdered?"

Violence erupted inside Jack, and he suppressed the urge to smash Newland's dirty face with his fist.

Jack shook the man by his shirt. "Did you kill her?"

"No! I loved her!"

The denial was delivered with such vehemence, that either Newland was an excellent actor or he was telling the truth. Jack released his shirt and stepped back.

The two constables ushered Newland out of sight.

"He's dying," Jack told Floyd. "What are you going to do with a peer of the realm?"

"We'll contact his family."

"He has none. His heir's in India."

"Then it's time the heir returned to England. Newland can be committed in his own home. Do you think he murdered Bess Whitfield?"

Jack hesitated. "Any man that tries to dig up a grave in the middle of the day is obviously insane. But I don't think he killed his obsession."

Chapter 37

Evelyn was sipping a glass of punch at a ball hosted by Lady Jersey when she learned of Earl Newland's run-in with the constables. The gossipmongers were wound up and excited, and the stories grew more and more outrageous as the evening progressed.

Evelyn immediately wanted to depart, but Lady Jersey was one of the powerful patronesses of Almack's. Evelyn had always dreaded the Wednesday night dance and supper at the private club on King Street. She had never wished to exhibit herself like all the young debutantes on the marriage mart, but she also did not want to cause trouble for herself or her father. So she dutifully thanked Lady Jersey and made her excuses, claiming a pounding headache.

As soon as her carriage was brought around, Evelyn instructed her driver to take her to St. James Street. It was close to midnight, and she did not bother to return home to summon Janet.

This was not the type of visit in which a chaperone was desired.

She stepped down from the carriage, pulled the hood of her cloak tightly about her face, and headed for the front steps. Lifting the brass knocker, she hoped Jack was home.

The butler opened the door. If he was surprised to see an unchaperoned lady of quality on his master's steps in the middle of the night, his expression remained impassive.

"Lady Evelyn Darlington. I shall summon Mr. Harding at once."

Relieved Jack was home, she stepped inside.

Just then Jack strode around the corner, a sheath of papers in his hand. With his shirtsleeves rolled up to his forearms, it was obvious that he was working late at home. He stopped short when he spotted her and grinned.

"Evie, to what do I owe this pleasure? Is anything amiss?"

"Please do not be alarmed. I'm fine, but may we speak in private?"

"Of course. No one will disturb us in my library office."

She gave her cloak to the butler, and followed Jack into the library. It was a cool June evening, and a low fire glowed in the fireplace. He closed the door behind him and motioned for her to sit, but she shook her head.

His gaze lazily roved her blue satin gown and the blond curls that brushed her bare shoulders. "You look lovely this evening, Evie. Please tell me you have had a change of heart regarding my proposal."

There was a tingling in the pit of her stomach at his heated gaze. "I was at Lady Jersey's ball tonight and heard the most fascinating tale. Gossip travels like wildfire among the *ton*."

"I take it you learned about Earl Newland's odd behavior digging up Bess Whitfield's grave in plain sight."

"Yes. How did you know?"

"I was at the Bow Street magistrate's office when Newland was dragged in like a dirty rat between two constables."

"Do you realize what this means?"

"Yes, yes. It's all helpful."

"Do you believe Newland killed her?"

"He denies it. He insists they were to marry. I believe Newland was Bess Whitfield's longtime lover and benefactor. She would have gained his wealth and influence, and he in turn would have had her in his bed. It would have been a mutually satisfactory affair."

"But do you believe the earl innocent?"

Jack shrugged. "He was very convincing, but who knows for certain? Without the diary, we're back to the beginning. Earl Newland and Viscount Hamilton are our prime suspects."

"Georgina confided in me that her father, Viscount Hamilton, had gambled away a fortune after Bess's death. His behavior has altered as well. He's moody and unstable."

Jack's eyebrow rose a fraction. "When did you learn this of Hamilton?"

"Georgina came to visit me the other day. I forgot to mention it because of my excitement with the experiment you had conducted on the shirt, and then later when you . . . when you—"

"When I offered marriage?" he asked.

At her silence, he strode to his desk and opened the top drawer. Withdrawing a small square box, he walked to stand before her. He dropped to one knee and looked up at her. He opened the lid to reveal a stunning emerald the size of a walnut surrounded by brilliant diamonds nestled in red velvet.

Heat throbbed in her cheeks, and she felt light-headed.

"I realize I started off on the wrong foot, and I had planned to visit you at your home tomorrow. But now that you are here, I want to seize the moment. Evelyn Darlington, I would be honored if you would be my wife."

She looked at the magnificent ring, then at the handsome man on his knee before her. Her mind whirled; the blood rushed through her veins like an avalanche. "Jack, I don't know if—"

"*Shh.* Don't answer yet, sweetheart. I want you to think about it."

He rose and slid the ring on her finger. "I've missed you, Evie. I want to show you how much. May I kiss you?"

Yes, she thought, *a thousand times yes.*

He did not declare his undying love for her, but he cared enough to buy her a betrothal ring and properly propose on his knee. Her firm resolve to hold out for nothing less than his heart weakened, and she seriously considered his proposal. The truth was she *wanted* to be his wife, wanted to spend the rest of her days gazing at him, sharing his bed, waking up beside him . . .

At last his mouth lowered, and she rose up on tiptoe to meet him. Their lips fused, their tongues caressed, and the hot tide of passion surged through her like fire to dry timber. He pulled her into his arms, and her soft curves molded to the contours of his hard body. He moaned.

Or was that she? Nothing was certain when he held her.

His lips seared a path down the column of her throat and he kissed the sensitive skin above the lacy edge of her bodice.

"For once I'm glad you came without your maid," he said in a hoarse tone.

Every nerve ending hummed in her body. He raised his head and looked in her eyes. His nostrils flared, and she realized he saw the lust that surely must be visible in her own eyes.

She wanted him. She was tired of caring about propriety and her tattered virtue, tired of living her life worrying incessantly about others—first her father, then Randolph. She yearned for joy and happiness of her own.

"I had not fully considered the consequences of arriving here alone, but I now believe it was for the best."

Satisfaction lit his eyes. "Good, because I can't keep my hands from you."

He swept her into his arms and carried her to his desk. When he sat her on the surface, her eyes opened wide.

"Jack, what are you doing?"

"I've dreamed of making love to you here."

With a wide sweep of his arm, papers, books, and paperweights flew to the floor.

Reclaiming her lips, he crushed her to him. Whatever control she had shattered beneath the hunger of his kiss. Fierce and vivid desire coursed through her like an awakened river. She wound her arms around his neck and pulled him closer. Her passion was equal to his and she met him kiss for kiss.

His nimble fingers made fast work of the hooks of her gown and her breasts were free. She had what she wanted then as his lips and mouth ravished her aching breasts. She worked the buttons of his shirt, and he impatiently ripped it from his body and tossed it aside. His hands went under her skirts and he cupped her mons. He pulled her hips to the edge of the desk and her gown slipped off her legs to the carpet. Next went her drawers, leaving her clad only in her silk stockings and garters.

She raised her arms, expecting him to come to her, but instead he sank to his knees and positioned her buttocks closer to the edge of the desk. Confused, she rose on her elbows, then was shocked as he spread her thighs and blew his hot breath on her sensitive mons.

Sweet heaven, could a man do that to a woman?

He lowered his head and licked her core, once, then twice, then over and over. She cried out and grasped fistfuls of his hair as intense pleasure spiraled through her. Her legs tensed, her heels digging into his back. She was powerless to protest, completely at the mercy of his lips and tongue. Her hips arched off the desk, her head thrashed from side to side and her mouth formed an O as she climbed toward a pinnacle, then was hurled beyond.

Completely sated, she lay sprawled and panting on the desk. Opening her eyes, she was startled by the savage, possessive look in his eyes as he hovered above her.

He may not love me, but he is consumed with need for me.

Her heart swelled in her chest, and she raised a hand. "Come to me, Jack."

It was all the encouragement he needed. He shed his clothes and reached for her. He gently raised her to sit on the edge of the desk, stepped between her spread legs, and sheathed himself inside her with one powerful stroke.

They both cried out. Her body melted against his and the world was filled with him. Not just where he physically touched her, but deep within her pounding heart. He thrust into her and together they found the tempo that bound their bodies together. Roused to the peak of desire, a moan of ecstasy slipped through her lips and she gave in to the wild wantonness.

Jack went rigid above her. He closed his eyes, and for a heartbeat she sensed his utter vulnerability as he poured himself inside of her.

He brushed a tender kiss across her forehead and

carried her to the thick carpet before the fireplace. He stretched out beside her and gathered her into his arms.

Papers from his desk littered the carpet around them and she laughed. "Will we never make love in a bed?"

"After we marry, we can spend half our lives in the bedroom."

She stilled. "Jack, you said I could think about it."

He made a show of looking at the long-case clock in the corner. "You've had an hour, my lady. Please say yes."

She smiled, certain now of her decision. "Yes, Jack. I will marry you, but I do not want to officially announce our engagement until *after* Randolph's legal troubles are resolved."

He grinned in conquest.

She felt an instant's panic. *He is so used to winning that he never doubted my answer.*

He was a dominant, predatory male, one who thrived on challenge and conquest. After they married, would he file her away and forget her like one of his many trial victories? Or would she be the unforgettable adversary and make him love her?

Chapter 38

The following morning, Jack decided to return to the Drury Lane Theatre and speak with Mary Morris. He found her in a dressing room, hemming a costume of Henry VIII. A royal red cape with fur trim, a velvet doublet with jeweled buttons, and knee high boots were spread out on a nearby table.

Jack stood in the open doorway. "Pardon, Mrs. Morris. Do you remember me?"

Mary looked up, her lips puckered with annoyance at the interruption. Jack knew the moment she recognized him for her sour expression changed.

"Aye, I remember ye. Yer the fancy barrister askin' questions about me Bess Whitfield. Where's the pretty blonde ye were with before?"

"I'm alone today."

"Ye bed her yet?"

Jack grinned. No sense lying to the perceptive old woman.

Mary nodded and set down the costume and needle. "I was right. Ye did. I can tell a randy male a mile away."

Jack laughed. He supposed he had appeared randy the last time Mary had seen him. It was an instinctive reaction every time Evelyn was near.

Jack's mind turned to last night. Evelyn had agreed to marry him. He had kissed her good night and for the first time in his life he had wanted a woman to spend the night. But he knew that wasn't possible and so he had allowed her to depart in her carriage.

Despite his overwhelming desire, Jack had the good sense not to follow her. Getting caught sneaking into her father's home in the middle of the night a second time would not sit well with Lyndale. If she returned alone, no one would question her whereabouts and the household would assume she had stayed at Lady Jersey's ball.

"What do ye want from me now?" Mary asked.

"We can't locate the diary. We know of two of Bess Whitfield's last lovers—Viscount Hamilton and Earl Newland, but you had mentioned a dark-haired commoner. A man named Sam."

"Funny ye came today. Sam was just here to see me. Askin' about the diary too."

"He was here?"

"Aye, an odd sort if ye ask me. 'E tries hard to blend in, but old Mary can see behind 'is mask. Soulless eyes that one 'as. Never did understand what Bess saw in 'im."

"When did he leave?"

"He asked to look in Bess's old dressin' room. I didn't care as I had searched it myself after 'er death and found nothing.' He may still be there—"

"Where is it?"

"Down the 'all. Second door to yer right."

Jack sprinted out of the room and down the hall. He threw open the door to Bess's old dressing room.

Empty.

Then he heard it. Footsteps outside the open window.

He flew to the window and saw a dark-garbed figure running down the back alley.

"You! Stop!"

The man stopped, turned. The low-crowned brim of his hat concealed his features. He moved automatically, and a pistol emerged in his right hand as if from thin air. Jack froze as the man raised the pistol and took aim. Then instinct kicked in and Jack leapt to the side, pressing his back to the wall just as the glass window exploded and a potted plant on the windowsill shattered like a projectile. Jack sprang forward and jumped from the second-story window.

He bent his knees, preparing for the impact, and the air rushed out of his lungs with a great *whoosh.* By the time Jack looked up, the man had taken off. Seconds later, Jack was on his feet in a flat-out run.

The man had a solid head start, but Jack was fast. The man knew the neighborhood well for he kept to the desolate backstreets. He looked back twice, but beneath the hat Jack couldn't make out his face.

Jack pumped his arms and legs, shortening the distance between them until he was within a yard of him. Then, gathering his energy, Jack leapt on the man's back.

They hit the cobbled street hard. Jack jarred his elbow and his ankle burned. The gun appeared in the man's grasp, and Jack got a good look at it.

Christ, it's a double-barreled pistol! A rarity that carried one more shot than a standard pistol.

Jack lunged for the pistol, and the pair rolled and grasped in a macabre dance of death for control. The man's hat flew off, and Jack's breath stalled as pulse-pounding recognition struck him.

"Simon!"

Jack's grip slipped, and the pistol fired. White-hot pain shot through his upper arm.

Simon Guthrie wrested the gun away and scrambled to his feet.

"You couldn't leave it alone, could you, Harding? I'll have to kill you like I did Bess."

Voices sounded at the end of the alley. Simon jerked around, and Jack took advantage of the distraction. He rolled to the side, prepared to tackle Simon's legs and bring him to the ground. But he never got the chance. Simon swung the pistol and struck Jack on the temple.

"Will you help me shelve these books, Evelyn? I just received a new set of treatises discussing the merits of tort law."

Evelyn took a thick book from her father's hands. "I'd be delighted to organize them." She studied her father's features and frowned. There were deep shadows under his eyes, and his shoulders slumped forward in fatigue. "You've been up all night preparing for your next lecture. You should rest and let me take care of these."

"You are a treasure, Evelyn. I am pleased that you have accepted Mr. Harding's proposal. He is a good match for you."

She had told her father this morning of her decision to marry Jack. "We agreed not to announce the betrothal until after Randolph's trial."

He shook his head regretfully. "Don't wait too long, my dear. You must seize every happiness life offers you."

He spoke with such uncharacteristic sadness, that Evelyn assumed he was thinking of her mother.

"I'm worried about you," she said.

"Don't trouble yourself. I deserve what God has in store for me."

Whatever did that mean? He needed to rest. Now.

"You should rest. I'll tell Hodges not to disturb you."

Thankfully he didn't argue and dutifully left the library.

Evelyn turned back to the crate of books on the floor. Seven treatises in all. She would look through them at her leisure another time. Perhaps even discuss the contents with Jack.

Her thoughts cast back to last night, her memories vivid and clear. Jack had done such glorious, wicked things to her body, and the degree to which she had responded stunned her. Her heart had swelled with love, and she had agreed to marry him. She knew he cared for her and that he desired her, but she wanted more.

Could she make Jack Harding love her?

She sighed and forced her attention to her father's crowded bookshelves. Where in the world would she put the new ones? She'd have to reorganize and move some of the existing books.

She noticed a set of old treatises that took up eye-level space on the center bookshelf. A thin layer of dust covered them, and she knew her father hadn't touched them in quite some time. She decided to move them one by one to a higher shelf. As she retrieved the last one, it was much lighter than the others. Curious, she opened the cover and was surprised to find that it was a false binding.

Stunned, she stared at a cut-out slot with a smaller, black book nestled inside.

She removed the small, leather-bound book and opened it.

Dear Diary,
   Maxwell Stanford came to my bed last night. He was voracious with his sexual demands, wanting me to straddle him and hold down his arms and legs as I impaled his shaft. Who would have thought the great Viscount Hamilton desired to be dominated?

Dear Lord, it's Bess Whitfield's diary! Evelyn thought. *What on earth is it doing in Father's library?* Fascinated, she read on.

Dear Diary,
   Newland acted more crazed than usual tonight. Crawling around on hands and knees, howling like a hound, begging for forgiveness. I'll demand nothing less than a diamond bracelet for his antics.

As if in a trance, Evelyn turned the page and continued to read.

Dear Diary,
   Lord Lyndale insists I call him Emmanuel as when we first met ten years ago. I could not have asked for a more generous benefactor and lover. His health is failing, and I fear our time together is running out. Newland is a disappointment, but Emmanuel insists I marry the crazed earl to protect my future.

A cold wave entered the room, and Evelyn's body stiffened in shock.

Lyndale, her father? Her father was Bess Whitfield's longtime lover and mysterious benefactor?

She stumbled back and grasped a chair for support.

She felt sick, nauseated. She forced herself to breathe, to understand.

Throughout the years, she had overheard her father's friends argue that he should have a lover, a companion. Evelyn's mother had died when she was an infant. She knew it was unrealistic to have expected him to remain faithful to a dead wife.

Still, the pain of betrayal was raw and sharp.

Her bewildered thoughts veered like quicksilver, and a feeling of dread pierced her brain. Did his affair have anything to do with his insistence she not marry Randolph Sheldon? After all, Randolph was Bess's cousin, her only living kin. Father knew they had been frantically searching for the diary.

Did he know it was hidden in his library all along?

A knock on the door startled her, and she jumped. The door opened and Hodges stood in the doorway. She recognized the taller figure standing behind the butler.

"Mr. Simon Guthrie is here to see you, my lady. He said you have been expecting him."

Chapter 39

"Jack! Wake up, man!"

Jack's eyelids cracked open. A lamp was brought close, and he winced in pain. Despite the pounding in his head, he forced his eyes to remain open. Anthony, Brent, and Devlin hovered above him.

He was lying on a settee, his head resting on a rolled-up coat. Jack struggled to rise, but Anthony placed a large hand on his shoulder and pushed him down.

"Easy, Jack."

"Where am I?" he demanded.

"Your office in chambers. Dr. Astor has been treating you."

"I was at the theater. I was shot." Jack's arm throbbed, a different pain than in his head. He glanced down and saw a thick bandage wrapped around his bicep. His shirt-sleeve was cut.

"You were lucky. The bullet just grazed you. An inch to the left and it would have shattered the bone," Brent said.

"How did you find me?"

"Shots were fired and people came running from the theater. They found you unconscious in a back alley.

Mary Morris sent a note here. We came as soon as we heard and sent for Dr. Astor," Devlin explained.

Jack's memory returned with a vengeance. "It was Simon Guthrie. He shot me. He murdered Bess Whitfield."   -

"Guthrie? Randolph's friend?" Anthony asked.

"Yes. He was known as Sam and one of Bess's last lovers. He must have been searching for the diary."

"Do you think Randolph knew his friend killed Bess?" Anthony asked.

No, Jack didn't believe Randolph knew. "I think Simon duped us all, Randolph included."

But Simon was still free and he was dangerous. There was no doubt in Jack's mind that Simon would have killed him if he had the opportunity. Simon had to know that Jack would hunt him down. Simon would be desperate. He would go to Evelyn.

Christ, Evelyn! She was in danger. "How long have I been out?"

"At least three hours," Brent said.

Three hours!

Jack swung his legs over the side of the settee, gritting his teeth as pain shot through his head and arm.

"I have to go to Evelyn. That bastard will go to her next."

Anthony, Brent, and Devlin exchanged worried looks.

"We'll all go with you," Anthony said.

"Simon, I wasn't expecting you," Evelyn said.

Simon shut the library door and turned back to Evelyn. He glanced at the book in her hands. "What do you have there, Evelyn?"

"You wouldn't believe it! I found Bess Whitfield's diary."

He stepped forward, hand outstretched. "Let me see it."

She frowned, some instinct making her fingers tighten on the diary. Simon's normally impeccably styled dark hair was disheveled, and there was a fresh cut on his cheekbone. She looked closer, noting the dirt smudges on his fawn-colored trousers. Simon had always appeared mature for his age, but today he seemed a decade older.

She bit her bottom lip. "Did you get in a fight? Is all well with Randolph?"

He laughed and shook his head. "I'm embarrassed to admit that I fell from my horse this morning. Now let me see the diary."

He came close, and Evelyn backed up a step. She wasn't certain she was ready to share that her own father was Bess Whitfield's longtime lover and benefactor.

He stopped and cocked his head to the side. "Where did you find it?"

"I've only just discovered it on the bookshelf. It was hidden in a false book. I want to read more."

He waved his hand. "Go on and read."

She flipped the pages. "Bess writes about Viscount Hamilton and Earl Newland. I want to find her entries on Sam. Perhaps we can learn his full identity."

Simon's voice was level. "Perhaps."

"Here! I see something." She read out loud.

Dear Diary,
Sam tried to persuade me to use the diary to blackmail many of my current and past lovers. As if I would! That's not the purpose of its existence. He's a fool! I would blackmail him with his true identity

*as a respectable Oxford student, before I would turn
on the others. I refuse to destroy my diary, and
therefore, I must take efforts to hide it from him.*

Evelyn's brows knit. "Bess doesn't mention Sam's full
name. Only that he was a respectable Oxford student. It
couldn't have been Randolph. Mary Morris had said
Sam was dark-haired. Who else at Oxford could it be?"

Her mind was racing now. The only other Oxford student she knew was Simon. . . .

Simon and Sam. Their names were frighteningly
similar.

Evelyn looked up as the shock of discovery hit her full
force. "You! You are Sam, Bess's lover!"

"So you have finally figured it out," he said in a low,
composed voice.

"You don't deny it?"

He shrugged matter-of-factly. "It makes little difference now."

Will it never end? First her father, then Simon. Had all
of London slept with the actress? Or just the important
men in her life?

"So you knew about the diary and wanted it for your
own purposes?"

He chuckled. "Is that all you believe? You are a grave
disappointment, Evelyn Darlington. As the daughter of a
professor and a self-proclaimed scholar, haven't you
guessed that I killed Bess Whitfield?"

Her breath caught in her lungs; her mind spun in
shock. Through the roaring din in her ears, she breathed
one word. "Why?"

His lips curved, and he replied with heavy irony, "She
got in the way, and I had to dispose of her."

She was shocked as she saw him with abrupt clarity. It

was like the final pieces of a puzzle that fit into place. The acquaintance she had been fond of for years no longer stood before her. Instead of the studious intelligence she had always admired, a predatory gleam shone in his eyes.

"I suspect you know the truth about your father, too?" Simon asked.

She gasped. "You knew all along?"

"So did Randolph."

Her composure was as fragile as an eggshell. Fear and horror at the evil before her battled with her need to know the truth.

"Tell me everything," she demanded.

"You want the truth?"

"I have a right to know!" Her voice was shrill to her own ears.

Simon laughed. "Bess was right. I did plan on using her diary to blackmail her rich lovers—one of whom was your father. But the bitch refused to go along with my plans. She cared more for the fickle affection of her lovers than wealth. She was an emotionally weak creature, but a crafty whore. Unbeknownst to me at the time, she gave the diary to her cousin Randolph for safekeeping. Randolph must have read it and learned that your father was one of Bess's lovers. Randolph idolizes your father and must have hidden the diary inside one of the books in an attempt to protect him."

"But Randolph said he went to Bess's home that night for her to give him something of great importance. We all assumed it was the diary."

"He lied! He already had the diary. I suspect he went to Bess's home that night to tell her he had successfully hidden it."

"Did Randolph know you were Bess's lover?"

"Ha! Randolph thinks he's so smart, but he's an idiot. He hadn't the slightest notion that I was swiving his cousin."

"He was smart enough to hide the diary where you never found it," she countered.

His eyes narrowed to slits. "I searched all over for the diary. I was searching Bess's bedroom when she came home unexpectedly early one night. I questioned her about it, but she would not tell me where it was hidden."

"So you murdered her when she refused to speak? Viciously and repeatedly stabbed her?"

"No. I murdered her because she was a whore and she deserved to die."

She heard the bitterness spill over into his voice and a sudden anger lit his eyes. Her stomach clenched tight.

"What about Randolph?"

"The fool just walked in. I never intended to frame Randolph for the murder. But it worked out conveniently nonetheless."

Another revelation. "You were the one that broke into our home and ransacked my father's library!"

"Yes. I searched here too, but I underestimated Randolph's creativity."

Simon picked up the false book, opened the cover, and stared at the empty compartment where the diary had been hidden. With a loud curse, he threw it across the room. It hit the fireplace with a thud and landed on the carpet.

Alarm bells went off in her head. Simon wouldn't confess everything unless he planned on killing her.

He was in front of the door and blocked her escape, but she began to retreat inch by inch, determined to put as much distance between them as possible.

"You won't get away with any of it," she said.

In two quick strides he had her cornered and snatched the diary from her hands. "I already have, Evelyn."

"You're crazy! Jack Harding will come for you."

"Mr. Harding is lying unconscious in an alley behind the Drury Lane Theatre. By the time he wakes, I'll have you with me."

Simon had harmed Jack? "If you think I'll go anywhere with you, then you are insane."

He pulled a knife with a wicked-looking blade from his coat pocket.

"I'll scream."

"I'll kill everyone in this house. Don't think I can't overpower two old men—your ancient butler and your father. Your robust housekeeper and your maid won't make it down the stairs. I'm aware of the skeleton staff of servants your father keeps and that there are no others. They stand little chance against me."

Fear battered at the remnants of her control. Her heart jumped in her chest at the fearful images of Hodges's and her father's bloody bodies.

He strode to her father's desk and withdrew a piece of foolscap. "I want you to write a note to Mr. Harding."

"What for?"

"To tell him where you will be waiting for him, of course."

He forced her to sit in the chair behind the desk, then started dictating. With a shaky hand, she scrawled his fearful instructions, all the while her mind racing with thoughts of escape.

He can't mean what he says. I'll never willingly walk out of this house with him, knife or not!

Lamplight flickered off a gold letter opener resting in the corner of the desk. It had been a commemorative item from Lyndale's peers, inscribed with the date he had left Lincoln's Inn. But its significance or inscription was not what interested her, rather its razor-sharp edge and pointed tip.

Simon paced in front of the desk as he dictated, and when he pivoted, she deftly swiped the letter opener from the desk and slipped it into her skirt pocket.

She wrote the last of his instructions and pushed the note away.

He walked behind her chair, his fingers biting into the tender flesh of her shoulder. He leaned down, his sour breath hot against her cheek. "Time to leave."

She recoiled at his touch and expected him to jerk her out of the chair.

A foul-smelling cloth was pressed to her mouth and nose instead. She struggled wildly, but was no match for his wiry strength.

Then there was nothing at all as blackness enveloped her.

Chapter 40

Panic and rage spurted through Jack as he read the note.

> *Mr. Harding,*
>   *I have someone you want. Kindly pay your*
> *respects to Bess Whitfield at your earliest*
> *convenience.*
>
>   *SG*

"We're too late! He has her!"

"Too late? Where is my daughter?" Lord Lyndale asked.

Jack's gaze snapped to Lyndale. They were in his library. Jack had left his chambers and sped here, his mind a crazy mixture of hope and fear. Anthony, Devlin, and Brent had followed and they now waited outside.

"Simon Guthrie has Evelyn. He was one of her lovers and murdered Bess Whitfield," Jack said, his voice rough with anxiety.

"Dear God!"

"I'm going after him."

Jack made for the door, not wanting to waste another

minute speaking with Lyndale when Evelyn was in the hands of that madman.

Lyndale grasped Jack's arm, his hold surprisingly strong. Unspoken pain was alive and glowing in the older man's eyes.

"You don't understand," Lyndale said. "This is my fault. Bess Whitfield was my mistress for over ten years. I supported her lifestyle and ensured the success of her acting career."

Jack halted. "Did you know Simon Guthrie was Bess's lover?"

"No! I knew Bess kept a diary naming her lovers, but I never read it."

Silence loomed between them like a heavy mist. Jack eyed the fake book with the hidden compartment now resting on Lyndale's desk. When Jack had first entered the library, he'd spotted it on the carpet by the fireplace and had immediately concluded that the diary had been hidden there.

It all made sense now. The break-in at Lyndale's home weeks ago. The ransacking of the library. Simon had been searching for the diary, but had never found its hiding place.

"Did you know the diary was hidden in your library?" Jack asked.

Lyndale shook his head. "No. As my Fellow, Randolph had access to my library. He must have hidden it here. Never did I suspect it was right under our noses the entire time."

Questions flew through Jack's mind, but he bit his tongue. Jack had lain unconscious for hours. It was now dark outside, and Evelyn was alone with a murdering monster in an isolated graveyard.

"I will find her." His voice was like steel.

Jack ran out of the house, panic such as he'd never experienced before rioting within his chest. The thought of Simon hurting Evelyn, or worse—killing her—tore at his insides.

Don't think of how he savagely murdered Bess Whitfield!

His breath caught in his throat, and his thoughts turned to the last time they had made love. He would never forget a single detail of her lovely face as she cried out his name in ecstasy. Afterward, he had once again asked her to marry him, and she had accepted his proposal. He was well aware that she sought his love, and yet he had remained stubbornly silent.

How could he have been such a fool?

Fearful clarity opened his eyes. He loved Evelyn. His vow not to become involved, not to love someone in an effort to stay focused on his legal career, shattered like broken glass. His insistence to marry her and keep her out of Randolph's arms or any other man's had nothing to do with honor or repayment of a debt to her father and had everything to do with love.

When he first left his father's home and entered Lincoln's Inn, Jack had little ambition in life. He thought he would fail as a barrister until Emmanuel Darlington had taken hold of him. But the true change in Jack had occurred once he had a taste of his first trial, had experienced his first victory; he had thought that he had found his calling and would want for nothing else in life.

But then Evelyn had approached him in the spectators' gallery after Slip Dawson's trial, and Jack's life had been turned upside down. Her golden beauty and blue eyes had initially attracted him, but it was her sharp intelligence and unfailing courage that had stolen his heart. Nothing that he had believed was most important in his

life—his career and status as a highly paid barrister—
was as important as Evelyn. The harder he had tried to
ignore the truth, the more it persisted.

He loved her.

And now it may be too late to tell her.

Jack ran to the parked carriage on Park Lane. He
barked directions to the driver and flung open the door.

Three pairs of eyes looked at him.

"Where is she?" Anthony asked.

"The graveyard where Bess Whitfield was buried."

The carriage jerked forward. Jack handed Anthony the
note, and it was passed to Devlin and Brent.

"The good news is she's alive, Jack," Devlin said.
"The bad news is he's using her as bait to get to you."

Anthony handed Jack a pistol. "It's a trap. But the bastard doesn't know there are three of us to back you."

Devlin nodded. "We're all armed and crack shots."

Brent remained silent, then reached out to touch Jack's
sleeve. "Don't worry, Jack. You'll yet be able to tell her
you love her before the end of the night."

Chapter 41

She woke cold and aching. Sitting upright, her back was pressed against a hard object. Her arms were behind her, and when she tried to move them her muscles screamed from the pain. She felt drained, lifeless, and she fought the urge to drift back into wisps of sleep.

She opened her eyes, disoriented.

Her hands were tied behind her back.

"Good. You're awake."

She recognized the voice moments before Simon Guthrie's face came into view.

She remembered. Dear Lord, she remembered everything.

"What did you do to me?" Her tongue was thick in her throat.

"Ether is potent and works quickly. As an Oxford Fellow, I have access to all types of useful chemicals."

A tight knot formed in her stomach. "Where are we?"

"Bess Whitfield's grave site."

As the final traces of the ether wore off, Evelyn noticed the odd shapes of the tombstones looming in the distance. A sliver of a moon cast them in shadows. Gooseflesh rose on her arms.

She recalled the location of Bess's grave from the last time she had been here with Jack spying on Earl Newland. Bess's grave was in the center of the graveyard, three rows from the stone path. She swallowed hard as she looked around. No mourners were present at this time of night.

"Untie me," she demanded, her voice shrill.

He laughed. "All in good time."

He paced before her, the diary in his hands, the hilt of the knife visible in the waistband of his trousers. Her vulnerability struck her like a blow to her chest.

She was alone after dark in an empty graveyard with a killer.

Simon stopped suddenly and rubbed his temples. Cursing beneath his breath, he muttered incoherently seemingly oblivious to her presence.

Evelyn's eyes widened as she stared at his bizarre behavior. But then just as suddenly he dropped his hands to his sides and squatted down before her. His black eyes impaled her.

She jerked, pulling at the bindings behind her back. The letter opener in her pocket jabbed her thigh. Her mind raced. If she could just reach it, she may be able to cut through the bindings on her hands.

She had to keep him talking, distracted.

"How do you intend to use the diary now? You are a known murderer. The authorities will search for you," she said.

He waved a hand dismissively. "There are those that will still pay to keep the diary out of the hands of the press."

"You mean Viscount Hamilton, Earl Newland, and my father."

"As well as several other influential past lovers Bess entertained."

"It won't work. You'll be caught."

"By your lover Jack Harding?"

At her shocked expression, he laughed. "Don't act so surprised. I know you are lovers."

"Mr. Harding has nothing to do with this."

"You're wrong. He saw me leaving Bess's old dressing room. He knows my identity. I have no choice but to silence him. That's what you are for, Evelyn. Bait. When Jack comes to save you, I'm going to kill him."

He stood and resumed his pacing. He went back to rubbing his temples, then stiffened in what appeared to be a seizure before relaxing and cradling his head in his limp hands.

He's ill and insane! she thought. *He has no conscience about taking human life.*

She shifted to the side, frantically trying to reach her skirt pocket. Fear spurted through her until at last she managed to grasp the letter opener. Twisting it in her hands, she worked her bindings. The opener slipped from her grasp twice, and the blade sliced her flesh. Blood made the handle slippery and hard to hold. Determination pulsed through her. She had to get free, had to act. She could not allow Jack to walk into Simon's trap.

Simon Guthrie must not harm another person.

He raised his head from his hands and regarded her with renewed interest.

"Does Randolph know of your plans?" she asked. *Keep working the bindings and keep him talking!*

"Randolph?" he scoffed. "He's too weak to stomach any of this. He would be happy to remain at university all his life."

"You were our friend! We trusted you!"

The opener cut through the last of the bindings, and her hands were free. She kept them behind her back waiting for the right moment.

Squatting before her, Simon's eyes gleamed. "I've always admired you, Evelyn. I even fancied having you for myself after Randolph was found guilty at trial and imprisoned." Reaching out, he wound a hand in her hair in a possessive gesture. "I planned to console you. I know you like intellectuals and University Fellows. I would have stepped into Randolph's shoes and married you."

It took Evelyn every ounce of willpower not to strike out and remove his hateful touch. *You must wait until he is most vulnerable or he will easily overpower you!*

She raised her chin in defiance. "I would never marry you, Simon."

His fist tightened painfully in her hair before he shoved her away. "You would have! But it doesn't matter now. You were stupid enough to sleep with Jack Harding and ruin everything. Randolph was too blind to see the lust between you two, but I knew all along. Disgusting!" he spat, spittle spraying her face. "You are a disgusting whore just like Bess. You'll help me kill Jack Harding, and then you will die the same way, by my hand."

He stood and turned his back on her.

The opening was all she needed. Springing to her feet, she raised the letter opener and stabbed him between his shoulder blades with all her might.

Simon's blood-curdling scream pierced the night air.

Grasping her skirts, she spun on her heel and sprinted in the opposite direction.

Tombstones loomed before her and she darted around them. Heavy footsteps sounded behind her, and she knew Simon was close behind. Sheer black fright swept through her. She tripped over a root and fell, her ankle turning on the uneven ground. She rose and took flight, each step bringing pain.

He was going to catch her. She would never make it to the main road.

She veered off the stone path. Moonlight glanced off the shape of the mausoleum. Making a split decision, she headed for the stone building. If the gates were open, she could lock herself inside, buy herself time until Jack arrived and she could scream a warning.

She reached the tall gate to the entrance of the mausoleum and prayed it wasn't locked. Her fingers curled around the wrought iron and pulled.

The heavy gate creaked loudly as it swung open, and she darted inside. She reached for the large padlock that hung on the gate. Her breath was shallow and ragged as Simon's footsteps came closer and closer. Her fingers trembled and she feared she wouldn't make it in time, then the lock slid in place.

A split second later, Simon crashed against the gate.

She jumped back.

"Bitch! You think this will stop me?"

"I'll scream a warning to Jack. He'll not walk into your trap!"

Simon rattled the gate. The sound battered her panicked senses.

She turned and plunged into the building. The torches in the sconces on the walls had long been extinguished, and blackness met her eyes. The heels of her shoes echoed off the stone floor and walls of the cavernous space. She pictured the burial chambers that lined both sides of the walls.

It was cold and deathly silent save for the sound of her harsh breathing. She could no longer hear Simon rattling the gate or his vicious curses. She stopped and leaned against the mausoleum's wall, surrounded by death.

Minutes passed. Jack would be arriving soon. She had to venture back and somehow shout a warning. The only comforting thought was that Simon could not hold her at knifepoint and threaten Jack with her life.

Then a terrible sound reached her as a gate in the rear of the mausoleum creaked open.

Simon! She never suspected there was a back entrance to the building.

Simon's shriek pierced her ears. "Stupid female! There's no place to hide from me."

Evelyn turned and flew to the front gate only to recall it was locked.

Trapped.

She gasped, panting in terror. He would kill her. She would never be able to warn Jack.

She reached the front gate, her fingers curling around the iron bars. She screamed, praying for someone to hear her, praying for a miracle.

"Evelyn!"

Jack's voice!

Crying out in relief, she grasped his arms through the gate. His green eyes blazed in the pale light of the moon.

"Where's Simon?" His tone was harsh.

"Close behind. He has a knife!"

"Step aside."

Jack pulled out a pistol and shot the padlock. It sheared clean off the gate, and then she was free. She desperately wanted Jack to hold her, but he held her away from him.

"It's over, Simon!" Jack shouted into the blackness of the mausoleum.

Heavy footfalls could be heard as Simon retreated back through the building.

Jack took off in pursuit.

She hesitated, uncertain what to do, and then went after them. Her ankle throbbed, but she ignored the pain. They ran through the building and out the back gate. She heard other male voices and saw Anthony, Brent, and James Devlin follow.

They chased Simon past the rows of tombstones and into the street.

Unlike the graveyard, the street was well lit. She could make out Jack and his fellow barristers pursuing Simon. Anthony was in the lead, gaining on Simon. Jack was a few steps behind, grasping his arm as he ran.

Simon glanced behind him, saw the pack of men chasing him, and sprinted heedlessly across the street toward a dark alley like hunted prey desperate to evade his pursuers. Just then a fast-traveling coach turned the corner and bore down on him. The driver yelled and tried to rein in the team of six horses. The horses reared and screamed as heavy traveling trunks flew from the top of the coach. But the coach failed to stop in time. Evelyn watched, aghast, as Simon was savagely trampled and crushed by flailing hooves and iron wheels.

Chapter 42

Hours later Jack found himself back in Lord Lyndale's library. Jack had previously sent for Constable Floyd Birmingham, and Simon's body had been carted away. Birmingham had questions before the murder investigation could be closed, and Anthony, accompanied by another constable, had been sent to fetch Randolph Sheldon from Newgate.

Jack glanced about the room. His fellow barristers, Randolph, and Lord Lyndale waited for Evelyn. Randolph stood awkwardly, his hands shoved in his pockets, his shoulders hunched forward. The spacious library appeared much smaller with everyone crammed inside, and a tense silence enveloped the room.

The seconds ticked by on the mantel clock. Jack's nerves wound tighter with each tick, and after ten minutes he decided to go in search of Evelyn.

Brent stopped him and spoke in his ear.

"Be patient, Jack. She's being tended."

The door opened, and Evelyn entered, escorted by Dr. Mason and Constable Birmingham. Leaning heavily on the doctor's arm, she limped forward and sat in a cushioned settee by the fireplace, her wrapped ankle resting on a stool.

Jack had not been able to speak with Evelyn privately since shooting the lock off the mausoleum gate and freeing her. After Simon's death, they had been swarmed by people—his friends, the neighbors who had come outside at hearing their shouts, and then the constables.

Evelyn noticed Randolph huddled in the corner. His normally thin face appeared gaunt, his cheekbones sunken hollows. Her blue eyes widened. "Randolph."

Randolph's voice was a low murmur. "Hello, Evelyn."

Evelyn turned to Jack, and their eyes held across the room. He watched the play of emotions on her face. Fear, relief, gratitude . . . and was that a glimmer of affection?

Jack wanted to rush to her side, pull her into his arms, and kiss her, but Brent's restraining grasp on his shoulder brought him to his senses. Even after what they had gone through, Jack had to maintain appearances before all these people.

Frustration roiled in his chest. She was so near, yet he was forced to wait.

Constable Birmingham cleared his throat. "Bow Street acknowledges that Simon Guthrie was Bess Whitfield's murderer. However, I have questions before Mr. Sheldon is free to leave."

"Wait," Lyndale said, and leveled his gaze at Randolph. "I have a question that cannot wait. When did you learn about my relations with Miss Whitfield?"

Randolph's face reddened. "Bess confided in me that you were her benefactor before I accepted the position as your Fellow, my lord. I've known for years."

Lyndale let out a long breath and reached out to touch his daughter's hand. "I owe you an apology, my dear. I'm sorry for not telling you about my indiscretion. My only excuse is that I acted out of loneliness."

Tears glistened in Evelyn's eyes. Nodding once, she squeezed her father's hand.

Birmingham cleared his throat and glared at Randolph. "Back to the matter at hand, Mr. Sheldon. If you had known about Lord Lyndale's affair with Miss Whitfield, then you must have known Simon was also intimate with her," he pointed out.

Randolph reluctantly nodded. "Bess did not begin her affair with Simon until years later. She had mentioned that she found an Oxford student interesting, but I didn't know it was Simon for certain until after she gave me her diary, and I concluded 'Sam' was Simon. I never told Simon that I knew."

"Why didn't you tell anyone about the diary?" Jack asked.

"Bess asked me to keep the diary a secret. But more than my vow to my cousin, I sought to protect my mentor and my best friend. I thought if I revealed the diary, and Lord Lyndale's and Simon's affairs with Bess Whitfield were discovered, then they would be suspected of her murder. So I hid the diary in Lord Lyndale's library. Never could I have imagined Simon was capable of murder!"

Evelyn spoke up. "Simon Guthrie was not in his right mind. I never noticed in the past, but tonight, when he drugged and kidnapped me, his behavior was bizarre. He would grasp his head in his hands and dig his fingers into his temples. At one point I thought he had a seizure."

Jack knew by the way Randolph hung his head that he'd been informed by Anthony of what Simon had done to Evelyn.

Randolph reached for a water glass with a shaky hand.

He swallowed the contents and set the glass down. "Although there is no excuse for his behavior, Simon was ill. I accompanied him a year ago to see a physician for his headaches. A tumor was suspected. We never said a word for fear he would lose his Fellowship position."

"Simon was not satisfied with his position at the university," Evelyn countered. "He planned to blackmail Bess's wealthy lovers, including my father."

"Simon's doctor bills had exceeded his university stipend," Randolph said. "The diary had mentioned that 'Sam' sought to blackmail Bess's lovers for money, and I assumed it was to pay off Simon's debts. But I also knew Bess would not go along with that, and without the diary, I thought Simon's plans were fruitless."

"You were wrong," Jack said.

Randolph's earnest eyes sought out Evelyn. "I never wanted to put you in danger, Evelyn. I had no idea as to the extent of Simon's depravity."

"I believe you. I don't blame you for his actions," Evelyn said.

"I felt sympathy for Simon because of his medical condition, and combined with the fact that I believed him to be my best friend, I never judged him for having an affair with my cousin. Neither did I judge Bess. Neglected as a child, she needed male attention like one needs water or air to survive. After Bess died, I sought only to protect Simon," Randolph said.

"Your loyalty almost cost you your life," Jack said, his tone harsh.

"There is one thing that remains unresolved," Evelyn said. "Why didn't Simon tell the authorities Randolph was hiding in Shoreditch? And why did he aid Randolph in a bar brawl? Simon easily could have allowed the Bow Street Runners to arrest Randolph."

"Simon didn't need Randolph arrested," Jack answered. "Simon was never under suspicion for the murder. I suspect Simon believed Randolph could have led him to the diary. Simon had already unsuccessfully searched for the diary on his own. He was desperate, and Randolph was his last hope of finding it. Randolph was closest to Bess. Perhaps Simon thought Randolph could help him."

Randolph sadly shook his head. "Simon often asked me about Bess's habits. I thought he was trying to solve her murder, but he was pumping me for information. He was brilliant, but manipulative."

"At least the culprit is dead. Justice has been served," Lord Lyndale said.

Jack clenched his jaw. "Justice? Simon intended to murder Evelyn. He died too honorably. As far as I'm concerned, I'd rather have seen him hanged."

Birmingham's lips twitched with amusement. "Despite Mr. Harding's thirst for blood, he was invaluable in solving the murder, especially considering the uncooperativeness of his client." The constable pointed a finger at Randolph. "As for you, Mr. Sheldon. You impeded our investigation. If it weren't for your barrister, you'd still be in jail rather than a free man."

Randolph looked at Jack. "He's right. How can I ever repay you, Mr. Harding?"

"I'm to marry soon. It would mean much to my bride if you came to our wedding," Jack said.

Confusion marred Randolph's brow. "I don't understand."

"You can ask Lady Evelyn to explain it to you. I've obtained a special license, and we're exchanging vows next week."

* * *

After everyone departed, Evelyn remained seated in the library. Her ankle no longer throbbed, but remained a dull ache. She exhaled slowly, her heartbeat calming for the first time that evening. The night had been frightful. There had been the shock of discovering Simon Guthrie was the murderer. Then she had roused from a drugged state bound in a graveyard, only to stab and flee Simon, and then unwittingly lock herself inside a mausoleum with him.

Despite the warmth in the room, she shivered.

Randolph was free and had left without shackles or a public taint on his name. But for as long as she lived, she would never forget the stunned, dazed look on his face after Jack's startling statement.

There was a low knock, and the door opened. Her head snapped up as Jack entered. He shut the door, and his eyes roamed over her face and rested on her wrapped ankle. His jaw clenched slightly. Then he came close, looking down at her with intensity, and sat beside her on the settee.

"You should have let me tell Randolph," Evelyn admonished.

He cocked his head to the side, his jade eyes compelling. "Why? You said as soon as Randolph's legal matters were resolved we could announce our betrothal."

"Are you always going to be this stubborn?"

There were traces of humor around his mouth and near his eyes. "I'm a barrister. I argue for a living."

Evelyn couldn't control her burst of laughter. "It is impossible to stay angry at you, Jack Harding."

"Evie, love. I've been waiting to speak with you alone."

Her breath caught at his endearment and the hopeful flint that lit his eyes. Dark tendrils of hair curled on his forehead, and she resisted the urge to brush them back.

"I have as well, Jack," she breathed.

He touched a finger to her lips. "*Hush,* darling. Me first. When I found Simon's note and I realized that murderer had abducted you, my heart stopped."

Evelyn's lip quivered. "Simon planned to court me, to take Randolph's place. But he knew about us. He decided to use me as bait to get to you. I was scared for my life. But what frightened me the most was that I wouldn't be able to warn you in time and that you would fall victim to Simon's trap. I couldn't allow that to happen. I thought if I locked myself in the mausoleum, I could stop Simon's plans and scream a warning to you."

He reached out, lacing his fingers with hers. "Evelyn, love. You were so brave to escape him. I don't know of a single woman that would willingly lock herself in an oversized tomb."

She choked, half laughing, half crying.

He raised her hand and pressed a kiss in her palm. His lips were warm and velvet soft, and her heart lurched in response.

"Do you know what I feared most?" he said. "I feared not being able to tell you the truth in my heart. My life is meaningless without you."

She looked at him in surprise. "Meaningless? What of your career?"

"Nothing. It means nothing to me if you are not by my side as my wife. I love you, Evelyn Darlington."

Tears welled in her eyes as she threw herself into his embrace. His arms tightened around her, and she could feel the strong beat of his heart through his shirt. "Oh,

Jack. I've waited for so long to hear that, but deep down I knew the truth."

He drew back and looked in her eyes. "How? I was a fool not to say the words."

She fingered his lapel. "I knew because of your actions. You've done everything for me. You represented Randolph even though you did not wish to. You accompanied me to the Billingsgate fish market because you knew of my stubborn nature and that I would have gone alone. You offered to marry me to protect my reputation after my father caught us together. And you rushed to a graveyard in the middle of the night to save me from a lunatic intent on killing us both. What man would do such things if he wasn't in love?"

He grinned and brushed a kiss across her forehead. "You pose an excellent case. I couldn't begin to compose a sufficient counterargument."

She shot him a saucy look. "I told you I'm quite good. Years of observation at Lincoln's Inn have honed my skills. You're fortunate I cannot become a barrister and oppose you in the courtroom. You would have met your match."

In one forward motion she was lifted high into his arms and settled on his lap. "I believe I already have," he whispered, his breath hot against her ear. And then he kissed her soundly on the mouth.

Author's Note

As an attorney in the United States, I have always wanted to write about two of my passions: romance and the fascinating aspects of legal history.

My research revealed just how vastly different jury trials were in early nineteenth-century England than they are today. Trials at the Old Bailey were short, averaging ten minutes or less, and took place in clusters. It was not uncommon for a jury to hear twelve or more cases in a day. Juries were expected to present their verdicts immediately after each case, without leaving the room, and they often gathered in the corner as they discussed their verdict.

Without modern science, DNA evidence or forensics, witness testimony was considered the best evidence. Judges often interrupted to ask questions of witnesses. As for a defendant's rights, there were few. There was no presumption of innocence, no right to remain silent. Rather than the prosecution presenting sufficient evidence to convince the jury that the defendant is guilty beyond a reasonable doubt, the defendant had the monumental burden of disproving the prosecution's evidence. This is a significant difference from modern trials and the adage "innocent until proven guilty."

In the beginning of the book, I took the liberty of hosting Slip Dawson's trial for "keeping a brothel" at the Old Bailey Courthouse in London. Typically, this offense was a misdemeanor and tried elsewhere. I also mention *pro bono* work, which is used today to describe volunteer legal services for the indigent, but it is not clear when the practice of *pro bono* actually began. Our modern legal system, although arguably not perfect, is a freedom that should not be taken for granted.

It was a pleasure to write this book, and I hope you enjoy reading my book as much as I have enjoyed writing it.

If you enjoyed IN THE BARRISTER'S CHAMBERS,
please look for Tina Gabrielle's other
two historical romances,
LADY OF SCANDAL and
A PERFECT SCANDAL.

Turn the page for an enticing excerpt
from each of these books!

LADY OF SCANDAL

Chapter 1

London, April 1812

"Rumor has it he's returned from the dead."

Victoria Ashton frowned at the young woman by her side. Jane Middleton, a robust debutante in her fourth Season, was a notorious gossip.

Victoria remained silent, her eyes scanning Almack's crowded ballroom.

"I've also heard he has amassed a fortune and is quite handsome as well," Jane said. "Why, all the mamas of the *ton* are throwing their daughters before him!"

Victoria feigned interest and nodded at Jane's comments. Shifting to the side, Victoria peered around Jane and studied the faces of the couples as they danced past on the full floor.

Her eyes then wandered to the entrance of one of Almack's gaming rooms. A cold knot formed in her stomach at the thought that Spencer had already gone inside.

Jane stepped in front of Victoria and blocked her view of the card room. Raising her voice an octave, Jane continued, "Blake Mallorey's new country home is so extravagant that the Regent himself visited to obtain ideas for the next royal residence."

Something about Jane's last statement gained Victoria's attention. "Whose residence did you say?"

"Why, the Prince Regent's new residence."

"No. Whose home did the Regent visit?"

Jane stared at Victoria in confusion.

"Victoria, haven't you heard a word I've said this evening? I'm speaking of Blake Mallorey's—although I suppose I now should use his proper title, the Earl of Ravenspear—return to Town after ten years. You do recall him and his family?"

A sudden chill ran down Victoria's spine.

Did she remember Blake Mallorey?

The name brought back a flood of childhood memories. Some were sweet and poignant; most were not.

Jane touched her arm and smiled slyly. "Oh, Victoria. I'm sure you remember. Wasn't there some sort of scandal between your families?"

Victoria shook her head. "It was so long ago. I hardly recall him."

"Well, he was invited to Almack's tonight by Lady Cowper herself. Perhaps you will recognize him when you see him."

Victoria whirled toward Jane. "Blake Mallorey is expected here? Tonight?"

"Why, yes. The entire town is gossiping about him," Jane said. "He is so wealthy now and so well connected. There are rumors that he has even loaned the Prince Regent money."

Jane patted Victoria's arm as if to soothe her. "You must not fret over a past scandal between your families. With his new status, Ravenspear would hardly concern himself with such a trifling matter as to settle old scores."

Biting her lip, Victoria looked away. "Please excuse me, I must find my brother, Spencer."

Grasping the skirt of her silk gown, Victoria wove her way through the crowded room. Was Blake the only Mallorey to return? What of his mother and sister? Victoria forced a smile and proceeded past the refreshment table and the dance floor.

She glanced at a small circle of ancient society ladies gathered near a potted palm. Their wrinkled mouths frowned as they glared.

Dear Lord, did they all recall the scandal?

As soon as Victoria entered the gaming room, she spotted Spencer through a haze of cigar smoke. His thick crop of yellow hair stood on end as if he had run his fingers through it in agitation. His green eyes were feverish and glittering as he held a hand of cards.

Bloody hell! Victoria straightened her spine and headed toward her brother. Men and women moved fortunes over the tables, watching cards and dice with avaricious intensity.

Spencer sat at a table in the far corner of the room. As she neared, a tall man appeared next to her brother and handed him a glass of punch. Victoria halted, shocked. Her mind whirled as pulse-pounding recognition struck her.

Spencer turned from his cards and smiled up at Blake Mallorey. Victoria watched in amazement as Blake grinned in return and slapped her brother heartily on the back at something he said. They rocked with the laughter of revelers and longtime friends.

Her mouth dropped open.

Blake leaned against the table and lazily picked up a hand of cards. He casually studied his cards before discarding one in a haphazard manner.

Her eyes were drawn to his face. She would have to be

blind not to acknowledge he was a startlingly attractive man. As a boy, Blake had been a good-looking youth on the pretty side of handsome.

But as a man . . .

His features were rugged and tanned. He had a straight nose and a chiseled jaw. His hair, dark as a raven's wing, was cut neatly to reach his collar. He was very tall and muscularly built, with deep blue eyes. His clothes were impeccable and obviously costly, but his taste for decoration was moderate, unlike most of the male members of the *ton*. His dark blue velvet jacket was stylish and perfectly tailored to fit broad shoulders, and was devoid of any lacings or silver brocade. His only jewelry was a diamond pin in his crisp knotted cravat.

Although he would be twenty-seven now, the same age as Spencer, Blake appeared older, more powerful. There was something dangerous and sinister about him that added to his attraction. A certain hardness to his features, an arrogance in his stance, proclaimed to all that this was a man who would not be dictated by society's rules, only his own.

Cobalt eyes rose to meet hers and she realized with dismay that she was standing still, staring openly at him.

Looking away abruptly, she feigned interest in an elderly man's cards sitting at the table before her. She slowly circled the card table twice before daring another glimpse beneath lowered lashes.

She drew a swift breath.

Blake Mallorey studied her as intently as she had him moments earlier.

As their eyes met and held across the room, a flicker of faint amusement crossed his face, and he nodded his head in greeting.

He recognized her!

Spencer sat beside Blake, engrossed in his cards, oblivious to Victoria's presence and Blake's interest.

Blake pushed himself away from the table, and with a pang she realized he intended to approach her. He moved without haste but with purpose, his gaze never leaving her face.

Her heart thumped madly, but she remained where she was, squaring her shoulders and raising her chin.

Halfway across the room from her he was overtaken by an eager crowd of females. Victoria observed with an odd bitterness that they were women of all ages, from society's latest crop of debutantes to the older patrons of the *ton*, all vying for his attention. He was politely attentive, but his eyes simultaneously roamed the room.

Victoria ran to her brother's side.

"Spencer!" She touched his shoulder. "Do you realize who you've been speaking with?"

Spencer turned bloodshot eyes toward his sister. The strong smell of alcohol wafted from his skin. "Vicki! You're ruining my concentration."

Victoria plucked the cards from her brother's hand and threw them on the table. "The gentleman folds," she announced to the wide-eyed dealer and the other startled players at the table.

Grasping Spencer's arm, she led him toward the opposite end of the room, where large French doors that led onto a terrace were open.

Spencer snatched his arm free. "Now why did you have to go and do that? I was ahead one hundred pounds."

Victoria glanced from side to side to ensure they were alone on the terrace. "One hundred pounds!" she whispered vehemently. "Wherever did you get the money to join a game with such high stakes?"

Spencer grimaced and rubbed his red eyes. "Damn, Vicki. I don't recall."

"That's because you arrived drunk," Victoria spat, "and why are you speaking with Blake Mallorey?"

Spencer's face lit up. "Why, now I remember. I borrowed the money to play tonight from Blake."

She gasped. "What? He loaned you money?"

"Of course. We've been out on the town all week together, and he has been enough of a gentleman to get me into both White's and Waiter's. I haven't been on the guest list at either establishment for over two years."

"You've been socializing with Blake Mallorey for over a week? Have you lost your wits? Have you forgotten the horrid scandal?" Glancing sideways, she lowered her voice further and added, "or the suicide?"

Spencer swallowed hard. "But that was so long ago, over ten years now. Blake is now an earl, and he has assured me that his wealth and status are secure. He has no interest in digging up old grudges."

"And you believed him?"

He shrugged dismissively. "Why not? I haven't had this much fun since I came into my inheritance from Aunt Lizzy at twenty-one."

Victoria reached out and clutched his hand. "It might have been ten years, but I have not forgotten, and I'm sure Blake's memories are stronger than mine. We must keep our distance from him. What would Father say if he learned you owed Blake Mallorey money?"

Spencer paled at the mention of disciplinarian Charles Ashton.

"Vicki, I owe Mallorey more than just the hundred pounds for tonight. He's been lending me money the entire week, and he has even purchased some of my outstanding markers."

Before Victoria could respond, the scrape of booted feet on the terrace cobblestones echoed through the night air.

Forcing a smile on her face, Victoria turned to greet the intruder as if she hadn't a care in the world. She stiffened.

Blake Mallorey's tall figure headed toward them, his eyes on her face. "I wondered what could be so appealing to lure you away from the tables, Spencer. Now I know."

Victoria's eyes met Blake's as he approached, and a shiver of apprehension coursed through her. She was keenly aware that he watched her with all his attention.

"How are you, Victoria?"

"Well, sir. Thank you," she said with rigid formality, refusing to use his deceased father's title.

His dark eyebrows arched mischievously. "Is this proper lady the same girl that followed me around and kicked the back of my heels to gain my attention?"

Victoria felt her face burn. "That was a long time ago. Children grow up."

"Ah, yes, they do. And you have grown into a stunningly beautiful woman. You have the same jade-colored eyes and sable hair that made you an adorable child, but as a woman your features are quite ravishing."

"We had heard you were killed at sea," she said, tossing her hair across her shoulders. "Some wicked, adventurous pirate story, as I recall, right, Spencer?"

Spencer coughed. "Vicki! That was just pure gossip. No truth behind it at all, I assure you, Blake."

An easy smile played at the corners of Blake's mouth. "I wouldn't want to discourage such rumors if they enhance my reputation."

She met his gaze without flinching. "In that case, there are numerous stories you may be interested in that I have overheard about you over the years."

"Vicki!" Spencer's face was bright red now.

"Perhaps," Blake said, "we could stroll the gardens and you could tell me all about these stories."

"I must decline." Victoria touched her temple with two fingers. "I seem to have developed a headache."

She swiveled quickly, turning her back on Blake. "Spencer, I'd like to leave now."

Spencer's mouth opened and closed like a fish's, then he merely nodded.

"Another time, then?" Blake pressed.

"I doubt our paths will cross again. Good night." Victoria entwined her arm with Spencer's and nearly dragged her brother from the terrace.

Victoria waited until they were safely seated inside a hackney cab, before she breathed a sigh of relief. She rested her head against the side of the padded coach and closed her eyes.

"I'm surprised at your rudeness," Spencer said, breaking the silence. "I consider Blake my new friend."

Victoria's eyes flew open. "Friend? He could cause the family a considerable amount of trouble should he choose to use his newly acquired wealth and power to do so. Don't forget that Father was recently appointed a Junior Lord Commissioner of the Treasury for the Regency and he would not want any blemish to tarnish his reputation."

"Blake's harmless, I tell you," Spencer said.

Harmless.

A picture of Blake Mallorey's face flashed before her. His wolflike grin, intense blue eyes, and powerful build.

She shivered.

"Harmless" was the last word she would choose to describe him.

She had an odd premonition that he would indeed seek retribution for the wrongs he believed were done to his family, and that, worst of all, her life would never be the same once he chose to do so.

A Perfect Scandal

Chapter 1

London, May 1814

"I've heard Lord Walling has depraved appetites in the bedroom."

Isabel Cameron's lips twitched at the words whispered into her ear by her close friend and fellow debutante, Charlotte Benning.

Isabel scanned the glittering ballroom, noting the magnificent chandeliers, the priceless artwork, and the crush of well-dressed people all vying amongst themselves for attention.

At Isabel's silence, Charlotte touched her arm. "What? Do not tell me that you of all people find such talk shocking?"

Isabel pushed a wayward dark curl off her shoulder and turned to Charlotte. "It's not the information that shocks me, but the thought of where you learned such private concerns regarding Lord Walling's bedroom antics. Have you been eavesdropping on your mother and her friends again?"

Charlotte chewed on her lower lip. "I cannot help myself. Those gossipers are an endless source of education."

Isabel glanced at Charlotte as her friend vigorously fanned her red cheeks. Charlotte was a petite, slender girl with a wealth of frizzy blond hair and round blue eyes.

Charlotte leaned close, covered her lips with her fan, and lowered her voice. "They even said Lord Walling pays a woman in Cheapside to indulge his fancy."

Isabel couldn't control her burst of laugher. "I pity the woman forced to endure his attentions, paid or not."

"Speaking of the man," Charlotte said. "Your soon-to-be betrothed waddles toward you as we speak."

Waddles.

Isabel's humor vanished, and she frowned. Lord Walling was indeed waddling. A portly man with fleshy jowls and a sagging stomach, he had strands of thinning hair, which he parted on the side and combed over a growing patch of shiny scalp. At fifty-three years of age, he was thirty-three years her senior.

"Can you imagine him intimate with a woman?" Charlotte asked.

Isabel's gut clenched tight.

Charlotte reached out and grasped her hand. "Dear Lord, what will you do if you cannot persuade your father against the match?"

Bloody hell! Isabel thought. *What will I do?*

"I've tried speaking with my father," Isabel whispered urgently. "He's unrelenting on the subject and insists that at my age I should be suitably settled. I've even attempted to dissuade Lord Walling of the notion that I would make a good wife, but to no avail. It's clear he is keenly interested in my family's reputation, title, and wealth. I'm afraid I have to take matters into my own hands."

"Oh dear," Charlotte said. "Not again, Isabel."

Lord Walling walked forward, directly toward her, nodding when she met his stare. His beady brown eyes reminded her of a ferret she had once seen at a country fair.

Walling bowed stiffly as he stood before Isabel and Charlotte. "Good evening, ladies. I trust you are enjoying Lady Holloway's ball."

"The evening is most entertaining, Lord Walling," Charlotte said.

He turned his attention to Isabel. "May I have the honor of the next dance, Lady Isabel?"

"I'm afraid I'm not feeling well tonight, Lord Walling, and would not be a suitable dance partner."

He looked at her in utter disbelief. "Oh? Your father told me that you had attended an exhibition at the Royal Academy of Arts just yesterday and that you were positively blooming."

"I found the art inspiring and must not have felt the effects of my illness until I arrived home."

"You shouldn't bother yourself with such artistic nonsense. A true lady, especially one of your age, should focus on domestic matters."

Charlotte took a quick sharp breath.

Isabel opened her mouth, then snapped it shut, stunned by his bluntness.

"My apologies, Lord Walling," Isabel said, finding her voice. "Perhaps another partner would be more willing."

"Should I tell your father to take you home, then?" he asked.

"No need to trouble yourself. My father is aware of my condition."

Lord Walling's lips thinned with irritation. "Nonsense. It is no trouble at all. I see the earl across the room, and we have much to discuss. I shall call upon you tomorrow then, Lady Isabel. I believe I have the earl's full approval on the matter," he said, a critical tone to his voice.

He bowed again and walked away.

"My goodness, Isabel. He's as persistent as a bloodhound during hunting season," Charlotte said.

"I fear he needs to marry for money. It's public knowledge that his country estate cannot sustain his spending habits. Even knowing this, my father is insisting upon the match."

At twenty, both Isabel and Charlotte were fourth-year debutantes on the marriage mart. One more Season to go and they would be official spinsters of unmarriageable age. While Charlotte sought a love match, Isabel wanted nothing more than to escape the marital web and return to Paris to live with her eccentric aunt and study her only true love—painting watercolors.

"I must be more creative in my efforts to dissuade him."

"As your best friend, Isabel, I implore you, please exercise more discretion than the last time," Charlotte pled.

Isabel looked away, uncomfortable with her friend's beseeching gaze.

It was then that she saw him. Two gentlemen had just set foot in the ballroom; both stood tall and straight and were dark-haired. Both were meticulously dressed in breeches and form-fitting double-breasted jackets. But whereas one carried himself with a commanding air of self-importance associated with the nobility, the other was shrouded in an air of isolation and aloofness.

It was the second man who captured her attention, the only one she knew—Marcus Hawksley. A childhood memory brought a wry, twisted smile to her face.

His profile was rugged, somber, and vaguely familiar. He was far from delicately handsome and effeminate as many of the dandies of the *ton*. His face was granitelike and striking, and his strong features held a raw sensuality, a smoldering dangerousness, which captivated her attention, and which she suspected women would secretly find deliciously appealing.

Hawksley's face was bronzed and his eyes sinfully

dark. His black curling hair was cut short and gleamed in the candlelight from the chandeliers above. He was tall and muscularly built. Even from across the room, Isabel could see the rich outline of his shoulders straining against the fabric of his jacket.

There was a restless energy about his movements as if he did not want to be in the ballroom with these people and wanted to depart as soon as his obligations of attendance were satisfied.

"Marcus Hawksley is here," Isabel blurted out. "I haven't seen him in years."

Charlotte shrugged. "That's because he hasn't been to a public event in years. He was quite the rogue in his youth. But then came the *horrific* scandal when he reformed and entered trade by becoming a stockbroker in the London Stock Exchange. Mother insists that trade is considered worse than the plague amongst the upper classes. Even his father, the Earl of Ardmore, and his older brother and heir, want nothing to do with him."

Isabel's lips puckered with disgust. It was just like the *beau monde* to overlook a gentleman's roguish behavior—his drinking, gambling, and womanizing— but consider it unforgivable when the same man reformed himself by becoming a successful businessman. Isabel had never paid much attention to the scandals, but Charlotte, whose mother was a close friend of Lady Jersey, one of the powerful patronesses of Almack's, was obsessed with gossip.

"Who is he with?" Isabel asked.

"Lord Ravenspear, the handsome earl whose wife, Victoria, is increasing with child."

"I wonder why Marcus is here tonight," Isabel said.

"Lady Holloway is his godmother. I suspect he has attended out of respect for her."

As if on cue, their hostess, Lady Holloway, approached the two gentlemen. Marcus bowed, and an easy smile played at the corners of his mouth. The smile was boyishly affectionate, softening his features, and it was clear he held Lady Holloway in high regard. He had the same look years ago when he had caught Isabel, an infatuated impetuous girl, filling his best riding boots with sand.

A sudden thought struck Isabel. "He caused a *horrific* scandal, you say? You are a genius, Charlotte!"

Charlotte's brows drew together. "Whatever do you mean?"

"I mean to gain my freedom."

Ignoring Charlotte's confused look, Isabel gathered her skirts and wove her way through the crowd.

The music from the orchestra grew louder as she walked, and couples whirled by in a colorful blur on the dance floor. Several older ladies glanced at her as she hurried past with a purpose—straight for Marcus Hawksley himself.

She came up to Marcus and Lord Ravenspear as Lady Holloway walked away to greet her other guests.

"Good evening, Mr. Hawksley. It has been quite some time since we have seen each other. Do you remember me?" Isabel asked.

Two pairs of eyes snapped to her face—Ravenspear's were deep blue; Marcus Hawksley's were dark and unfathomable.

One corner of Marcus's mouth twisted upward. "Lady Isabel Cameron. Of course I remember you. How many years has it been? Ten or more?"

Eight to be exact, she thought.

As an infatuated adolescent of twelve, she remembered him clearly. He had been a reckless rogue, a sworn bachelor at the age of twenty-two, and had been the object of her schoolgirl fantasies. Looking into his face now, there were no traces of the pleasure-seeking scoundrel.

Marcus Hawksley appeared severe and serious, and quite simply her savior if she played her cards right.

"It has been a while," she said.

"May I introduce Lord Ravenspear?" Marcus turned toward the earl.

"It is a pleasure to meet you, Lady Isabel," Ravenspear said.

Isabel raised her gaze to find Ravenspear watching her. His cobalt eyes sparkled with humor. Isabel could imagine what the earl was thinking—that a debutante approaching a bachelor without a chaperone or her father in a crowded ballroom was quite forward.

Good, Isabel thought. *May all of the upper crust watch, especially Lord Walling.*

"If you will excuse me, I see friends I'd like to speak with," Ravenspear said.

To Isabel's surprise, the earl gave a sly wink before departing.

She was left alone with Marcus. "Mr. Hawksley," she said, reaching out to touch his sleeve. "I'm afraid my request may sound forward, but I have not had a gentleman ask me to dance this evening. I cannot bear to be the talk of all the other debutantes here. Will you save me from such a fate?"

Marcus Hawksley's expression stilled and grew hard. His mercurial black eyes sharpened and blazed down into hers.

Her hand froze on his velvet jacket, and his muscles tensed under her fingertips. Heat emanated from his body, and he appeared as tightly coiled as a spring.

Suddenly, she was unsure of herself, of her outrageous behavior.

What if she had made a grave mistake? Had underestimated his reformation from rogue to serious businessman?

She took an abrupt step back, away from his tense, hard body, and made to turn on her heel. "Forgive me. I—"

He reached out and grasped her wrist.

"For old times' sake then," he murmured as he led her to the dance floor, leaving her no choice but to follow.

The orchestra had begun the waltz, and he swept her into his arms. It was the perfect dance for Isabel's intent. Known as the "forbidden" waltz because of the close contact of the dancers, she had a heightened awareness of their audience. As they started to dance, she wondered if he knew the steps since he hadn't been to any society functions in quite some time. But she needn't have worried for his tall frame moved with easy grace.

He looked down at her. "You realize that by dancing with me you may cause more gossip than by not dancing with any man the entire evening?"

She feigned innocence. "Whatever do you mean?"

"Don't pretend you don't know. There's a black mark on my name, Isabel."

A shiver of excitement ran down her spine. *I'm counting on it, Marcus!*

She was conscious of his hand touching hers, of his powerful body moving beside her, grazing her skirts. Her skin became increasingly warm, her breath short.

As they whirled across the floor, she glanced in the direction of her father and Lord Walling.

Her father appeared confused and agitated, and wiped at his brow with a handkerchief.

Walling looked furious, his fleshy face and neck mottled red.

Encouraged, she leaned lightly into Marcus, tilting her

face toward his. "A black mark does not scare me, Mr. Hawksley. I'm old enough to know that society can be harsh, can be too judgmental, and rarely is correct when it comes to a person's true character."

He looked at her in astonishment, and then grinned. "Not only have you grown into a beautiful woman with your raven hair and clear blue eyes, but an astute one as well. A true surprise you have become, Lady Isabel."

She didn't know whether it was the attractive smile that had transformed his face or his flattering words, but her pulse leapt to life, and her feet seemed to drift along on a cloud over the dance floor.

The bold passage of his jet eyes over her face and the curve of her neck heightened her senses. She found herself extremely attuned to his strength, his overwhelming masculinity. He was unlike any other male she had ever known. Here was no fop, no dandy that the young debutantes swooned over. Here was a powerful man whose dangerous nature was disguised by a thin veneer of respectability.

Reason told her to flee, to abandon her impulsiveness, but instead a thrill tingled along her nerves.

Their eyes locked, and his dark brows slanted in a slight frown.

He senses it, too! she thought.

As the dance neared its end, she realized with bewilderment that she was no longer acting the awed female entirely for the benefit of her father and Lord Walling, but that she indeed felt an undeniable attraction to Marcus Hawksley.